Chi's Sweet Home

チーズ スイートホーム

12

Konami Kanata

contents
homemade 201~218 +

homemade 201: a cat chases her memories

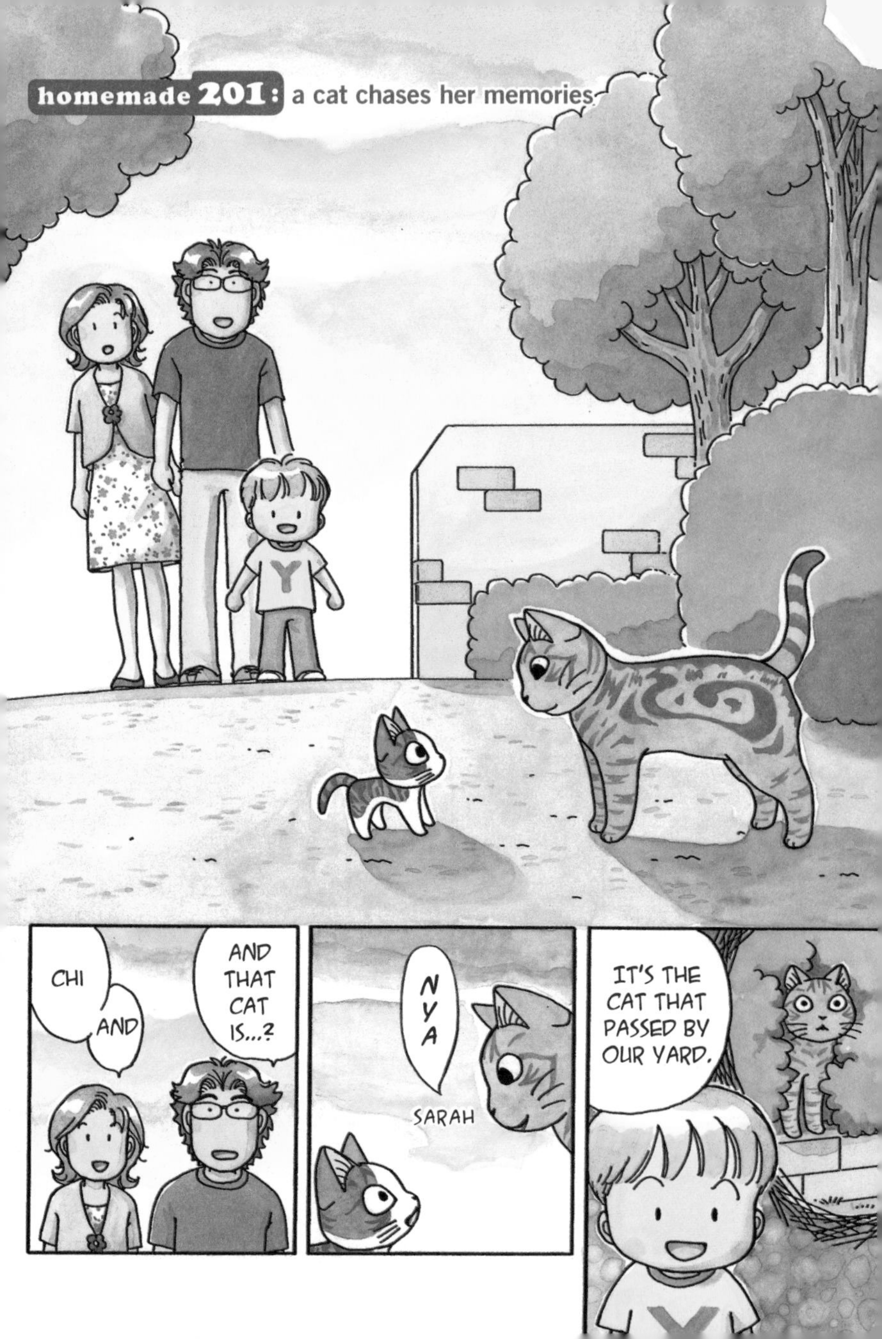
CHI
AND
AND THAT CAT IS...?
NYA
SARAH
IT'S THE CAT THAT PASSED BY OUR YARD.

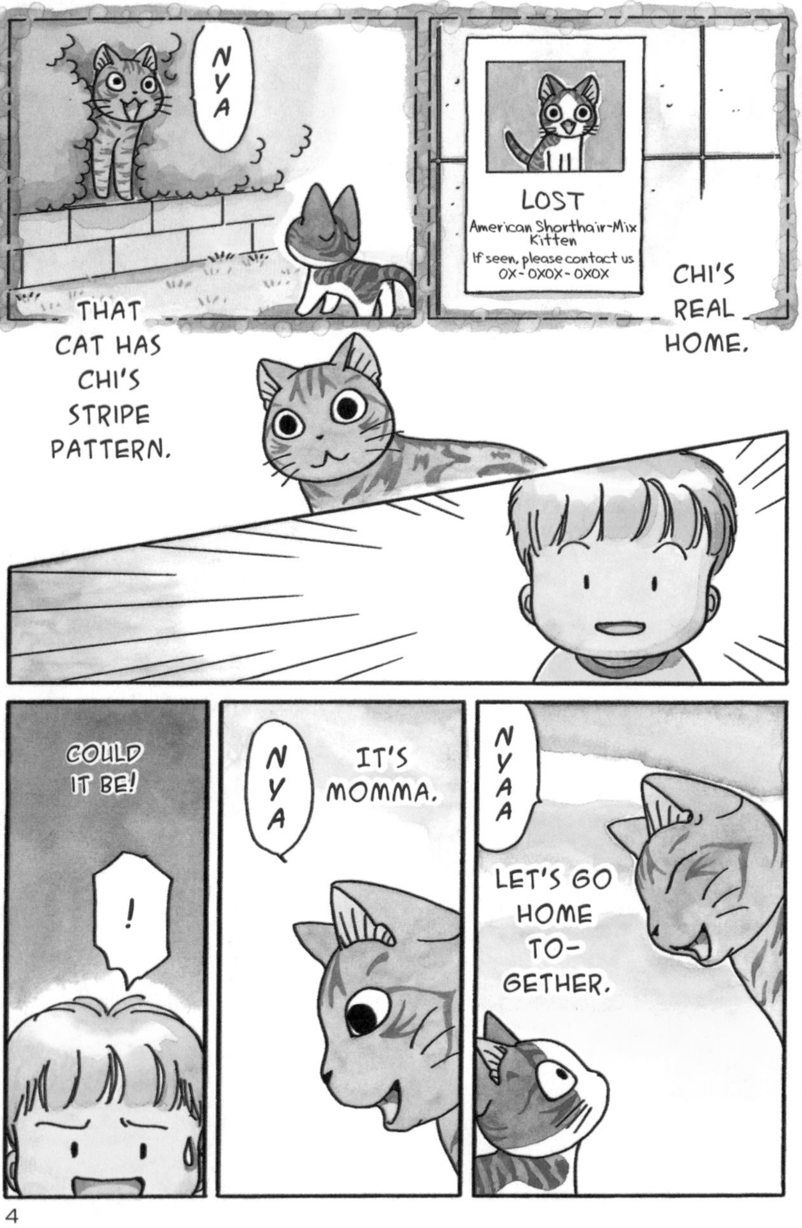
NYA
THAT CAT HAS CHI'S STRIPE PATTERN.
LOST
American Shorthair-Mix Kitten
If seen, please contact us
OX-OXOX-OXOX
CHI'S REAL HOME.
COULD IT BE!
!
NYA
IT'S MOMMA.
NYAA
LET'S GO HOME TO-GETHER.

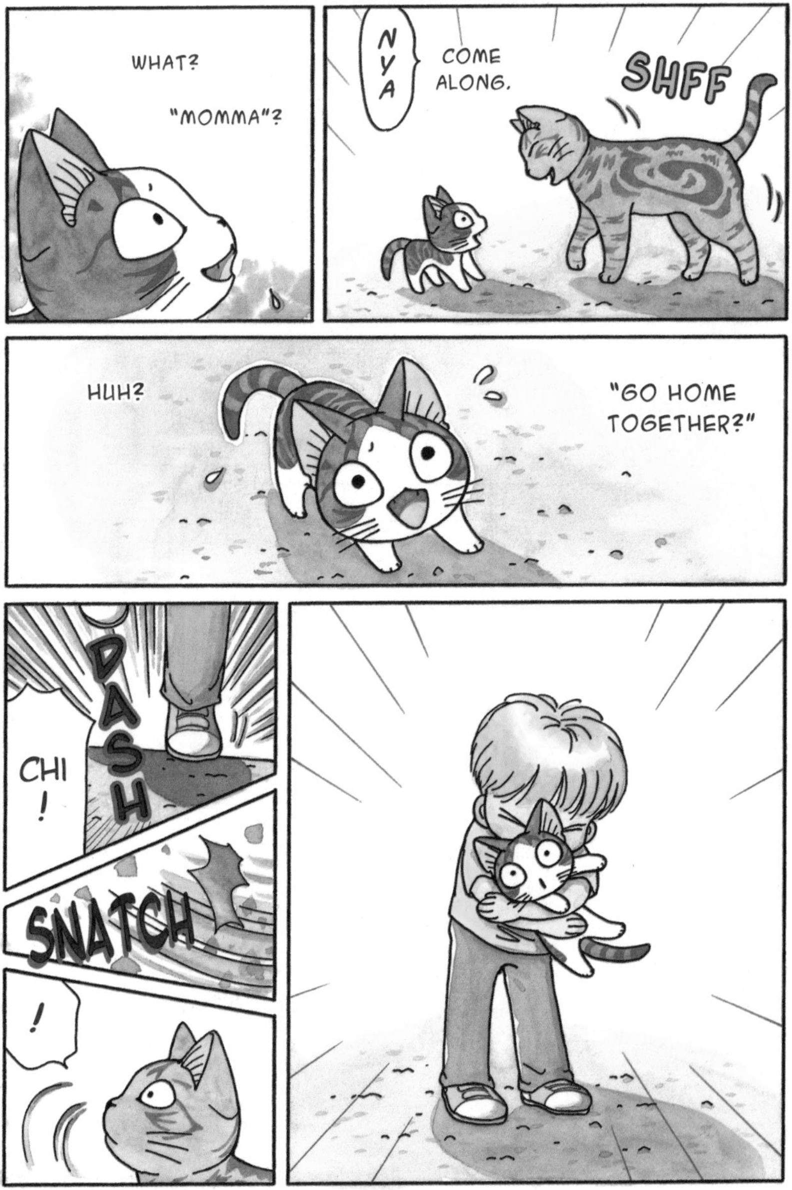
WHAT?
"MOMMA"?
NYA
COME ALONG.
SHFF
HUH?
"GO HOME TOGETHER?"
DASH
CHI!
SNATCH
!

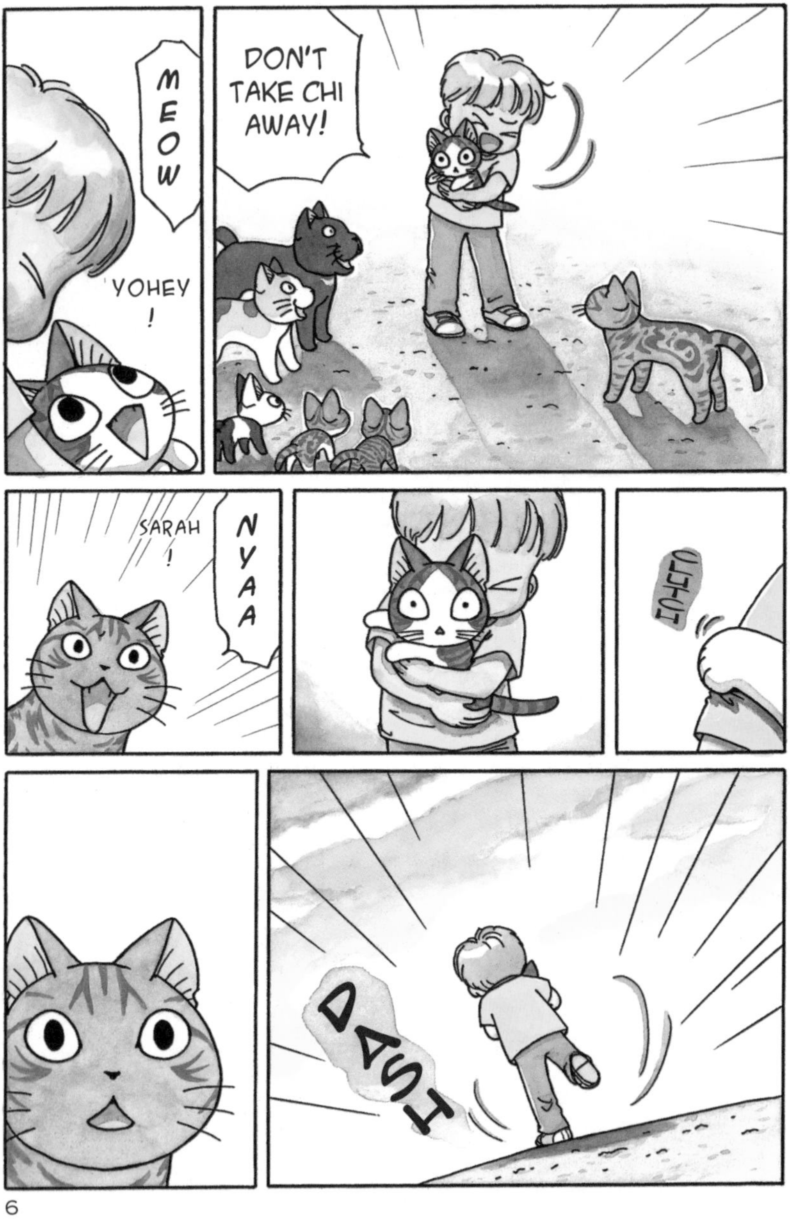
MEOW
YOHEY!
DON'T TAKE CHI AWAY!
SARAH!
NYAA
CLUTCH
DASH

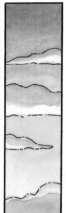

...

...

...

COULD THAT CAT... BE CHI'S MOTHER?

IS HERE GOOD?

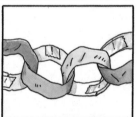

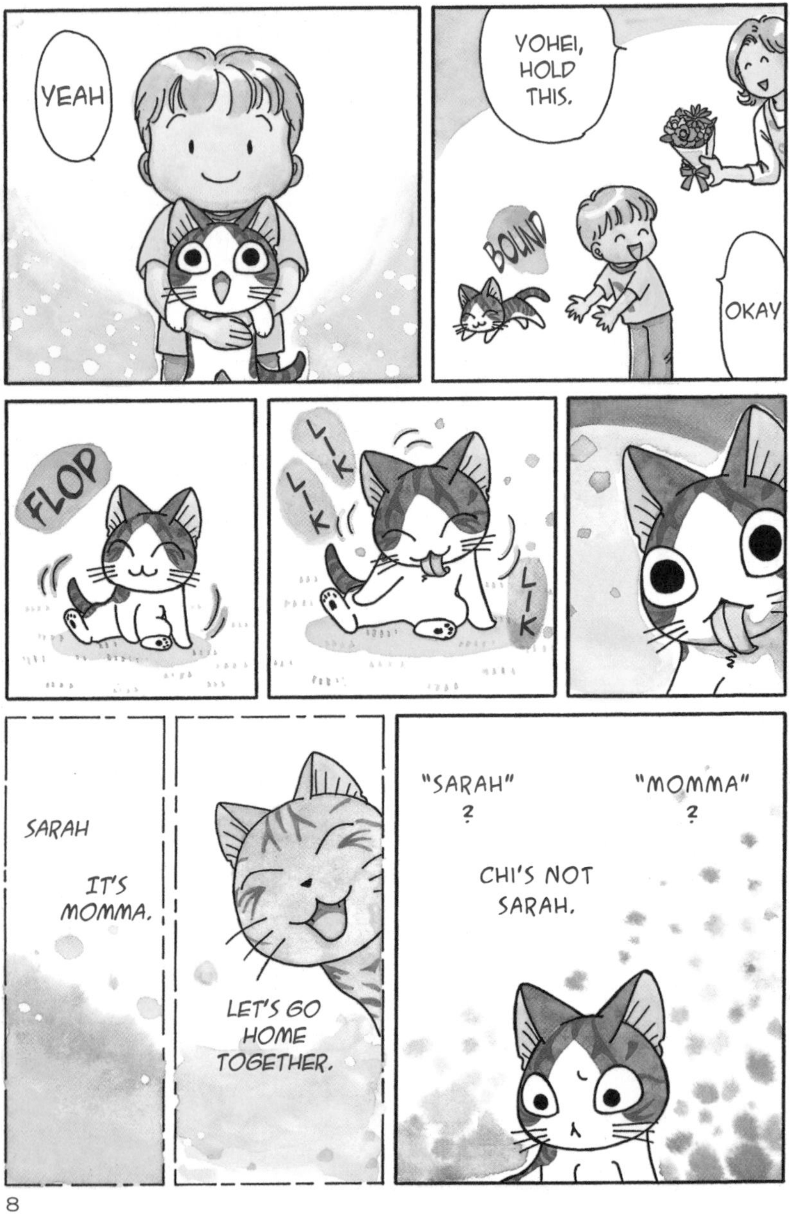
YEAH
YOHEI, HOLD THIS.
BOUND
OKAY
FLOP
LIK
LIK
LIK
SARAH
IT'S MOMMA.
LET'S GO HOME TOGETHER.
"SARAH" ?
"MOMMA" ?
CHI'S NOT SARAH.

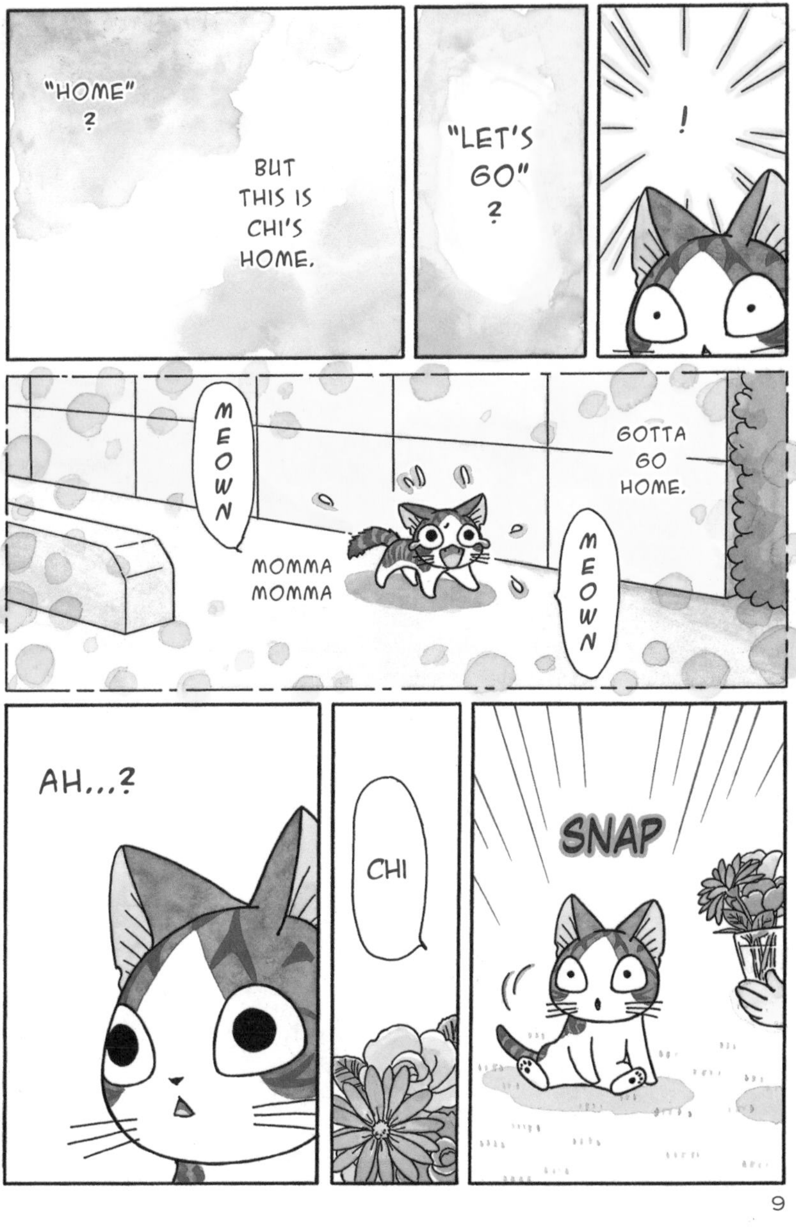
"HOME"
?
BUT THIS IS CHI'S HOME.
"LET'S GO"
?
!
MEOWN
GOTTA GO HOME.
MOMMA MOMMA
MEOWN
AH...?
CHI
SNAP

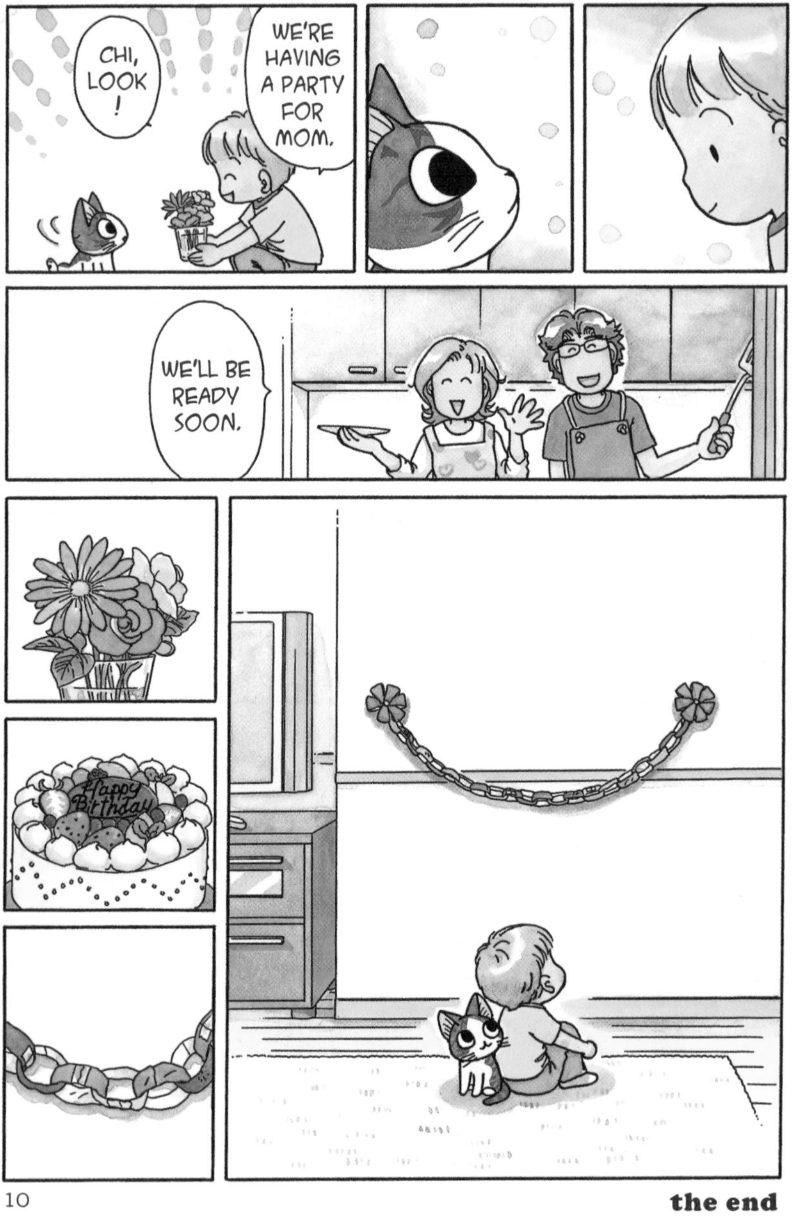
CHI, LOOK!
WE'RE HAVING A PARTY FOR MOM.
WE'LL BE READY SOON.
Happy Birthday

the end

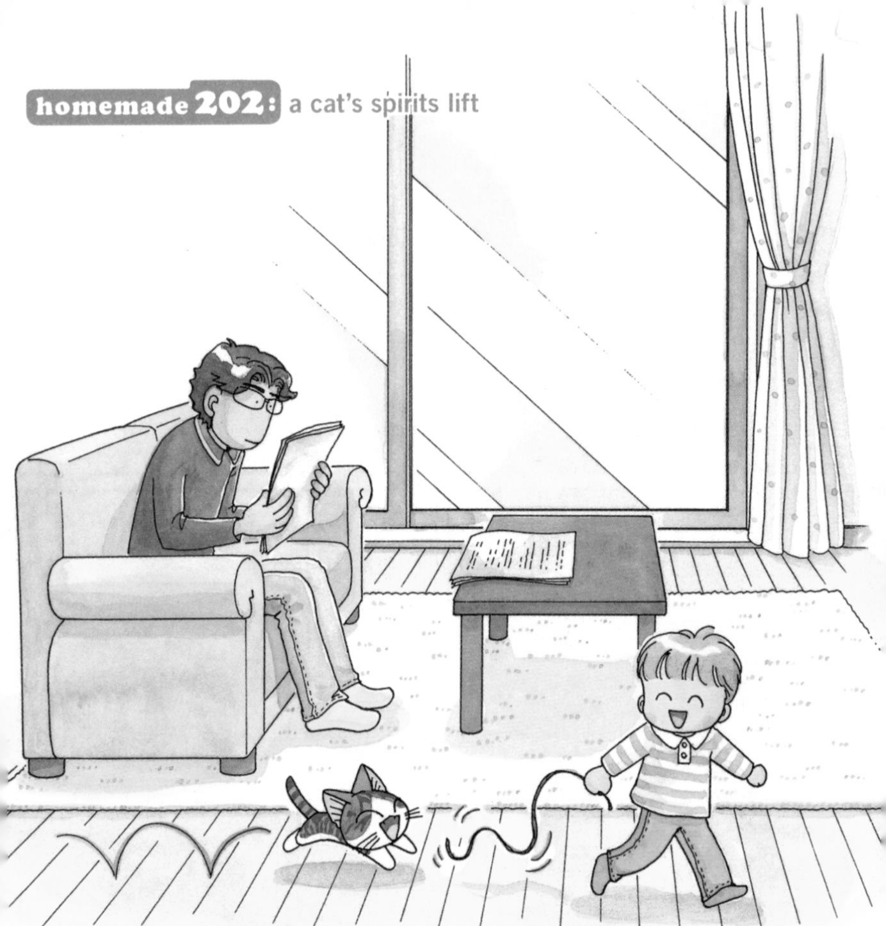
homemade 202: a cat's spirits lift

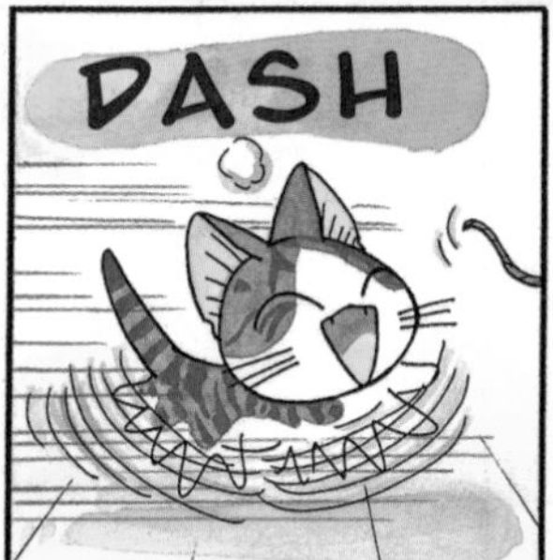
DASH

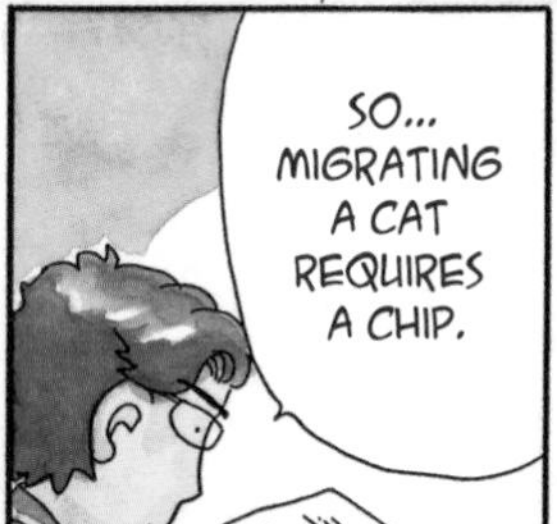
SO... MIGRATING A CAT REQUIRES A CHIP.

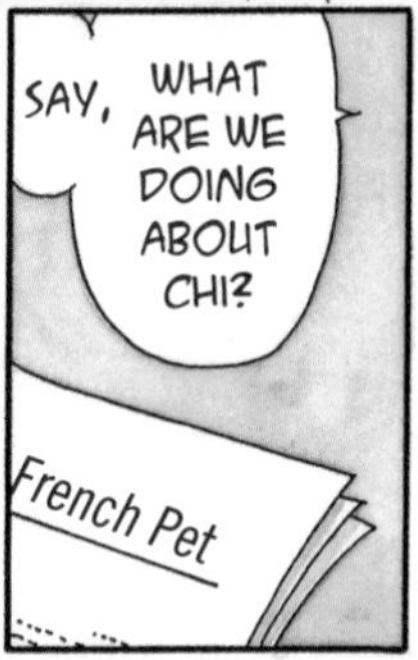
SAY, WHAT ARE WE DOING ABOUT CHI?
French Pet

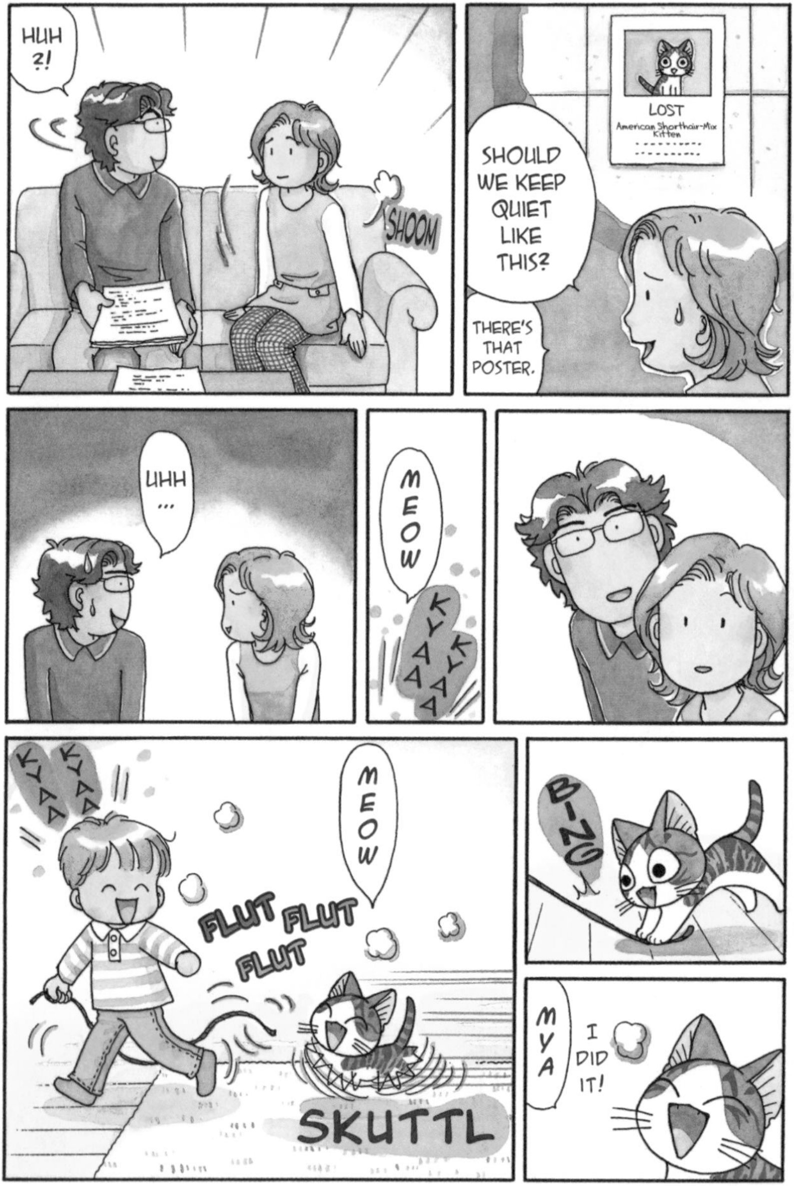
HUH ?!
SHOOM
LOST
American Shorthair-Mix Kitten
SHOULD WE KEEP QUIET LIKE THIS?
THERE'S THAT POSTER.
UHH ...
MEOW
KYAAA
KYAAA
KYAA
KYAA
MEOW
FLUT FLUT FLUT
SKUTTL
BING
MYA
I DID IT!

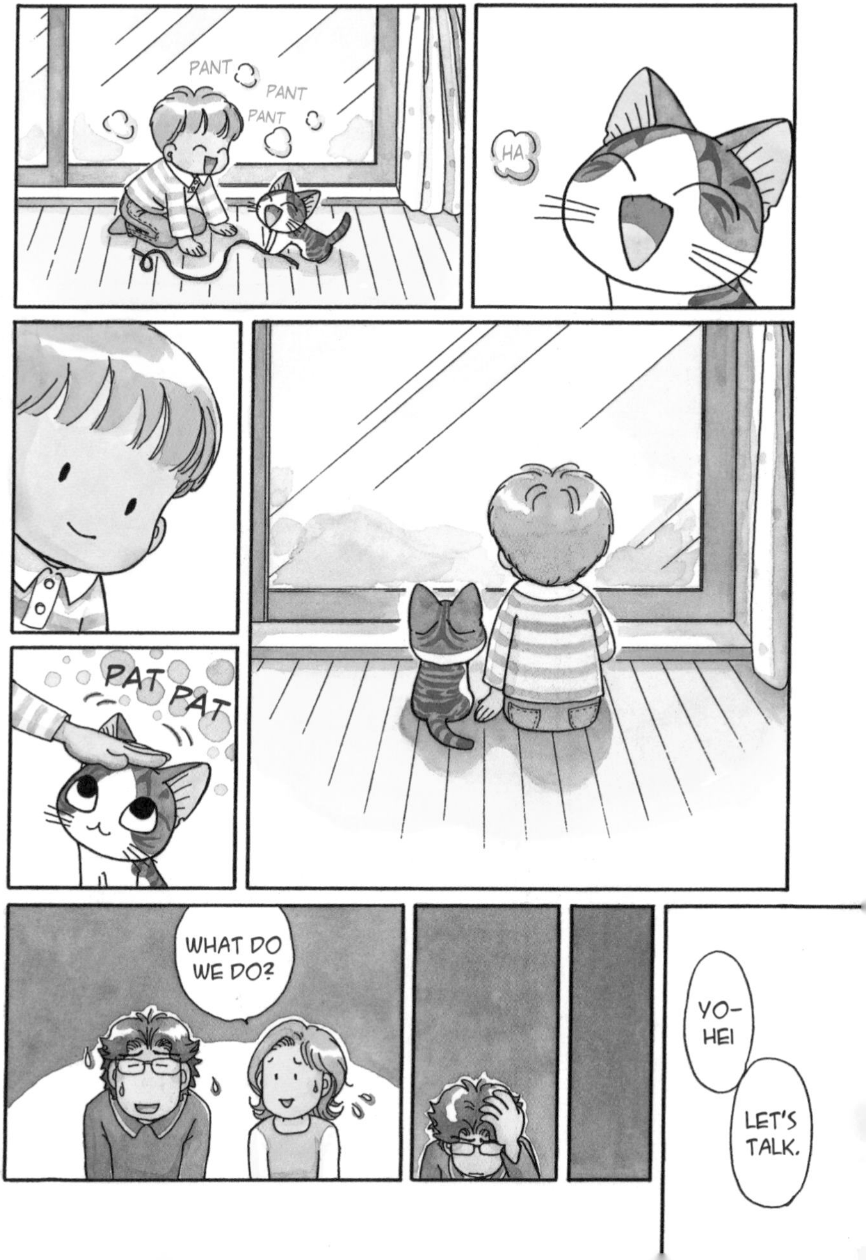
PANT
PANT
PANT
HA
PAT PAT
WHAT DO WE DO?
YO-HEI
LET'S TALK.

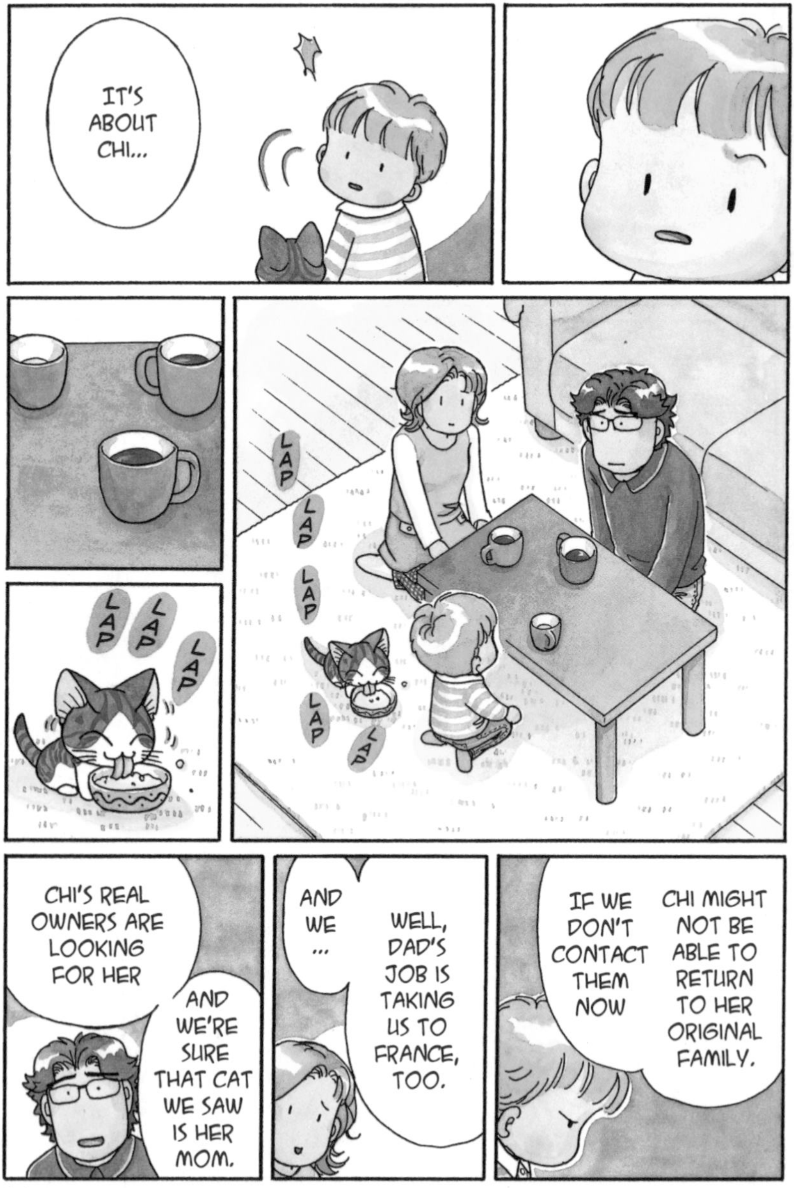
IT'S ABOUT CHI...
LAP LAP LAP LAP LAP
LAP LAP LAP
CHI'S REAL OWNERS ARE LOOKING FOR HER
AND WE'RE SURE THAT CAT WE SAW IS HER MOM.
AND WE ...
WELL, DAD'S JOB IS TAKING US TO FRANCE, TOO.
IF WE DON'T CONTACT THEM NOW
CHI MIGHT NOT BE ABLE TO RETURN TO HER ORIGINAL FAMILY.

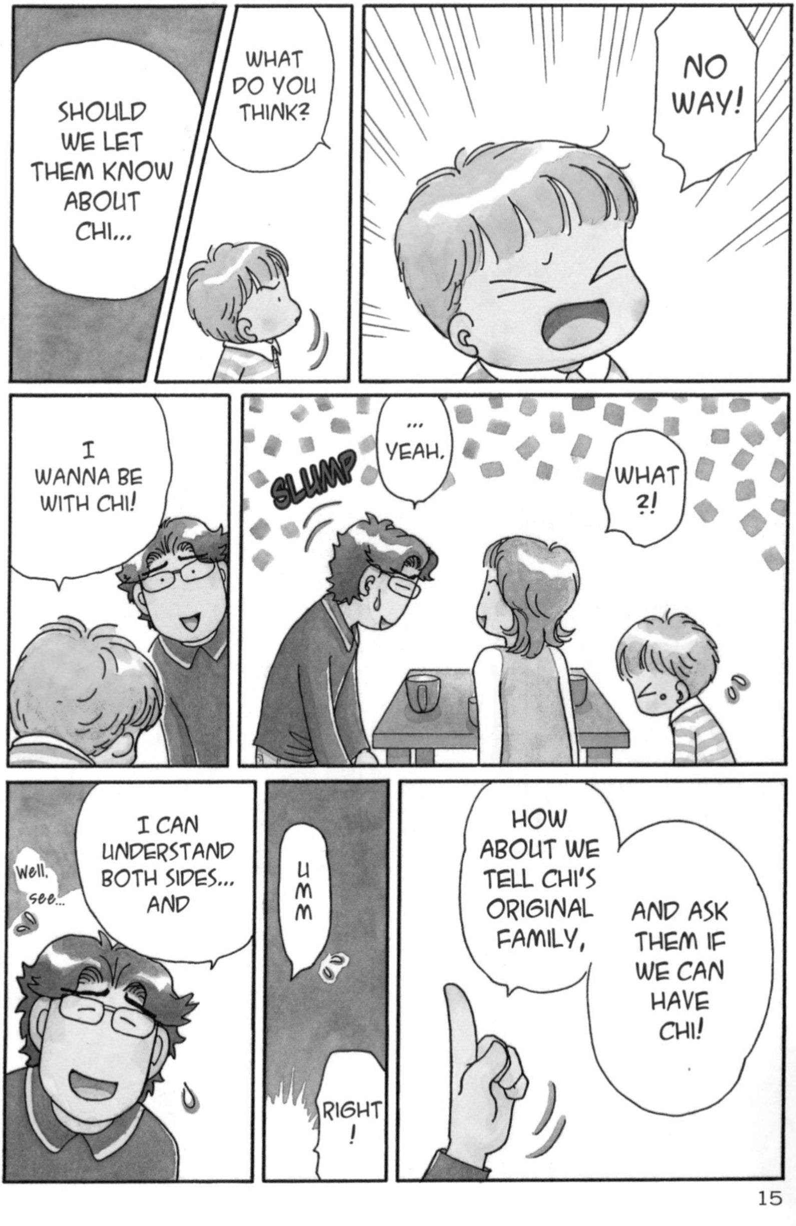

SHOULD WE LET THEM KNOW ABOUT CHI...
WHAT DO YOU THINK?
NO WAY!
I WANNA BE WITH CHI!
SLUMP
... YEAH.
WHAT?!
Well, see...
I CAN UNDERSTAND BOTH SIDES... AND
UMM
RIGHT!
HOW ABOUT WE TELL CHI'S ORIGINAL FAMILY,
AND ASK THEM IF WE CAN HAVE CHI!

YEAH!

RIGHT!

OKAY

BUT

THEY MIGHT NOT SAY YES.

...

...

...

...

OH

REACH

PUSH

MYA?

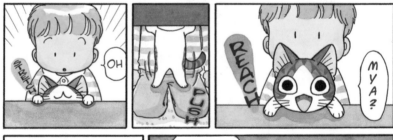

SEE...

NOPE NOPE

16

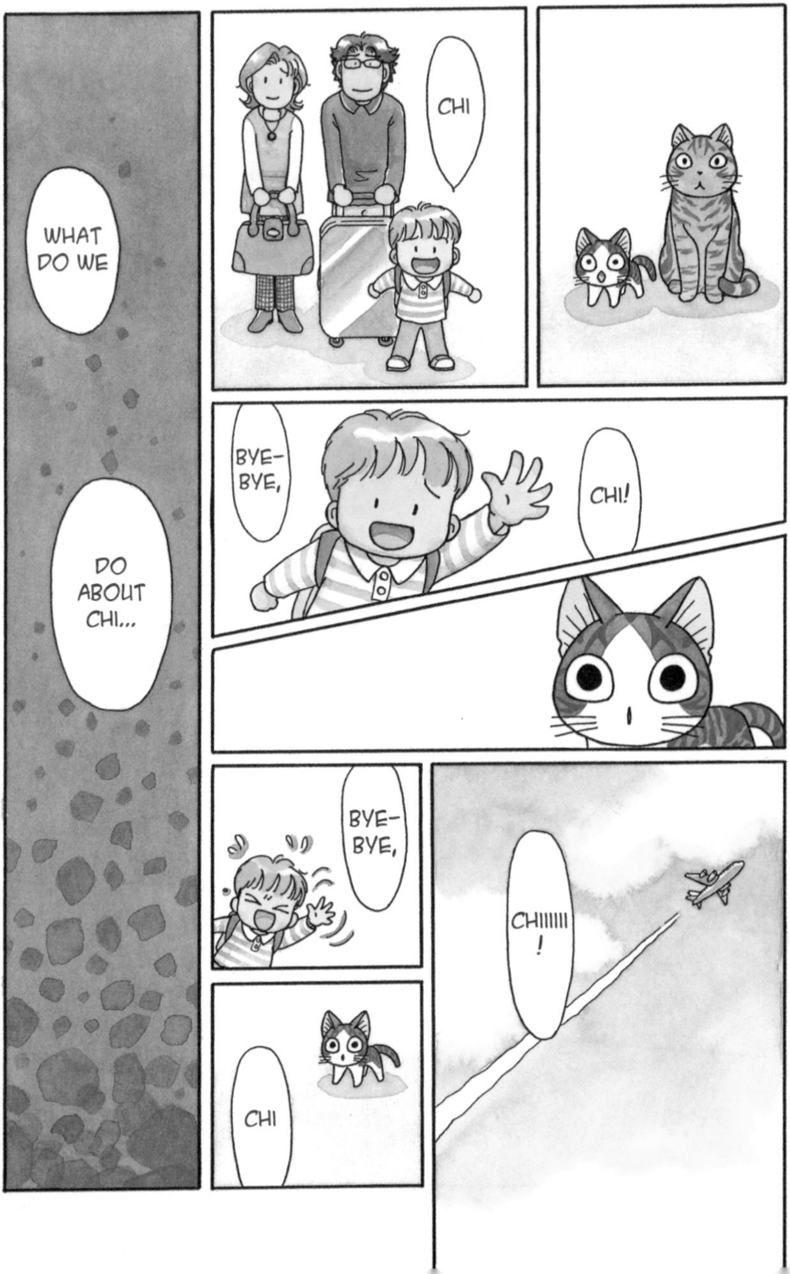
WHAT DO WE
DO ABOUT CHI...
CHI
BYE-BYE,
CHI!
BYE-BYE,
CHI
CHIIIIIII !

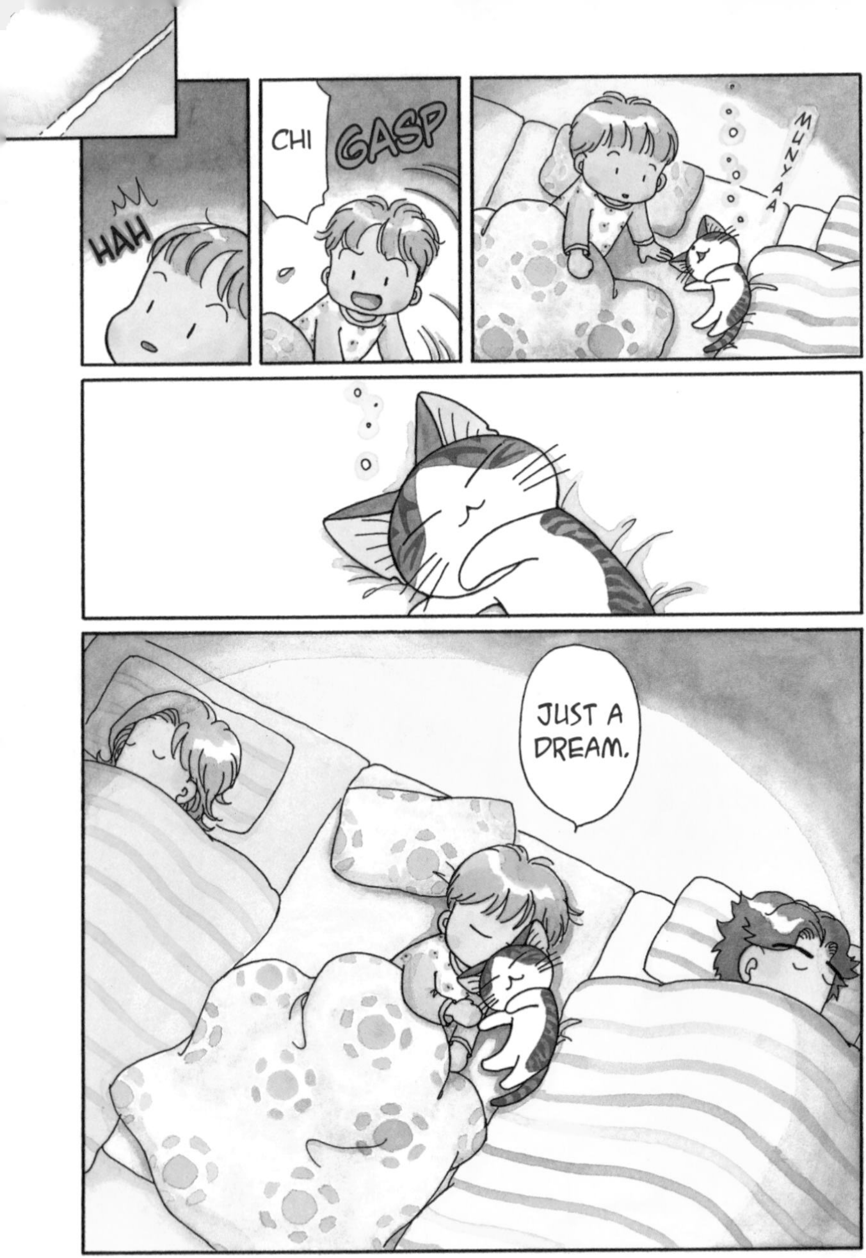
HAH
CHI
GASP
MUNYAA
JUST A DREAM.

the end

homemade 203: a cat meets trouble

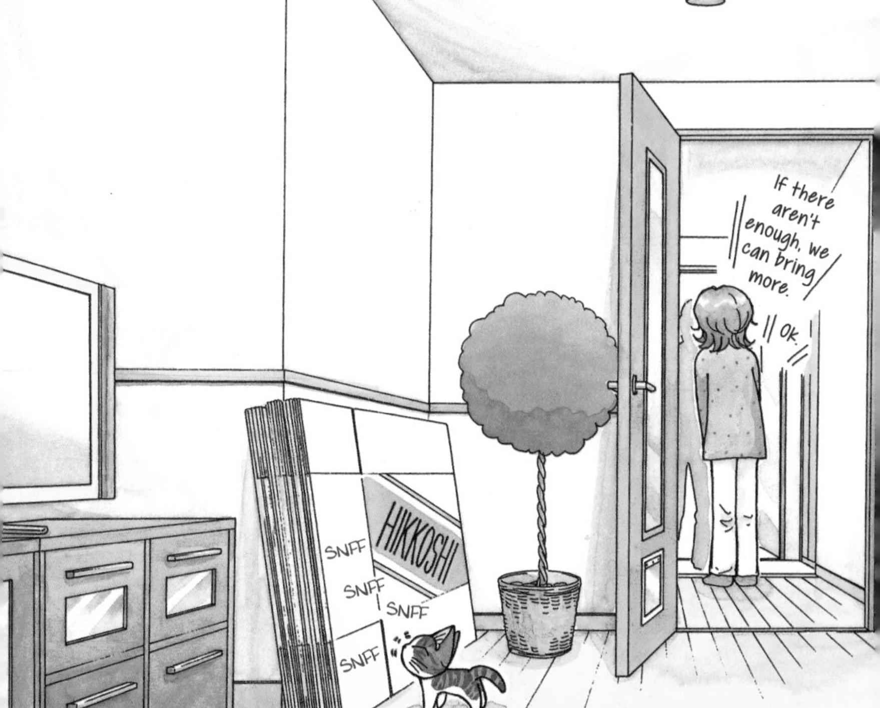
If there aren't enough, we can bring more.
Ok.
HIKKOSHI
SNFF
SNFF
SNFF
SNFF

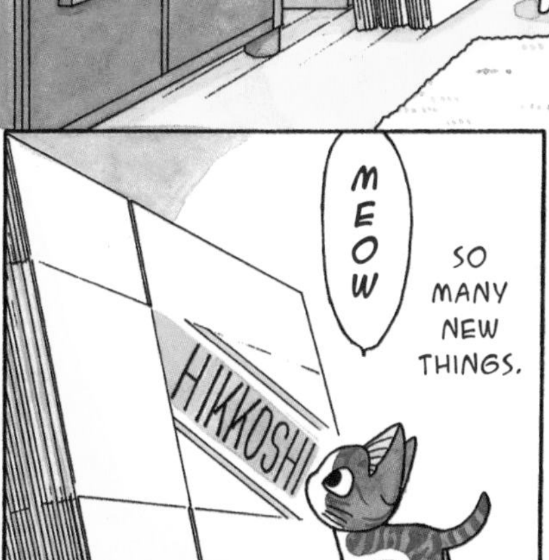
MEOW
SO MANY NEW THINGS.
HIKKOSHI

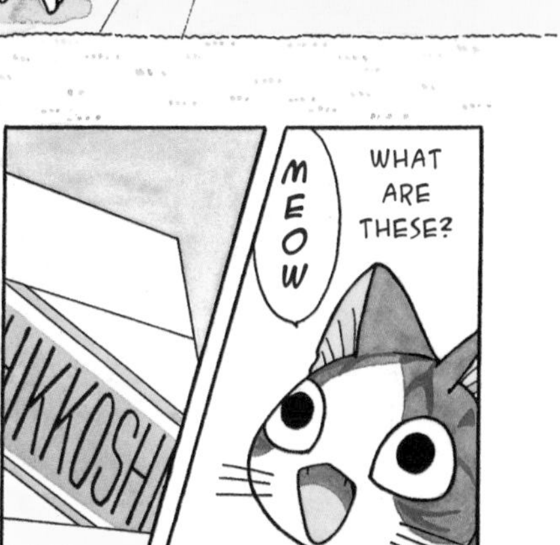
MEOW
WHAT ARE THESE?
HIKKOSH

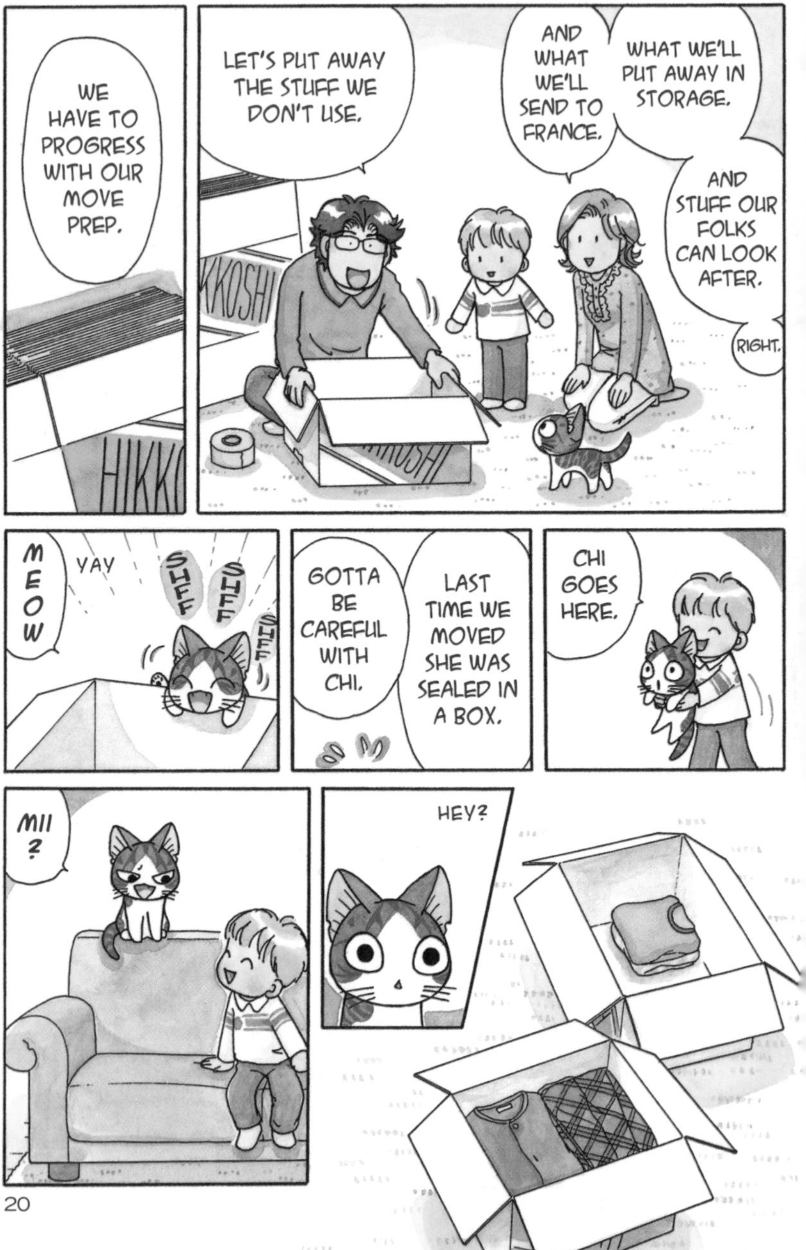
WE HAVE TO PROGRESS WITH OUR MOVE PREP.
HIKKO
LET'S PUT AWAY THE STUFF WE DON'T USE.
AND WHAT WE'LL SEND TO FRANCE.
WHAT WE'LL PUT AWAY IN STORAGE.
AND STUFF OUR FOLKS CAN LOOK AFTER.
RIGHT.
KKOSHI
MEOW
YAY
SHUFF
SHUFF
SHUFF
GOTTA BE CAREFUL WITH CHI.
LAST TIME WE MOVED SHE WAS SEALED IN A BOX.
CHI GOES HERE.
MII?
HEY?

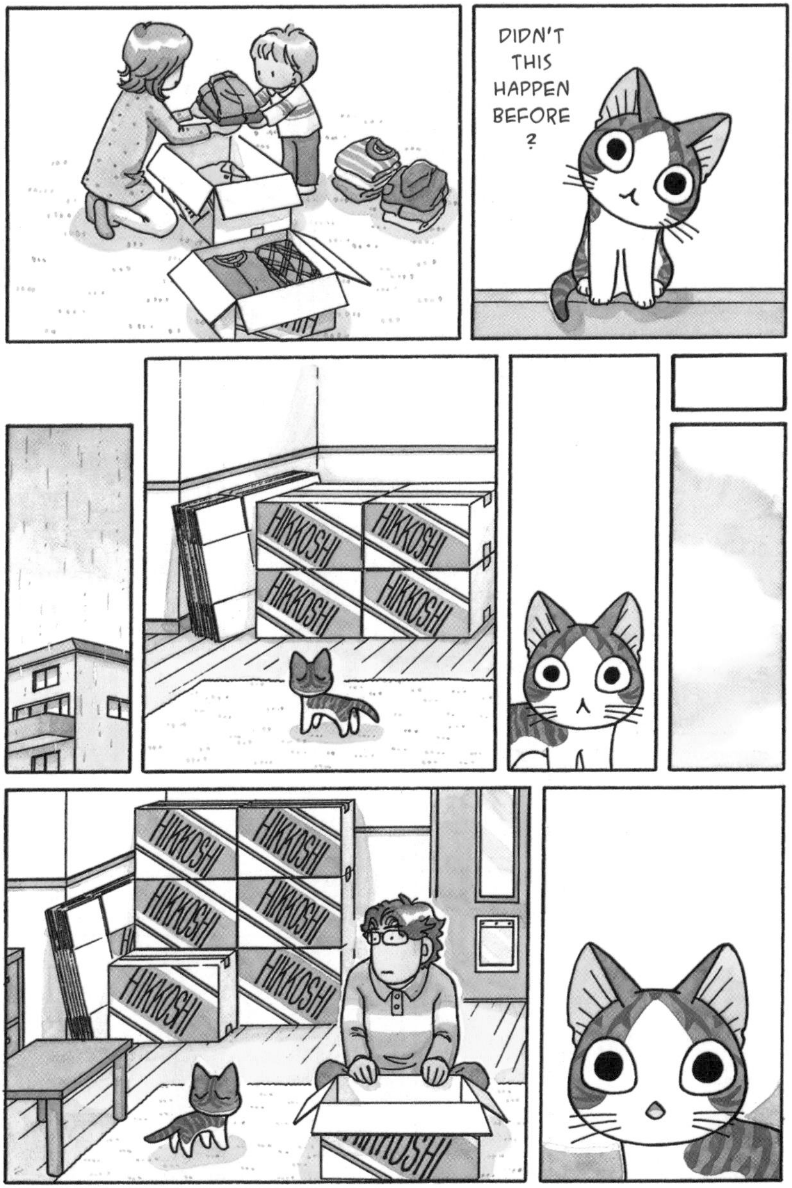
DIDN'T THIS HAPPEN BEFORE ?
HIKKOSHI

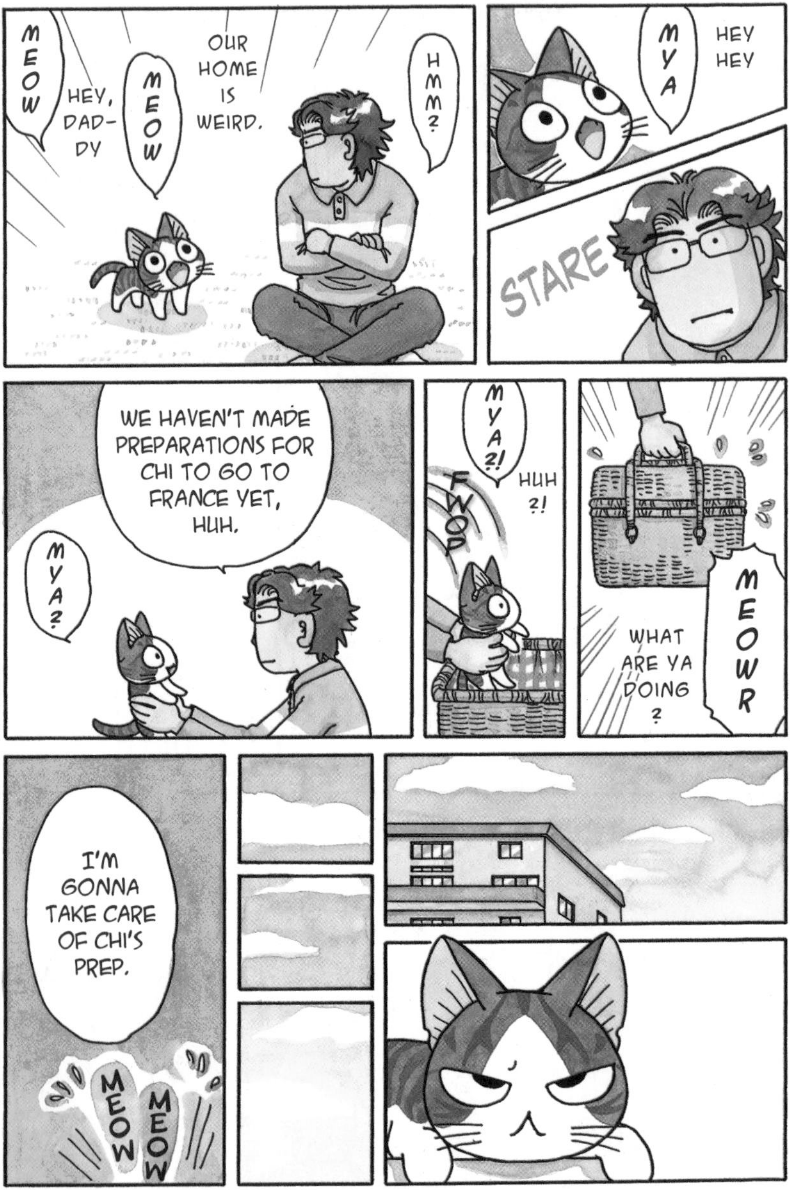
MEOW
HEY, DADDY
MEOW
OUR HOME IS WEIRD.
HMM?
MYA
HEY HEY
STARE
WE HAVEN'T MADE PREPARATIONS FOR CHI TO GO TO FRANCE YET, HUH.
MYA?
MYA?!
HUH?!
FWOP
MEOWR
WHAT ARE YA DOING?
I'M GONNA TAKE CARE OF CHI'S PREP.
MEOW
MEOW
MEOW

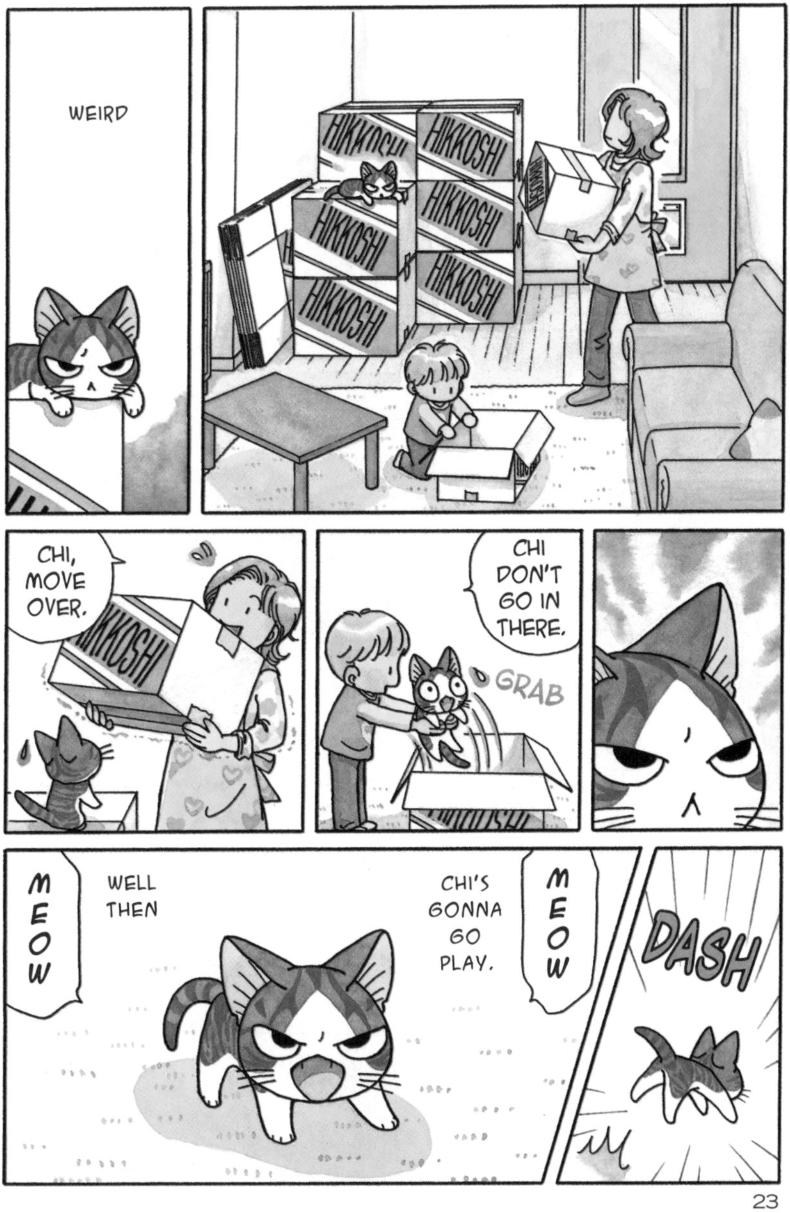

WEIRD
CHI, MOVE OVER.
CHI DON'T GO IN THERE.
GRAB
MEOW
WELL THEN
CHI'S GONNA GO PLAY.
MEOW
DASH

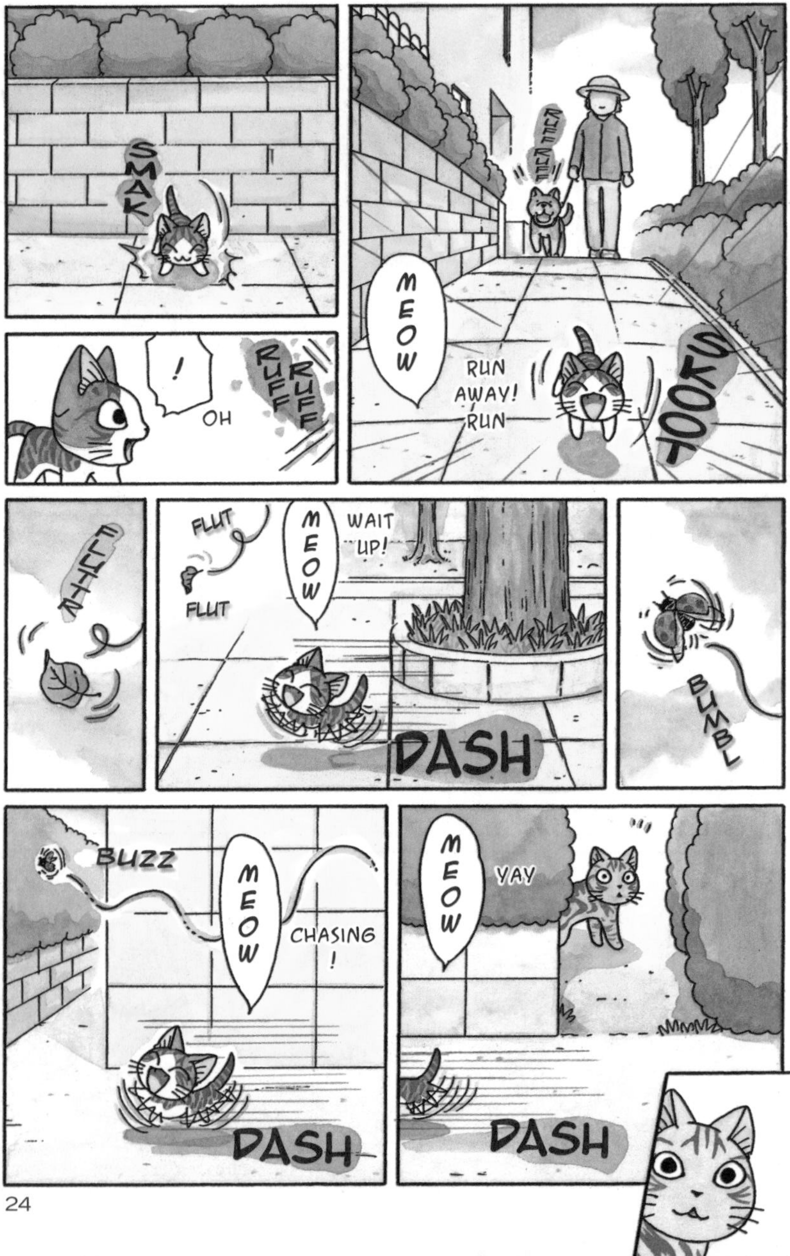
SMAK
!
OH
RUFF RUFF
RUFF RUFF
MEOW
RUN AWAY! RUN
SKOOT
FLUTTR
FLUT
FLUT
MEOW
WAIT UP!
DASH
BUMBL
BUZZ
MEOW
CHASING!
DASH
MEOW
YAY
DASH

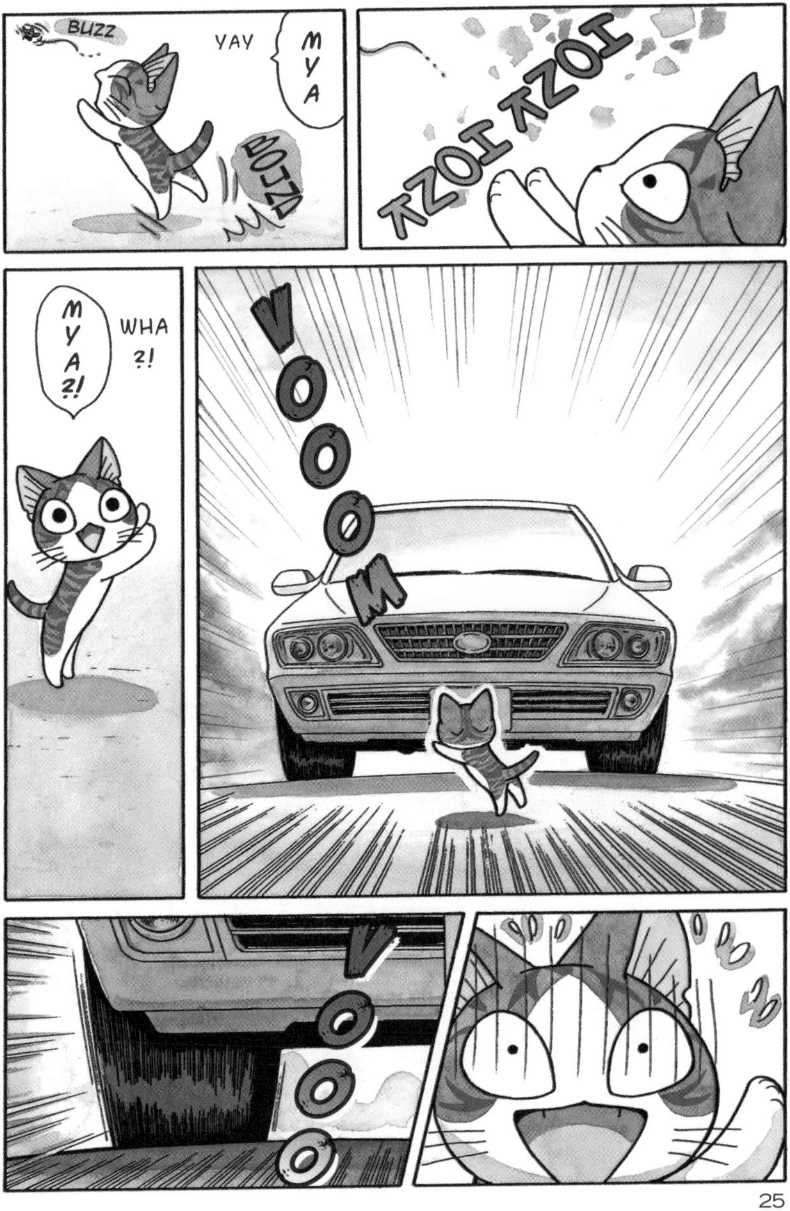
BUZZ
YAY
MYA
BOJZA
TZOI TZOI
MYA?!
WHA?!
VOOOOM
VOOOO

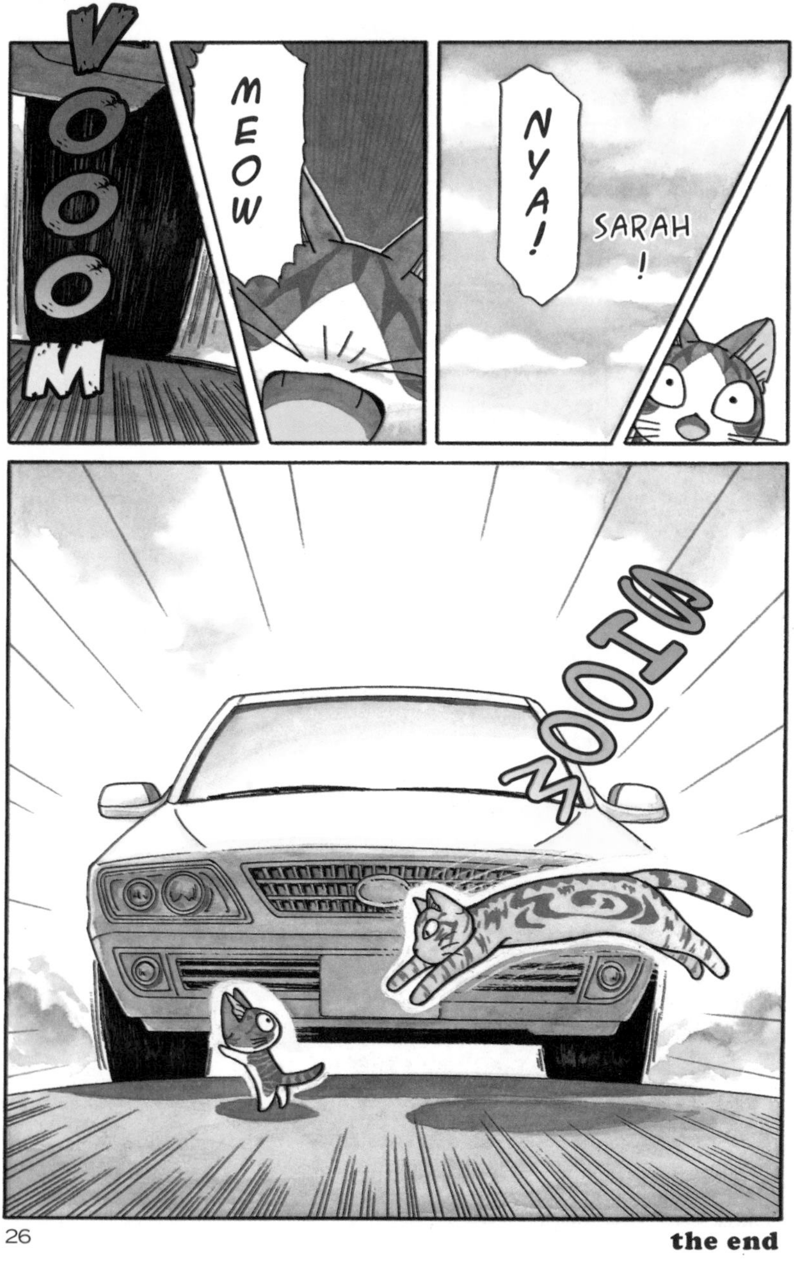
VOOOOM
MEOW
NYA!
SARAH!
SHOOOM

the end

homemade 204: a cat runs

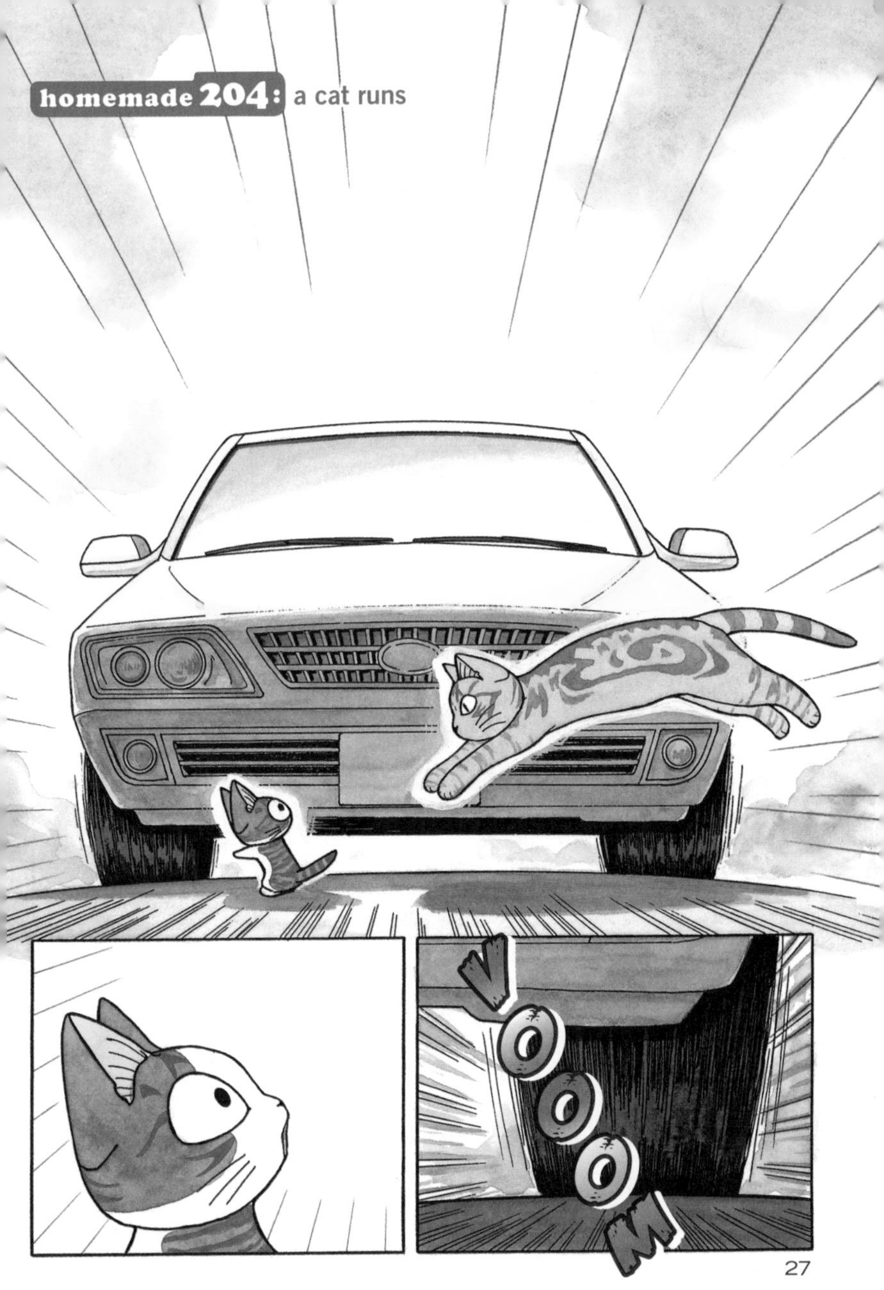
VOOOM

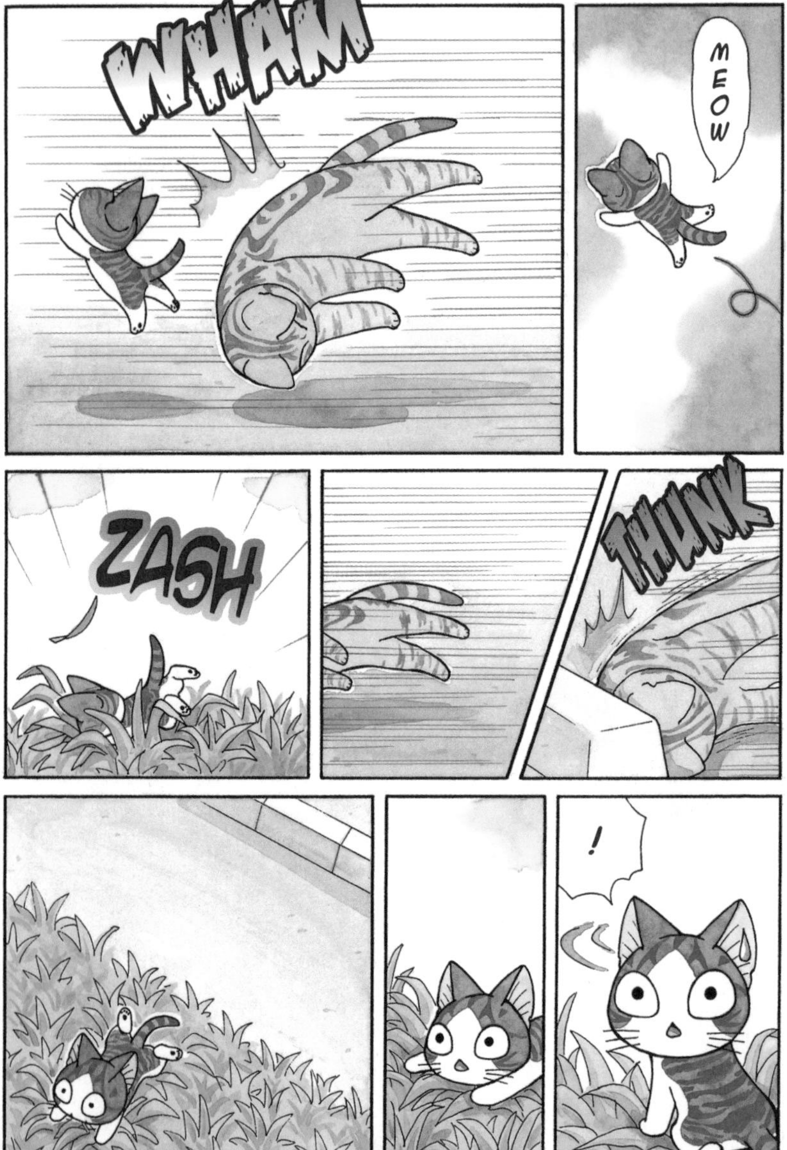
WHAM
MEOW
ZASH
THUNK
!

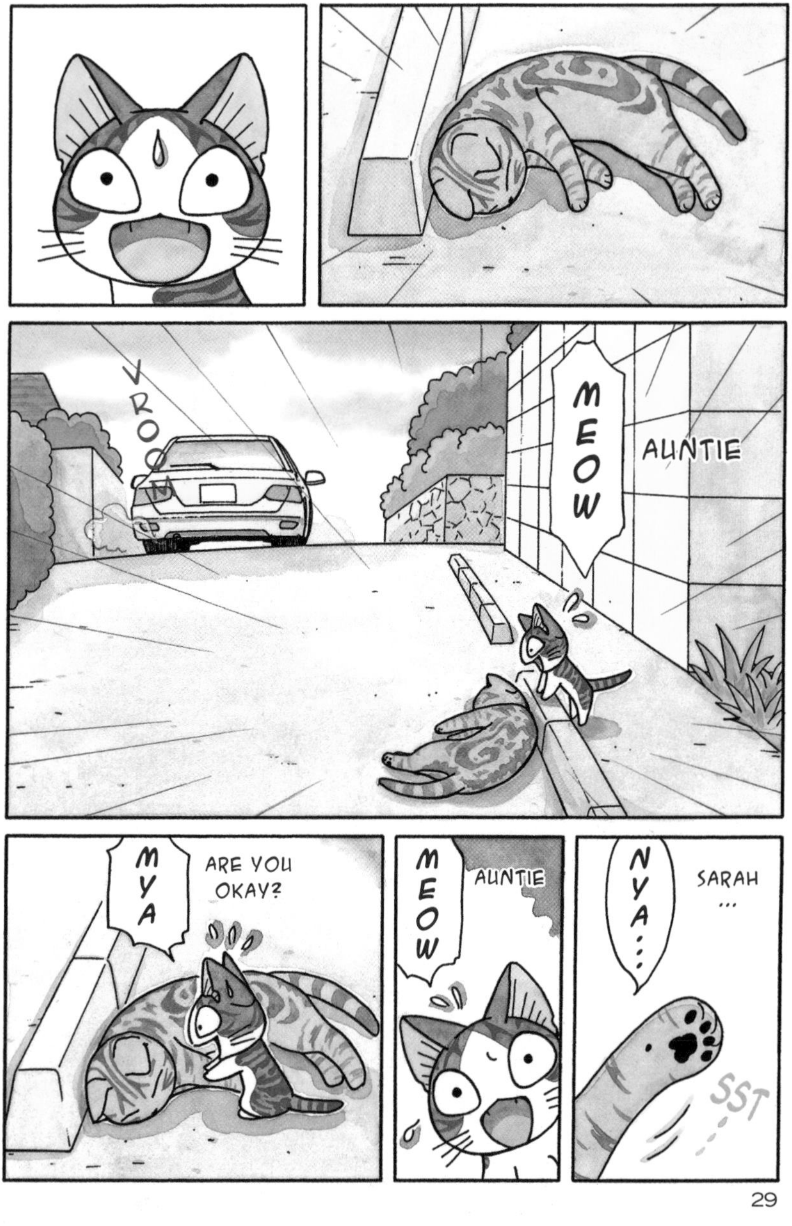
VROOM
MEOW
AUNTIE
MYA
ARE YOU OKAY?
MEOW
AUNTIE
NYA...
SARAH ...
SST

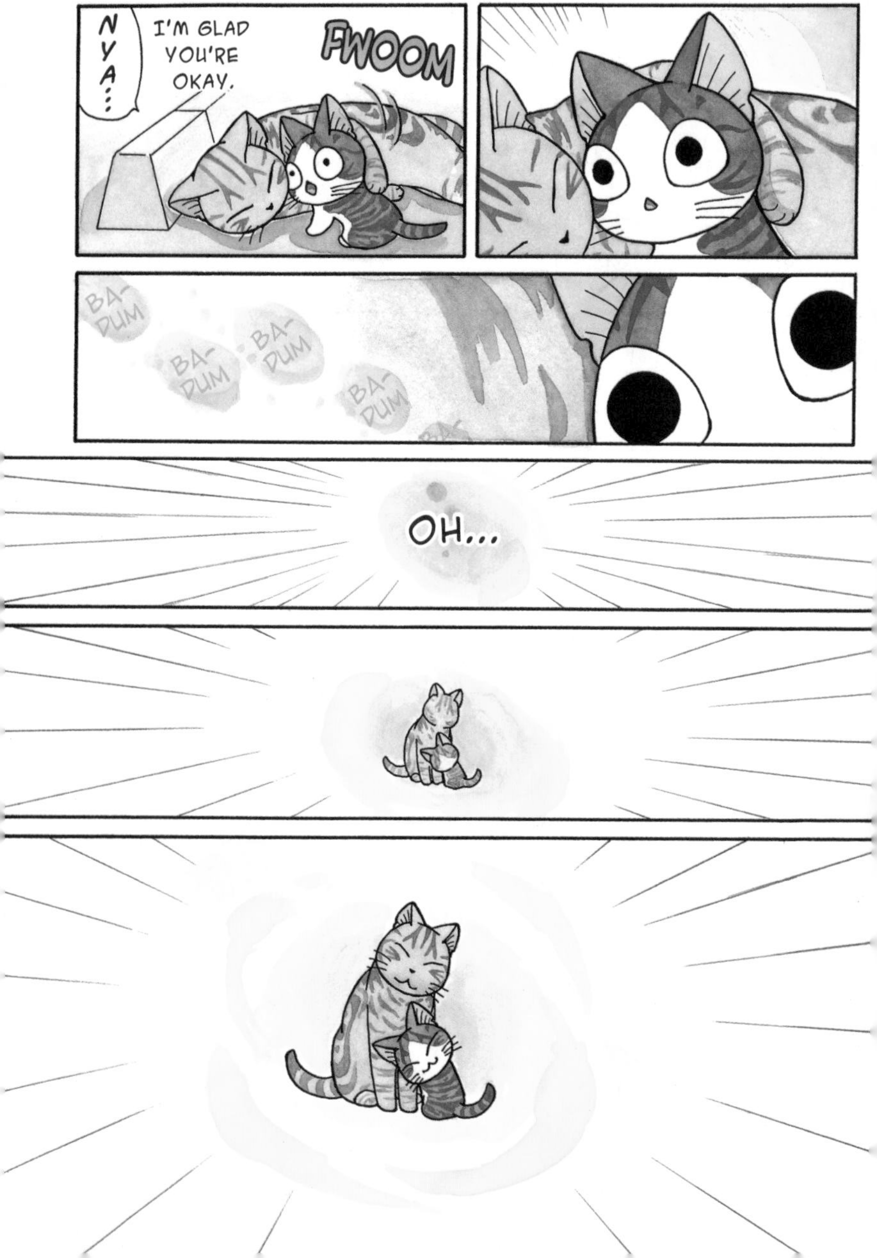
NYA...
I'M GLAD YOU'RE OKAY.
FWOOM
BA-DUM
BA-DUM
BA-DUM
BA-DUM
OH...

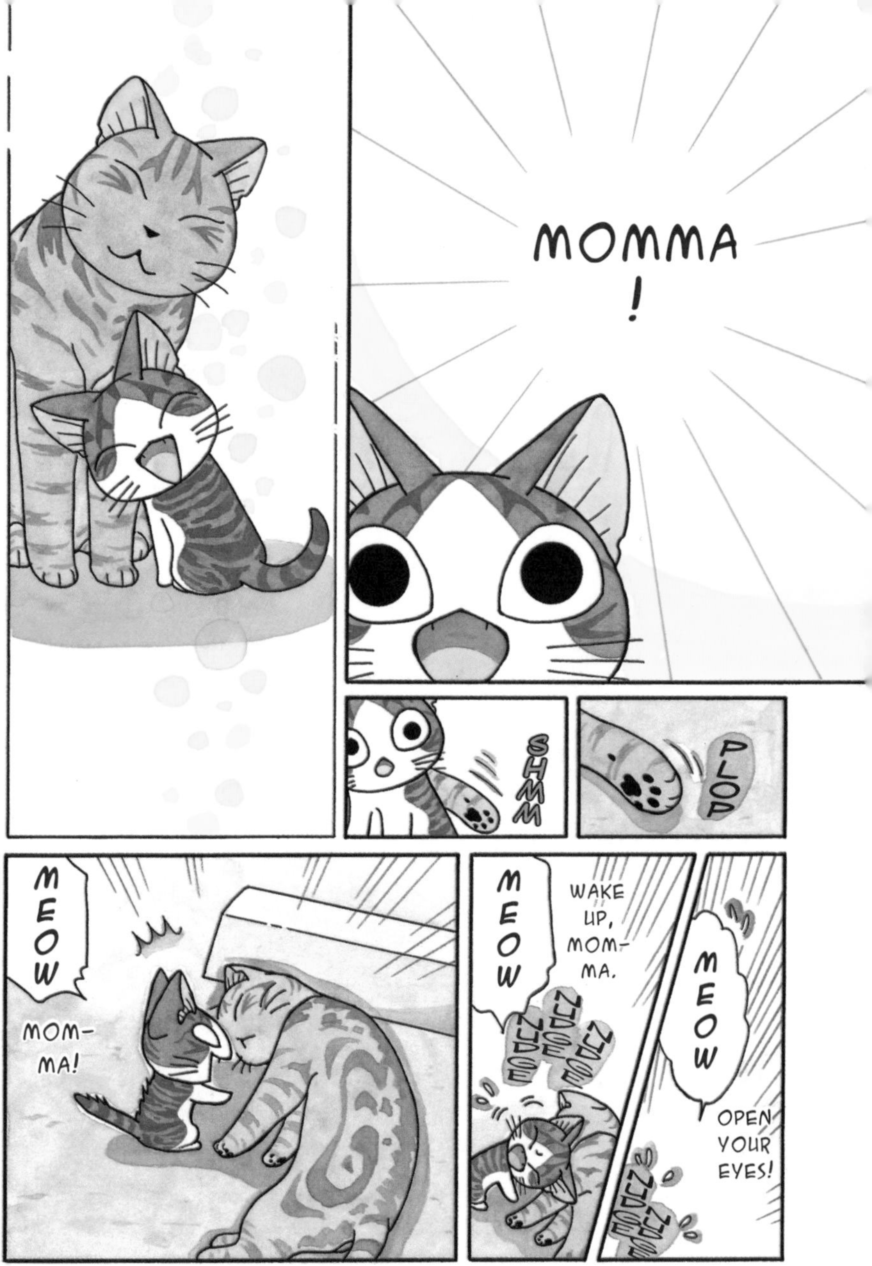
MOMMA
!
SHMM
PLOP
MEOW
MOM-
MA!
MEOW
WAKE
UP,
MOM-
MA.
NUDGE
NUDGE
NUDGE
MEOW
OPEN
YOUR
EYES!
NUDGE
NUDGE

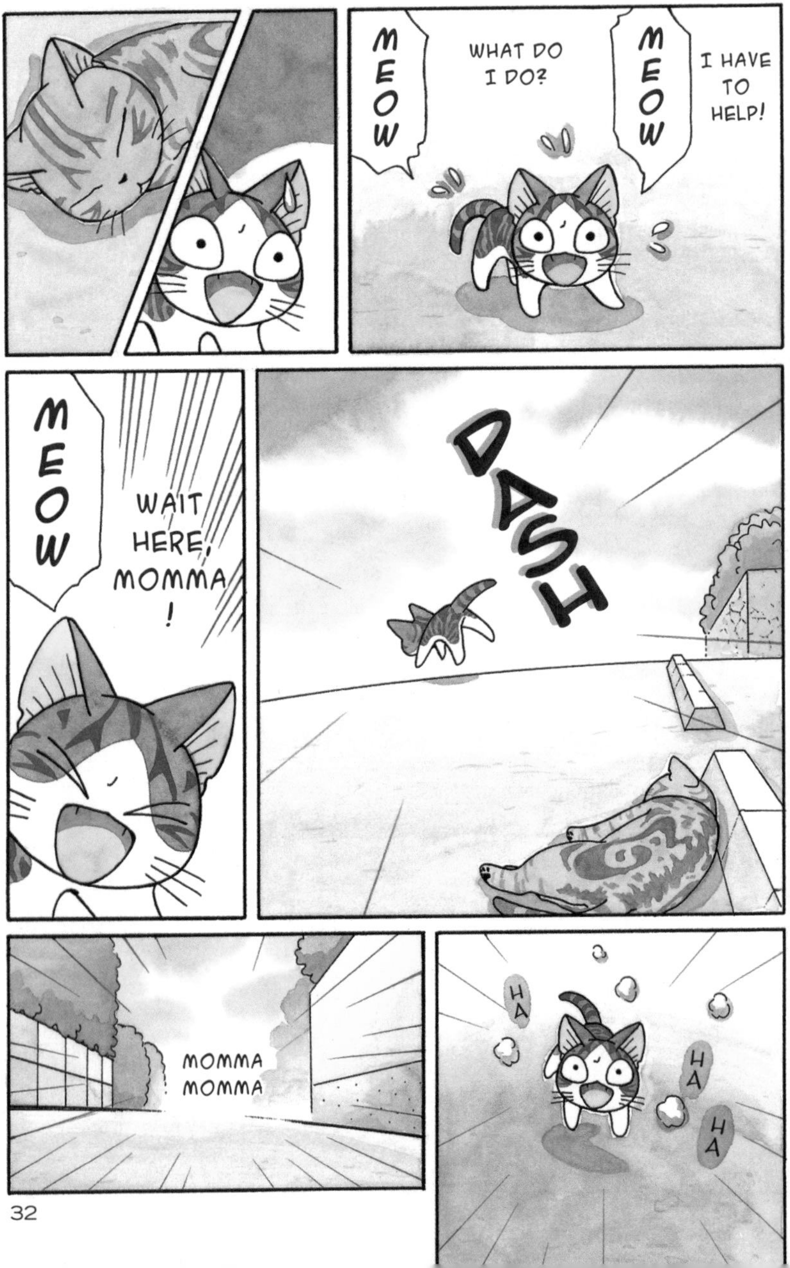
MEOW
WHAT DO I DO?
MEOW
I HAVE TO HELP!
MEOW
WAIT HERE, MOMMA!
DASH
MOMMA MOMMA
HA
HA
HA
HA

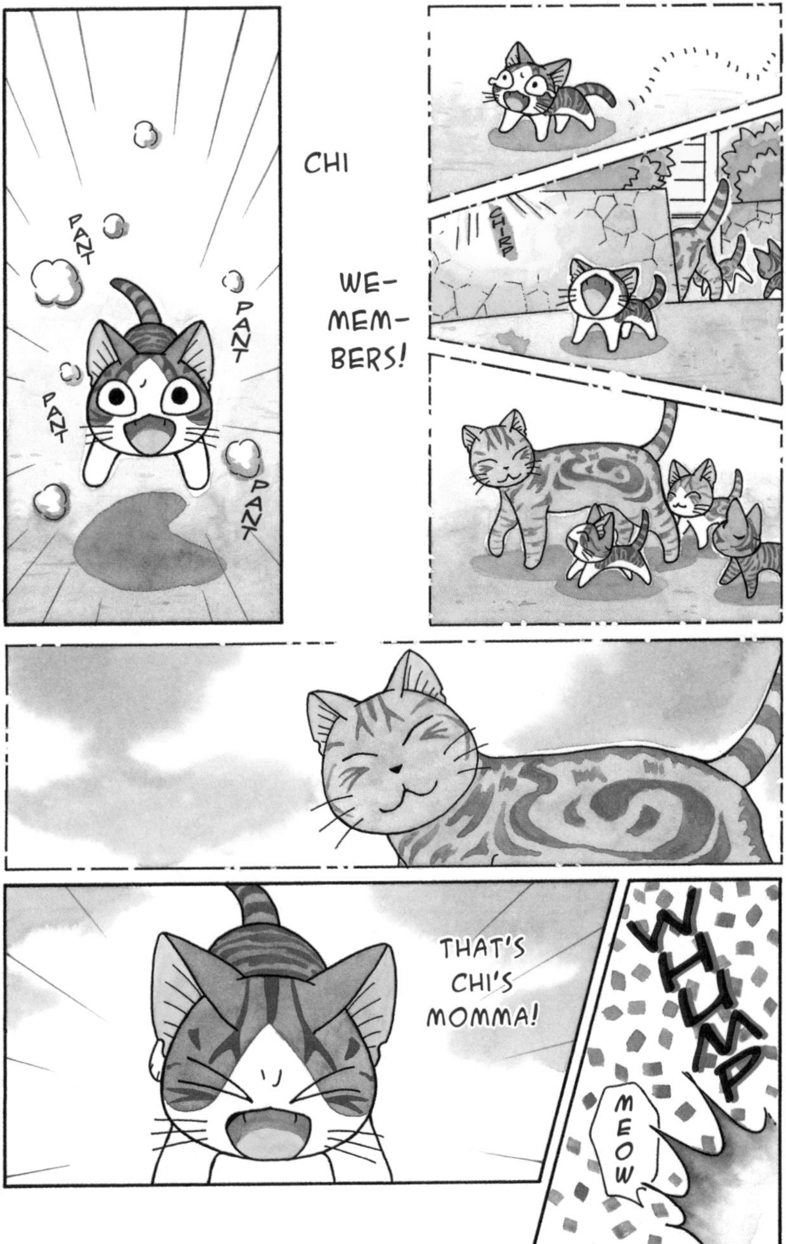
PANT
PANT
PANT
PANT
CHI
CHIRP
WE-MEMBERS!
THAT'S CHI'S MOMMA!
WHUMP
MEOW

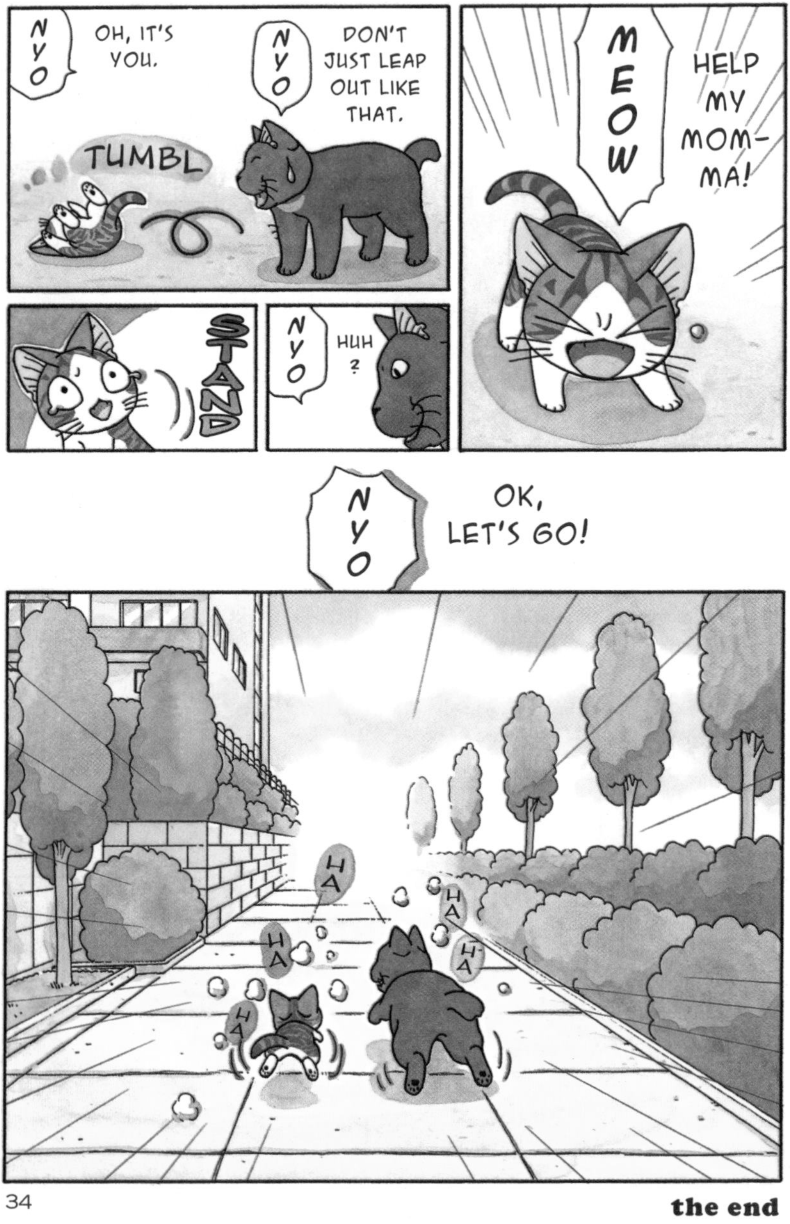
NYO
OH, IT'S YOU.
NYO
DON'T JUST LEAP OUT LIKE THAT.
TUMBL
STAND
NYO
HUH?
MEOW
HELP MY MOM-MA!
NYO
OK, LET'S GO!
HA
HA
HA
HA
HA

the end

homemade 205: a cat helps

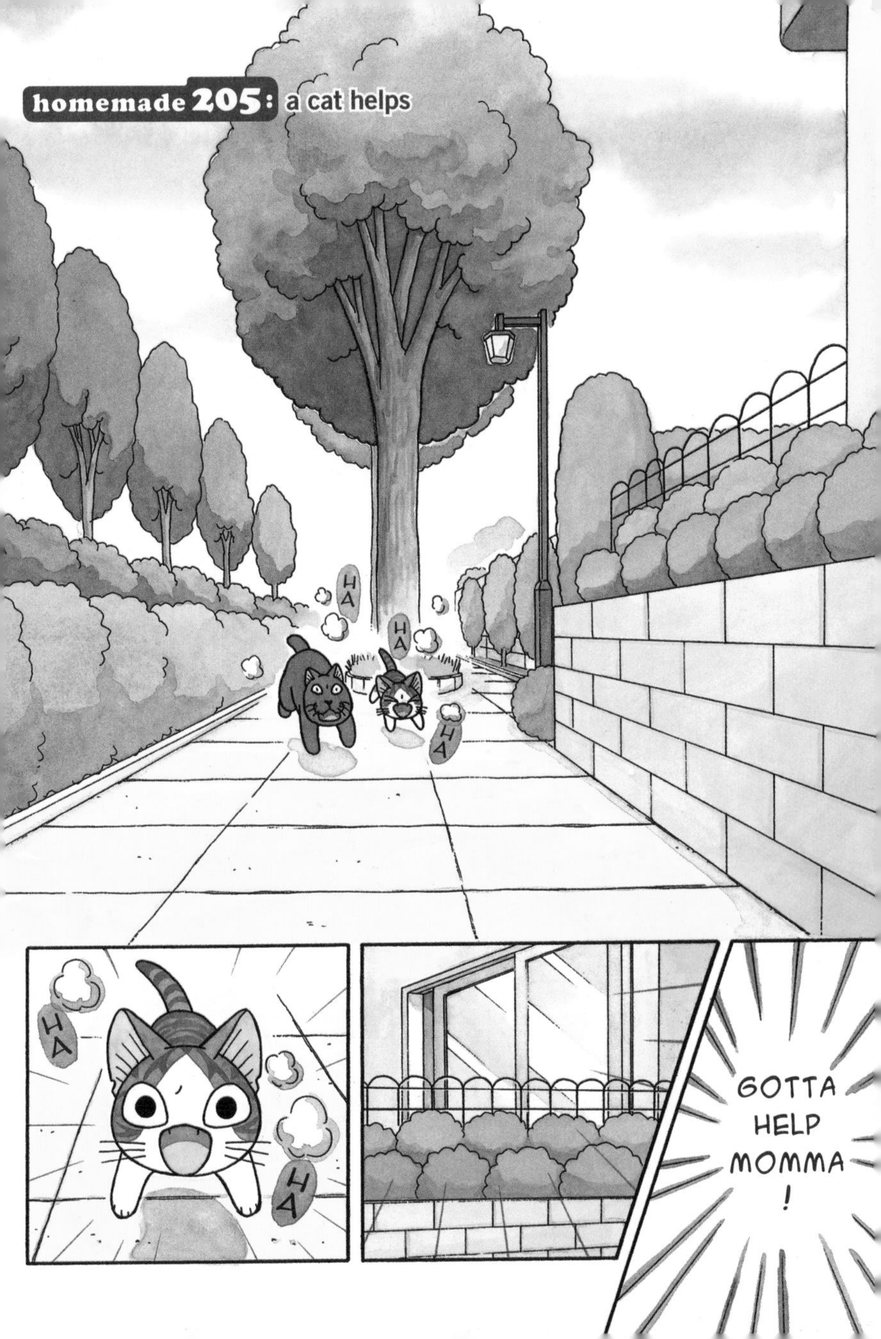

HA
HA
HA
HA
HA
GOTTA HELP MOMMA!

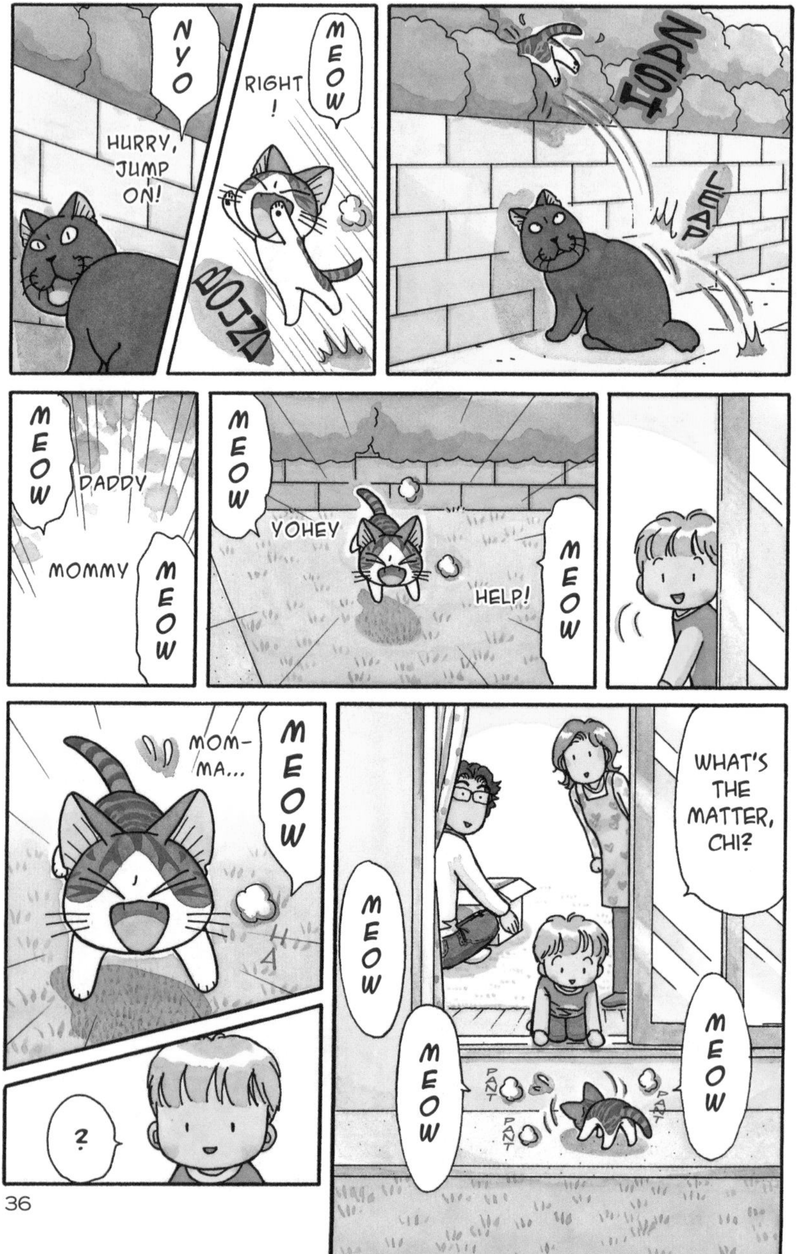

NYO
HURRY, JUMP ON!
MEOW
RIGHT!
ZOOM
HOP
LEAP
MEOW
DADDY
MOMMY
MEOW
MEOW
YOHEY
HELP!
MEOW
MOM-MA...
MEOW
?
WHAT'S THE MATTER, CHI?
MEOW
MEOW
MEOW
PANT
PANT
PANT

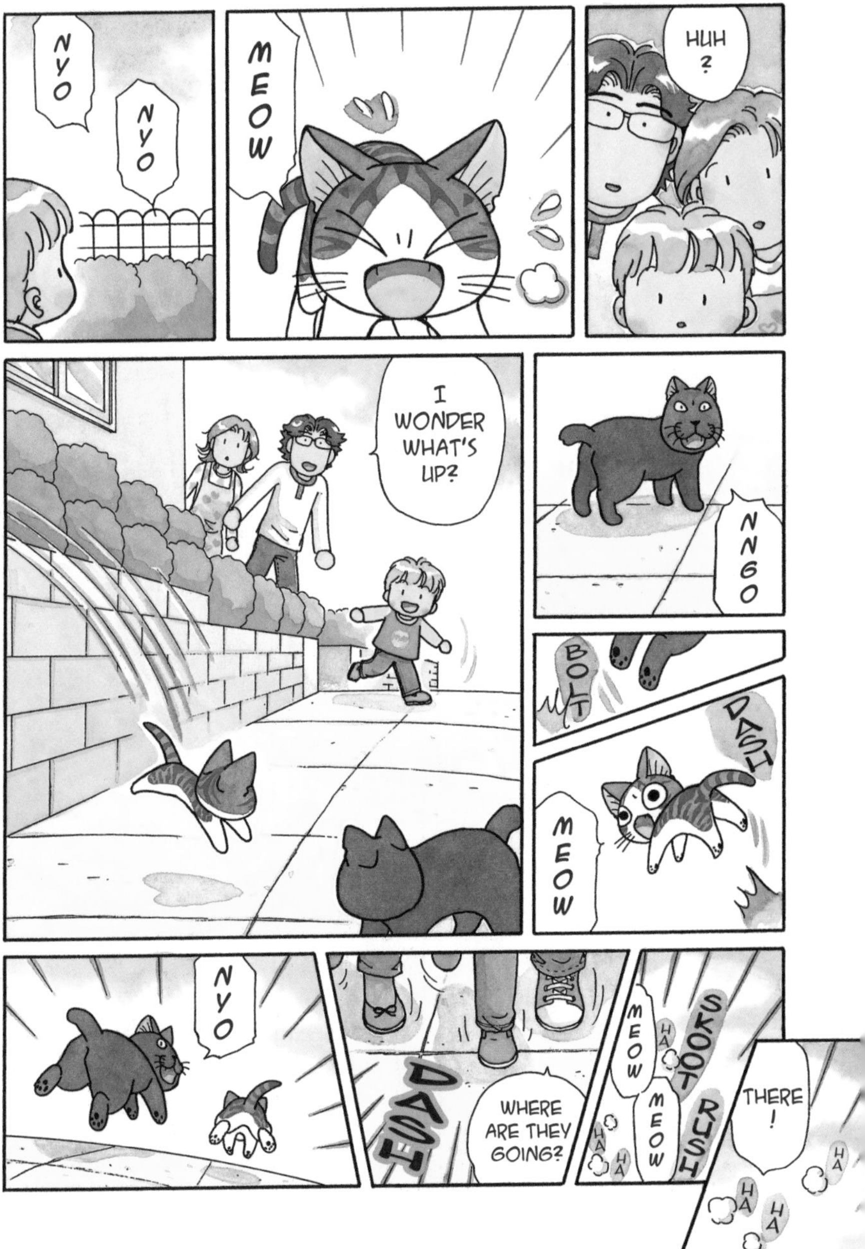
NYO
NYO
MEOW
HUH?
I WONDER WHAT'S UP?
NNGO
BOLT
DASH
MEOW
NYO
DASH
WHERE ARE THEY GOING?
MEOW
MEOW
HA
HA
HA
SKOOT
RUSH
THERE!
HA
HA
HA

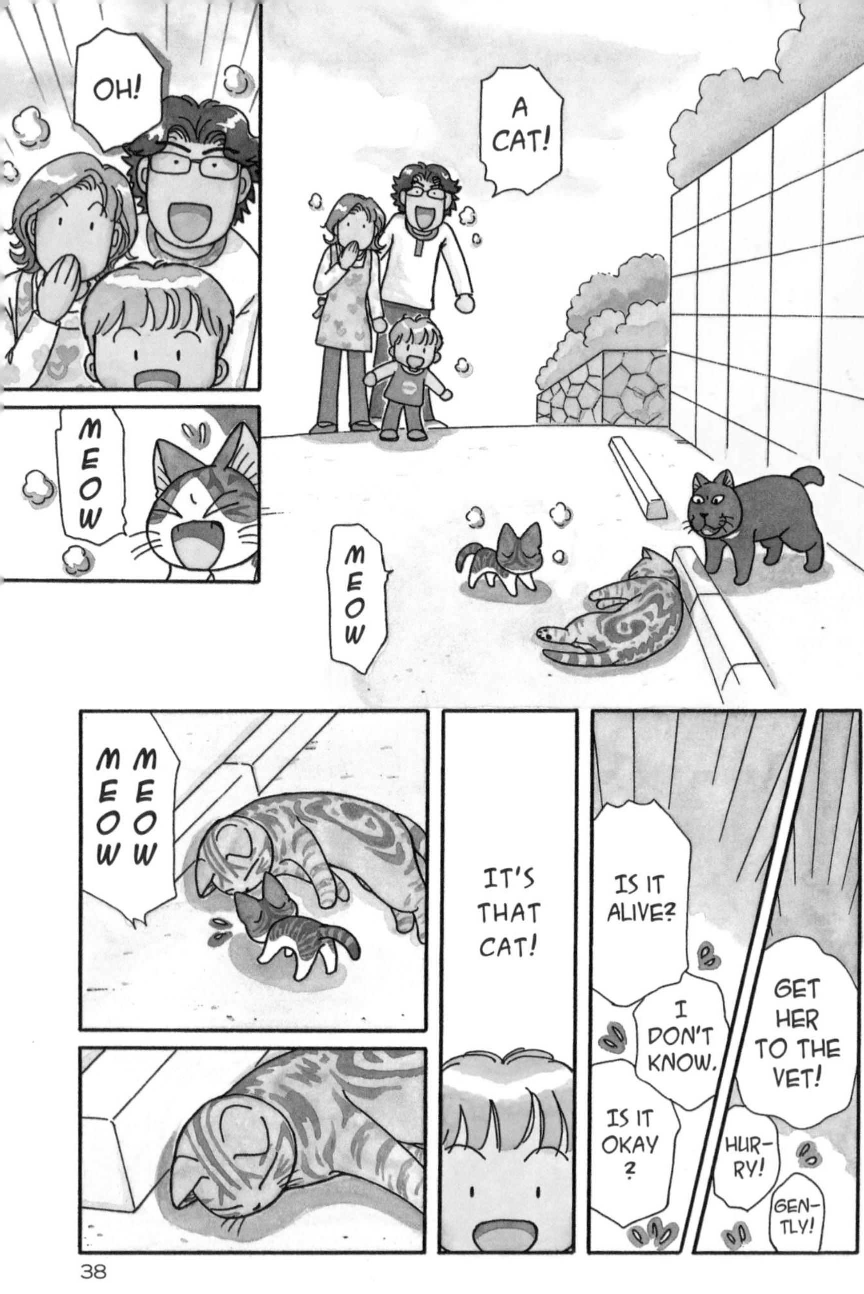
OH!
MEOW
A CAT!
MEOW
MEOW MEOW
IT'S THAT CAT!
IS IT ALIVE?
I DON'T KNOW.
IS IT OKAY?
GET HER TO THE VET!
HURRY!
GENTLY!

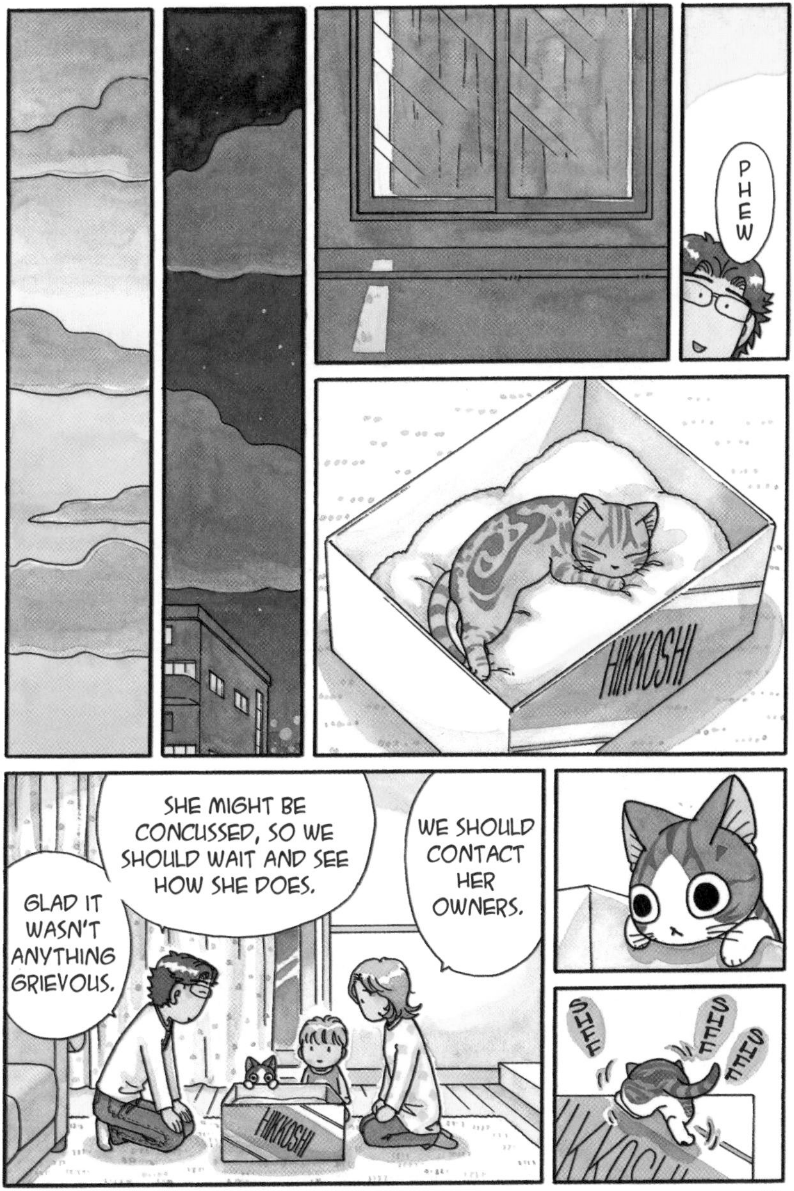
PHEW
HIKKOSHI
SHE MIGHT BE CONCUSSED, SO WE SHOULD WAIT AND SEE HOW SHE DOES.
GLAD IT WASN'T ANYTHING GRIEVOUS.
WE SHOULD CONTACT HER OWNERS.
HIKKOSHI
SHUFF
SHUFF
SHUFF

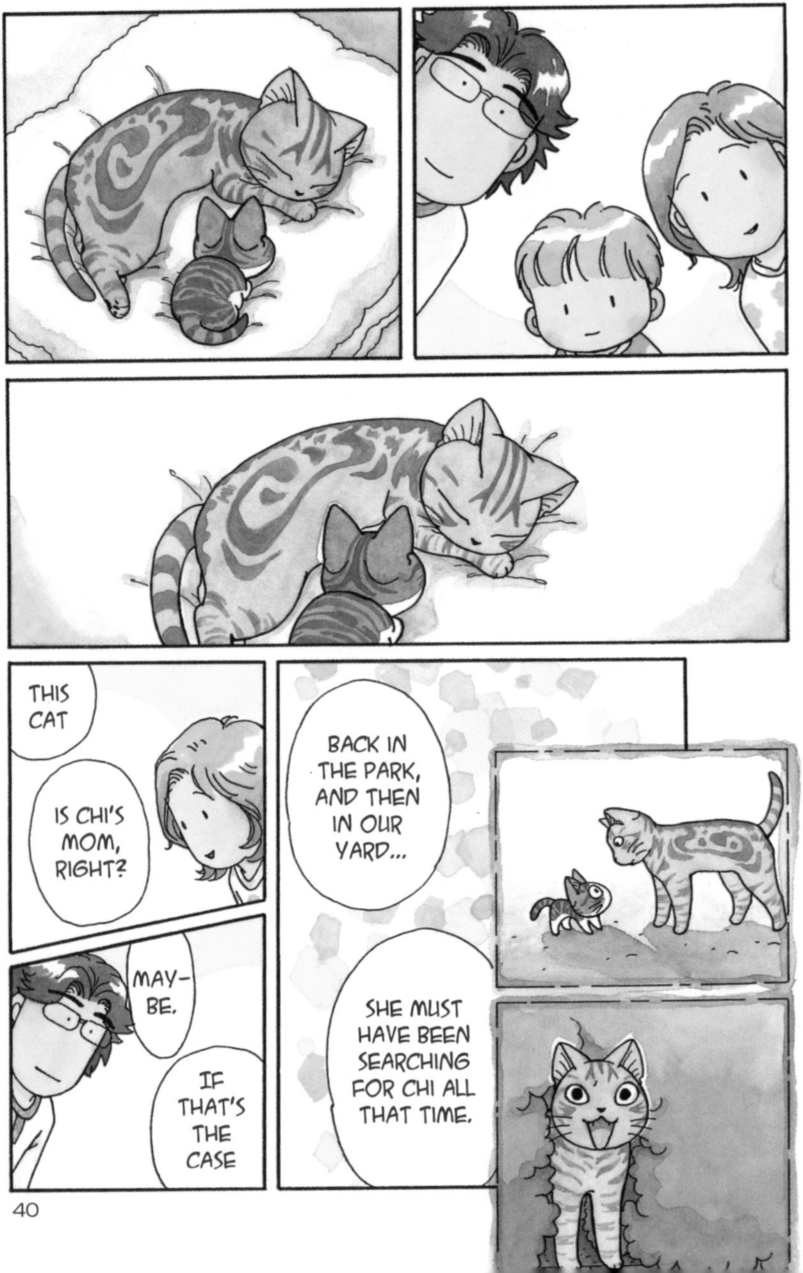
THIS CAT
IS CHI'S MOM, RIGHT?
MAY-BE.
IF THAT'S THE CASE
BACK IN THE PARK, AND THEN IN OUR YARD...
SHE MUST HAVE BEEN SEARCHING FOR CHI ALL THAT TIME.

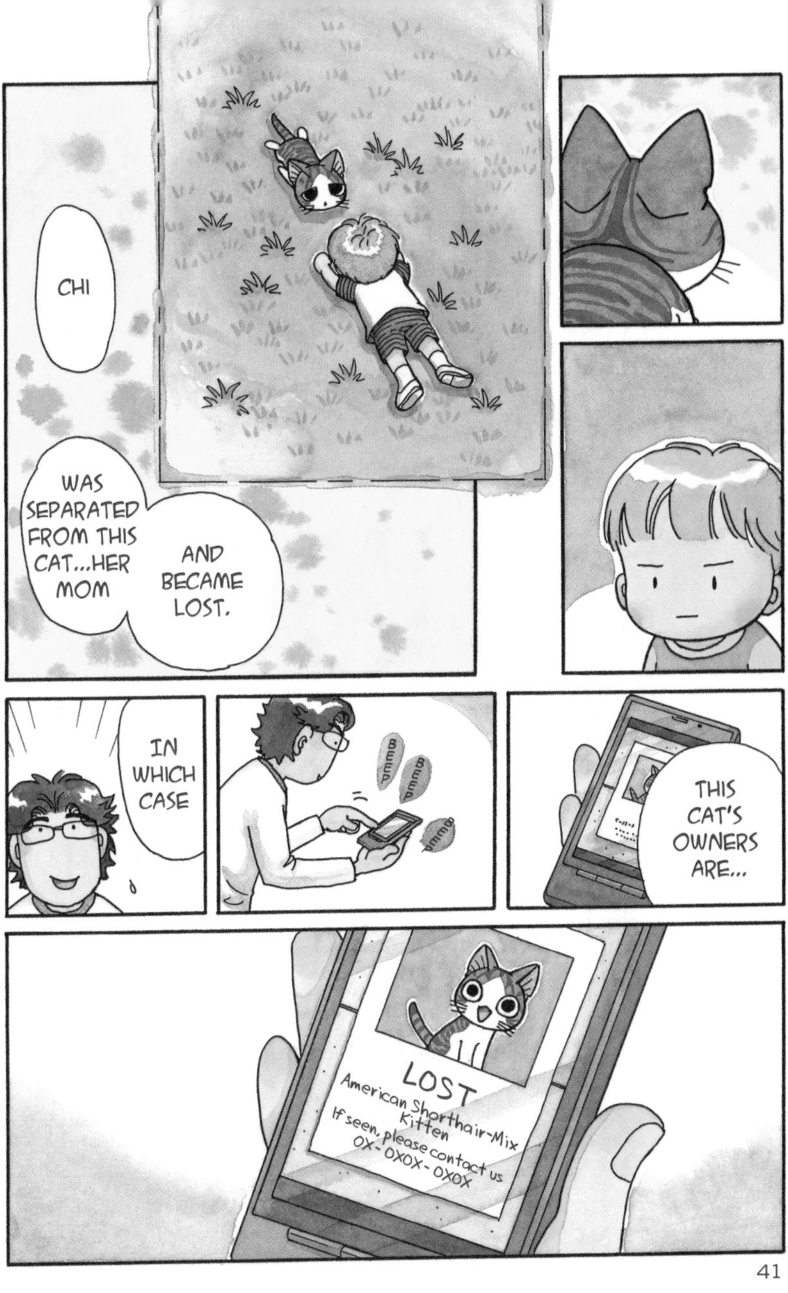
CHI
WAS SEPARATED FROM THIS CAT...HER MOM
AND BECAME LOST.
IN WHICH CASE
BEEP
BEEP
BEEP
THIS CAT'S OWNERS ARE...
LOST
American Shorthair-Mix Kitten
If seen, please contact us
OX-OXOX-OXOX

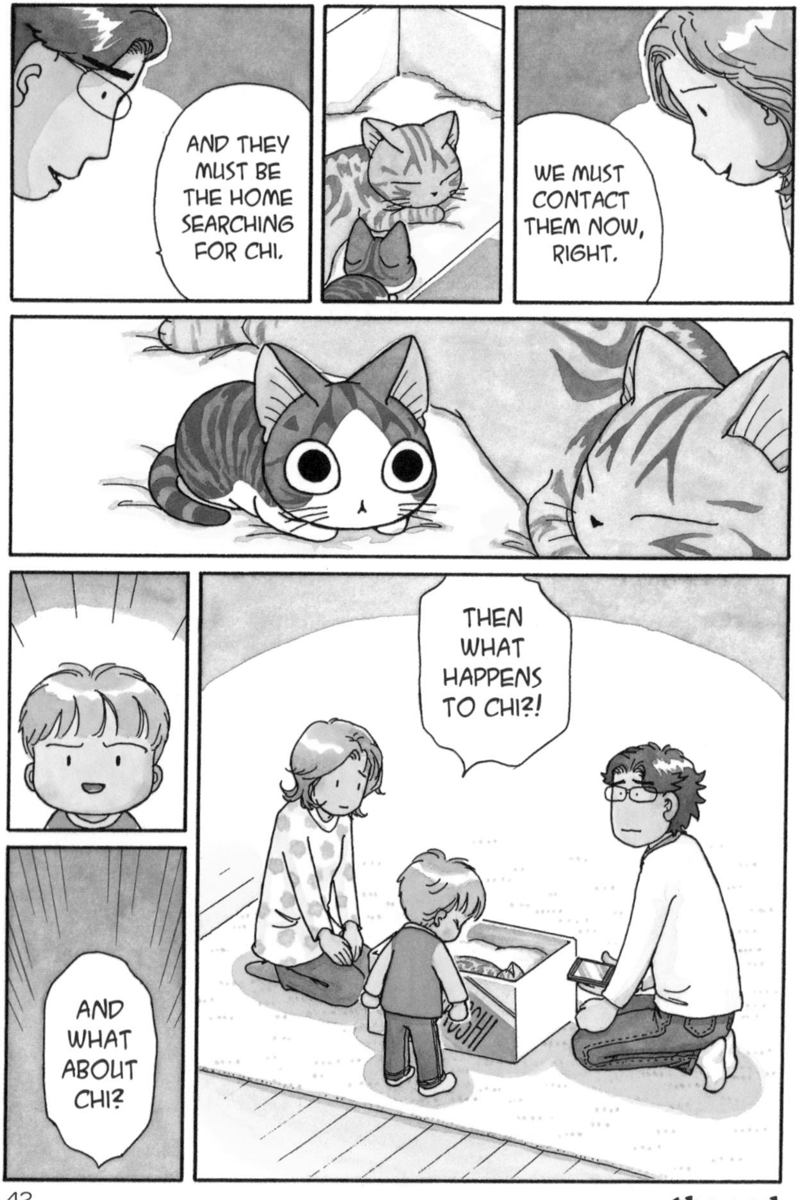
AND THEY MUST BE THE HOME SEARCHING FOR CHI.
WE MUST CONTACT THEM NOW, RIGHT.
AND WHAT ABOUT CHI?
THEN WHAT HAPPENS TO CHI?!

the end

homemade 206: a cat snuggles

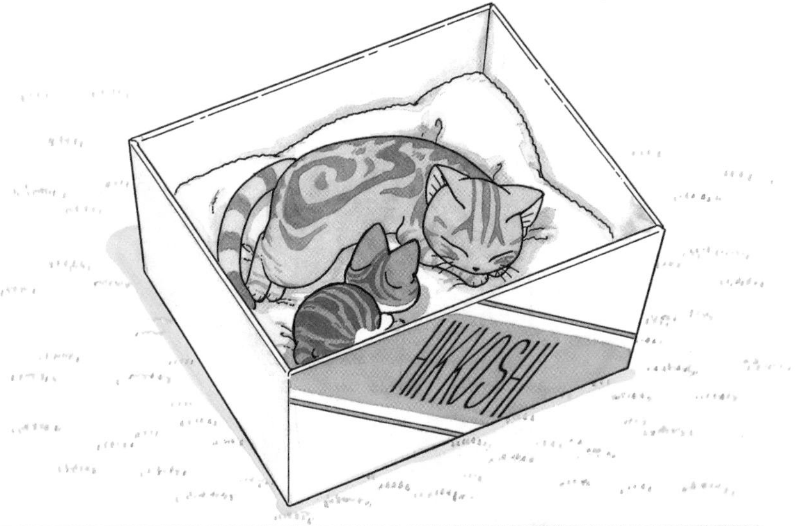
HAKKOSH

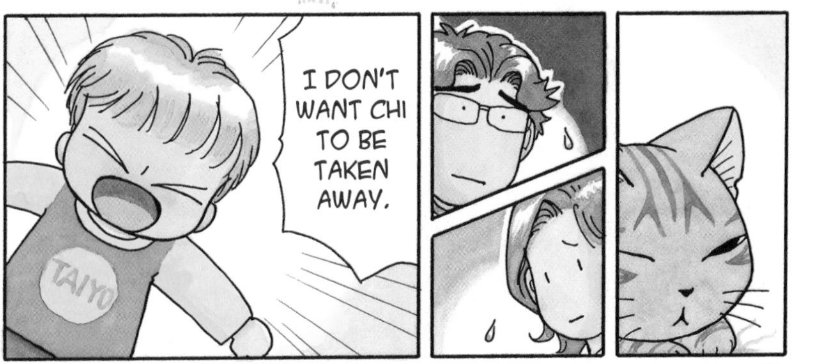
I DON'T WANT CHI TO BE TAKEN AWAY.
TAIYO

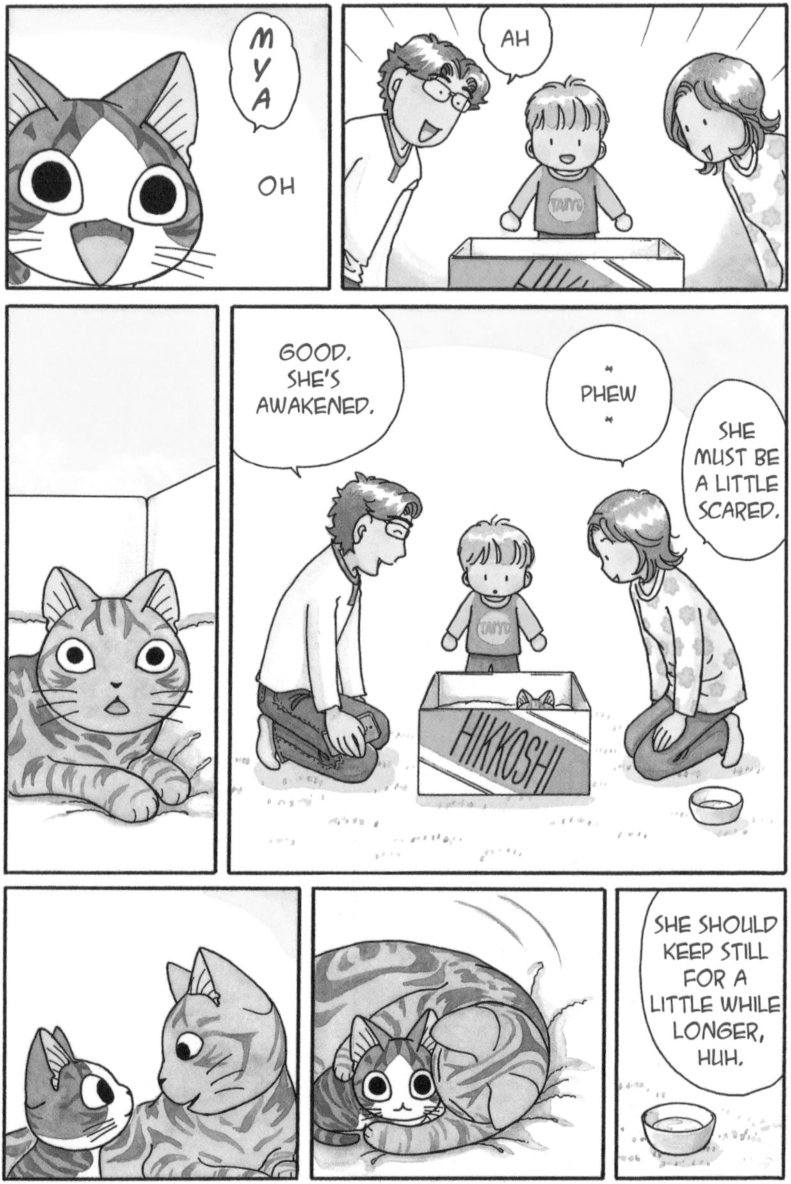
MYA
OH
AH
GOOD. SHE'S AWAKENED.
* PHEW *
SHE MUST BE A LITTLE SCARED.
SHE SHOULD KEEP STILL FOR A LITTLE WHILE LONGER, HUH.

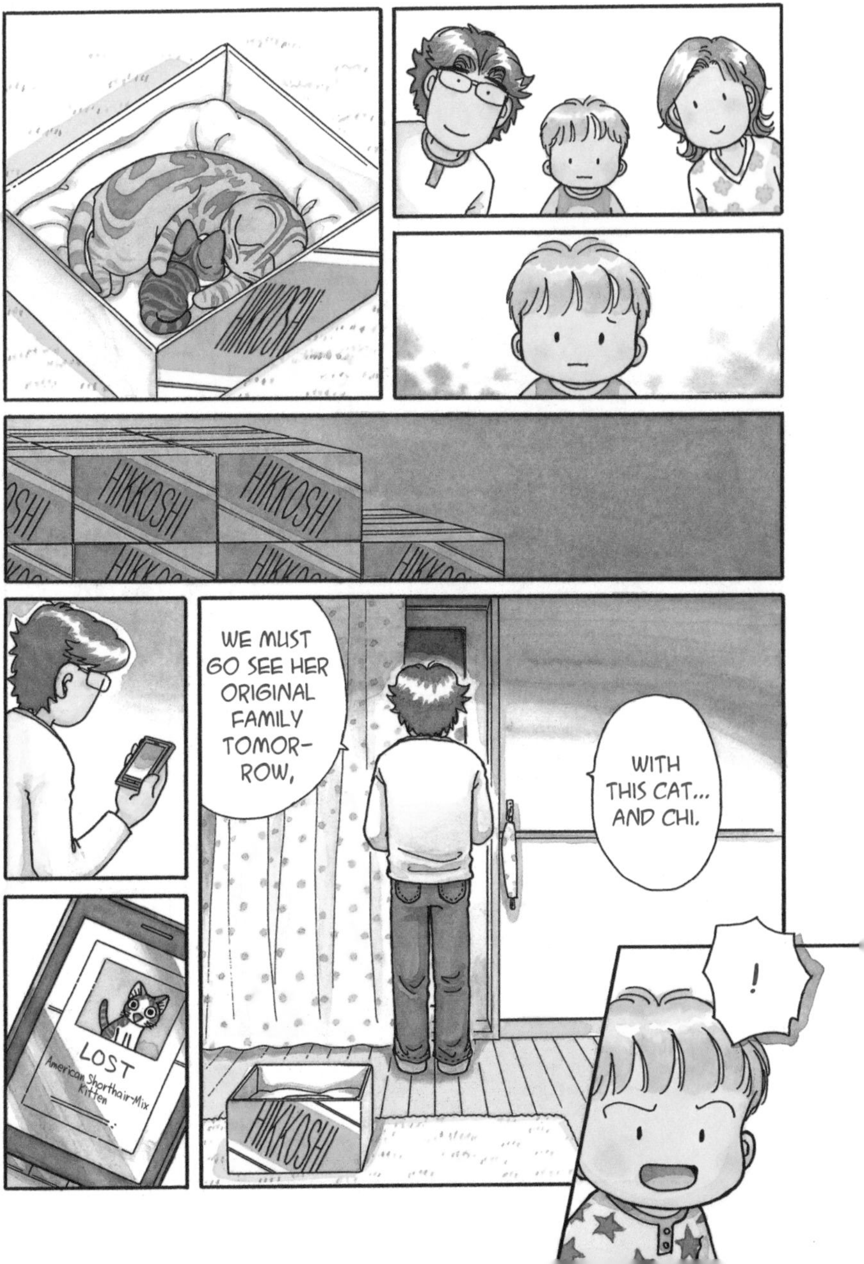
HIKKOSHI
HIKKOSHI
HIKKOSHI
LOST
American Shorthair-Mix Kitten
WE MUST GO SEE HER ORIGINAL FAMILY TOMORROW,
WITH THIS CAT... AND CHI.
HIKKOSHI
!

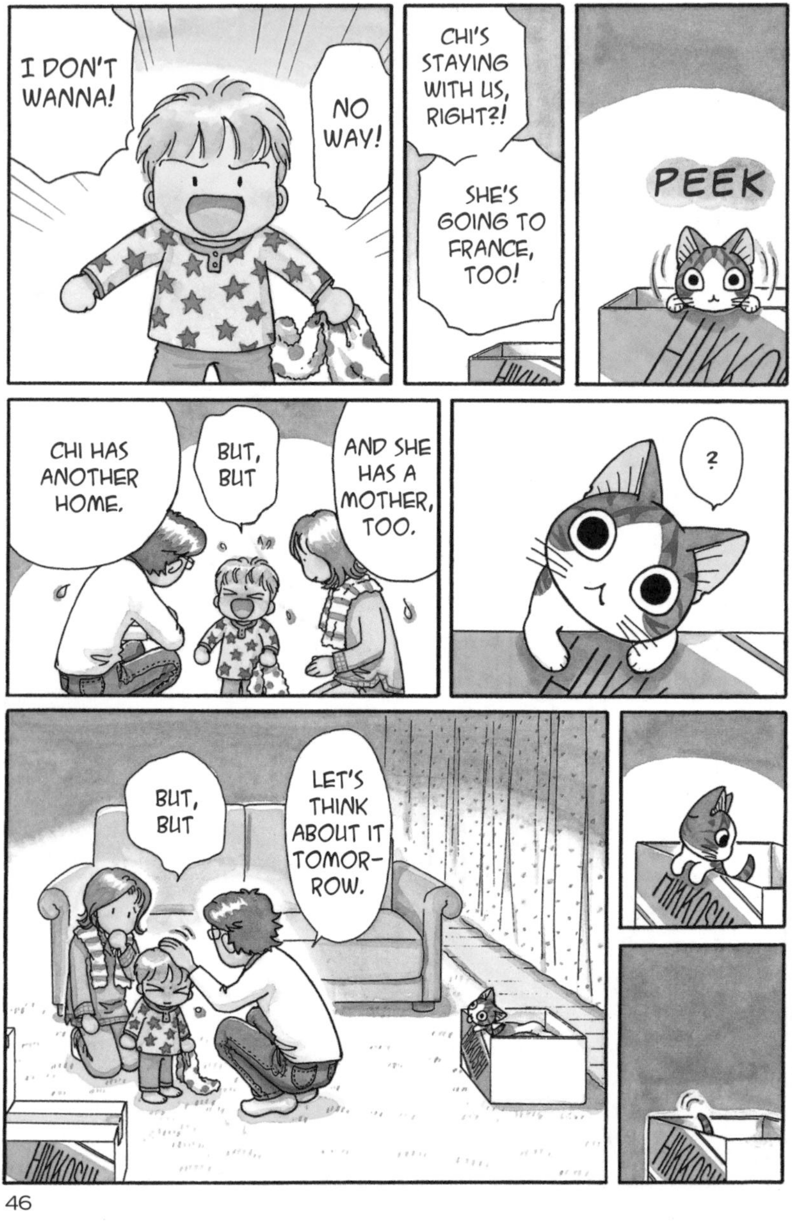
I DON'T WANNA!
NO WAY!
CHI'S STAYING WITH US, RIGHT?!
SHE'S GOING TO FRANCE, TOO!
PEEK
CHI HAS ANOTHER HOME.
BUT, BUT
AND SHE HAS A MOTHER, TOO.
?
BUT, BUT
LET'S THINK ABOUT IT TOMORROW.

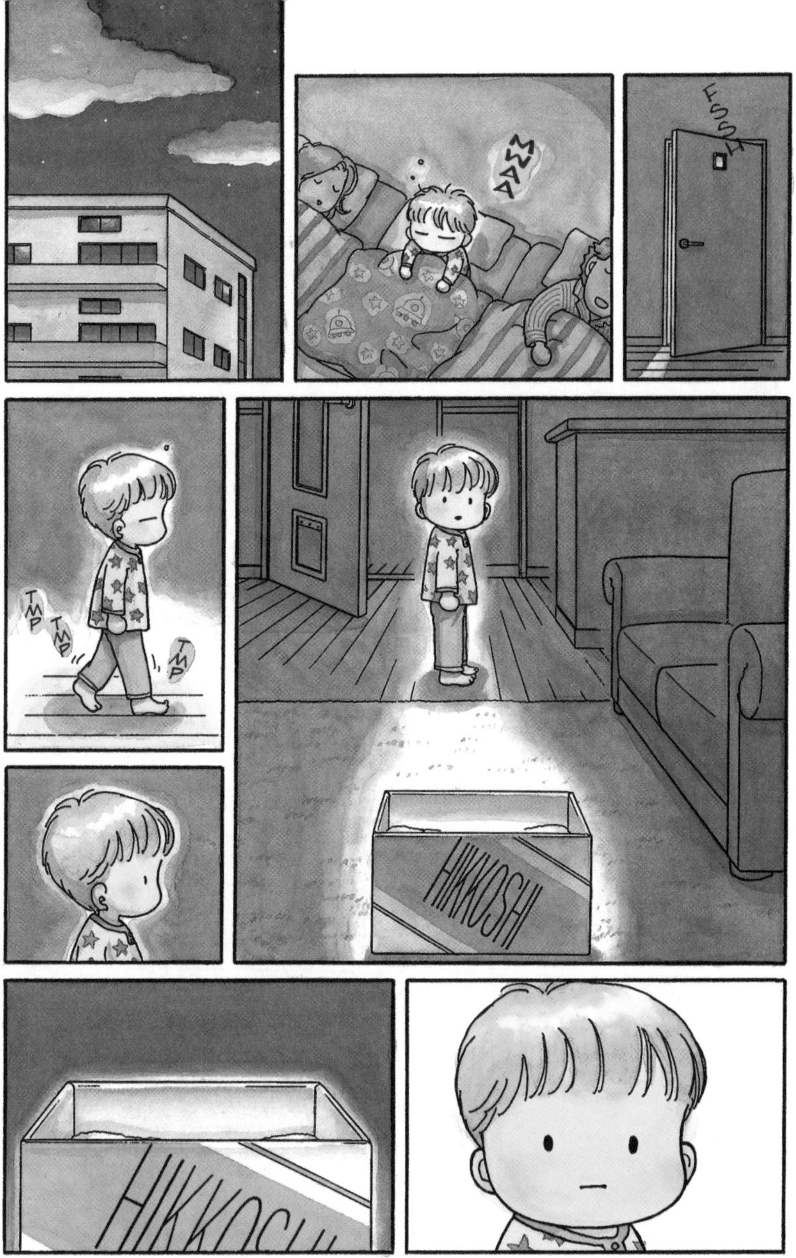
MWAA
FSSH
TMP TMP
TMP
HIKKOSHI
HIKKOSH

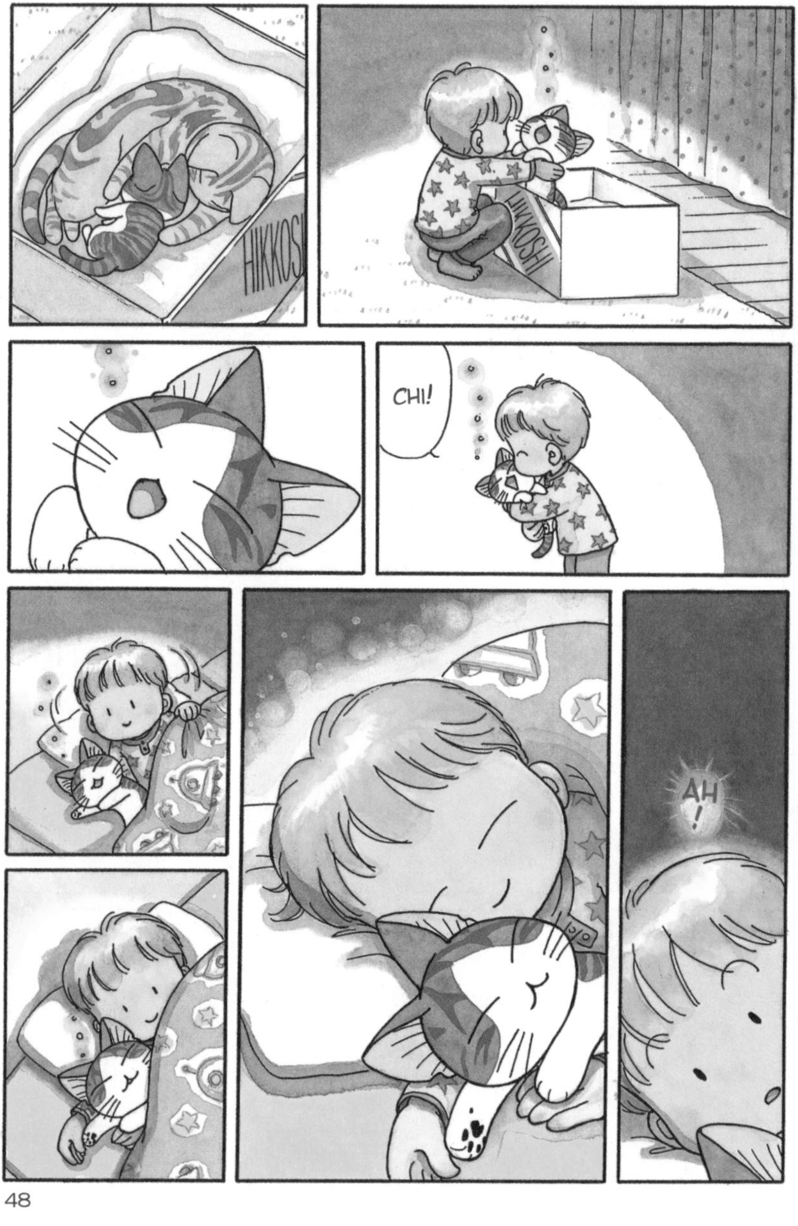
HIKKOSHI
HIKKOSHI
CHI!
AH!

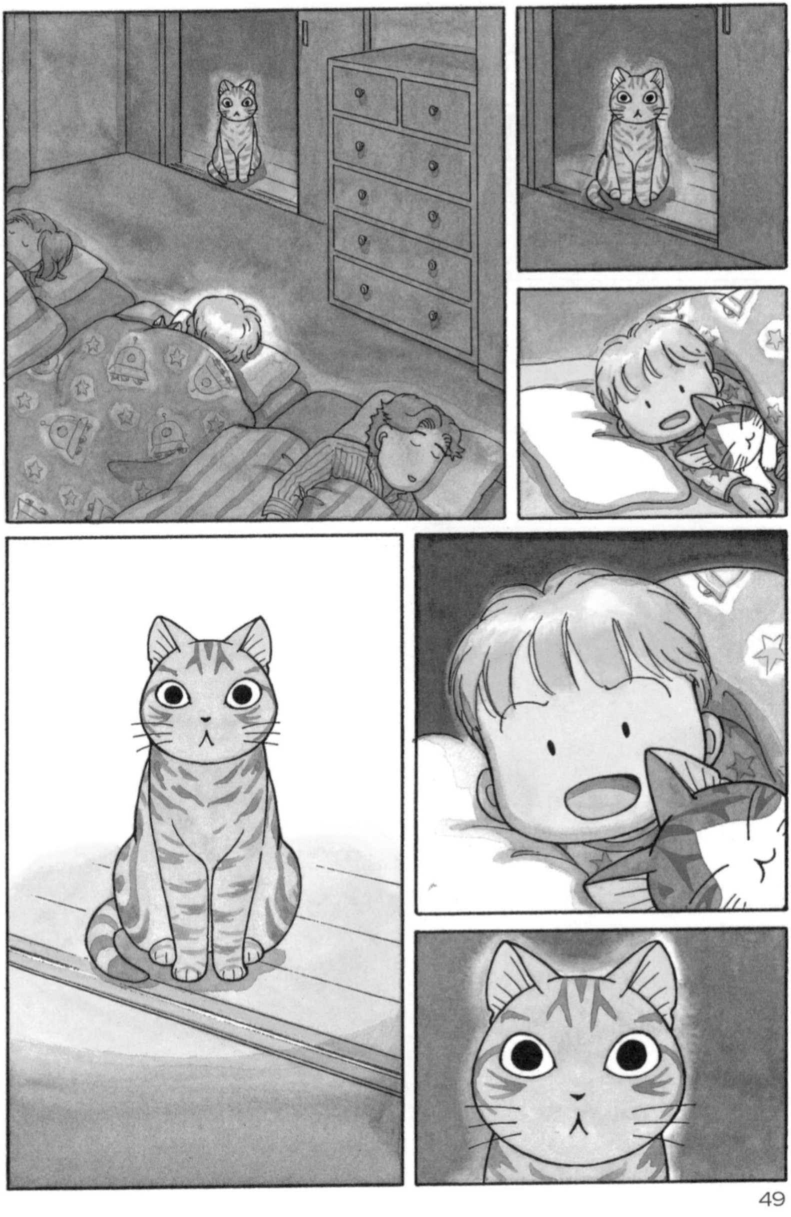

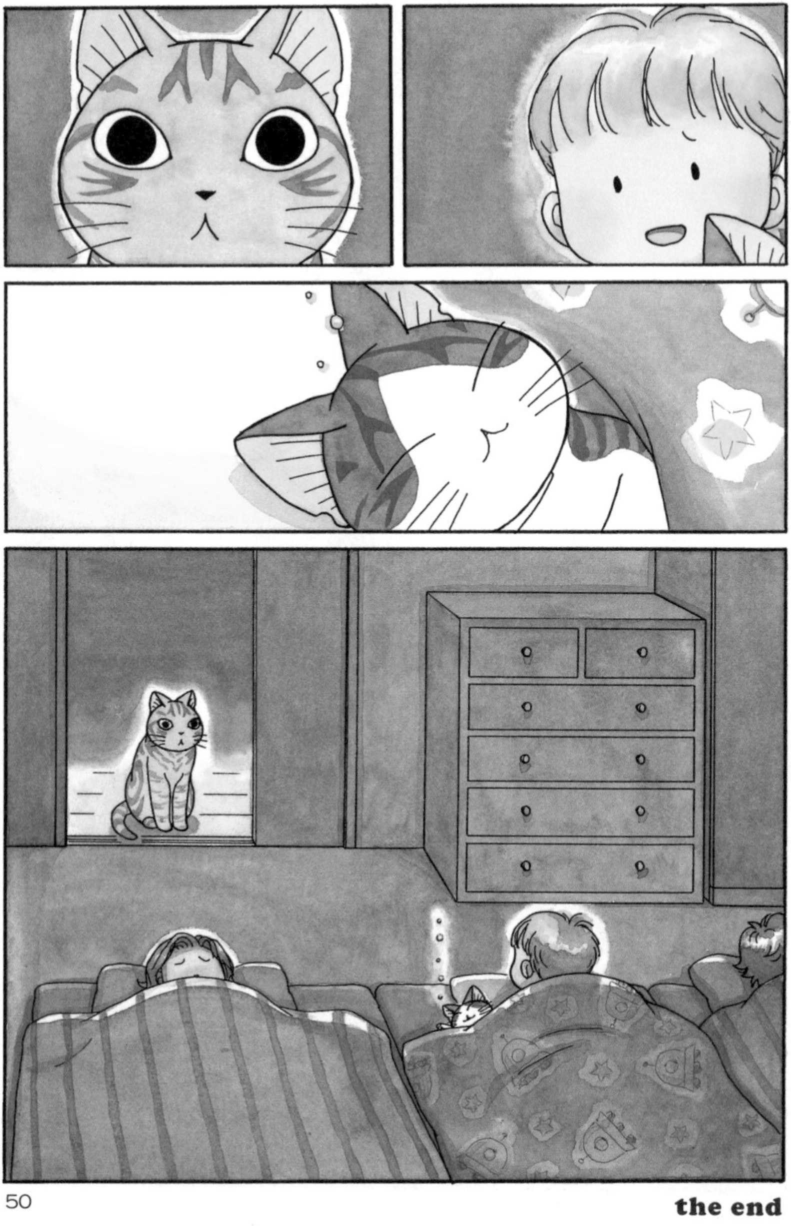

the end

homemade 207: a cat bonds

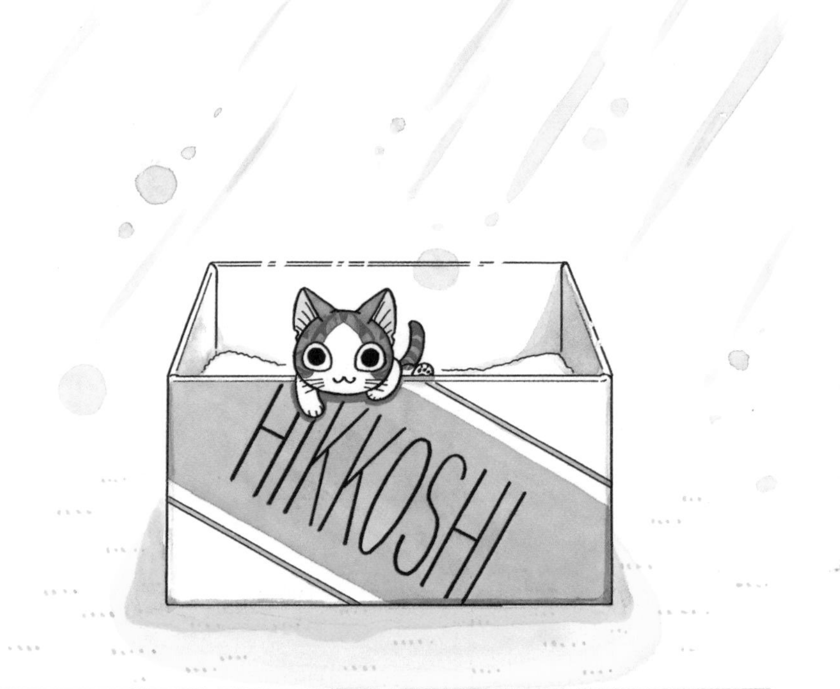
HIKKOSHI

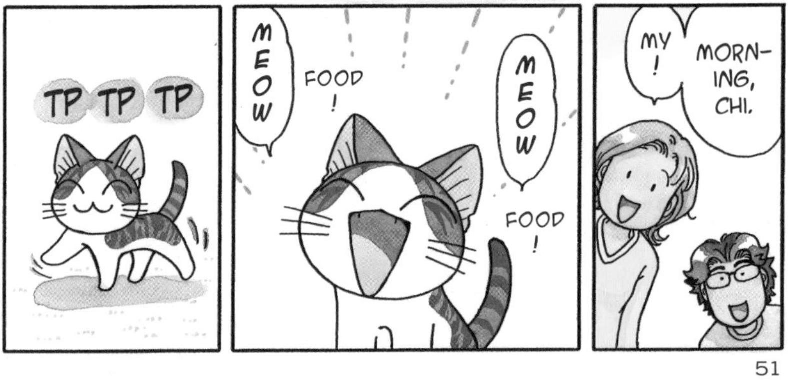
TP TP TP
MEOW
FOOD!
MEOW
FOOD!
MY!
MORNING, CHI.

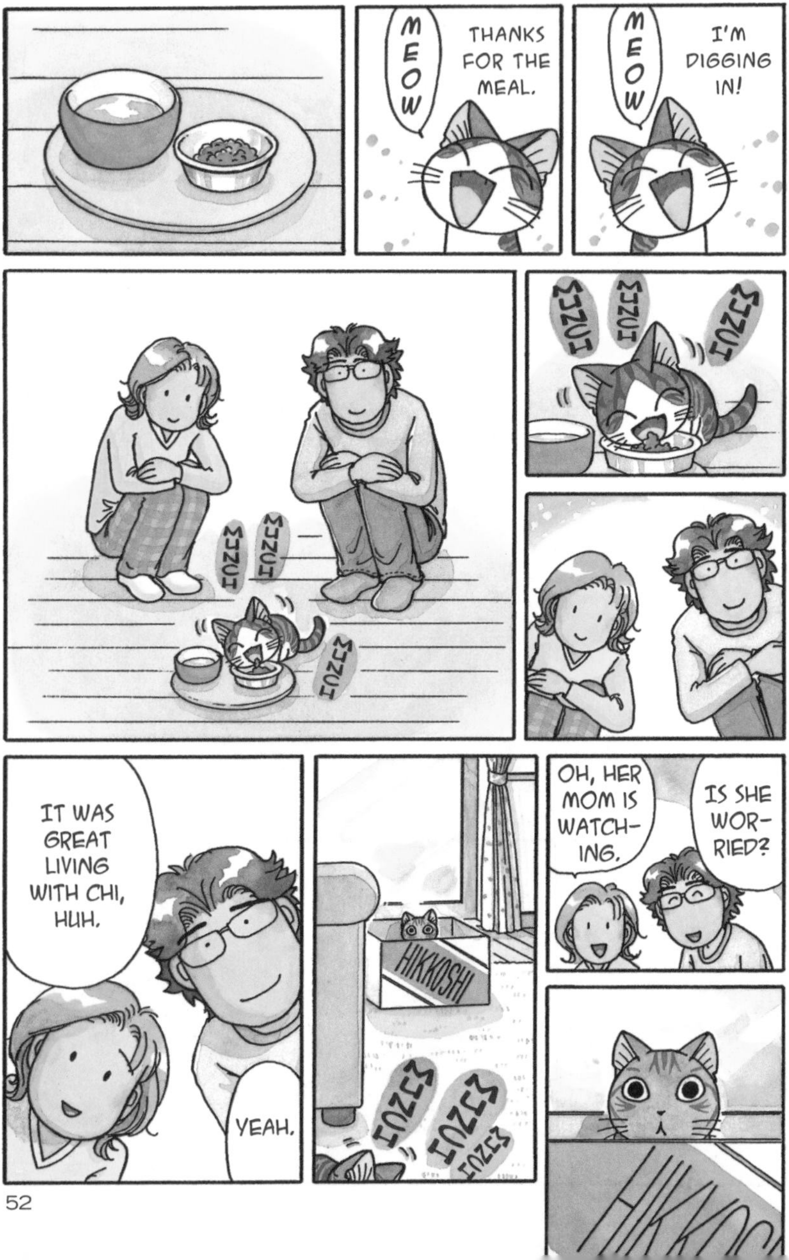
MEOW
THANKS FOR THE MEAL.
MEOW
I'M DIGGING IN!
MUNCH
MUNCH
MUNCH
MUNCH
MUNCH
MUNCH
IT WAS GREAT LIVING WITH CHI, HUH.
YEAH.
HIKKOSHI
MUNCH
MUNCH
MUNCH
OH, HER MOM IS WATCH-ING.
IS SHE WOR-RIED?

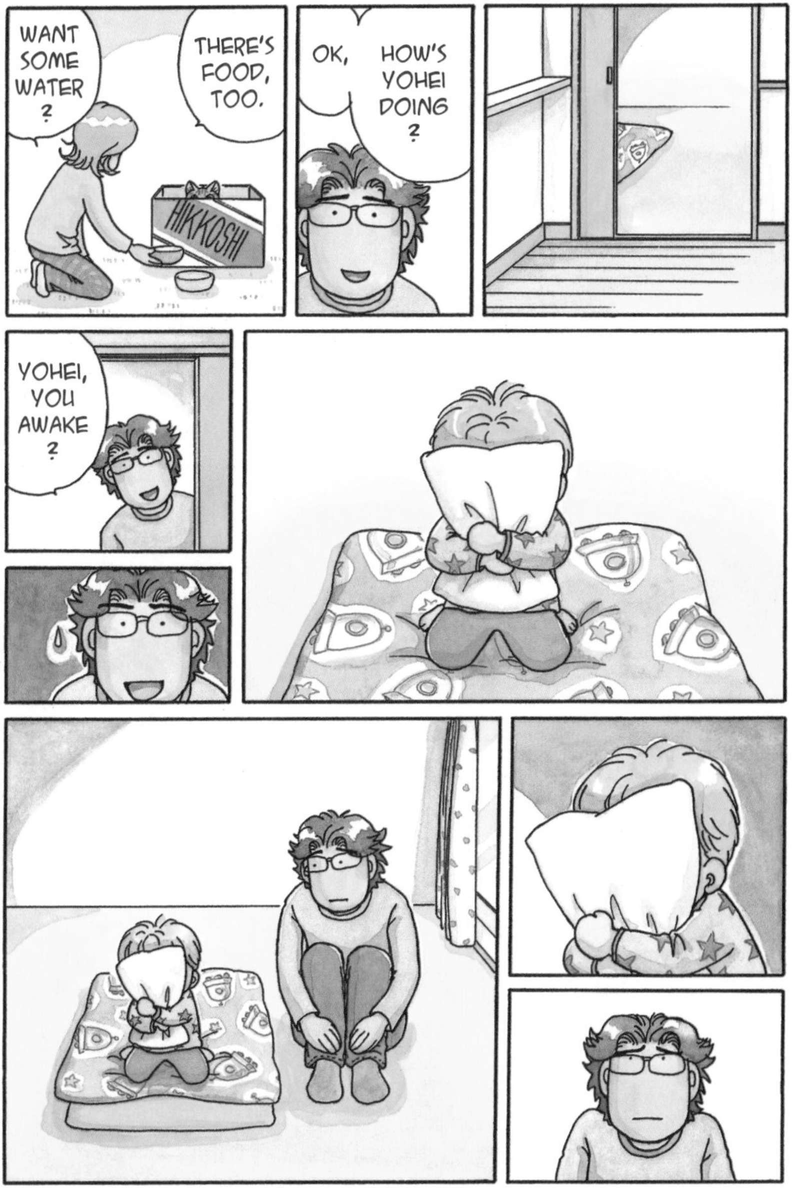
WANT SOME WATER?
THERE'S FOOD, TOO.
OK,
HOW'S YOHEI DOING?
HIKKOSHI
YOHEI, YOU AWAKE?

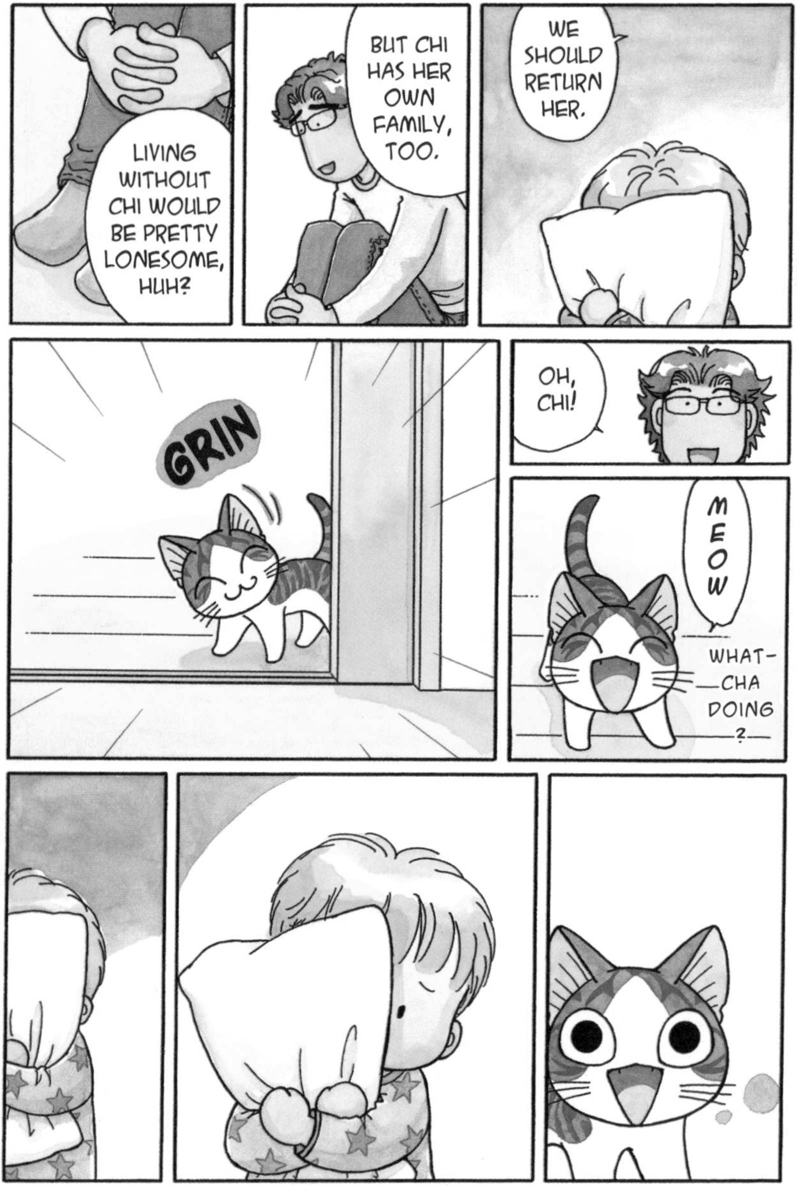
LIVING WITHOUT CHI WOULD BE PRETTY LONESOME, HUH?
BUT CHI HAS HER OWN FAMILY, TOO.
WE SHOULD RETURN HER.
GRIN
OH, CHI!
MEOW
WHAT-CHA DOING?

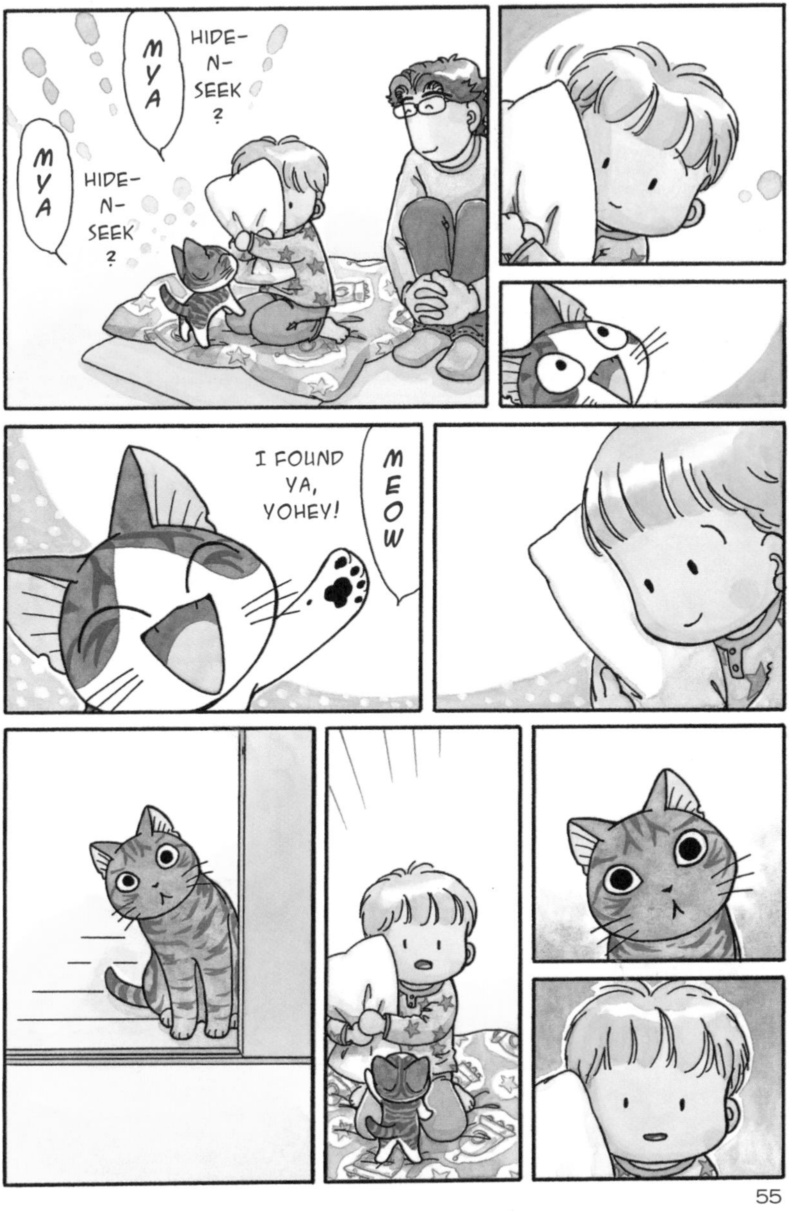
MYA
HIDE-N-SEEK?
MYA
HIDE-N-SEEK?
I FOUND YA, YOHEY!
MEOW

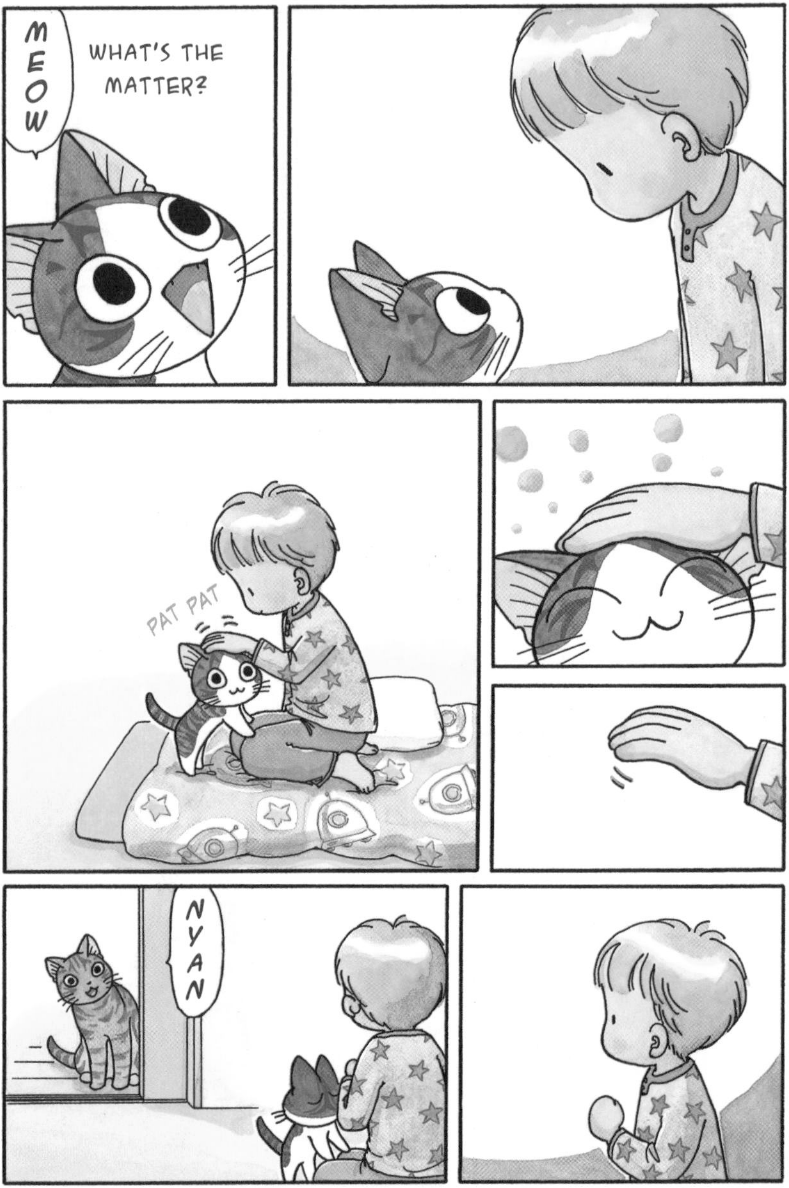
MEOW
WHAT'S THE MATTER?
PAT PAT
NYAN

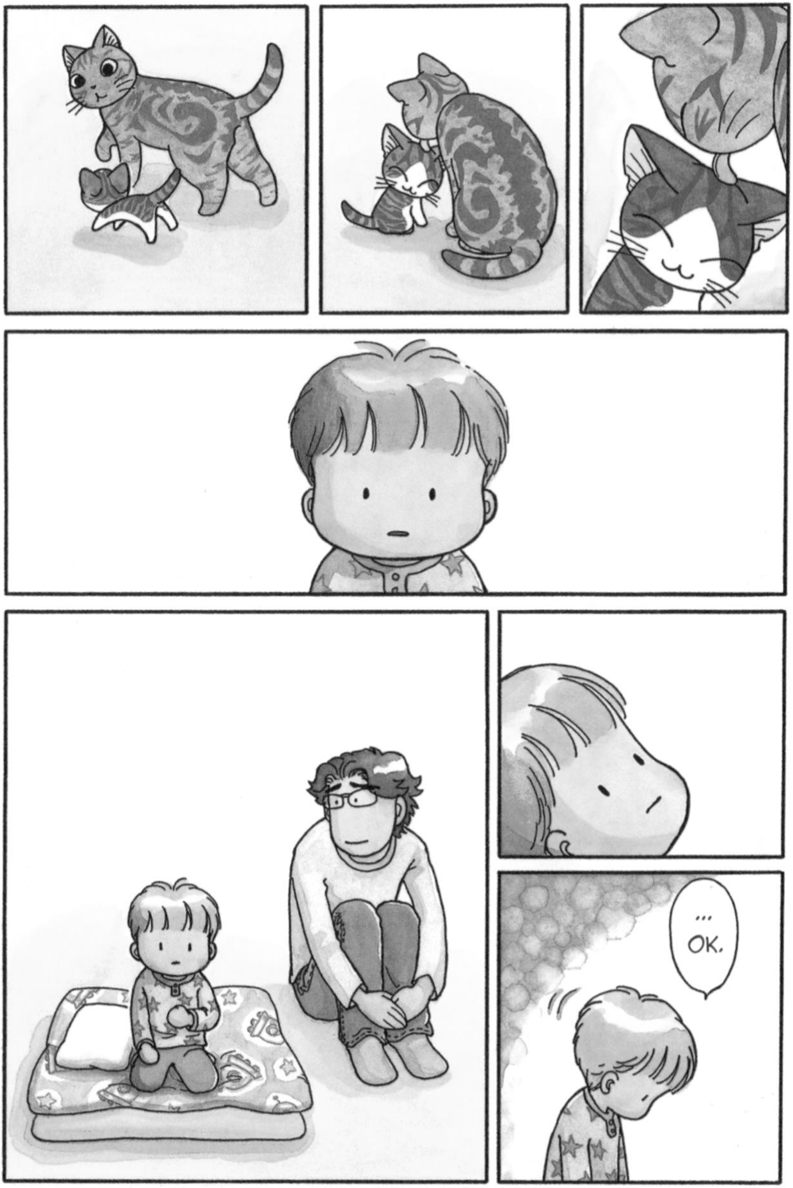
... OK.

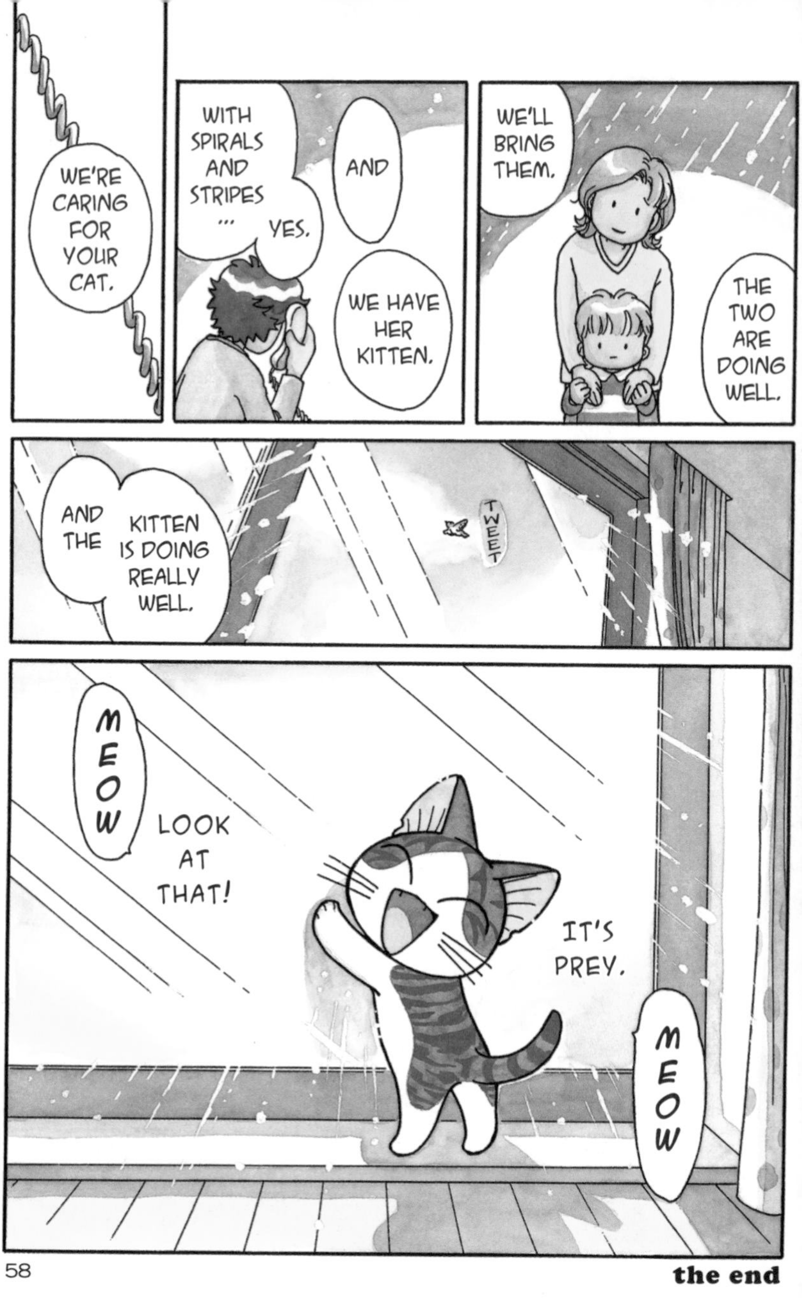
WE'RE CARING FOR YOUR CAT.
WITH SPIRALS AND STRIPES ...
YES.
AND
WE HAVE HER KITTEN.
WE'LL BRING THEM.
THE TWO ARE DOING WELL.
AND THE KITTEN IS DOING REALLY WELL.
TWEET
MEOW
LOOK AT THAT!
IT'S PREY.
MEOW

the end

homemade 208: a cat goes back

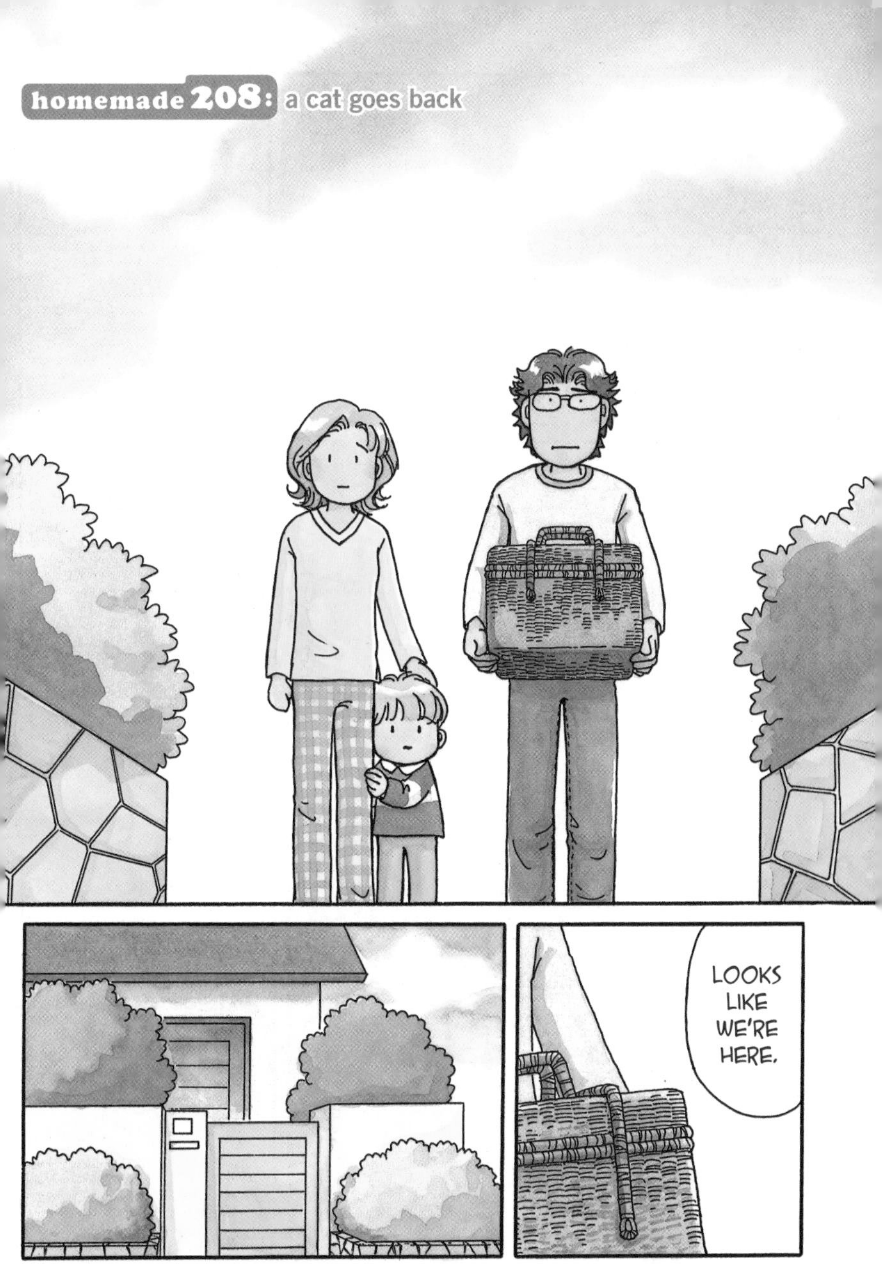
LOOKS LIKE WE'RE HERE.

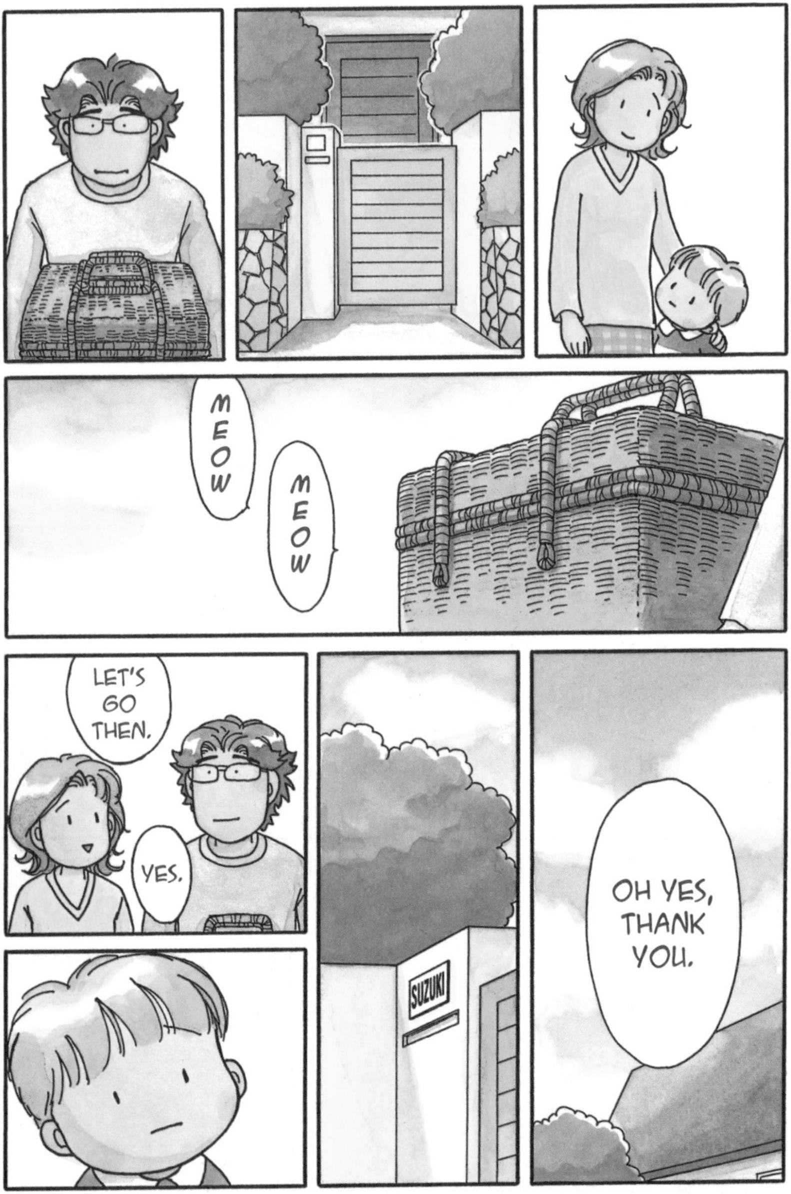
MEOW
MEOW
LET'S GO THEN.
YES.
SUZUKI
OH YES, THANK YOU.

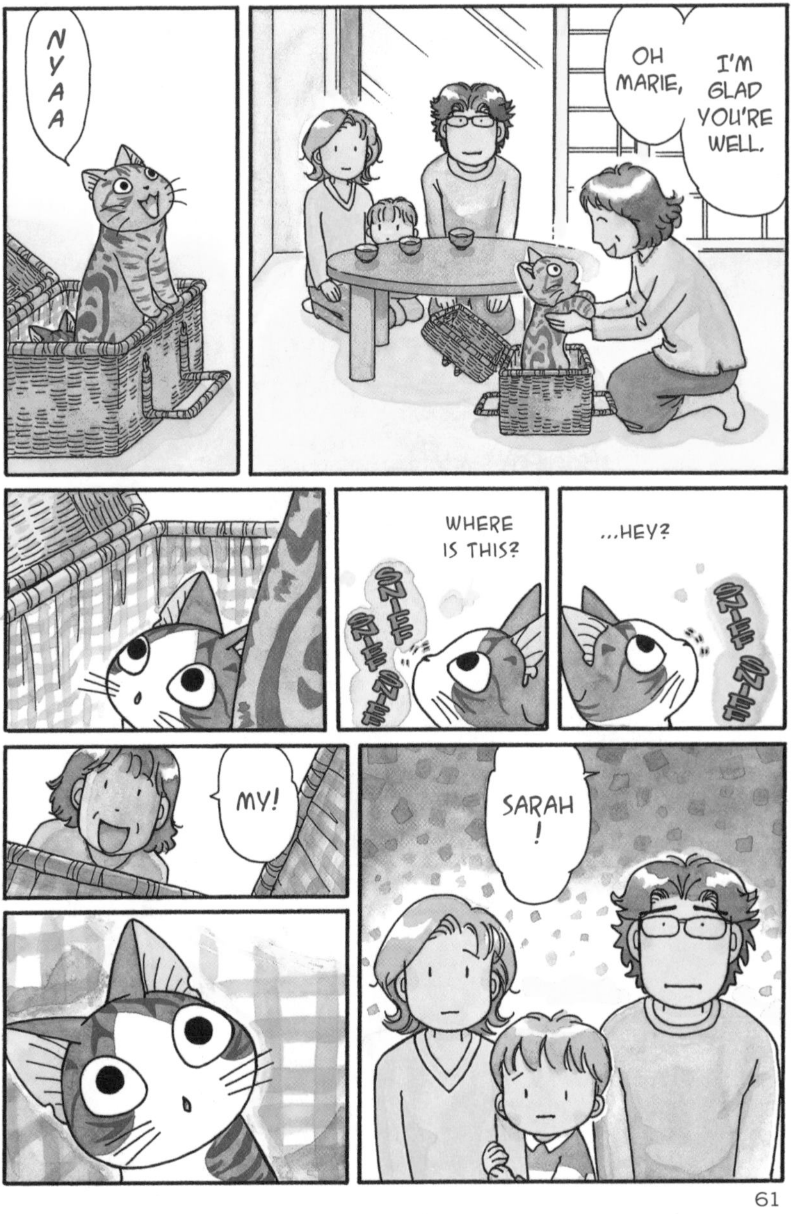
NYAA
OH MARIE,
I'M GLAD YOU'RE WELL.
WHERE IS THIS?
SNIFF SNIFF
SNIFF SNIFF
...HEY?
SNIFF SNIFF
MY!
SARAH!

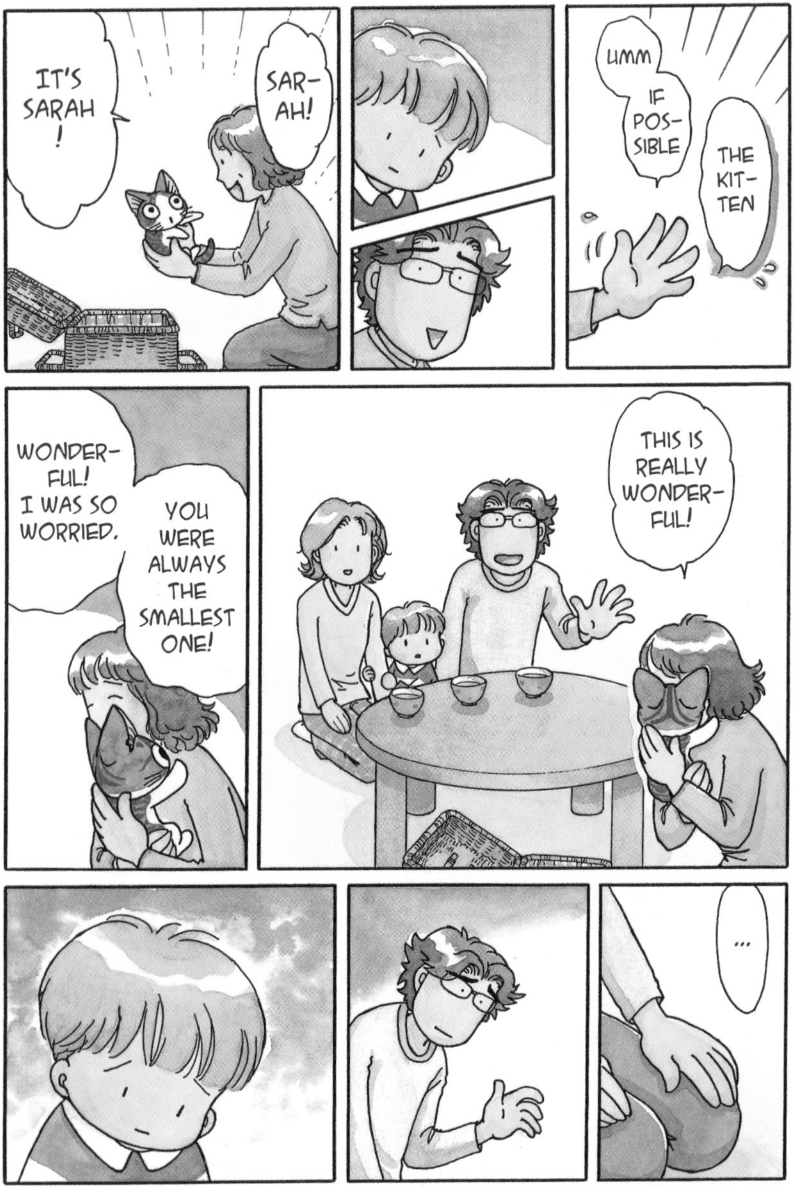
IT'S SARAH!
SAR-AH!
UMM
IF POS-SIBLE
THE KIT-TEN
WONDER-FUL! I WAS SO WORRIED.
YOU WERE ALWAYS THE SMALLEST ONE!
THIS IS REALLY WONDER-FUL!
...

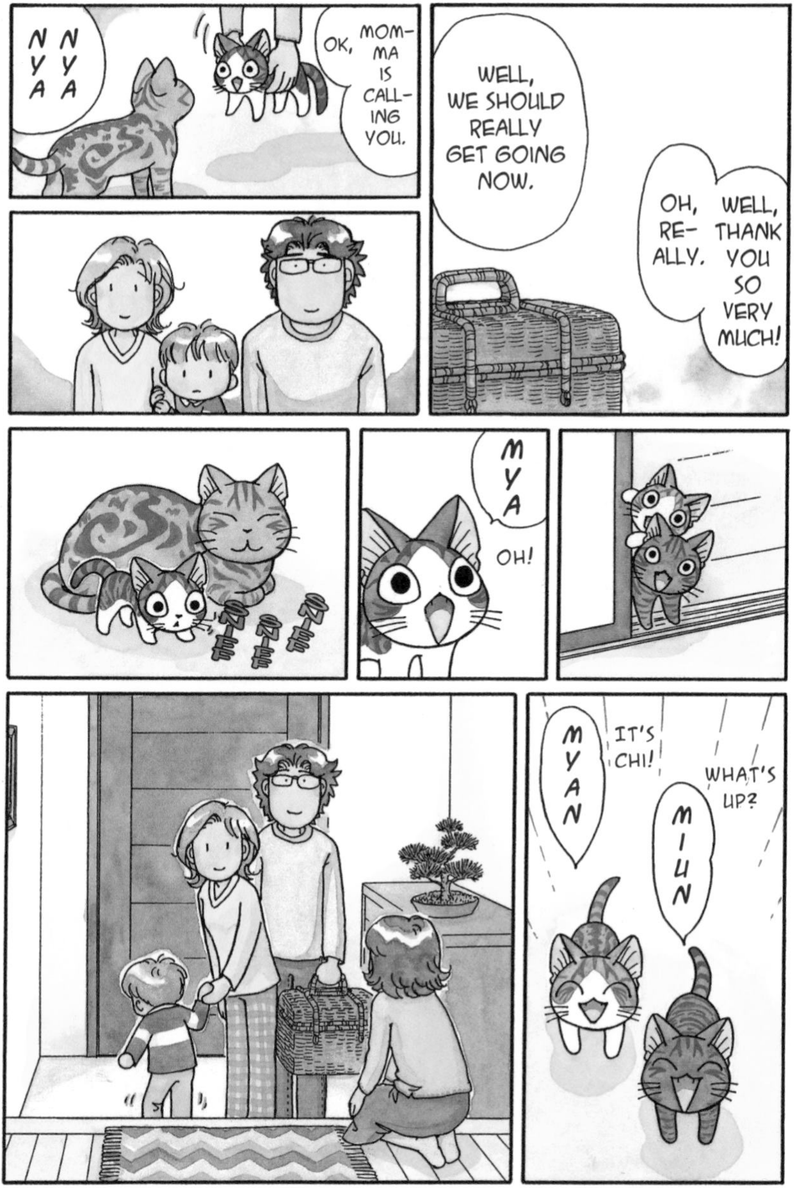
NYA NYA
OK, MOMMA IS CALLING YOU.
WELL, WE SHOULD REALLY GET GOING NOW.
OH, REALLY. WELL, THANK YOU SO VERY MUCH!
MYA
OH!
MYAN
IT'S CHI!
WHAT'S UP?
MIUN

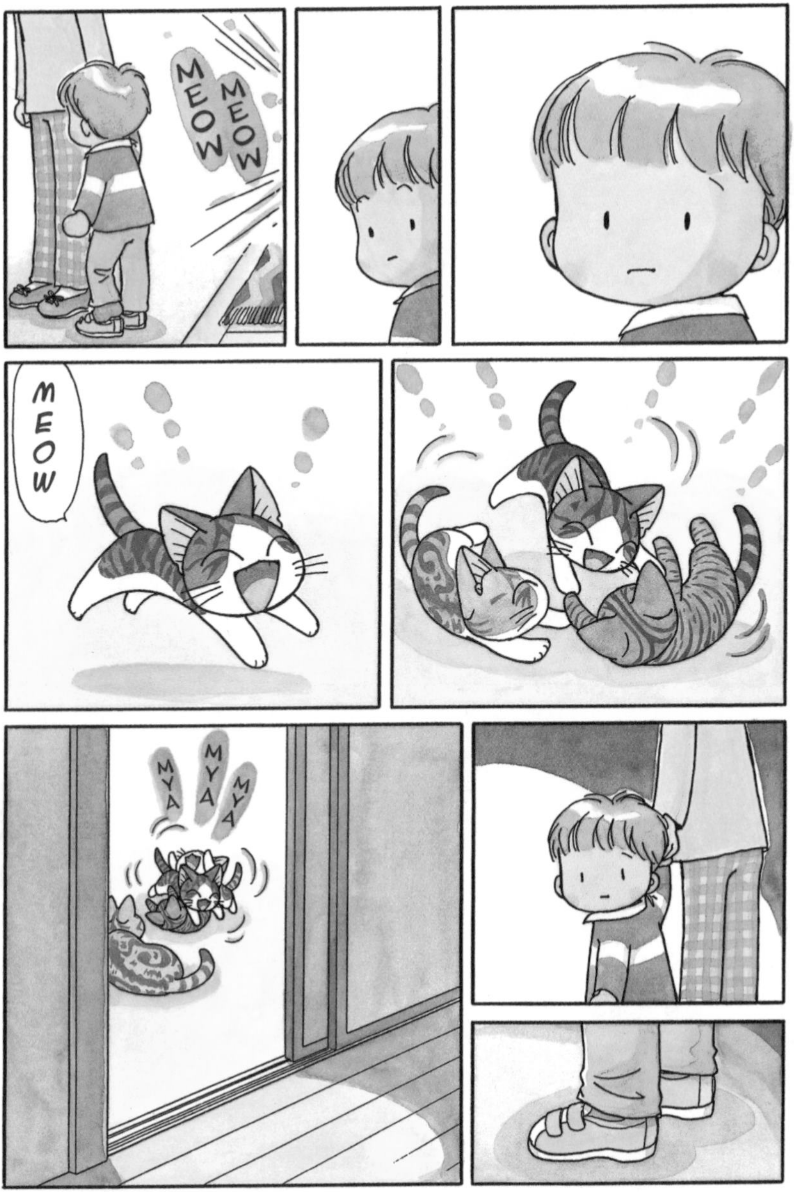
MEOW
MEOW
MEOW
MYA
MYA
MYA

THE BASKET IS SO LIGHT NOW.

WE BETTER GET READY TO GO TO FRANCE.

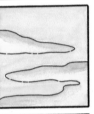

HAH HAH

MYA

THAT WAS FUN.

MEOW DADDY

MEOW MOMMY

MEOW YOHEY

MEOW HEY-YY!

65

HUH?

the end

homemade 209: a cat accepts

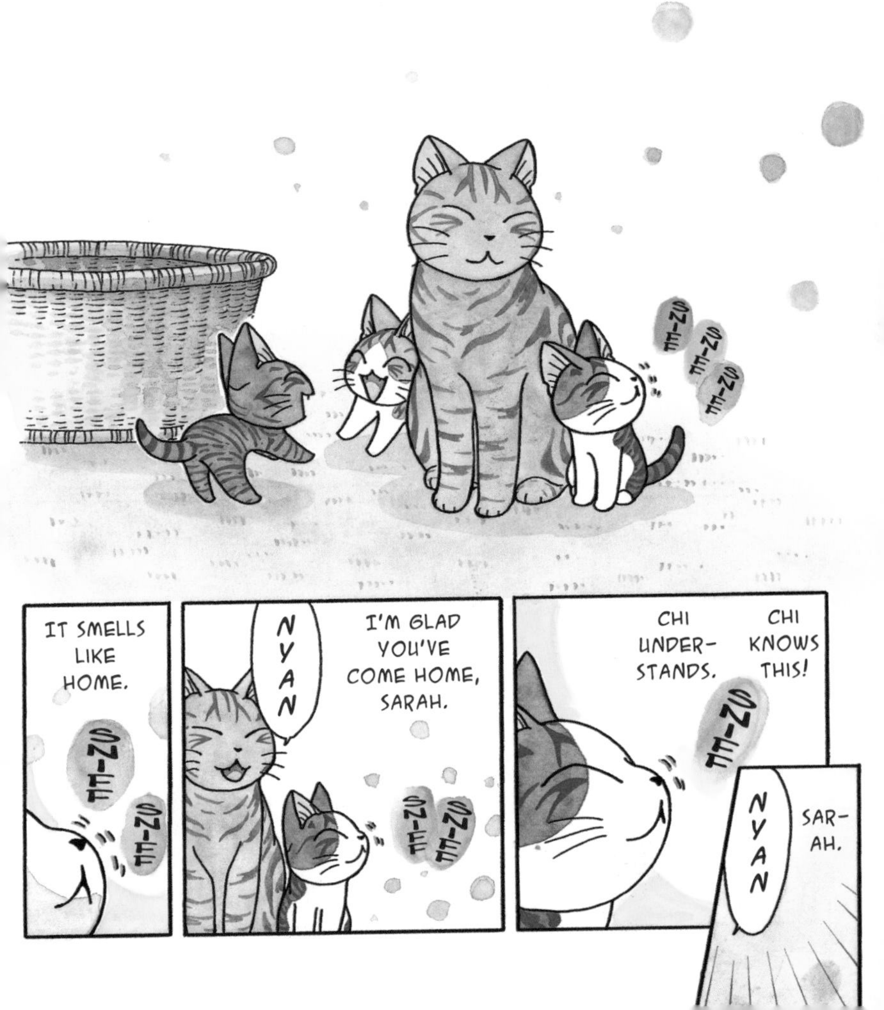
SNIFF
SNIFF
SNIFF
IT SMELLS LIKE HOME.
SNIFF
SNIFF
NYAN
I'M GLAD YOU'VE COME HOME, SARAH.
SNIFF
SNIFF
CHI UNDER-STANDS.
CHI KNOWS THIS!
SNIFF
NYAN
SAR-AH.

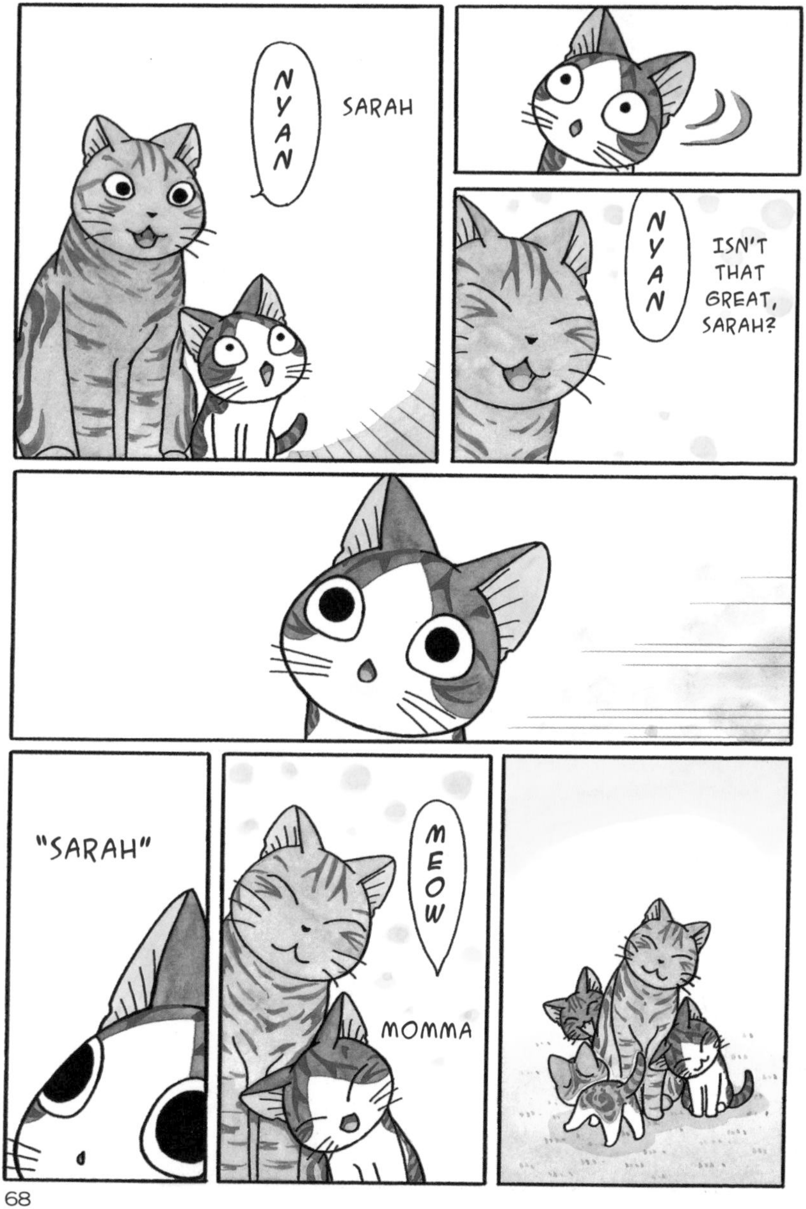
NYAN
SARAH
NYAN
ISN'T THAT GREAT, SARAH?
"SARAH"
MEOW
MOMMA

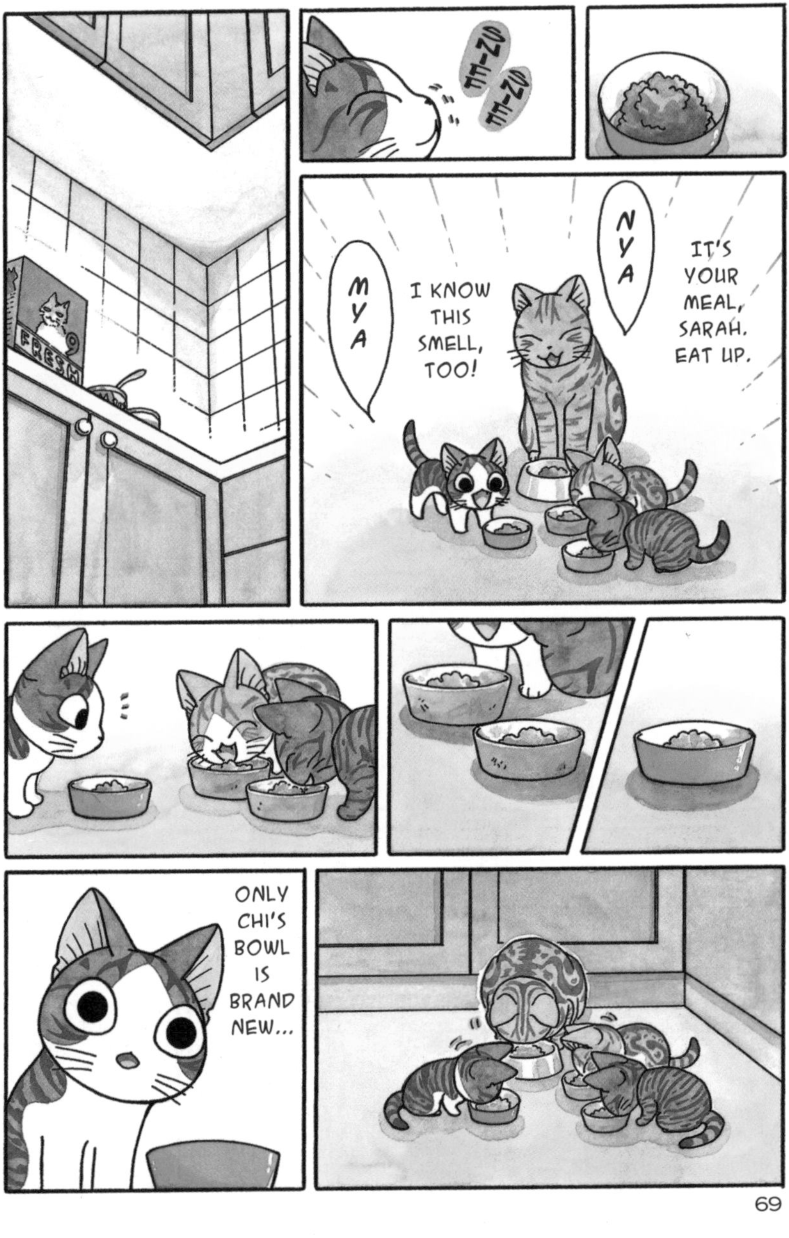
FRESH
SNIFF SNIFF
MYA
I KNOW THIS SMELL, TOO!
NYA
IT'S YOUR MEAL, SARAH. EAT UP.
ONLY CHI'S BOWL IS BRAND NEW...

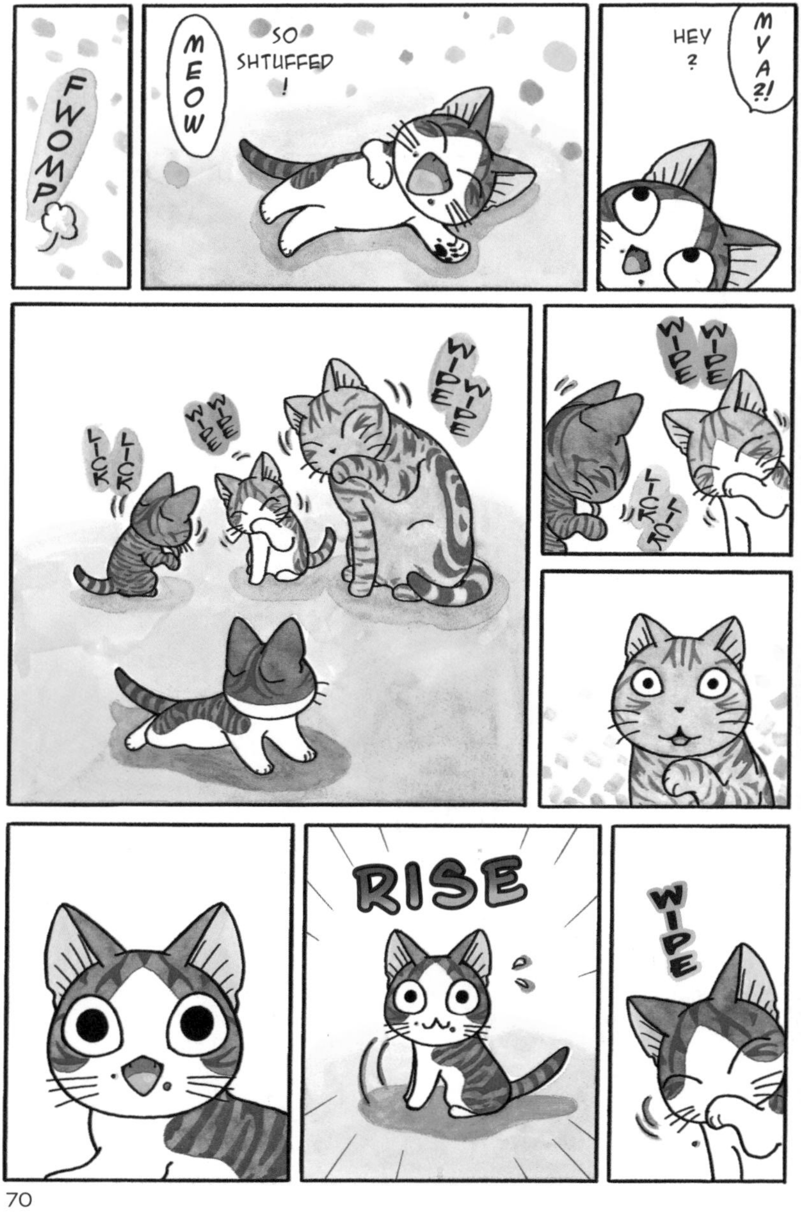
FWOMP
MEOW
SO SHTUFFED!
HEY?
MYA?!
LICK LICK
WIPE WIPE
WIPE WIPE
WIPE WIPE
LICK LICK
RISE
WIPE

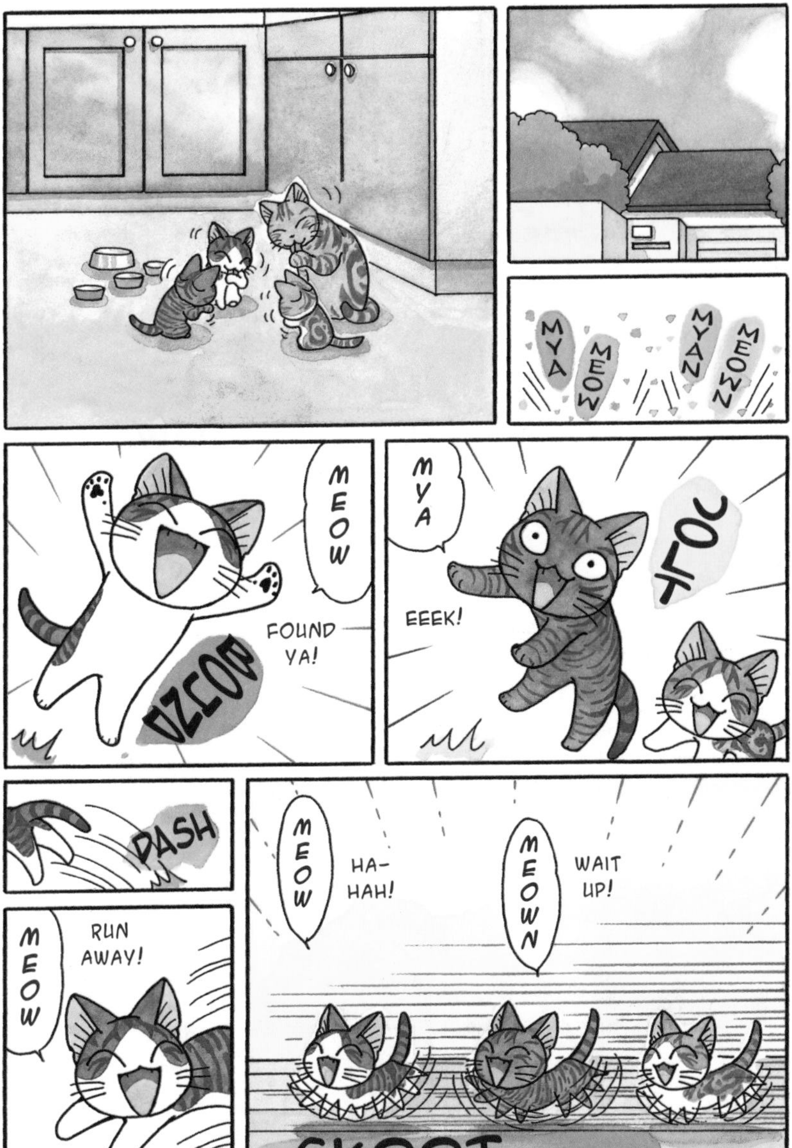
MYA
MEOW
MYAN
MEOWN
MEOW
FOUND YA!
MYA
EEEK!
DASH
MEOW
RUN AWAY!
MEOW
HA-HAH!
MEOWN
WAIT UP!
SKOOT——

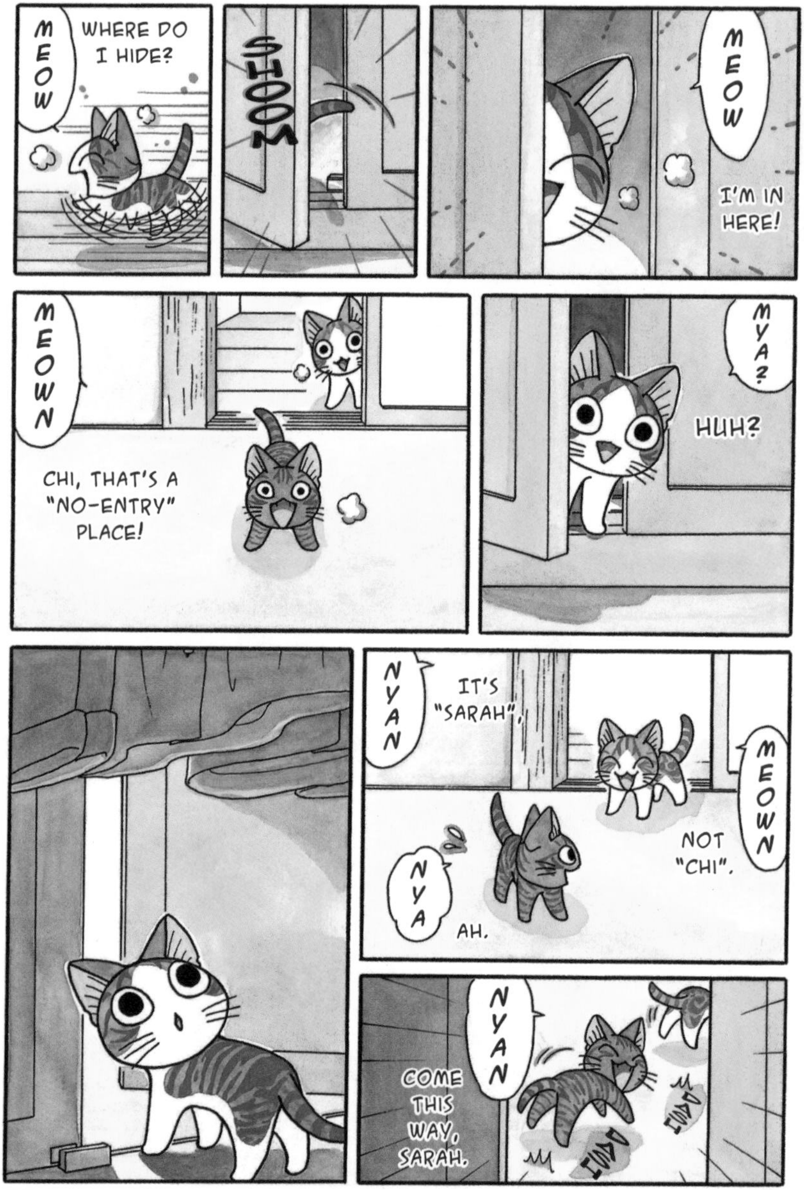
MEOW
WHERE DO I HIDE?
SHOOM
MEOW
I'M IN HERE!
MEOWN
CHI, THAT'S A "NO-ENTRY" PLACE!
MYA?
HUH?
NYAN
IT'S "SARAH",
MEOWN
NOT "CHI".
NYA
AH.
NYAN
COME THIS WAY, SARAH.

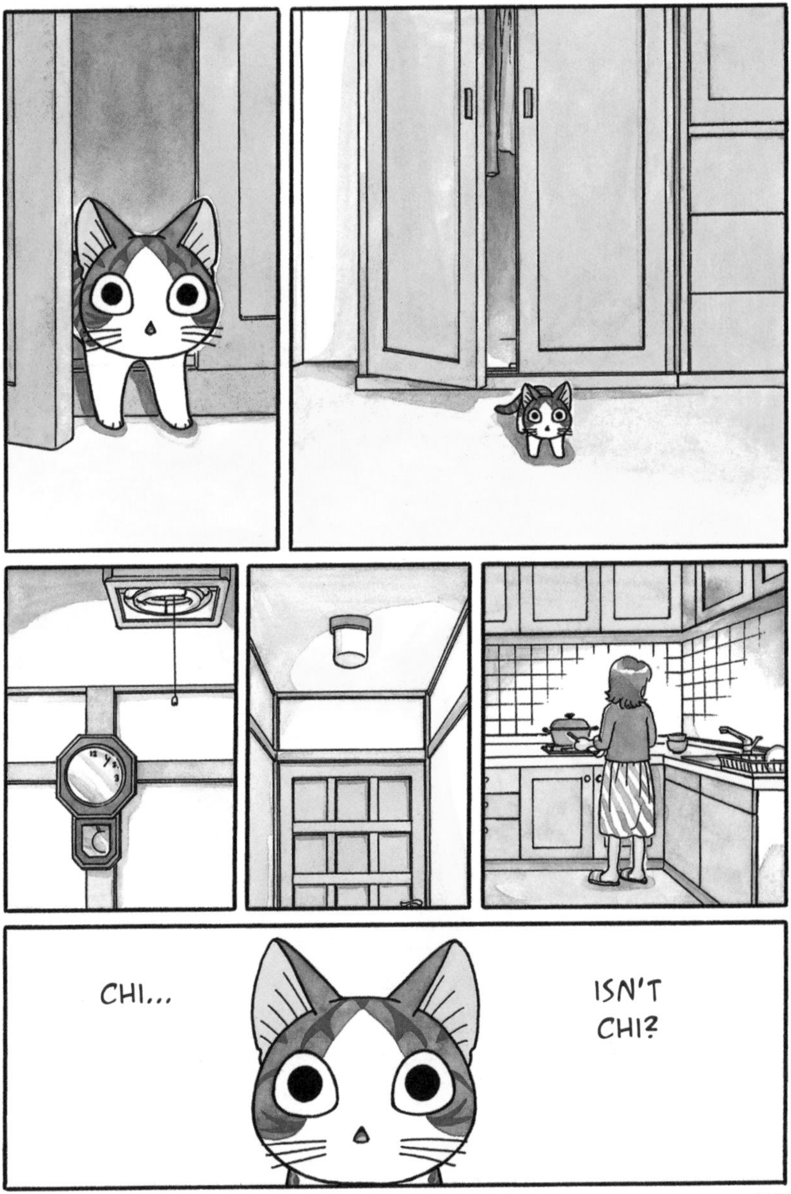
CHI...
ISN'T CHI?

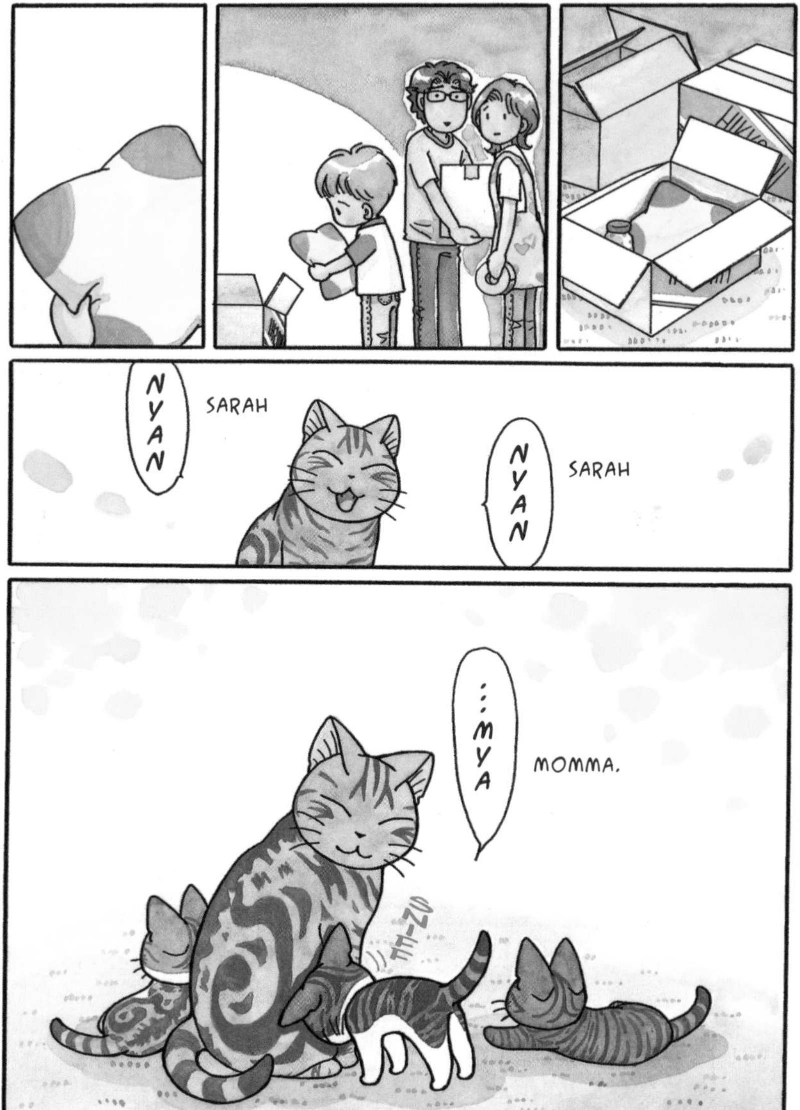
NYAN
SARAH
NYAN
SARAH
...MYA
MOMMA.
SNIFF

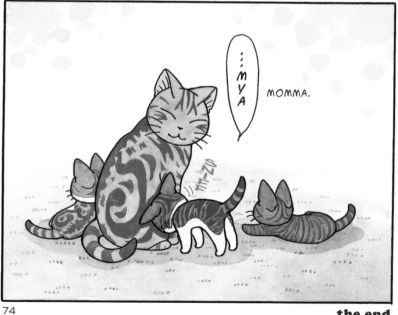

the end

homemade 210: a cat fits in

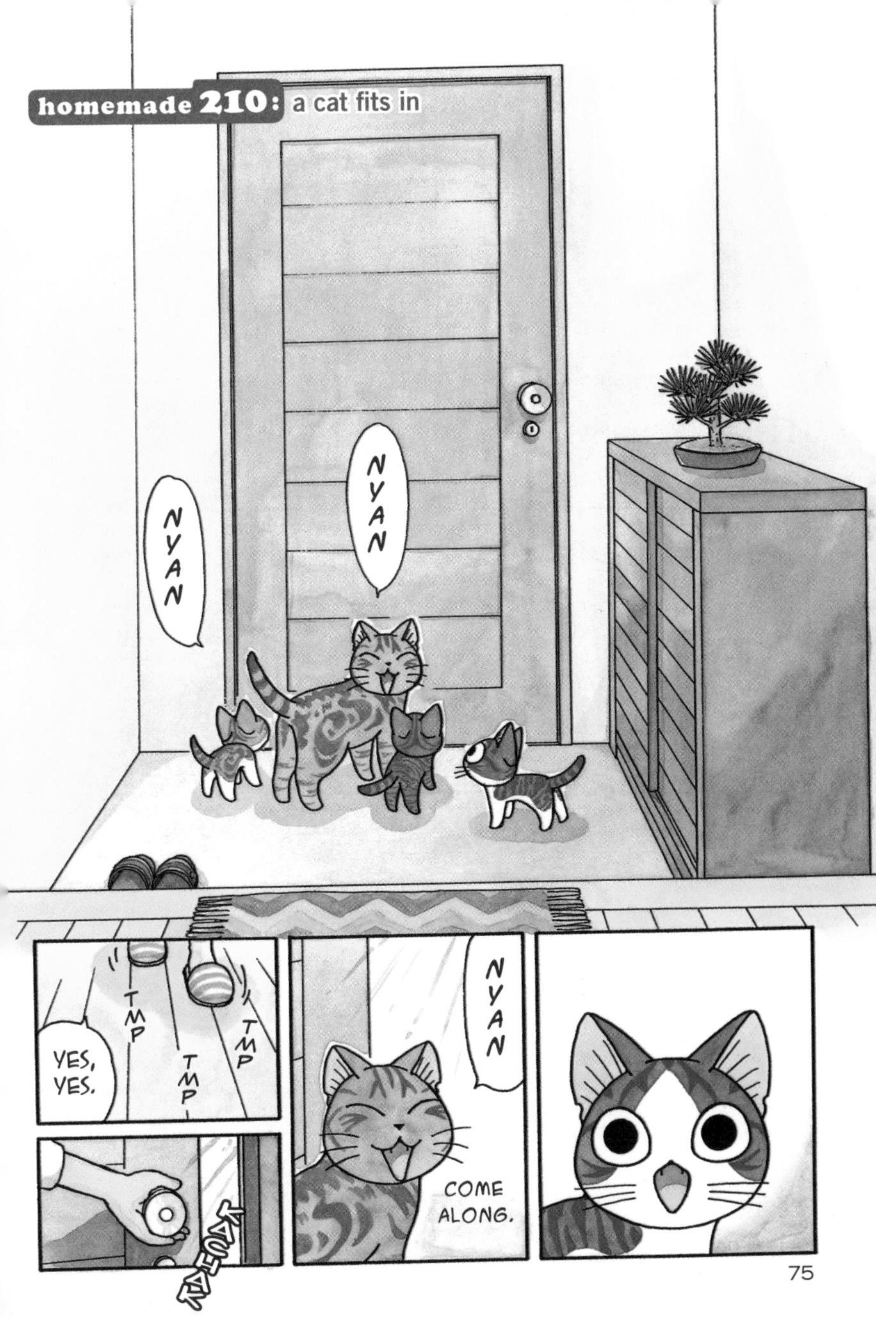

NYAN
NYAN
YES, YES.
TMP
TMP
TMP
KACHAK
NYAN
COME ALONG.

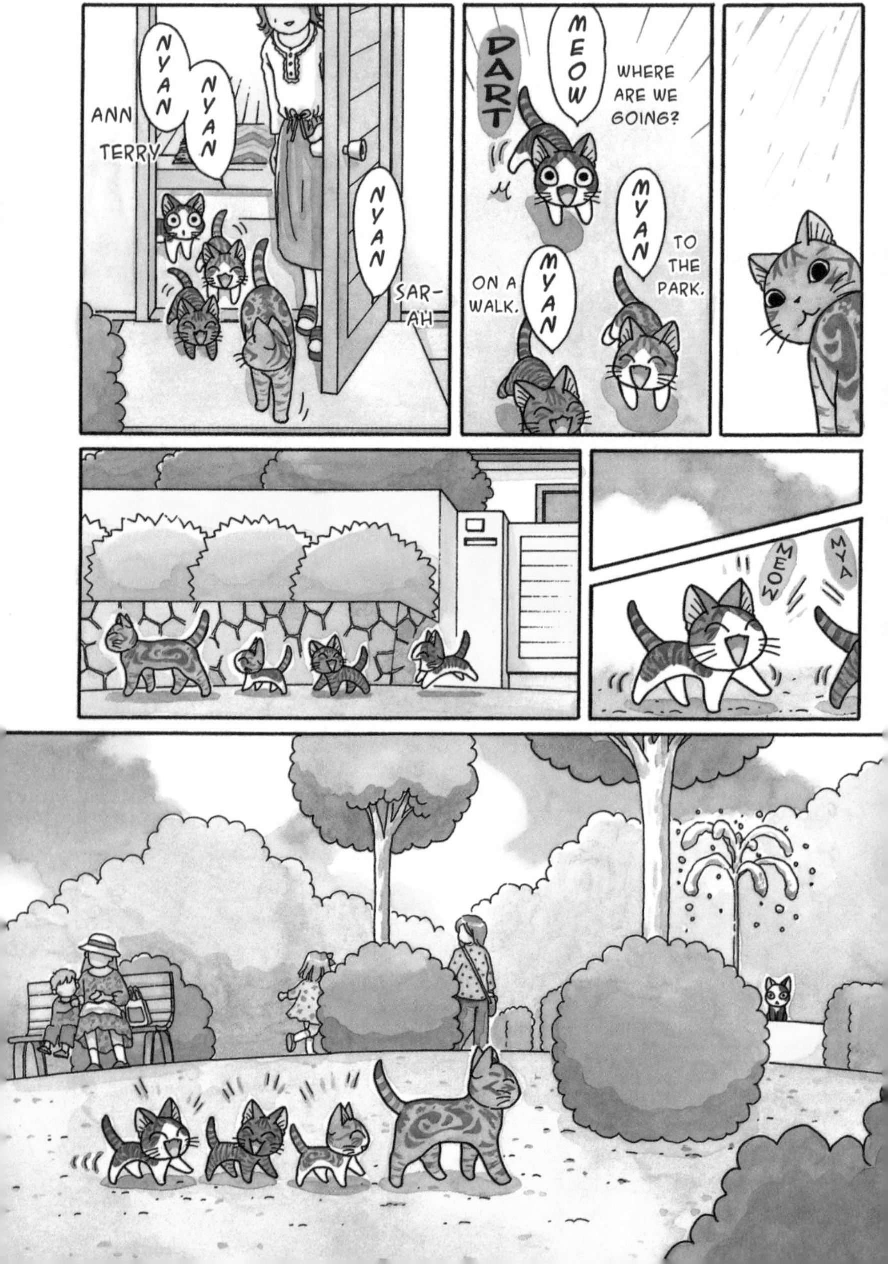
ANN
NYAN
TERRY
NYAN
NYAN
SAR-AH
DART
MEOW
WHERE ARE WE GOING?
MYAN
TO THE PARK.
MYAN
ON A WALK.
MEOW
MYA

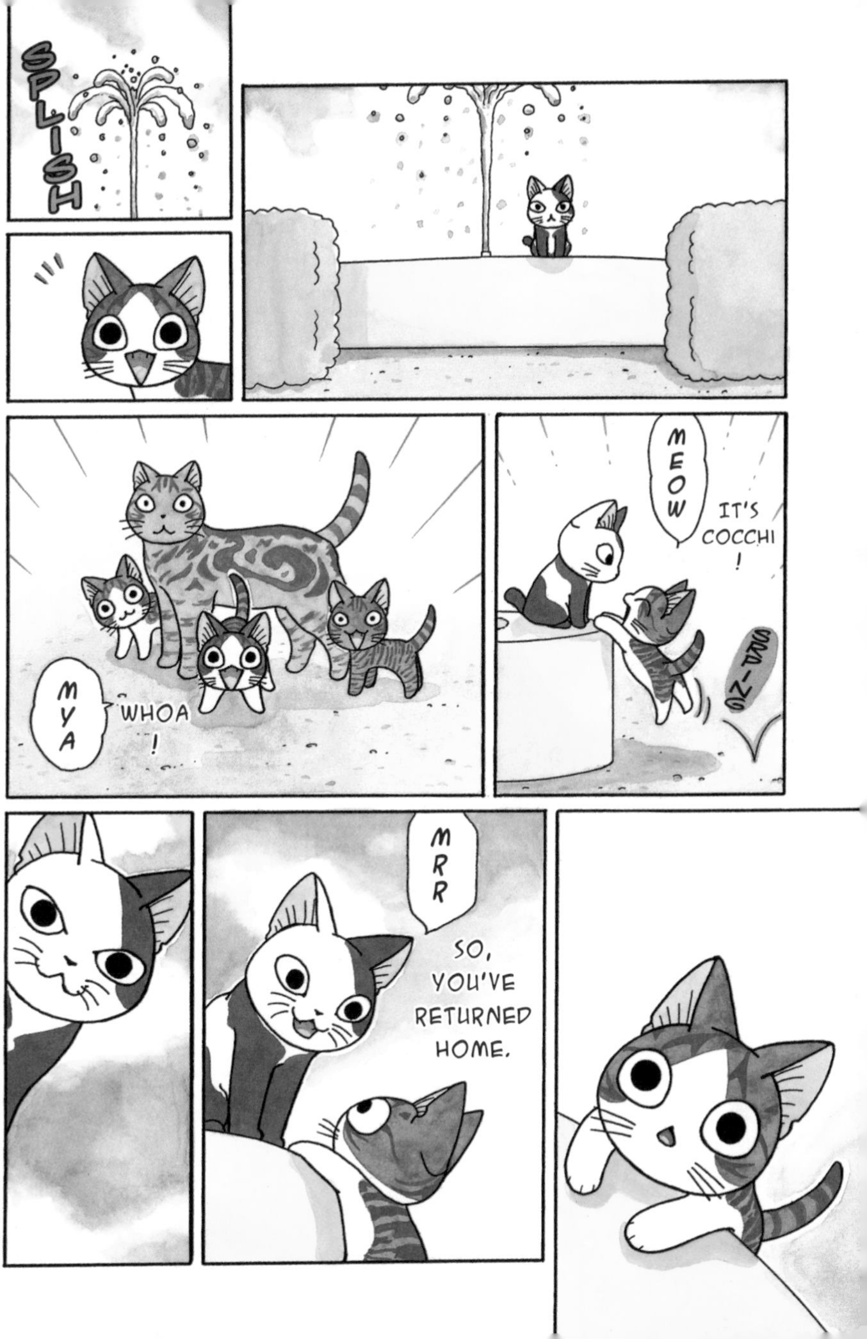
SPLISH
MYA
WHOA!
MEOW
IT'S COCCHI!
SPRING
MRR
SO, YOU'VE RETURNED HOME.

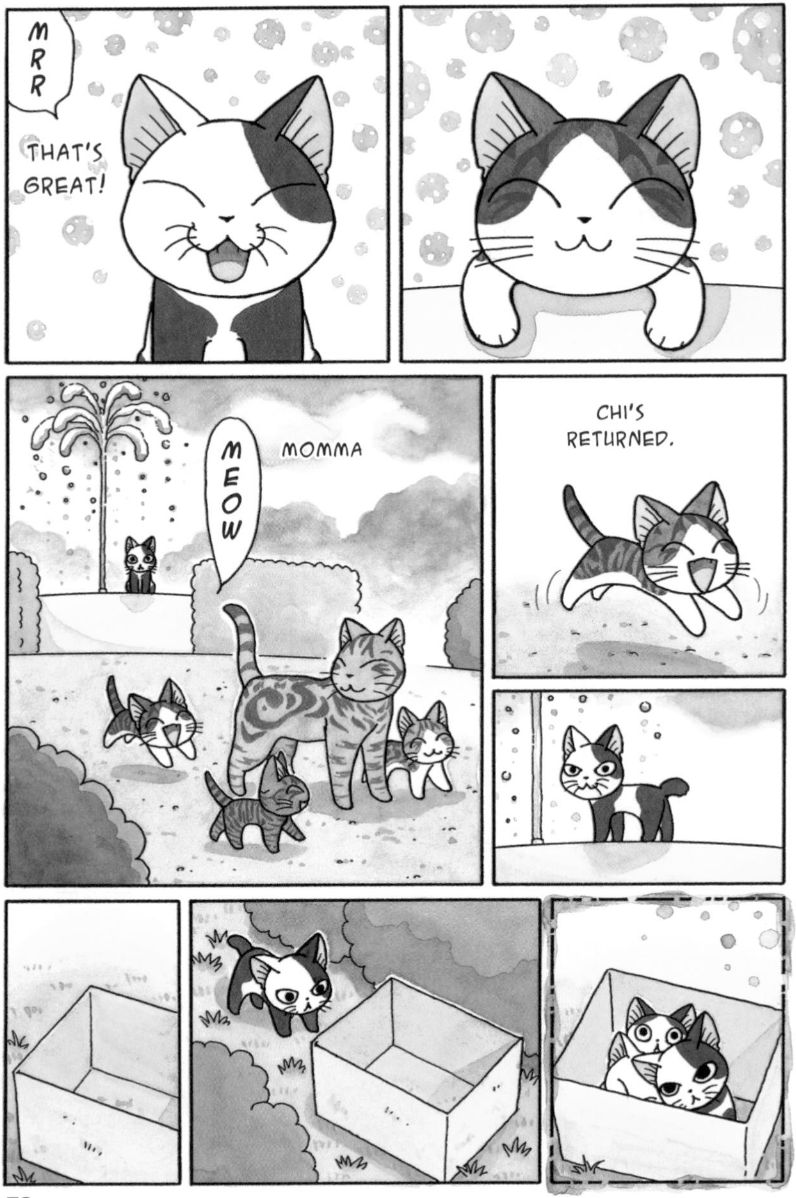
MRR
THAT'S GREAT!
MEOW
MOMMA
CHI'S RETURNED.

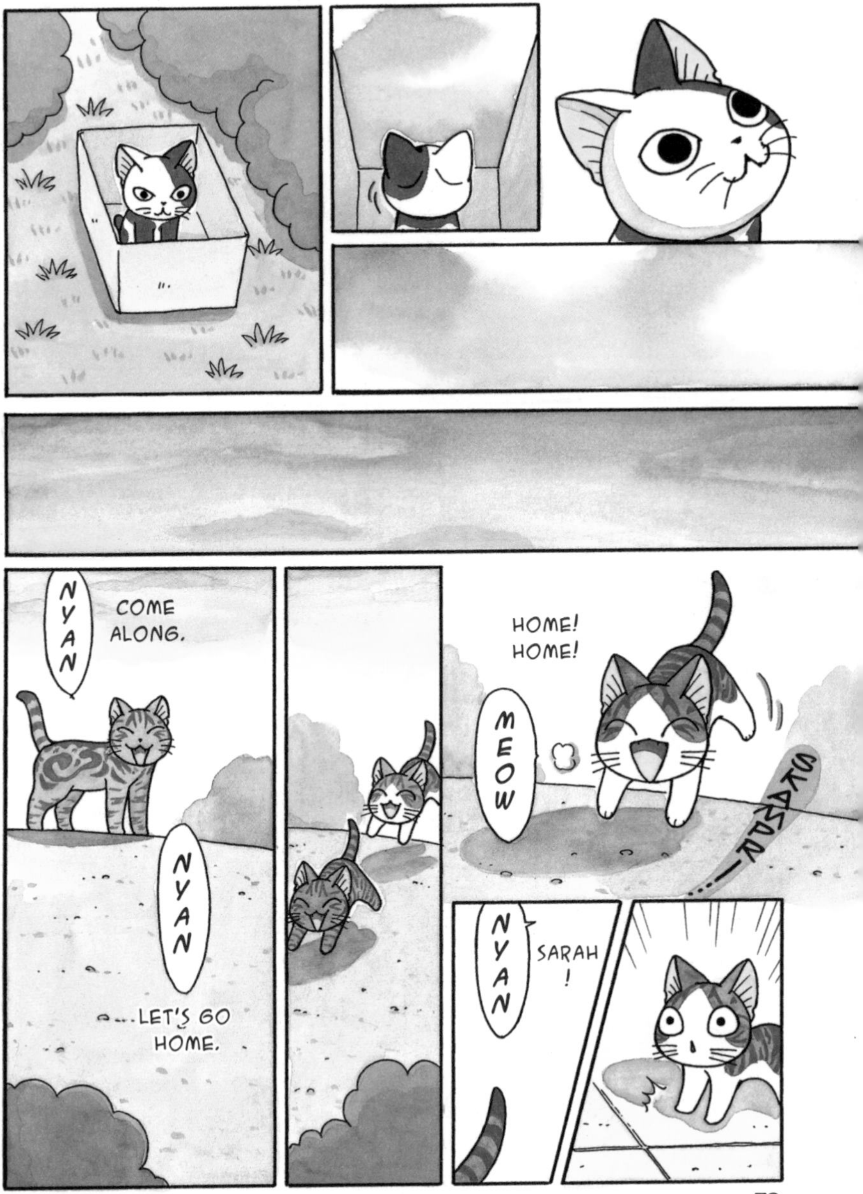

NYAN
COME ALONG.
NYAN
...LET'S GO HOME.
HOME! HOME!
MEOW
NYAN
SARAH!

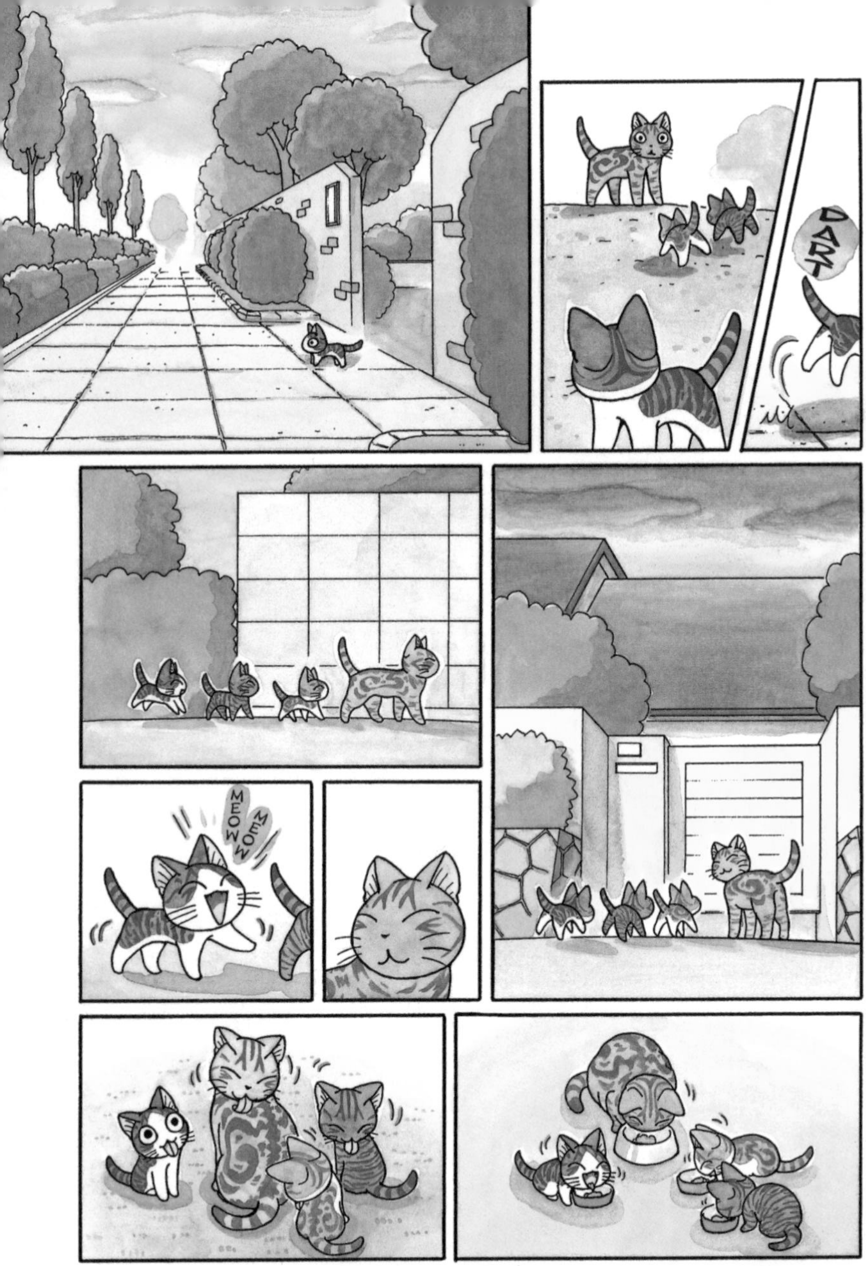
DART
MEOW MEOW

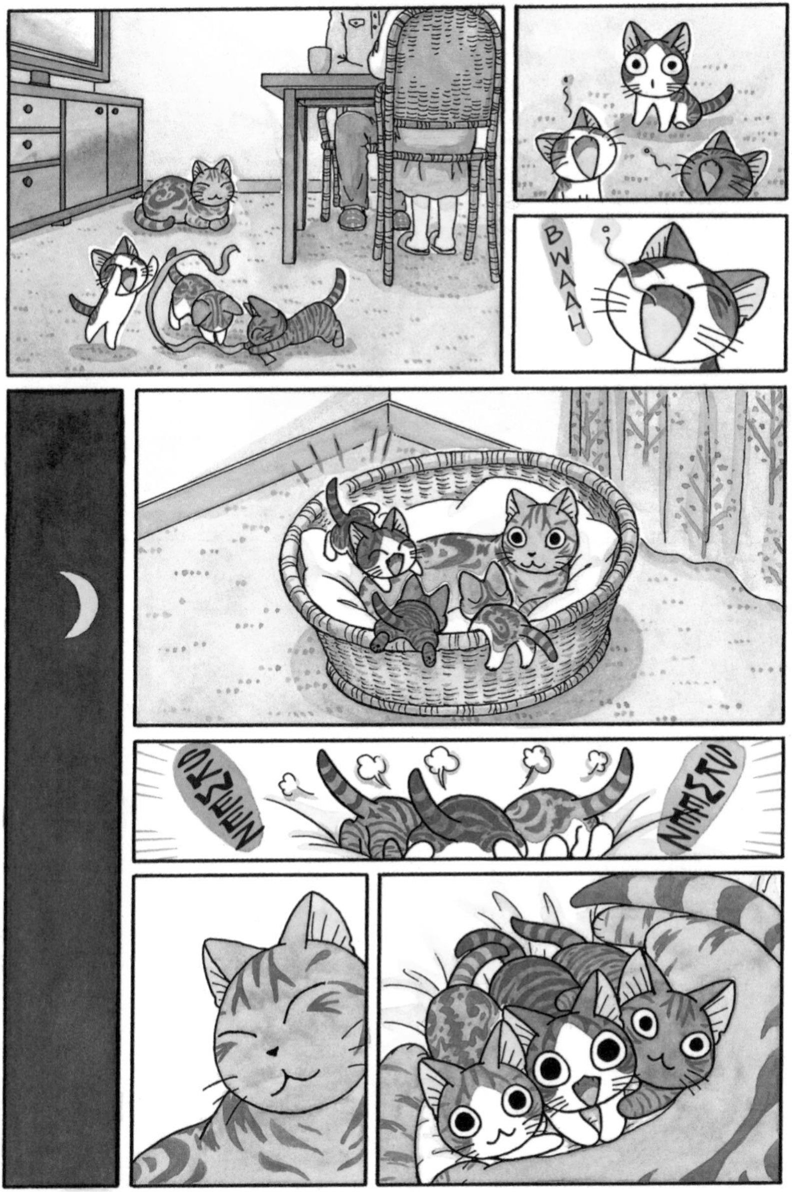
BWAAH

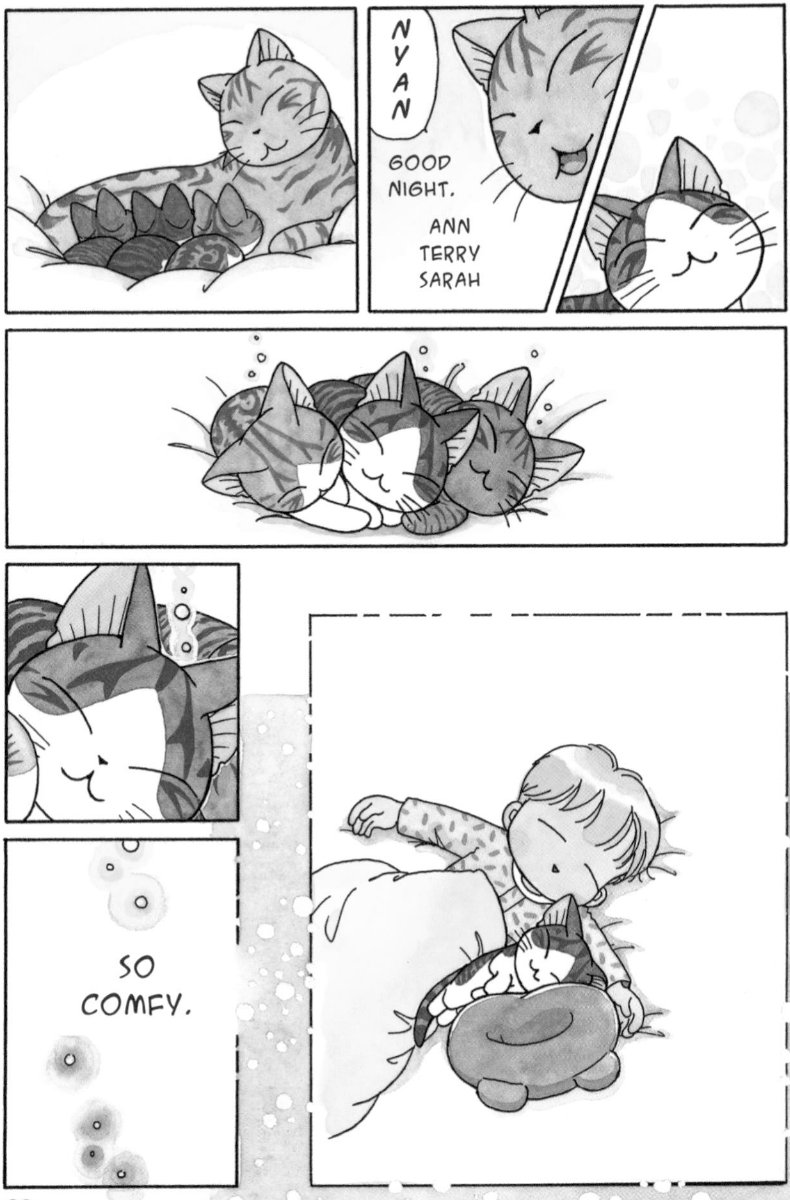
NYAN
GOOD NIGHT.
ANN
TERRY
SARAH
SO COMFY.

the end

homemade 211: a cat separates

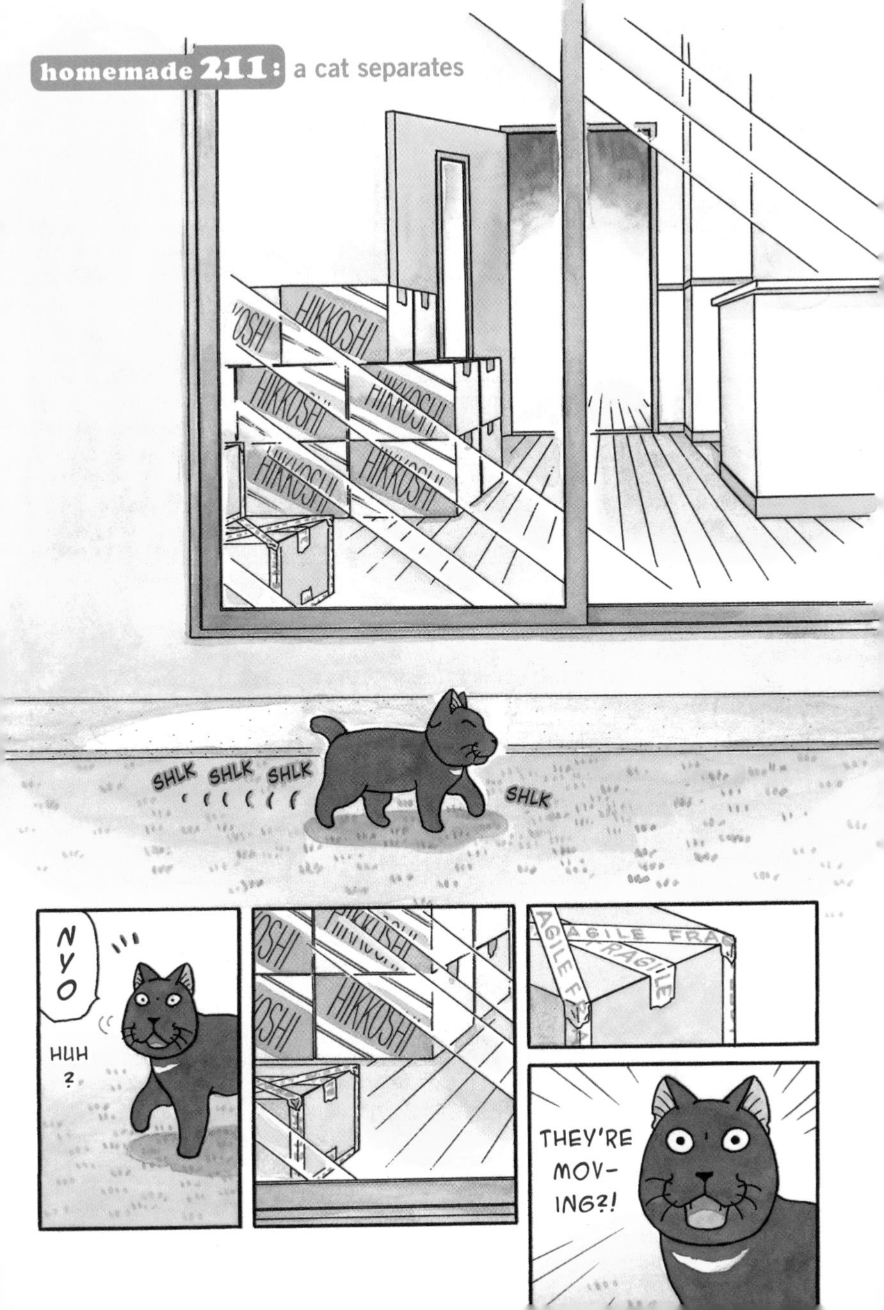

OSHI
HIKKOSHI
HIKKOSHI
HIKKOSHI
HIKKOSHI
HIKKOSHI
SHLK SHLK SHLK
SHLK
NYO
HUH?
OSHI
HIKKOSHI
OSHI
FRAGILE FRA
FRAGILE
AGILE FRA
THEY'RE MOVING?!

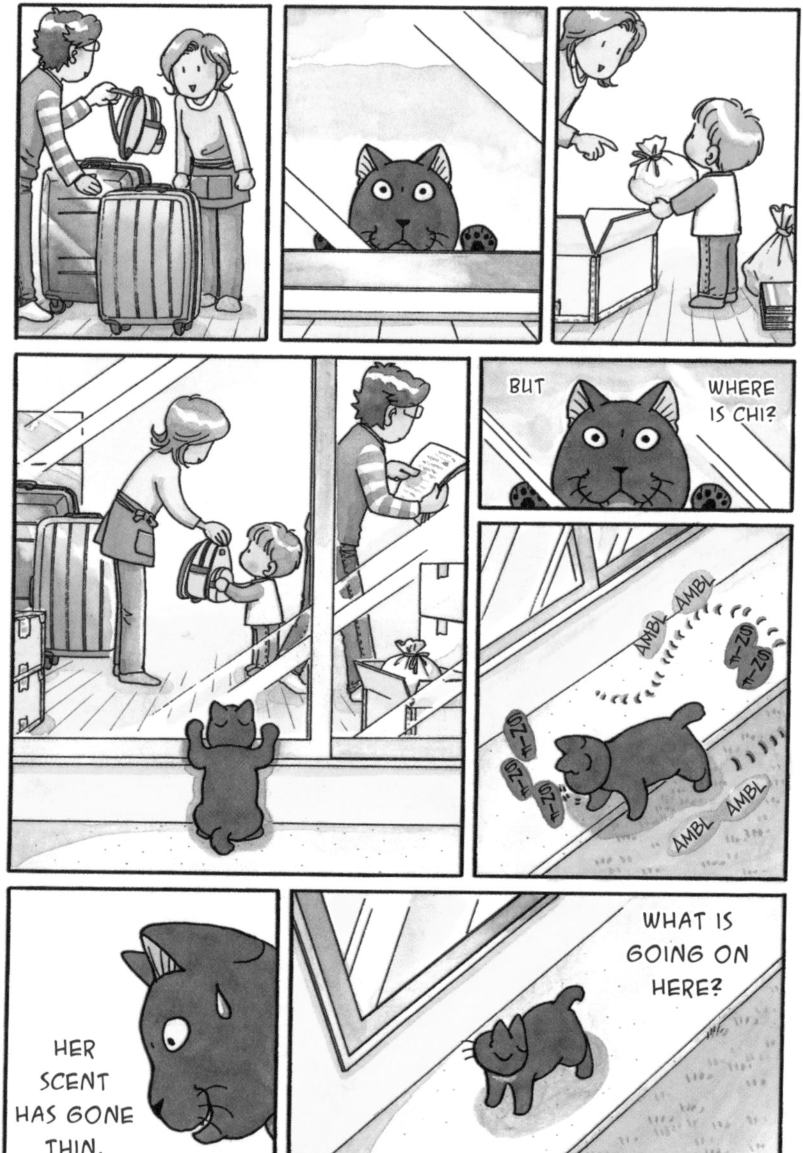
BUT
WHERE IS CHI?
AMBL
AMBL
AMBL
AMBL
HER SCENT HAS GONE THIN.
WHAT IS GOING ON HERE?

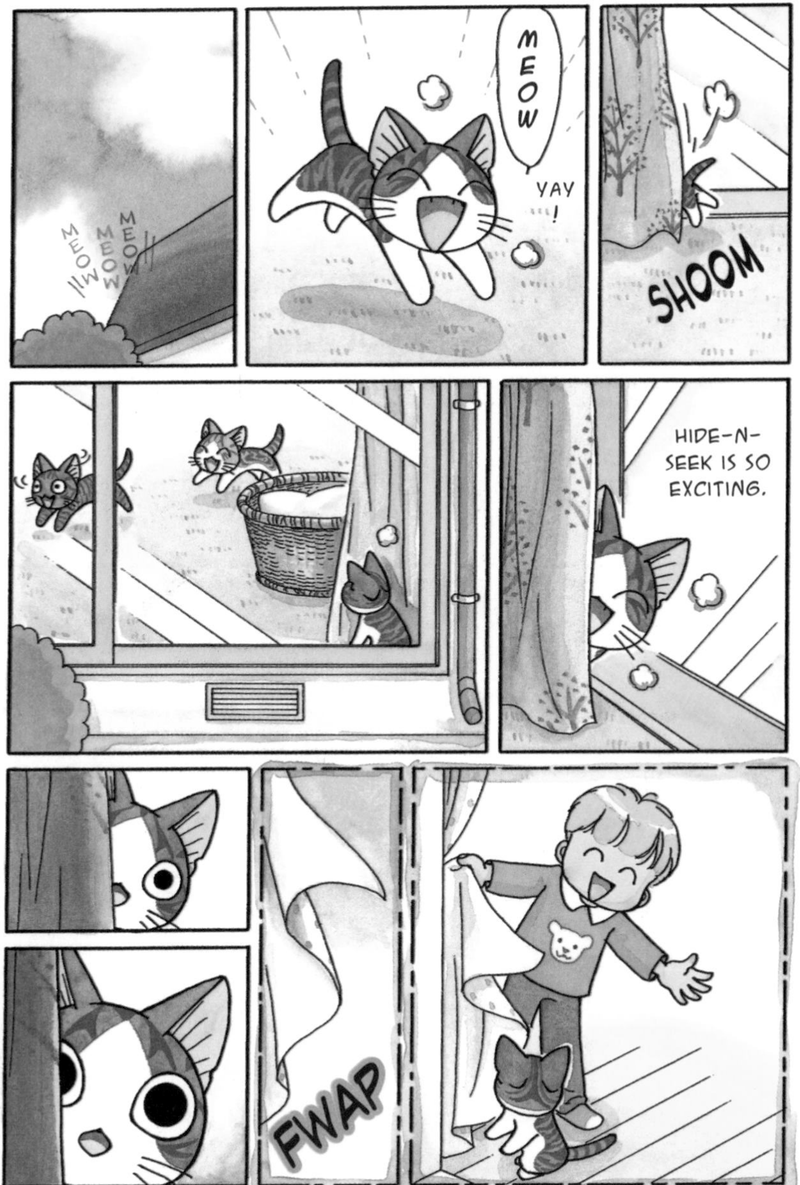
MEOW MEOW MEOW!!
MEOW
YAY!
SHOOM
HIDE-N-SEEK IS SO EXCITING.
FWAP

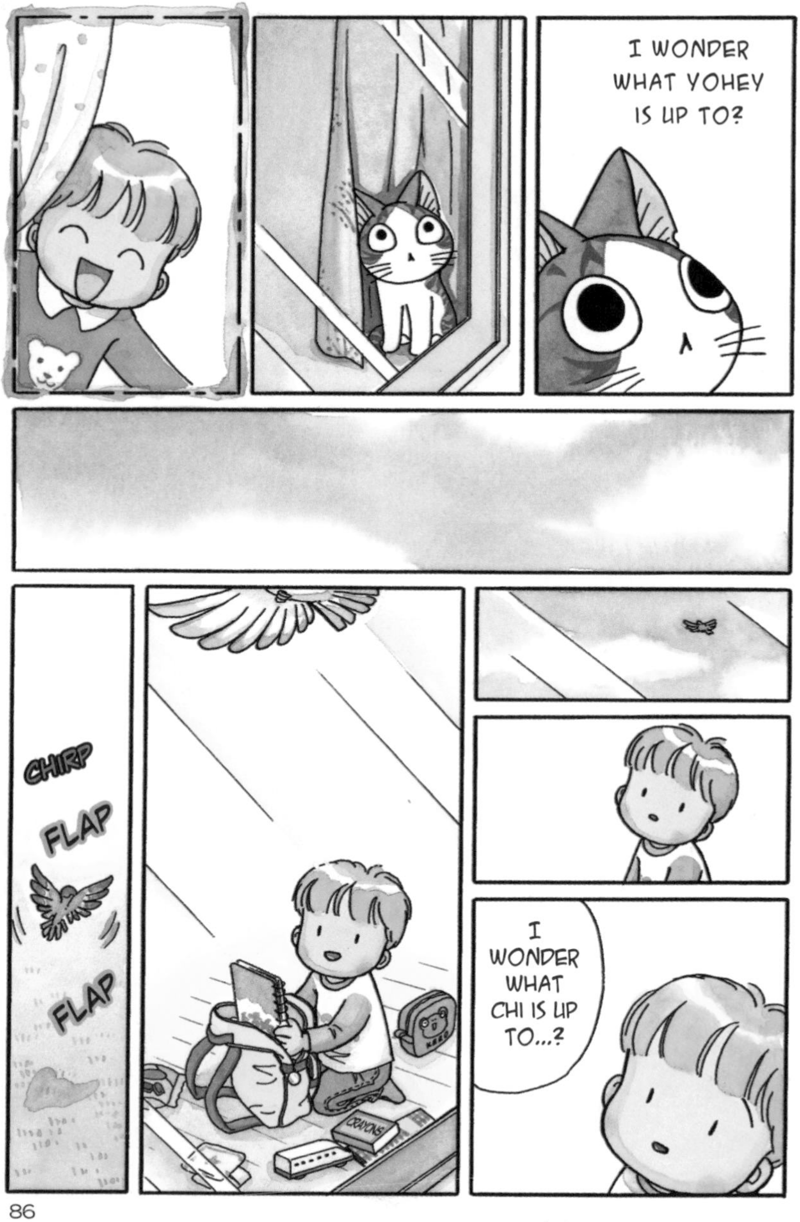
I WONDER WHAT YOHEY IS UP TO?
CHIRP
FLAP
FLAP
CRAYONS
I WONDER WHAT CHI IS UP TO...?

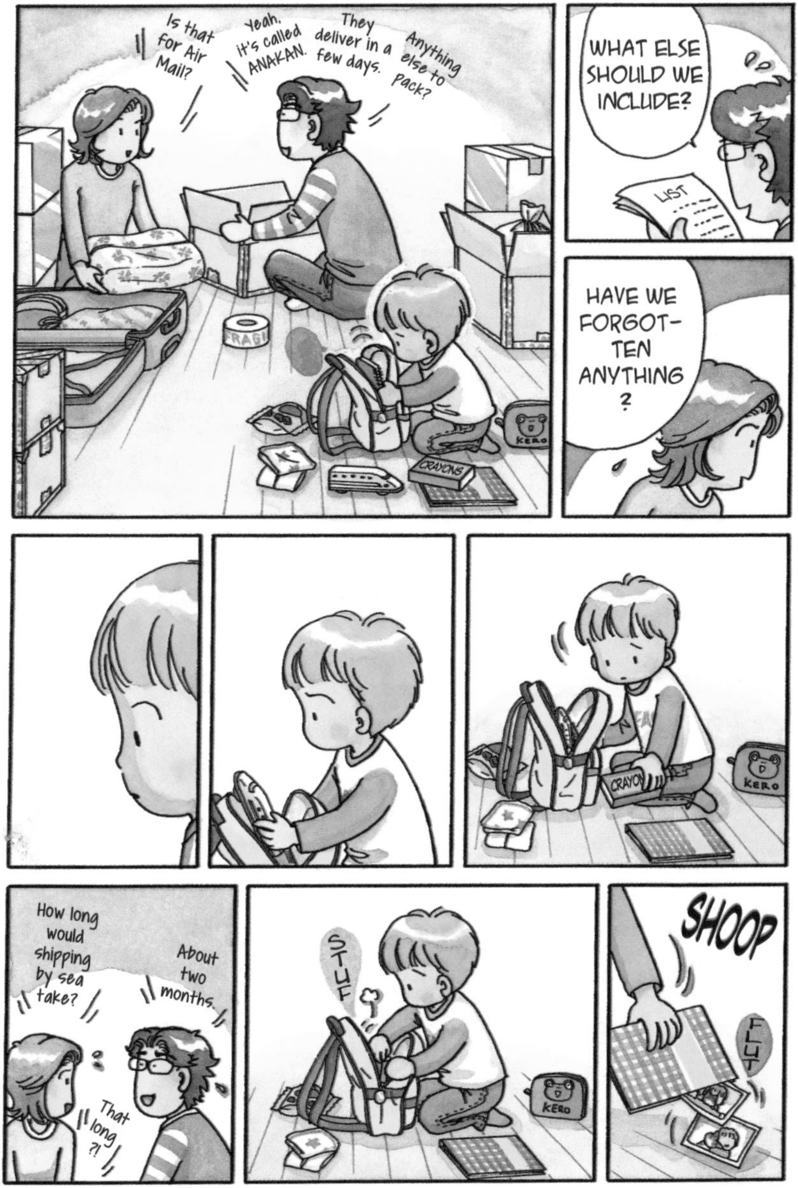
Is that for Air Mail?
Yeah. It's called ANAKAN.
They deliver in a few days.
Anything else to pack?
FRAGI
KERO
CRAYONS
WHAT ELSE SHOULD WE INCLUDE?
LIST
HAVE WE FORGOT-TEN ANYTHING?
CRAYON
KERO
How long would shipping by sea take?
About two months.
That long?!
STUF
KERO
SHOOP
FLUT

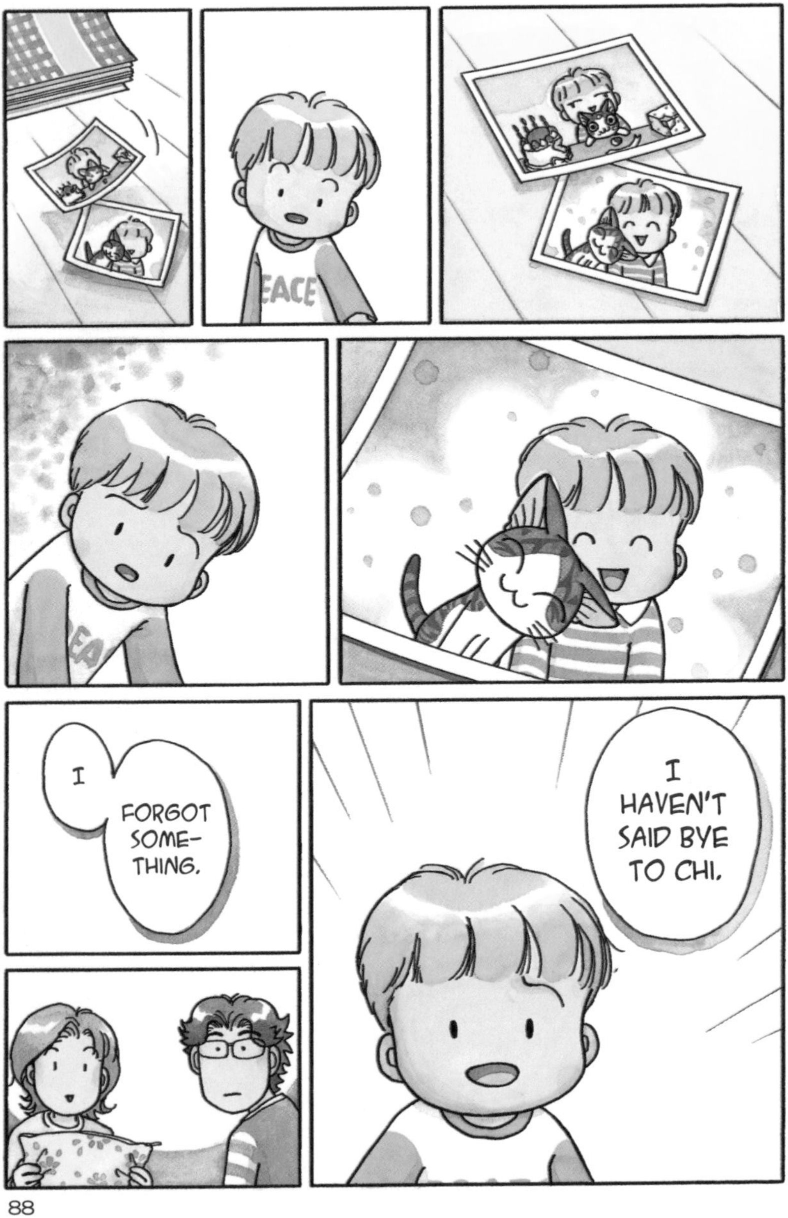
PEACE
PEA
I FORGOT SOME-THING.
I HAVEN'T SAID BYE TO CHI.

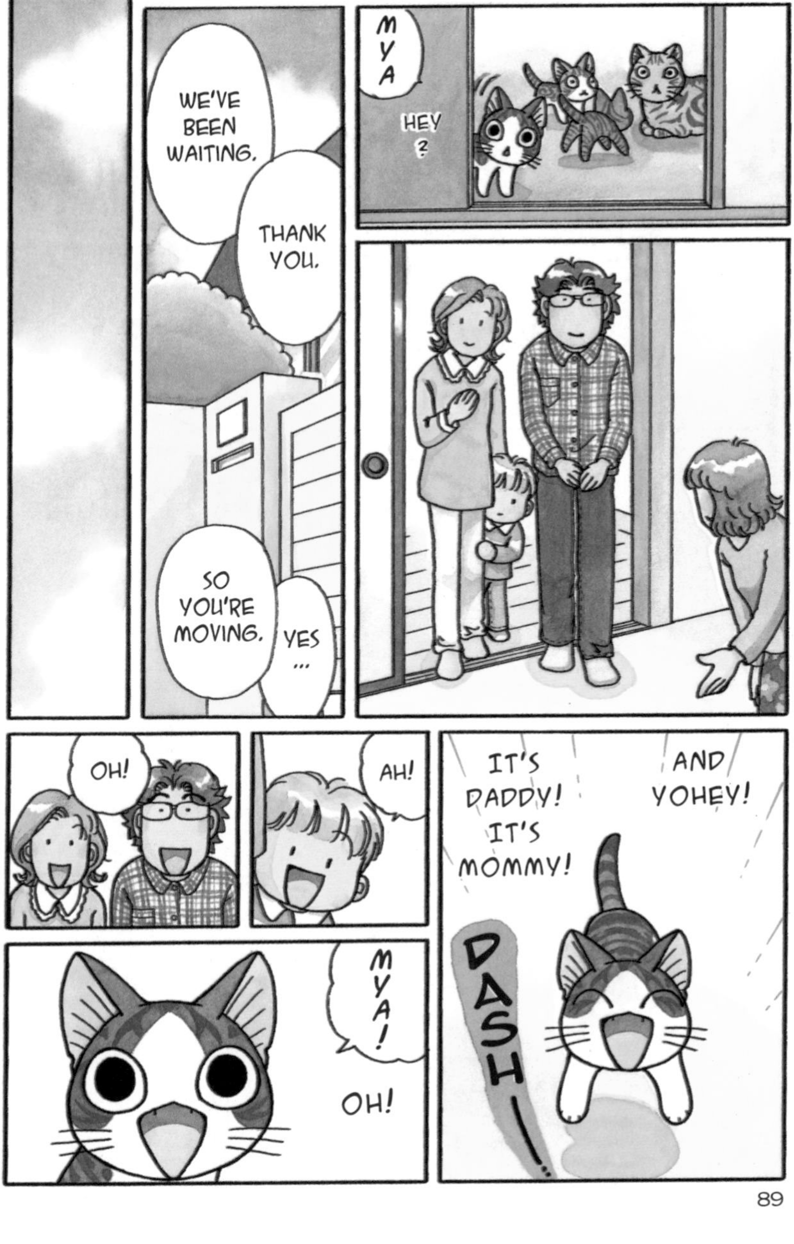
WE'VE BEEN WAITING.
THANK YOU.
SO YOU'RE MOVING.
YES ...
MYA
HEY?
OH!
AH!
MYA!
OH!
IT'S DADDY! IT'S MOMMY!
AND YOHEY!
DASH—!!

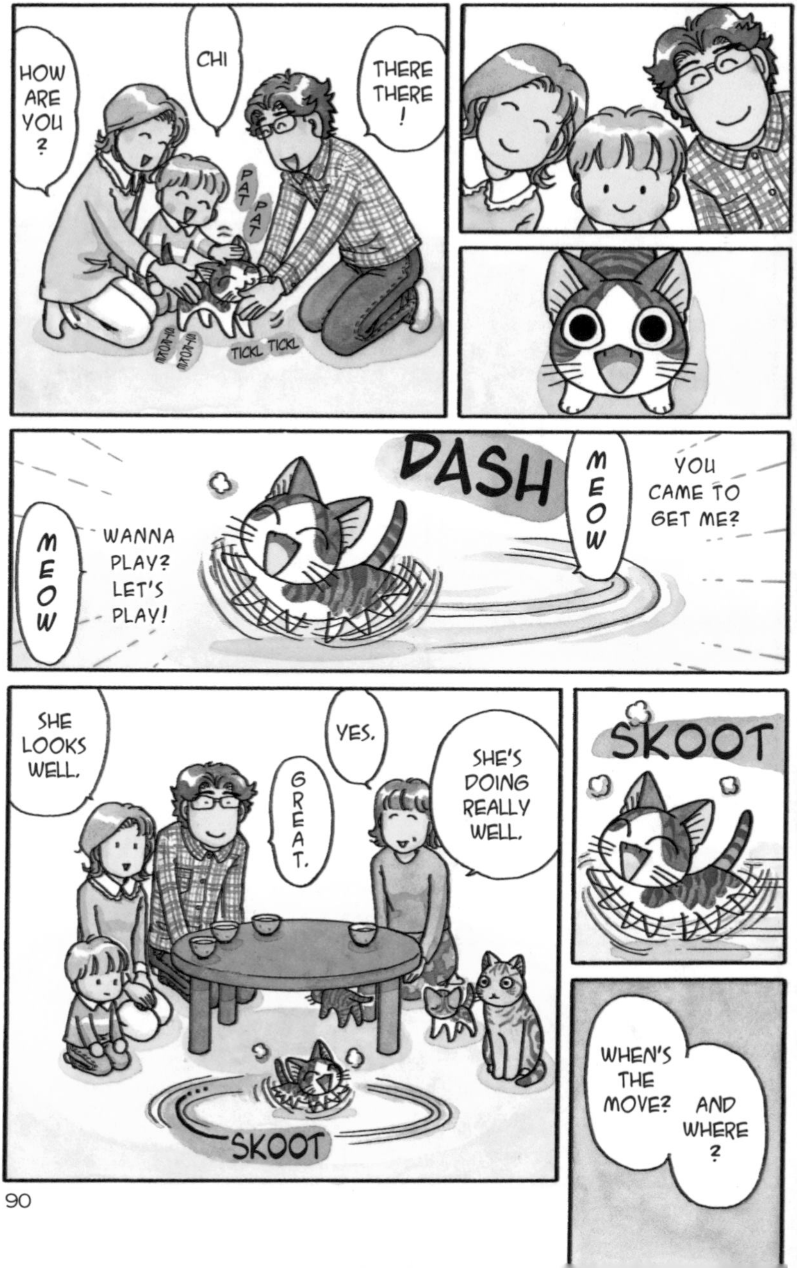

HOW ARE YOU?
CHI
THERE THERE!
PAT PAT
TICKL TICKL
MEOW
WANNA PLAY? LET'S PLAY!
DASH
MEOW
YOU CAME TO GET ME?
SHE LOOKS WELL.
YES.
GREAT.
SHE'S DOING REALLY WELL.
SKOOT
SKOOT
WHEN'S THE MOVE?
AND WHERE?

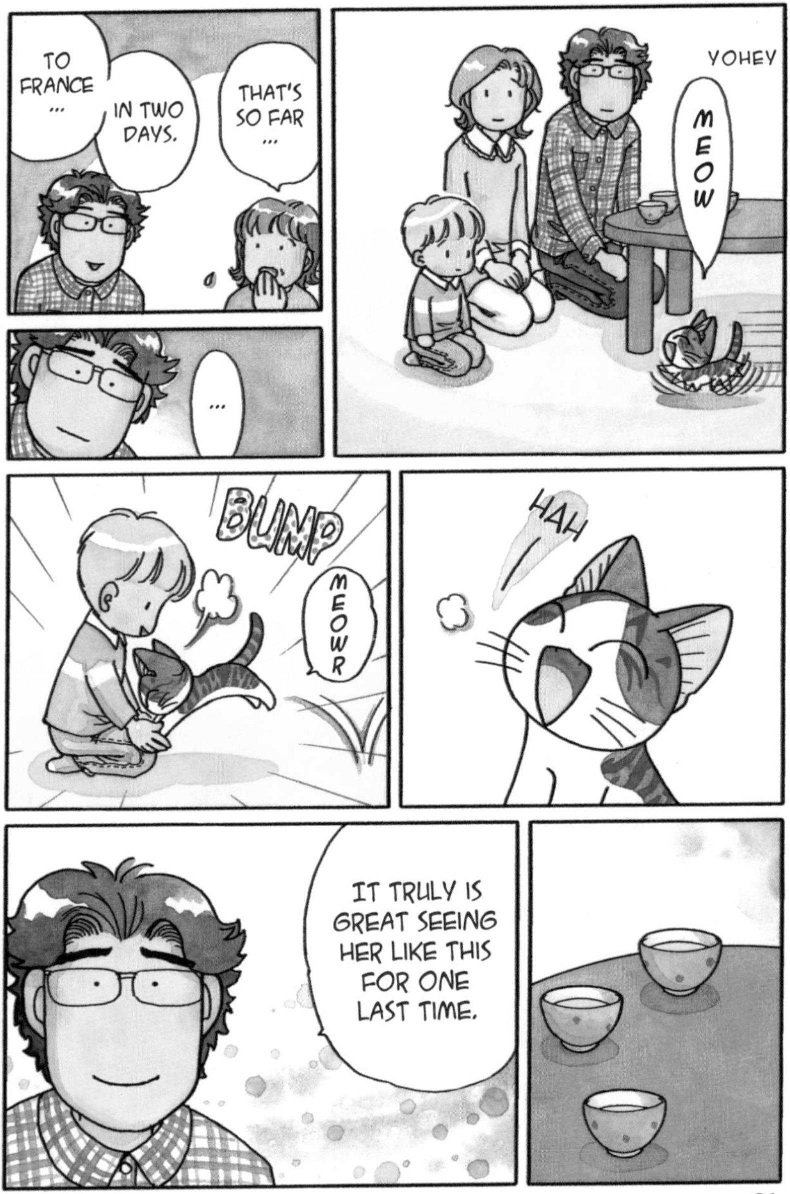

TO FRANCE ...
IN TWO DAYS.
THAT'S SO FAR ...
...
YOHEY
MEOW
BUMP
MEOWR
HAH
IT TRULY IS GREAT SEEING HER LIKE THIS FOR ONE LAST TIME.

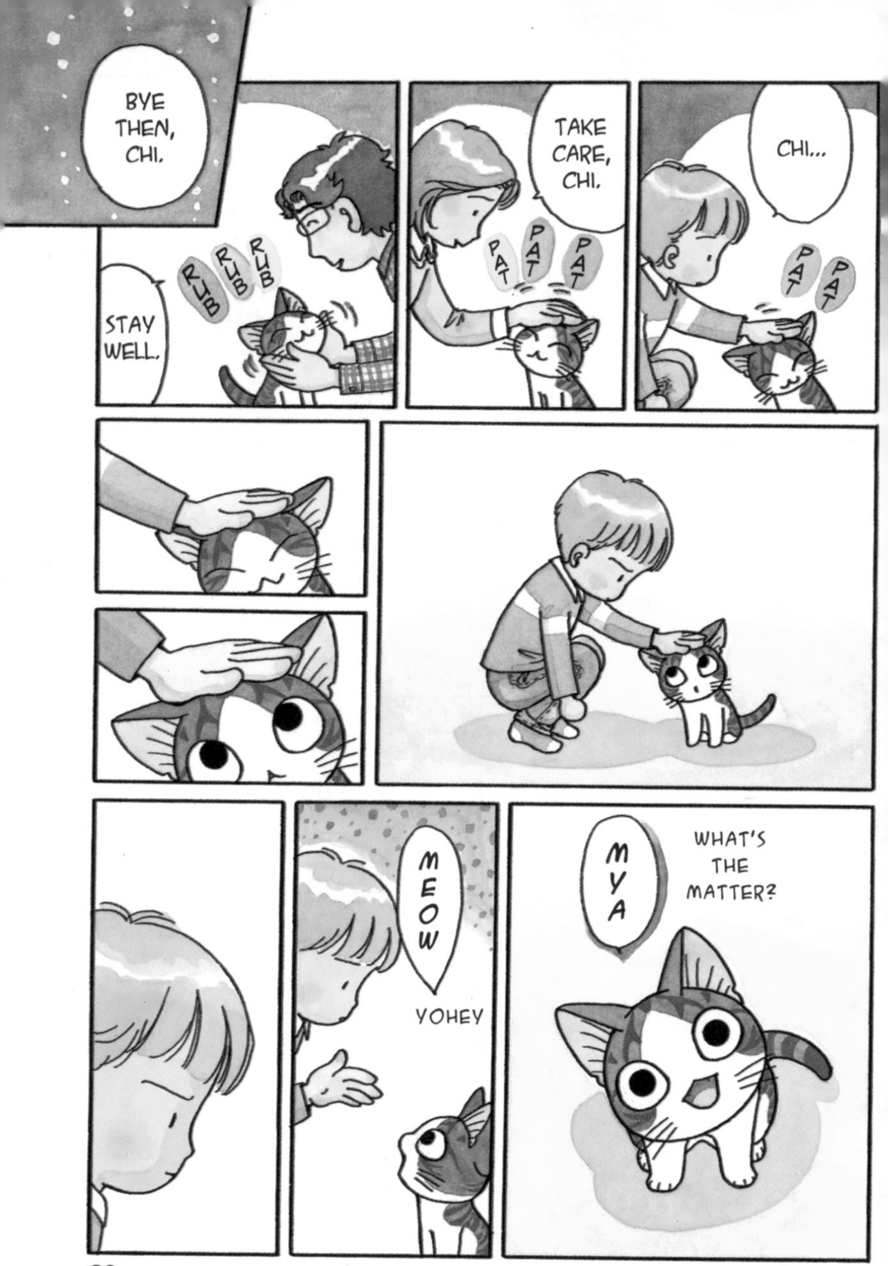
BYE THEN, CHI.
STAY WELL.
RUB RUB RUB
TAKE CARE, CHI.
PAT PAT PAT
CHI...
PAT PAT
MEOW
YOHEY
MYA
WHAT'S THE MATTER?

CHI
!

ZKUEEN

HUH
?

CHI
...

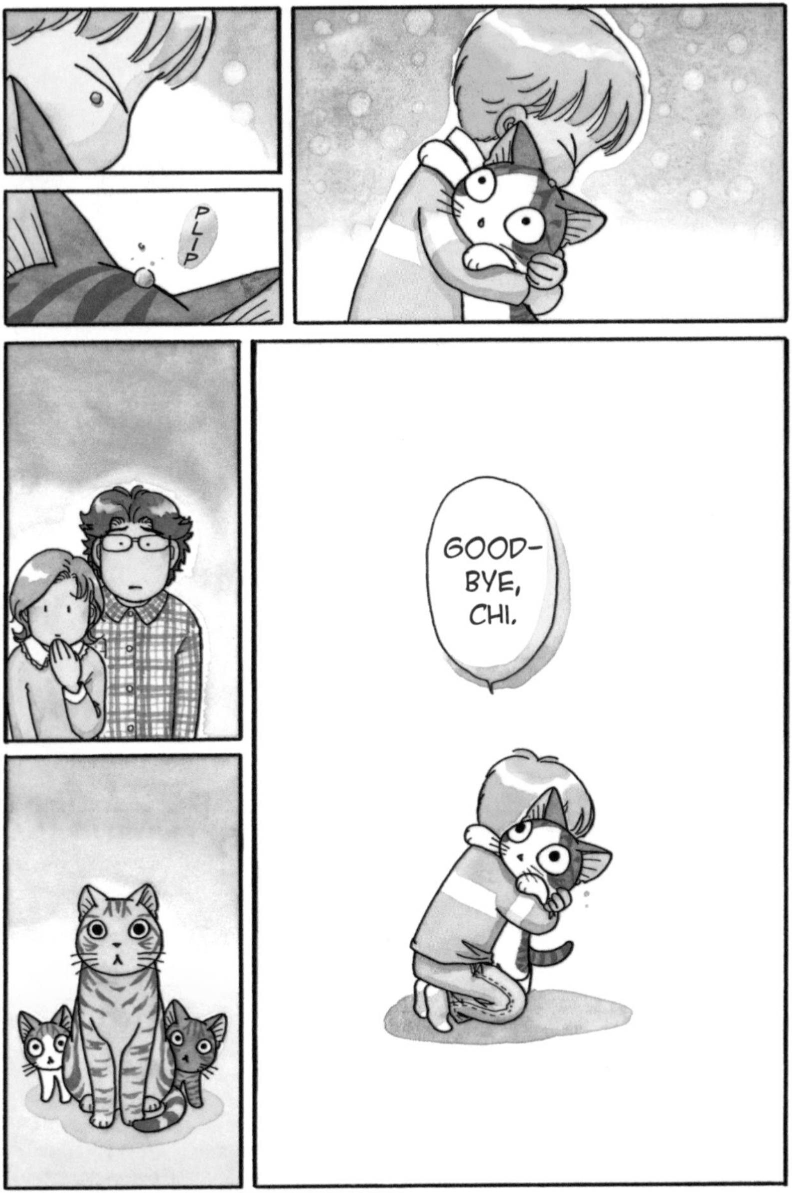
PLIP
GOOD-BYE, CHI.

the end

homemade 212: a cat confirms

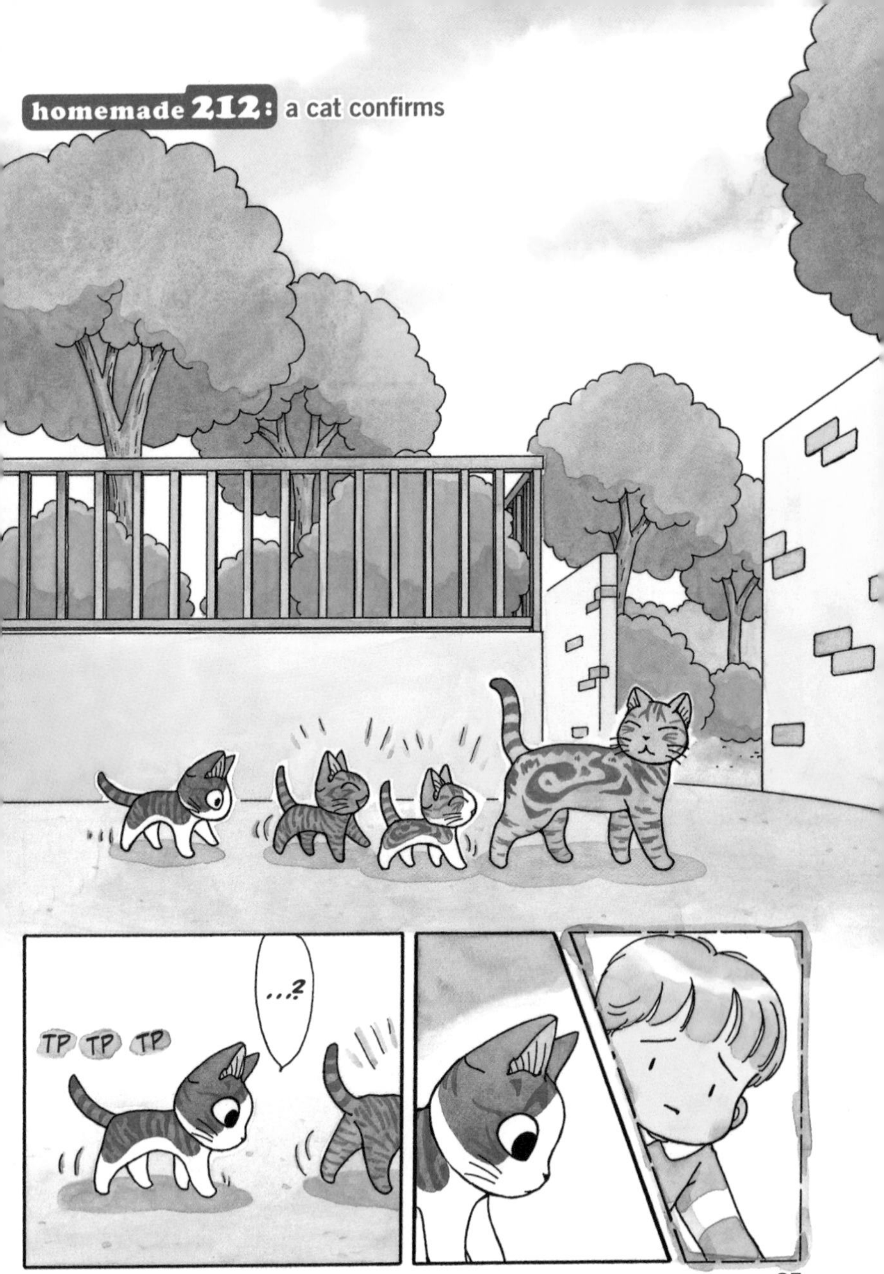
TP TP TP
...?

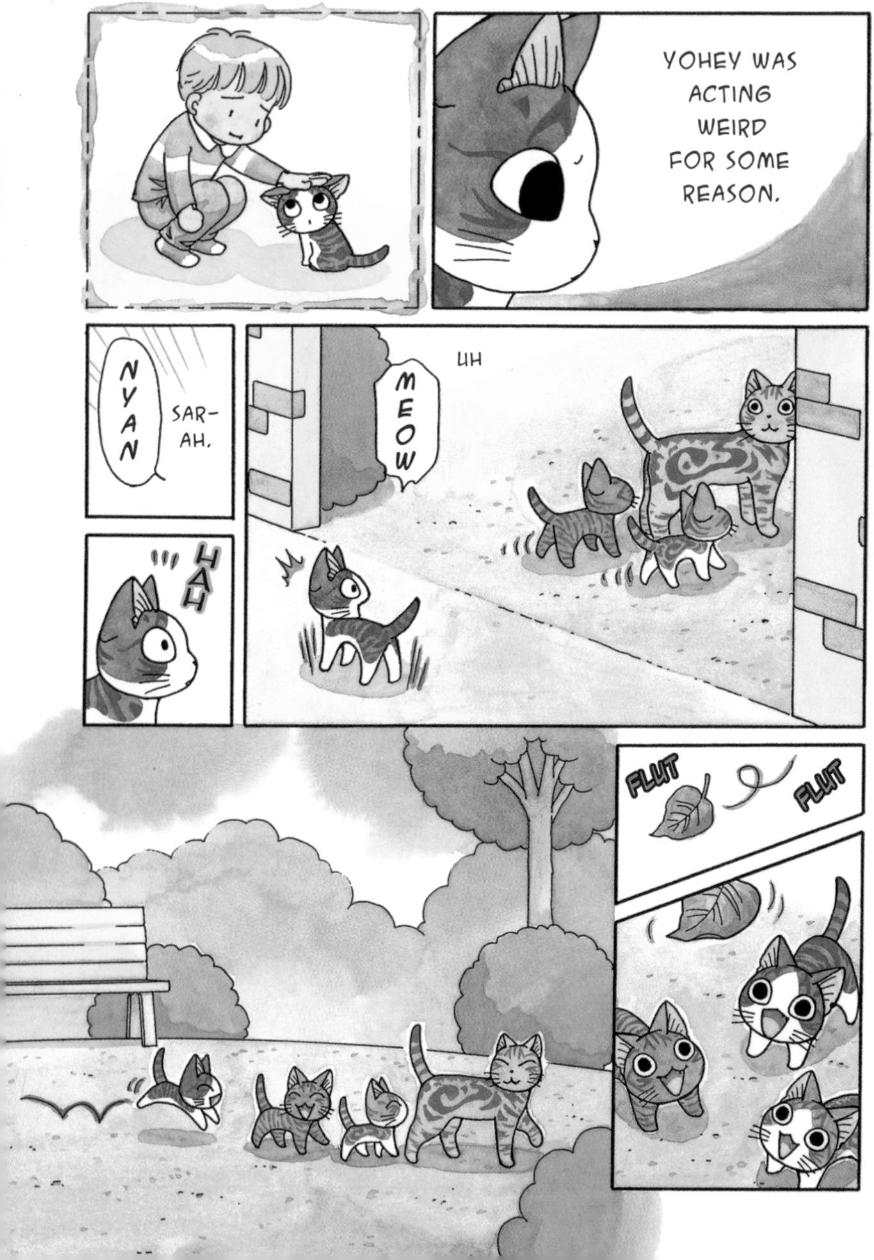
YOHEY WAS ACTING WEIRD FOR SOME REASON.
NYAN
SAR-AH.
HAH
MEOW
UH
FLUT
FLUT

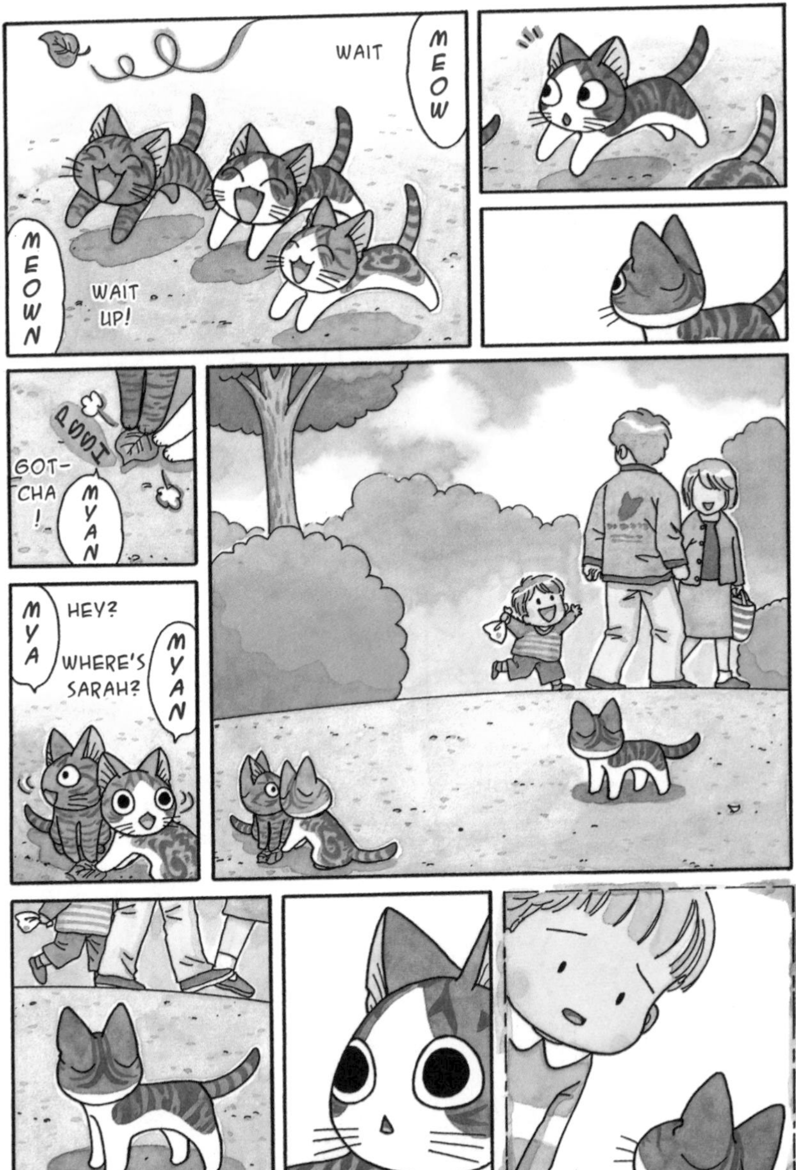
WAIT
MEOW
MEOWN
WAIT UP!
GOT-CHA!
MYAN
MYA
HEY?
WHERE'S SARAH?
MYAN

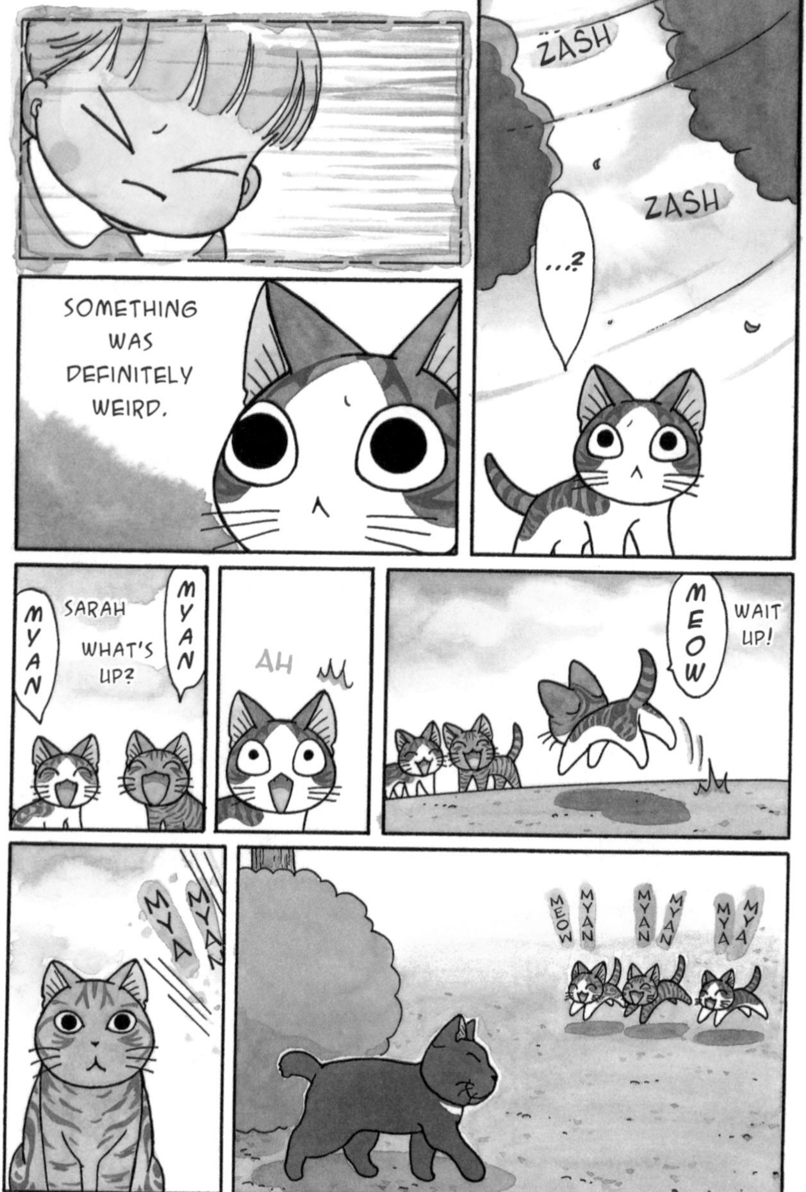
SOMETHING WAS DEFINITELY WEIRD.
ZASH
ZASH
...?
MYAN
SARAH
WHAT'S UP?
MYAN
AH
MEOW
WAIT UP!
MYA
MYAN
MEOW
MYAN
MYAN
MYAN
MYA
MYA

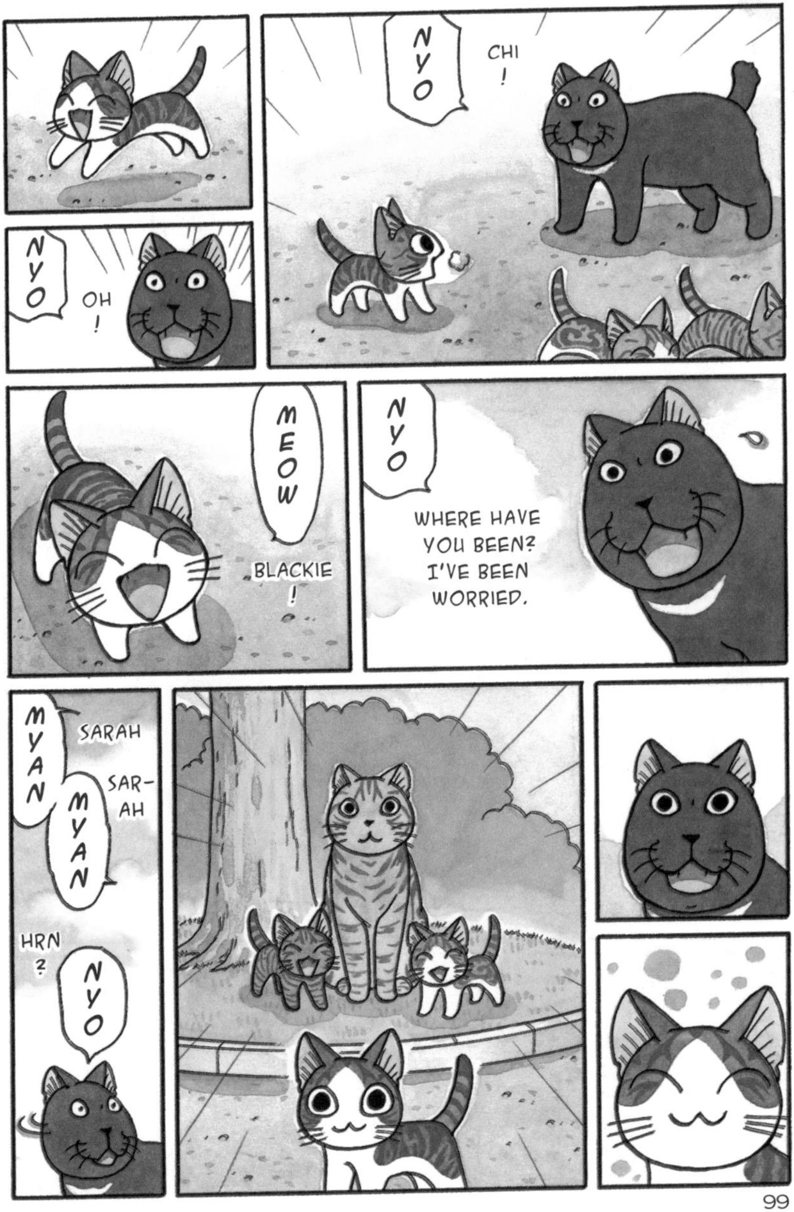
NYO
OH!
NYO
CHI!
MEOW
BLACKIE!
NYO
WHERE HAVE YOU BEEN? I'VE BEEN WORRIED.
MYAN
SARAH
MYAN
SAR-AH
HRN?
NYO

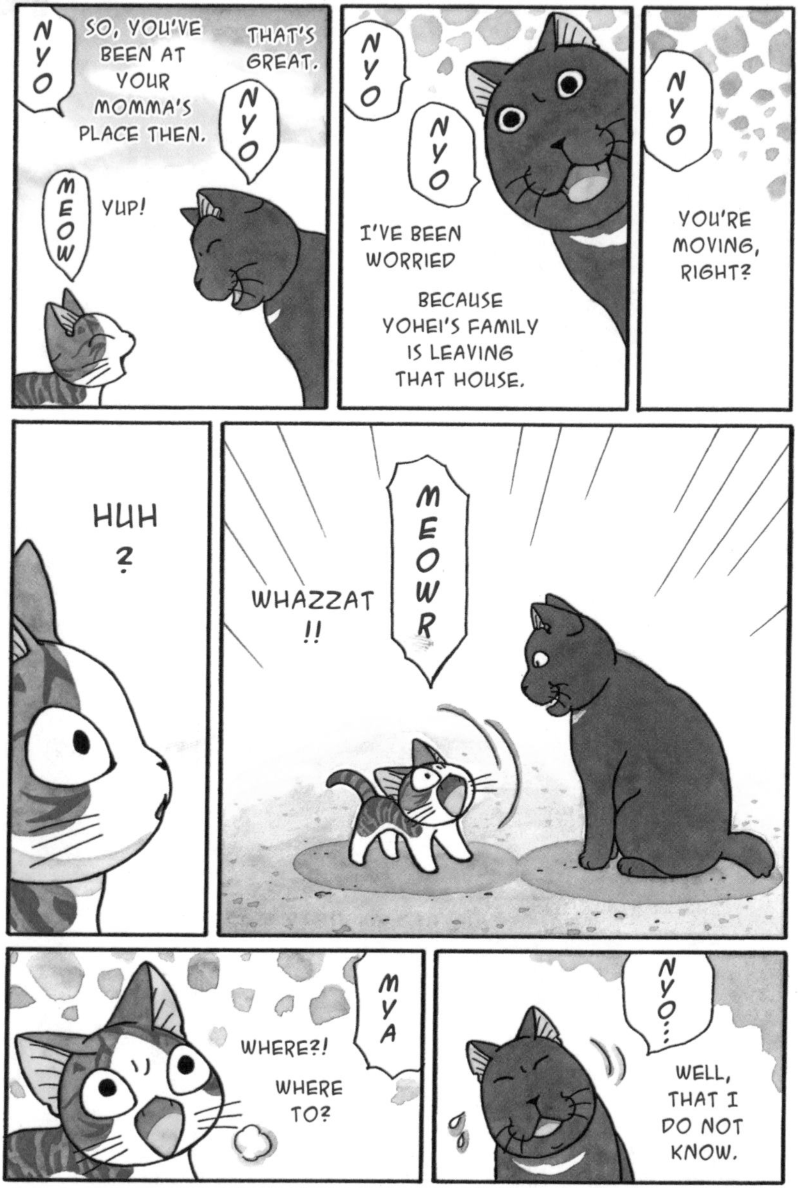
NYO
SO, YOU'VE BEEN AT YOUR MOMMA'S PLACE THEN.
THAT'S GREAT.
NYO
MEOW
YUP!
NYO
NYO
I'VE BEEN WORRIED
BECAUSE YOHEI'S FAMILY IS LEAVING THAT HOUSE.
NYO
YOU'RE MOVING, RIGHT?
HUH ?
MEOWR
WHAZZAT !!
MYA
WHERE?!
WHERE TO?
NYO...
WELL, THAT I DO NOT KNOW.

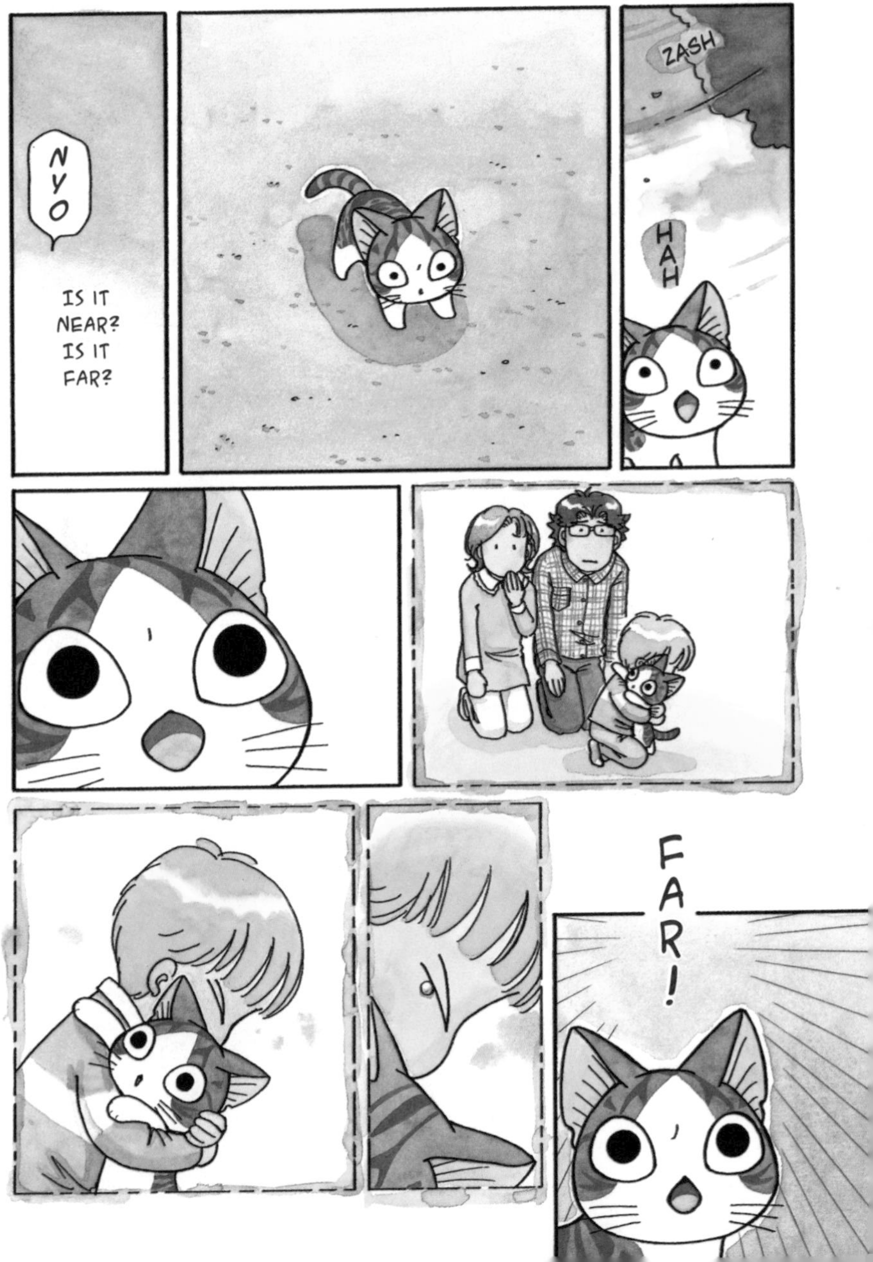
NYO
IS IT NEAR? IS IT FAR?
ZASH
HAH
FAR!

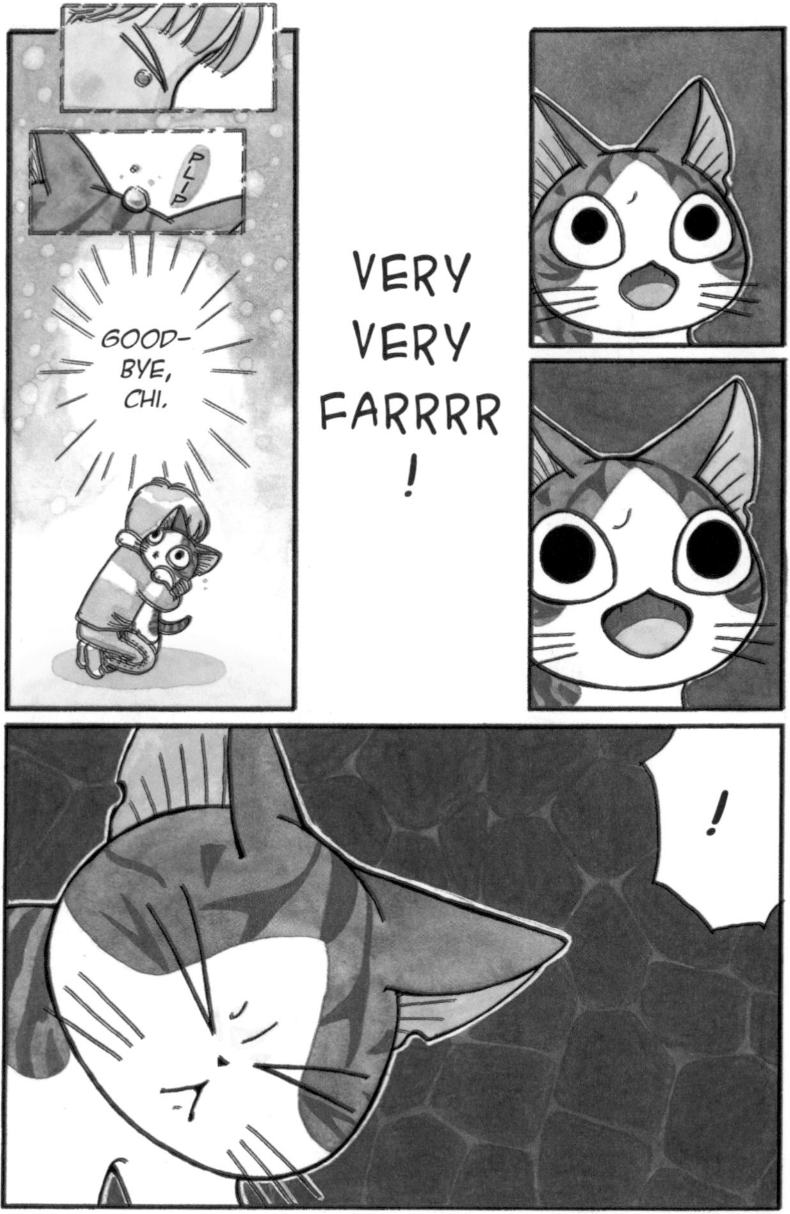
PLIP
GOOD-BYE, CHI.
VERY VERY FARRRR !
!

the end

homemade 213: a cat has to pick

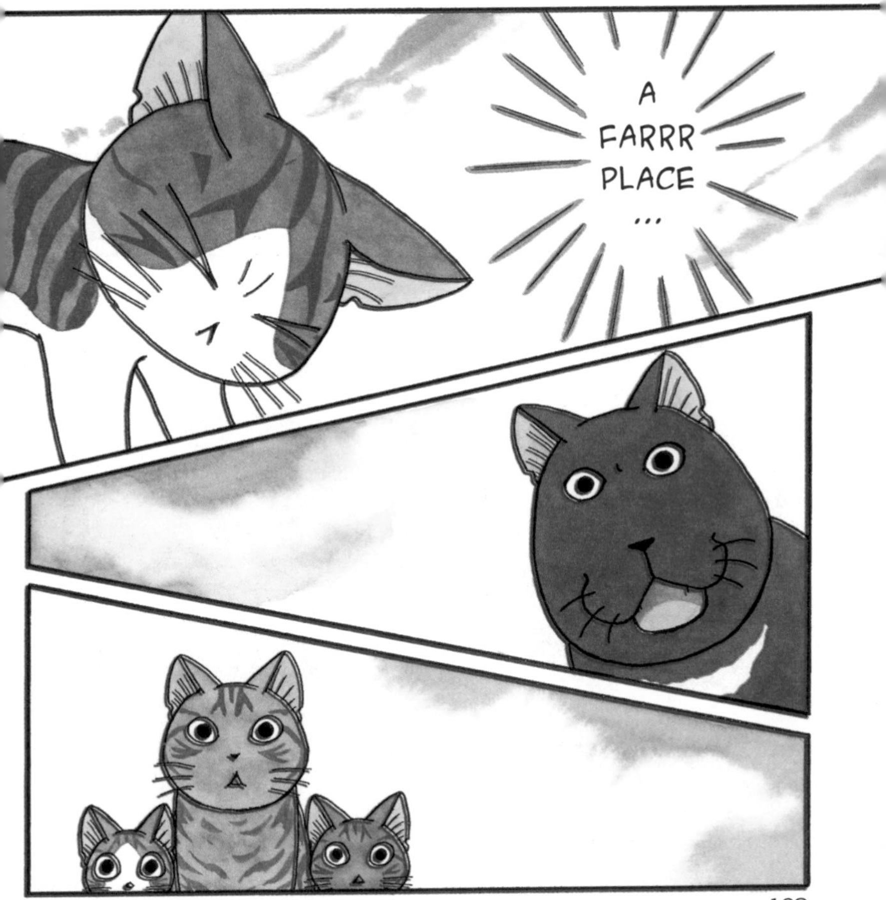
A FARRR PLACE ...

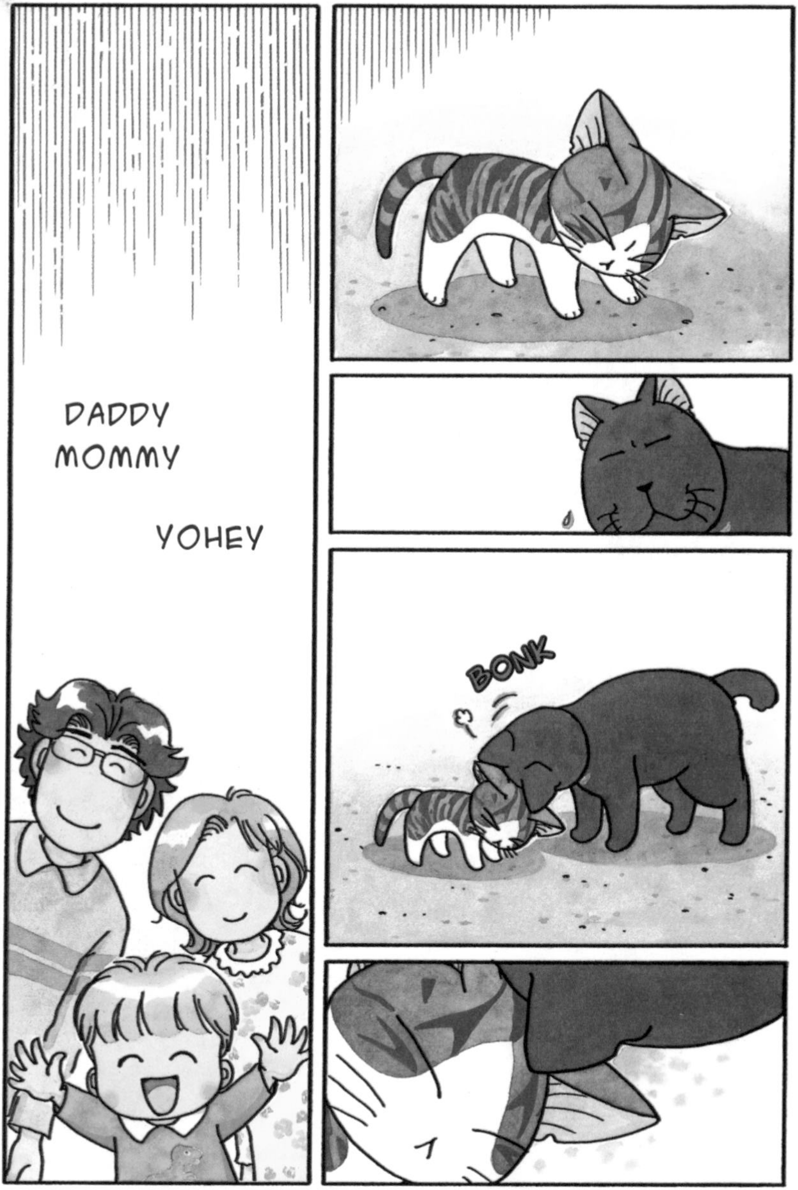
DADDY
MOMMY
YOHEY
BONK

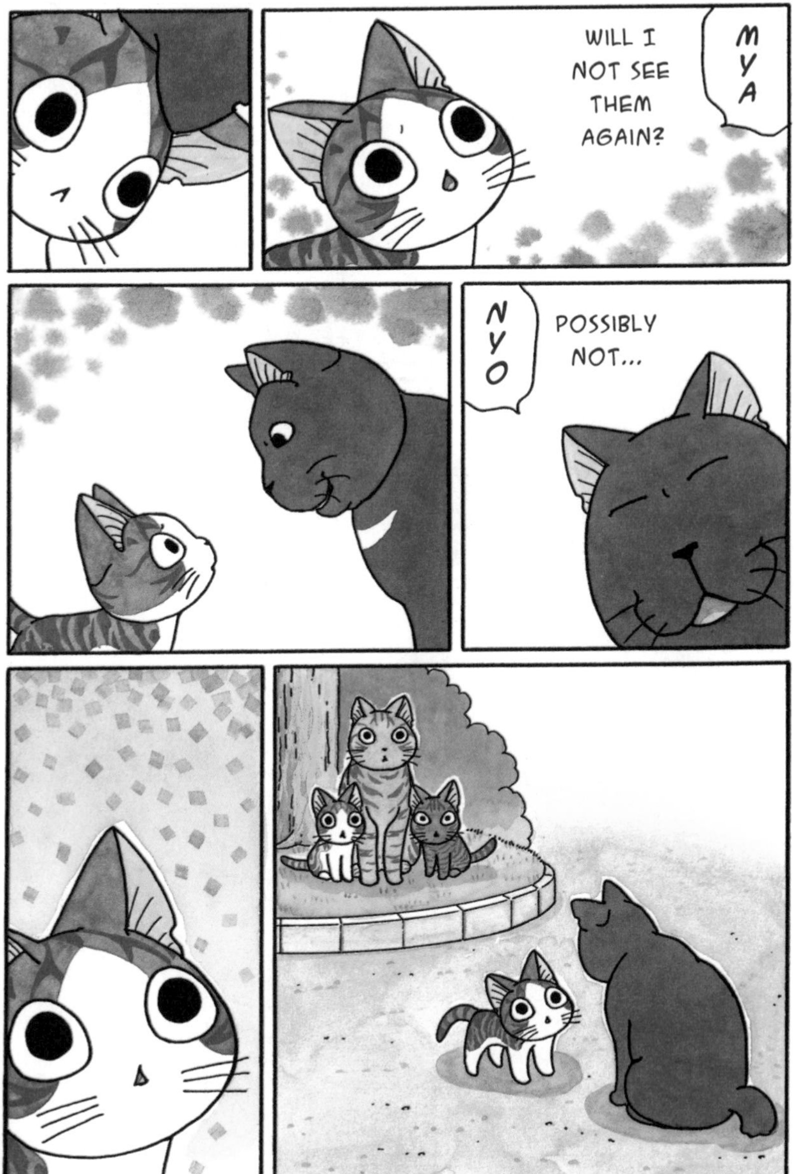
WILL I NOT SEE THEM AGAIN?
MYA
NYO
POSSIBLY NOT...

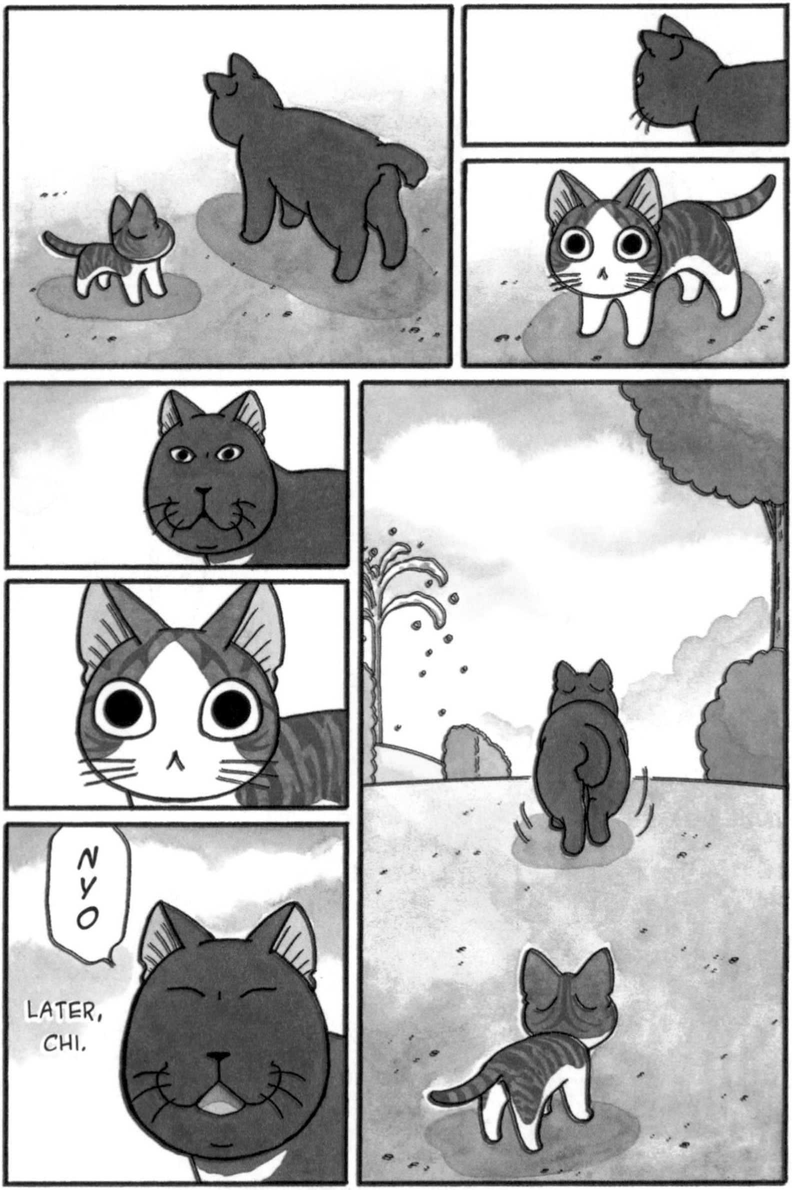
NYO
LATER, CHI.

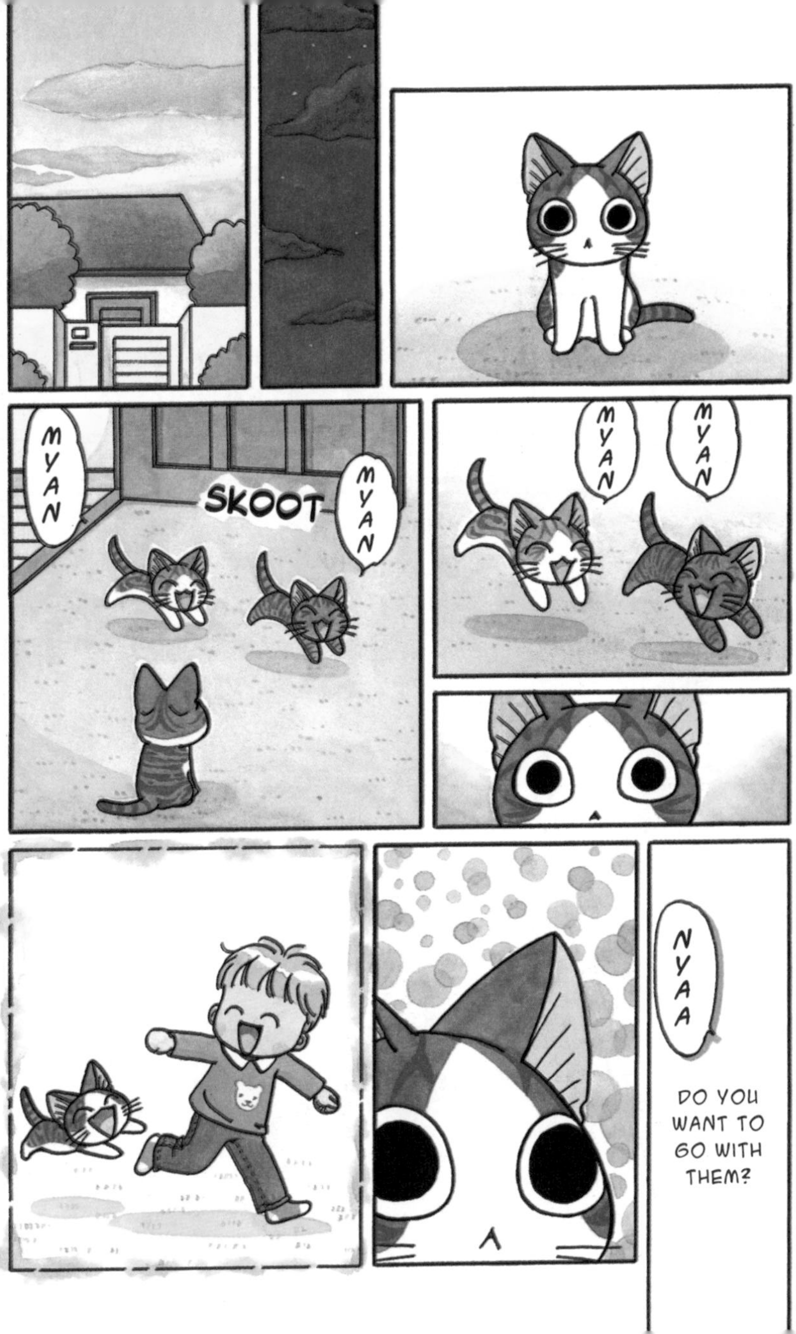
MYAN
SKOOT
MYAN
MYAN
MYAN
NYAA
DO YOU WANT TO GO WITH THEM?

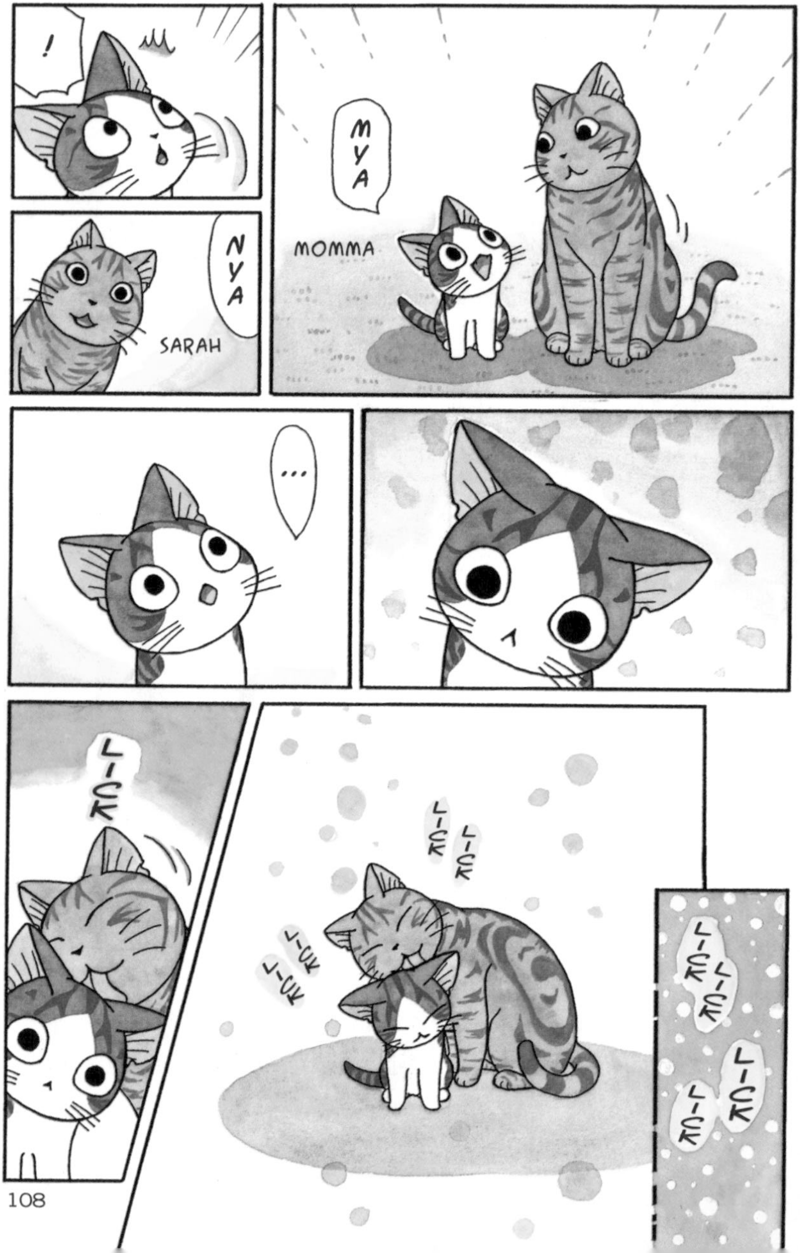
!
MYA
MOMMA
NYA
SARAH
...
LICK
LICK
LICK
LICK
LICK
LICK
LICK
LICK
LICK

NYA

SARAH,

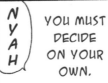

NYAH

YOU MUST
DECIDE
ON YOUR
OWN.

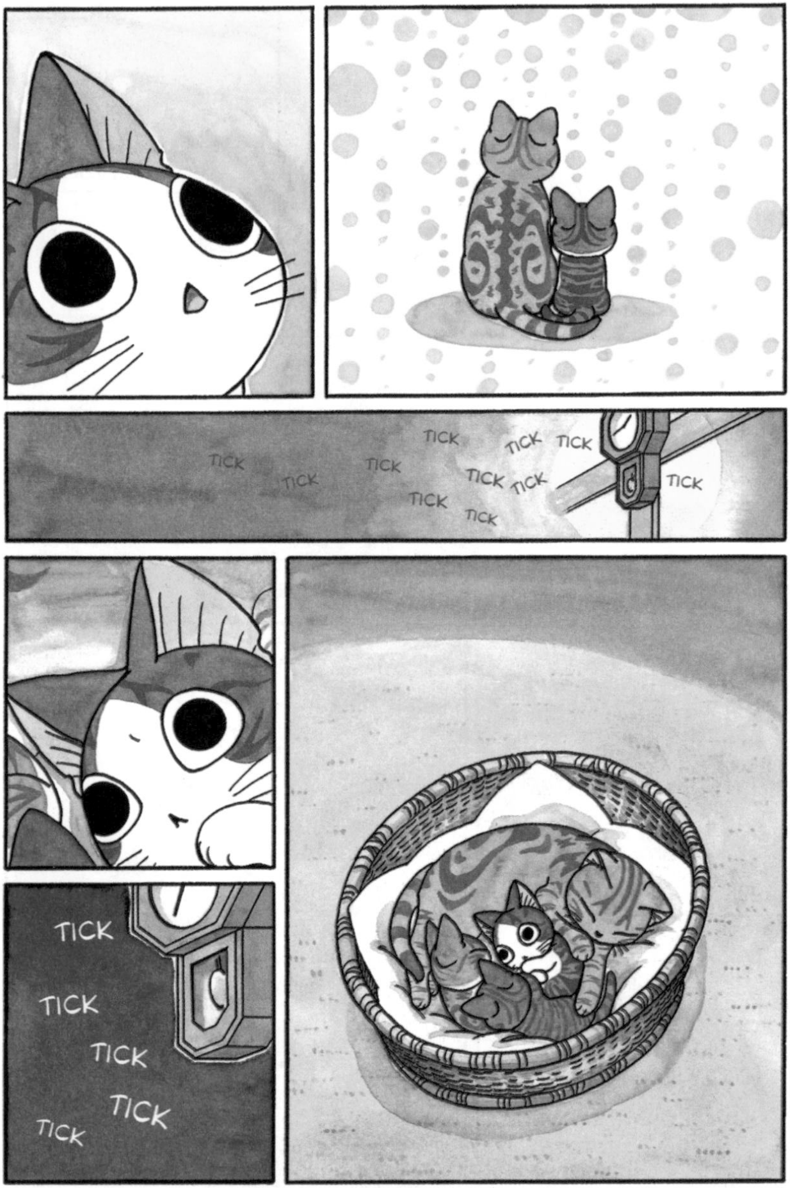
TICK
TICK
TICK
TICK
TICK
TICK
TICK
TICK
TICK
TICK
TICK
TICK
TICK
TICK
TICK
TICK

the end

homemade 214: a cat makes up her mind

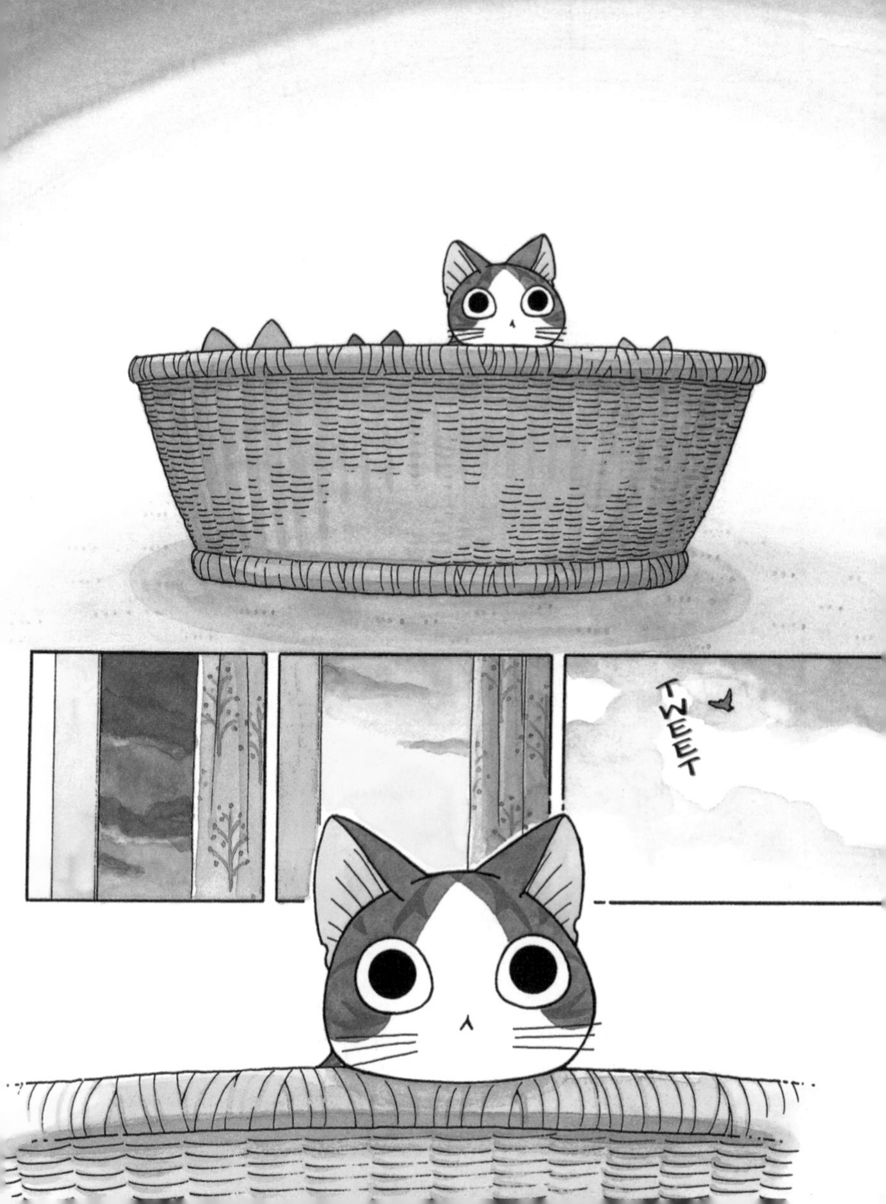
TWEET

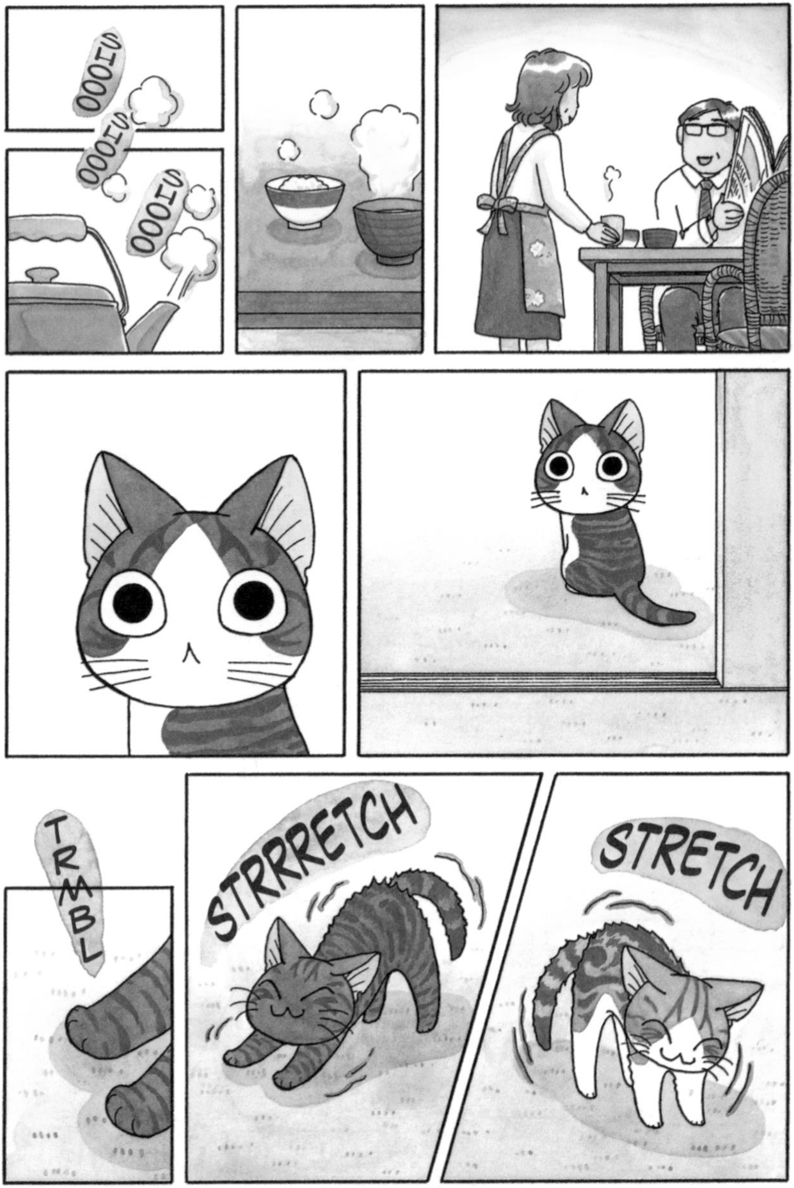
SIOOOO
SIOOOO
SIOOOO
TRMBL
STRRRETCH
STRETCH

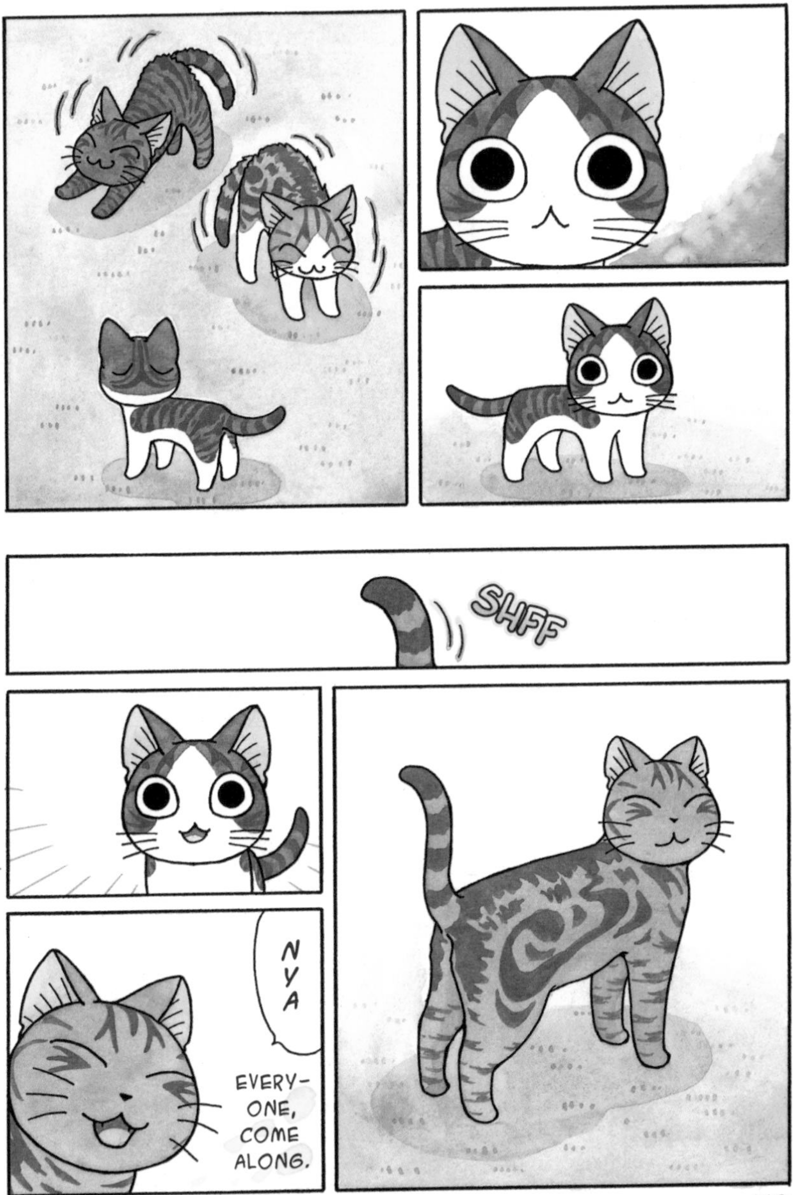
SHFF
NYA
EVERY-ONE, COME ALONG.

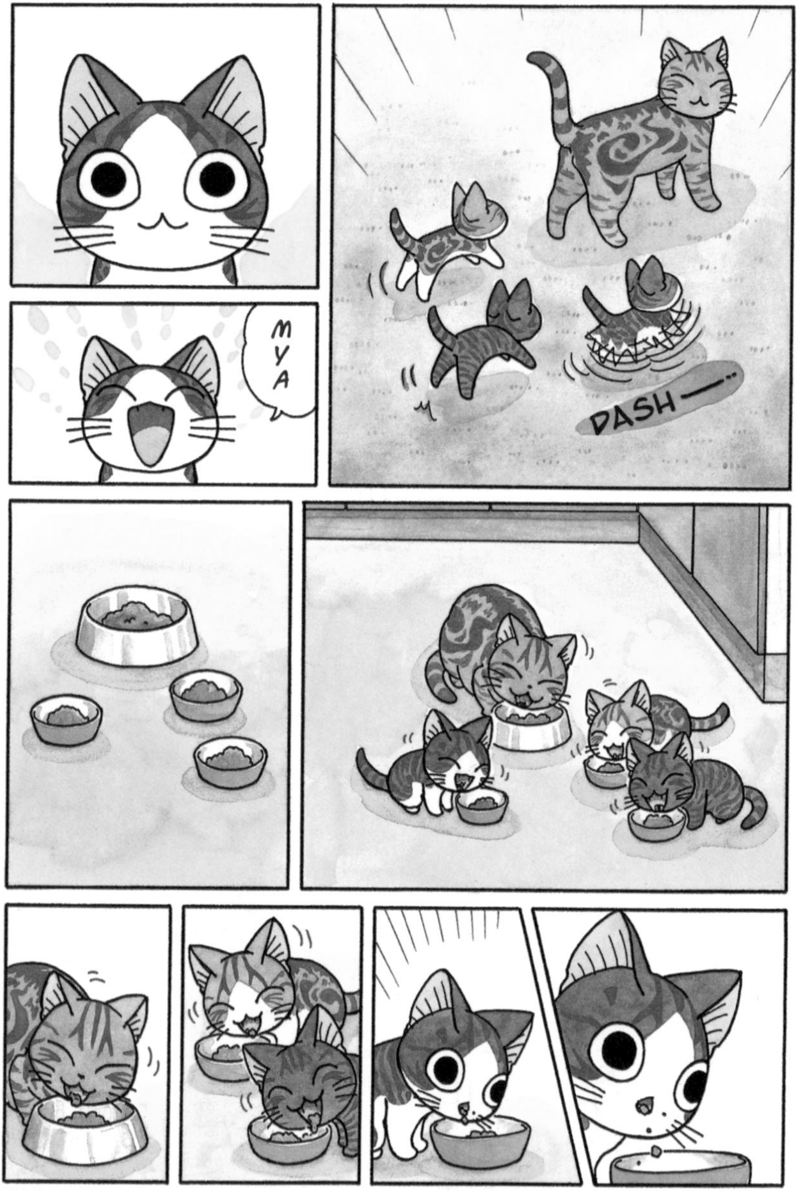
MYA
DASH

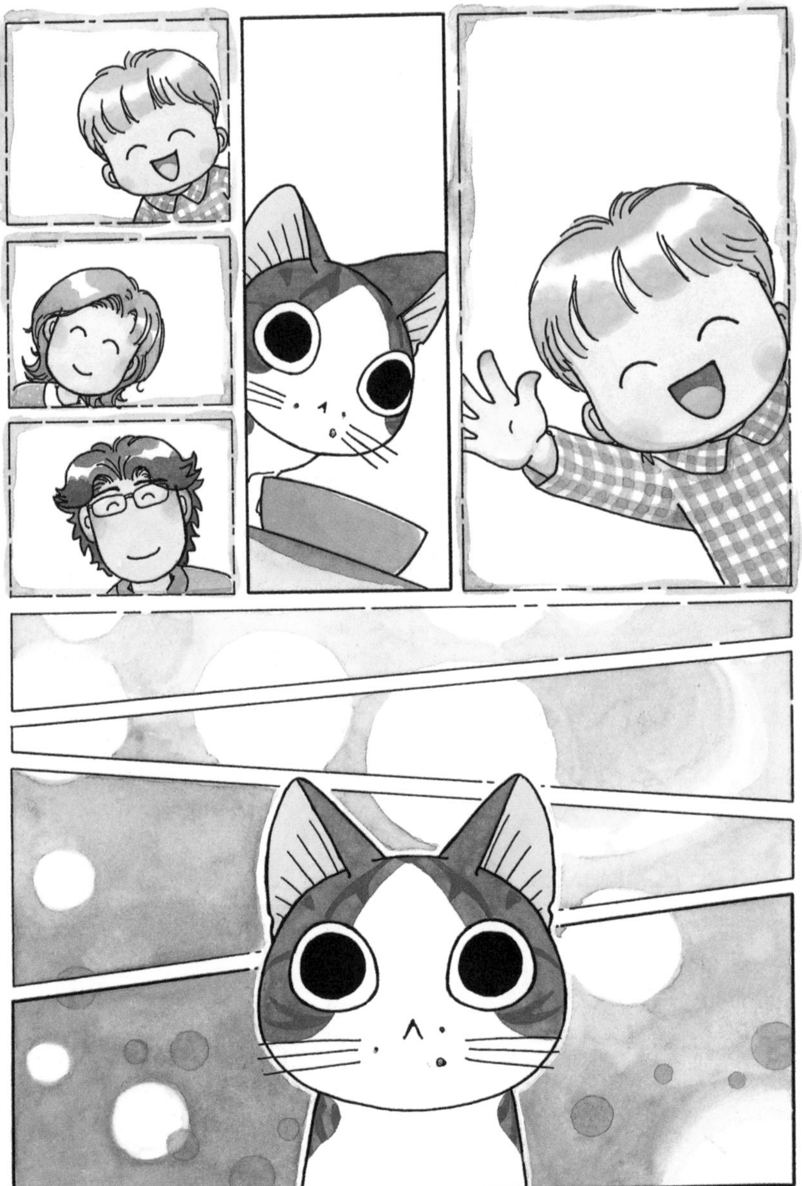

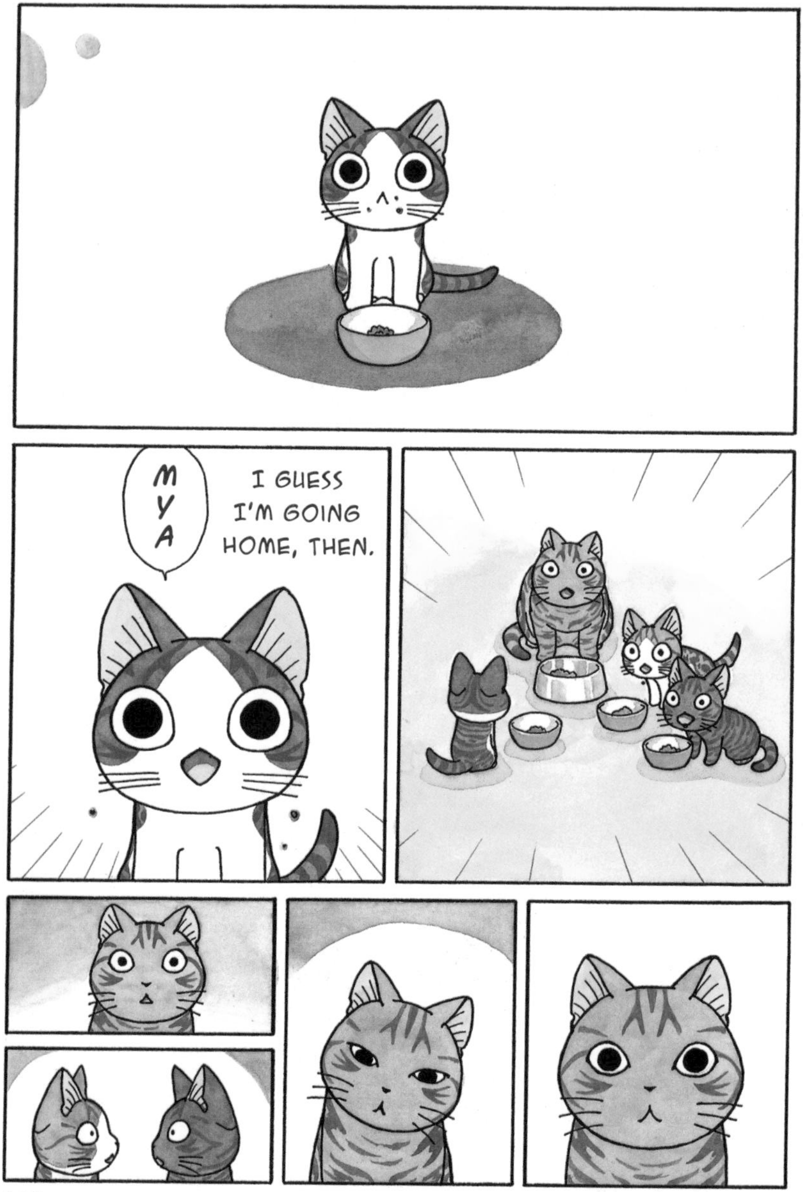
MYA
I GUESS I'M GOING HOME, THEN.

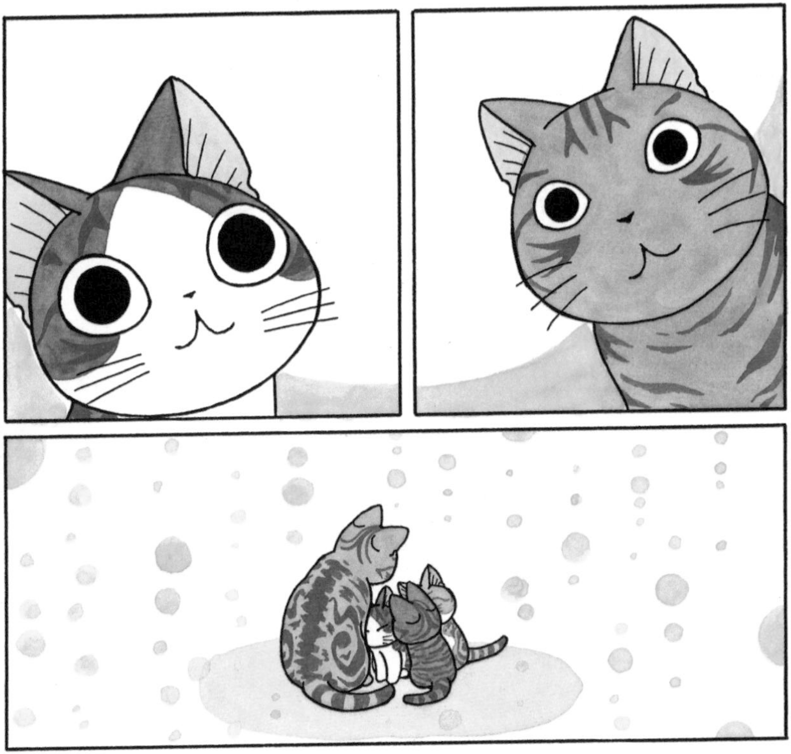

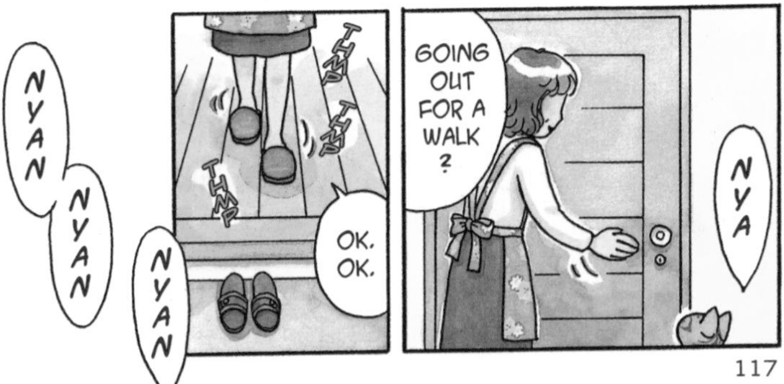
NYAN
NYAN
NYAN
THMP
THMP
THMP
OK. OK.
GOING OUT FOR A WALK?
NYA

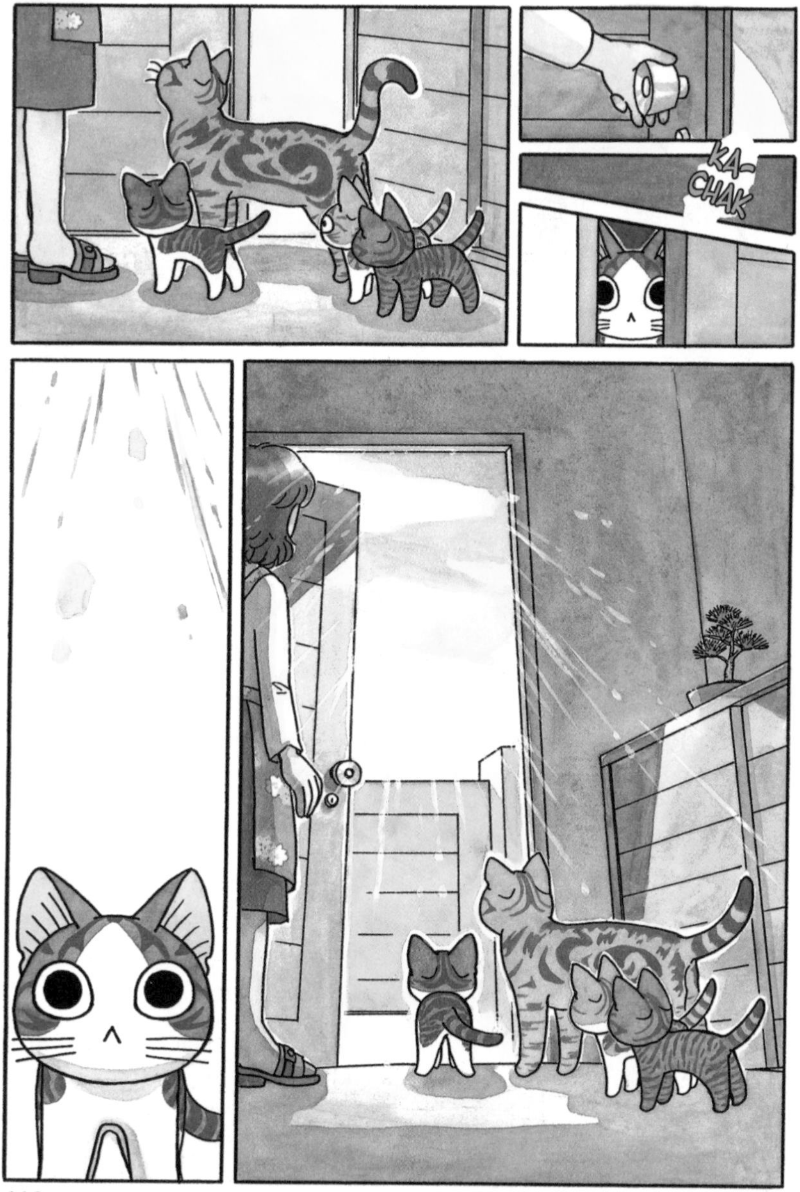
KA-CHAK

the end

homemade 215: a cat runs off

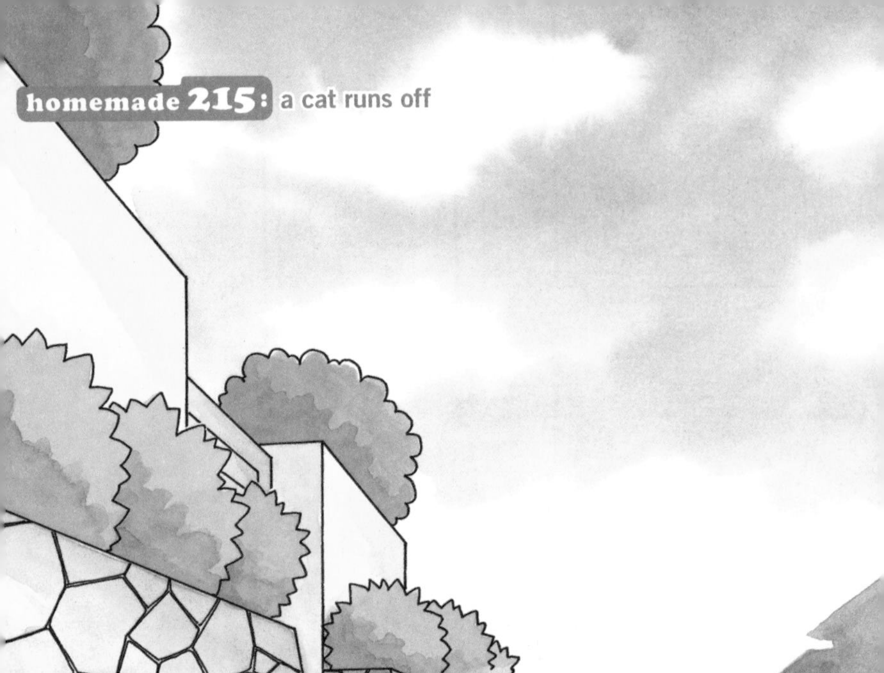

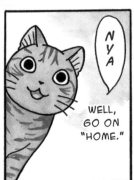

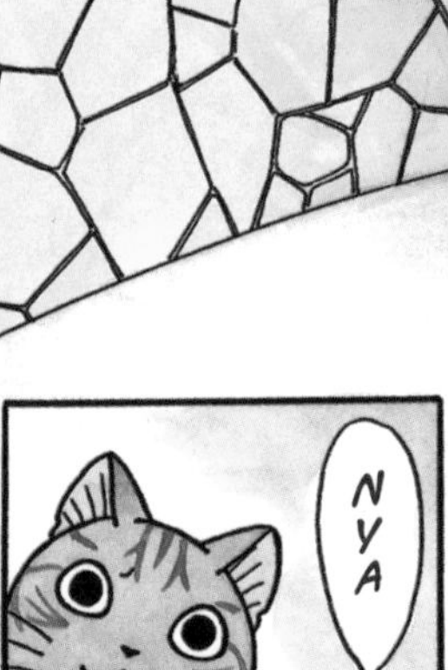
NYA
WELL, GO ON "HOME."

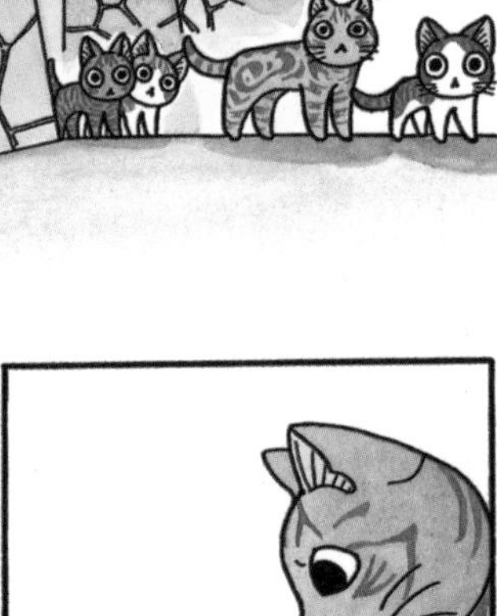

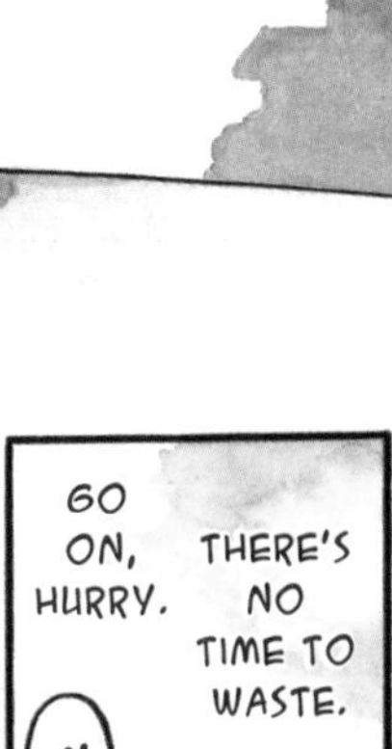
GO ON, HURRY.
THERE'S NO TIME TO WASTE.
NYA

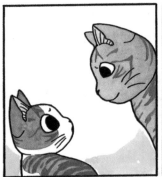

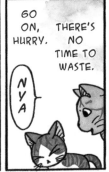

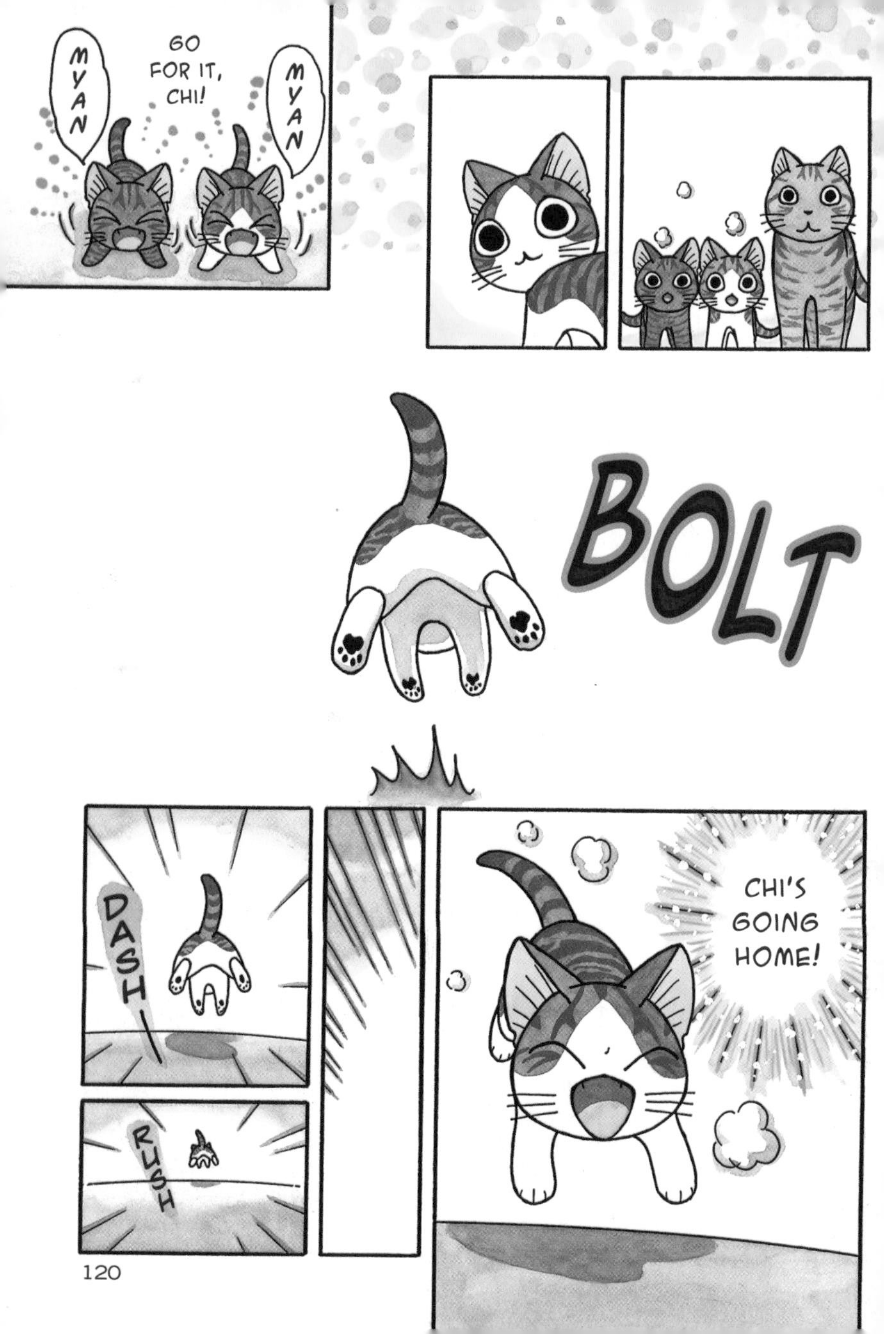
MYAN
GO FOR IT, CHI!
MYAN
BOLT
DASH
RUSH
CHI'S GOING HOME!

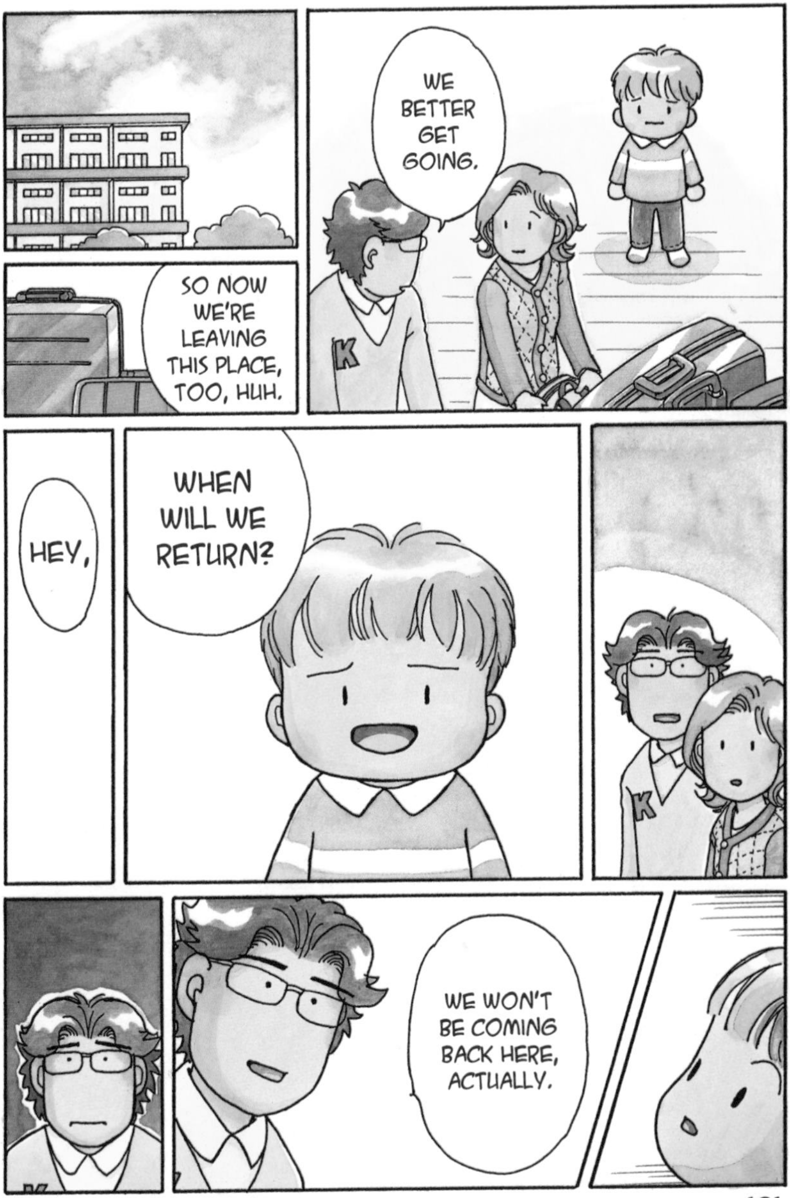
WE BETTER GET GOING.
SO NOW WE'RE LEAVING THIS PLACE, TOO, HUH.
HEY,
WHEN WILL WE RETURN?
WE WON'T BE COMING BACK HERE, ACTUALLY.

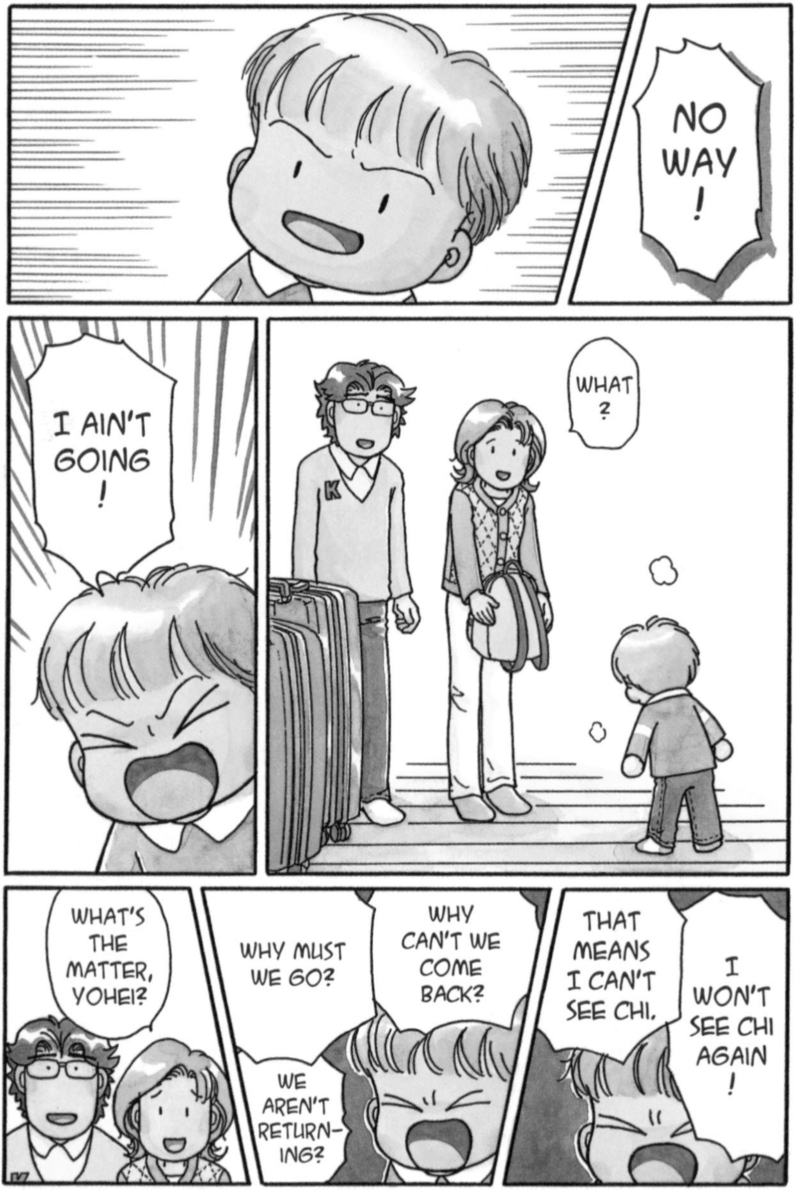
NO WAY!
I AIN'T GOING!
WHAT?
WHAT'S THE MATTER, YOHEI?
WHY MUST WE GO?
WHY CAN'T WE COME BACK?
WE AREN'T RETURNING?
THAT MEANS I CAN'T SEE CHI.
I WON'T SEE CHI AGAIN!

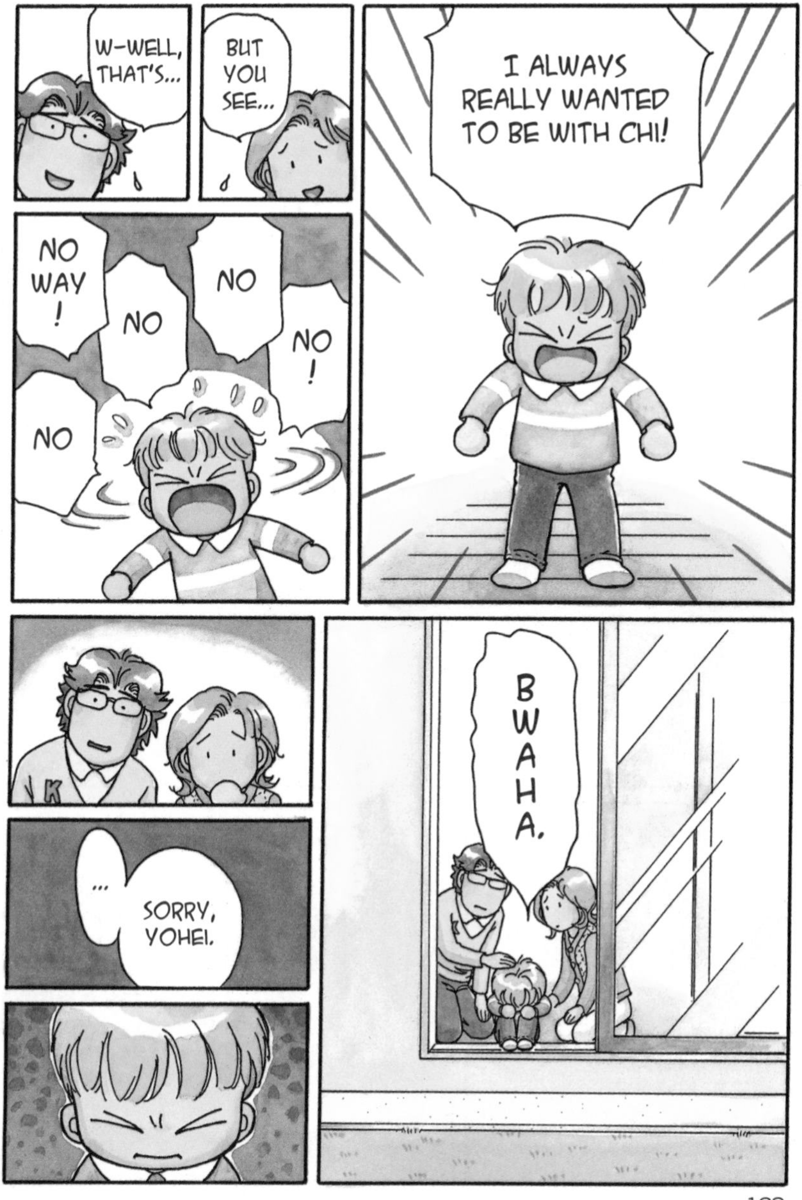
W-WELL, THAT'S...
BUT YOU SEE...
NO WAY!
NO
NO
NO!
NO
I ALWAYS REALLY WANTED TO BE WITH CHI!
... SORRY, YOHEI.
BWAHA.

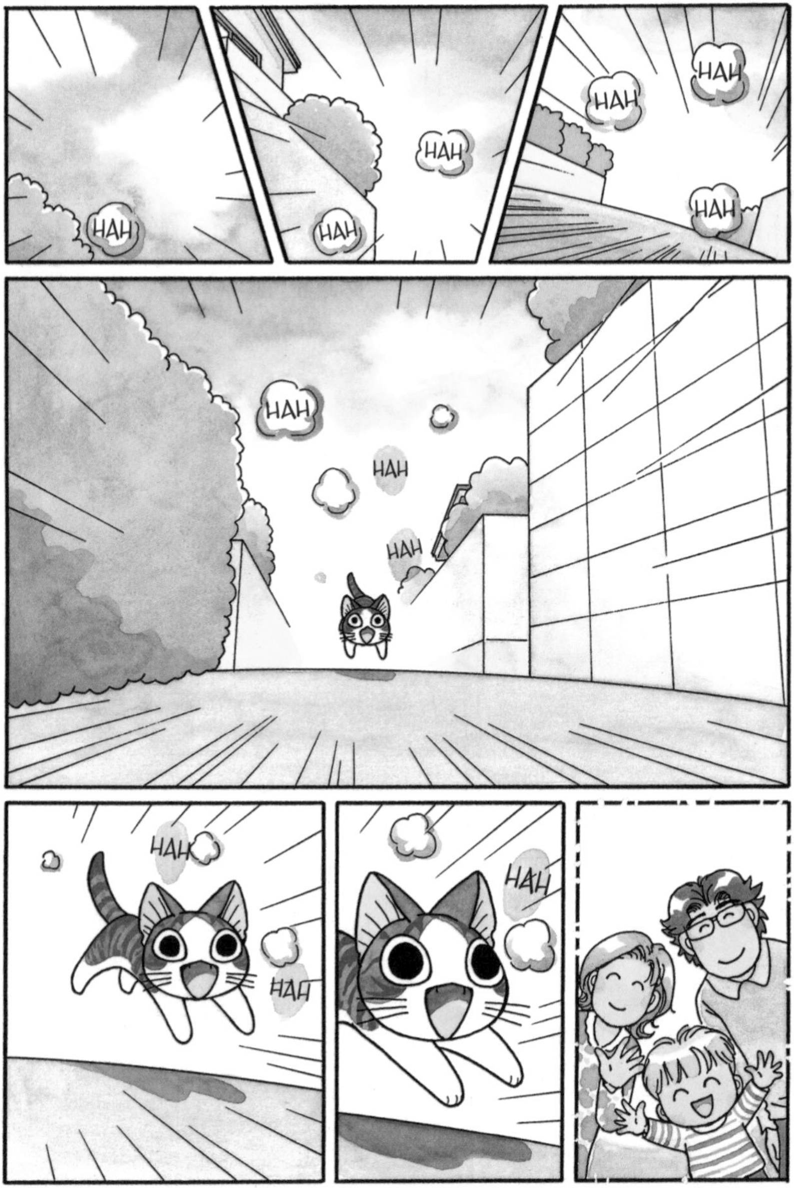
HAH
HAH
HAH
HAH
HAH
HAH
HAH
HAH
HAH
HAH
HAH
HAH

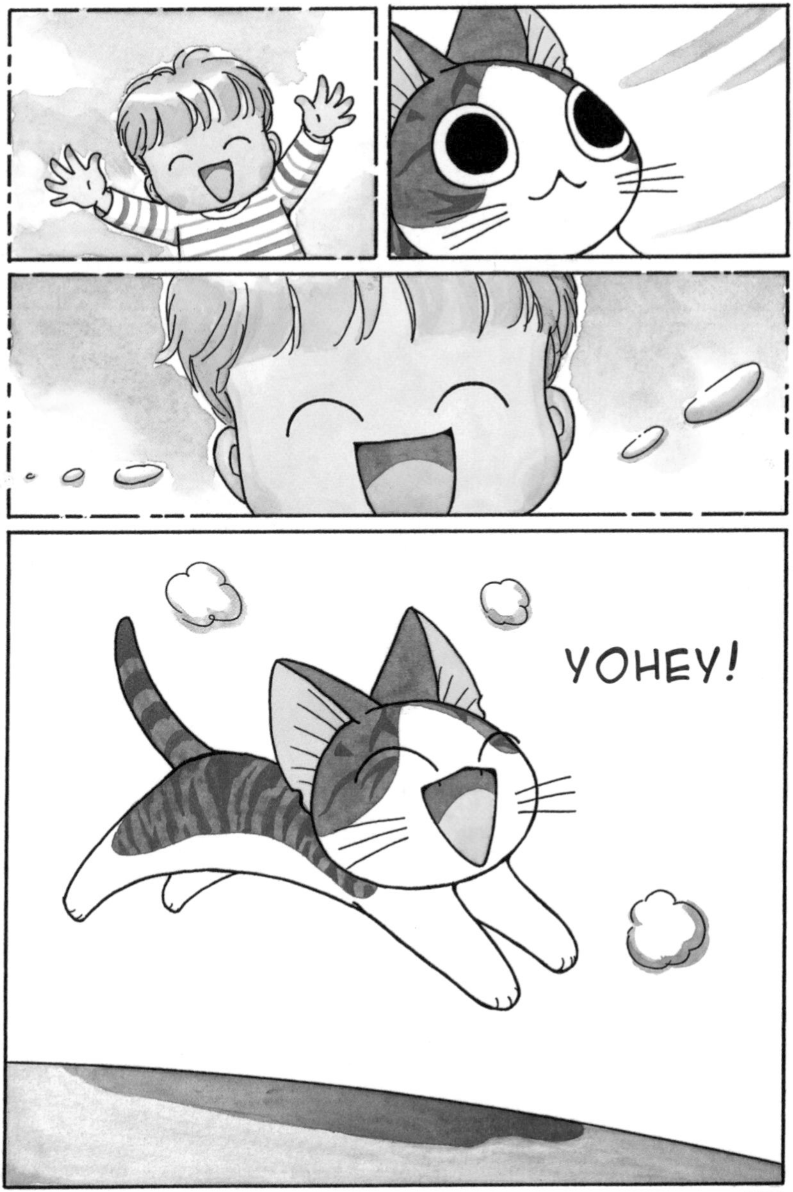
YOHEY!

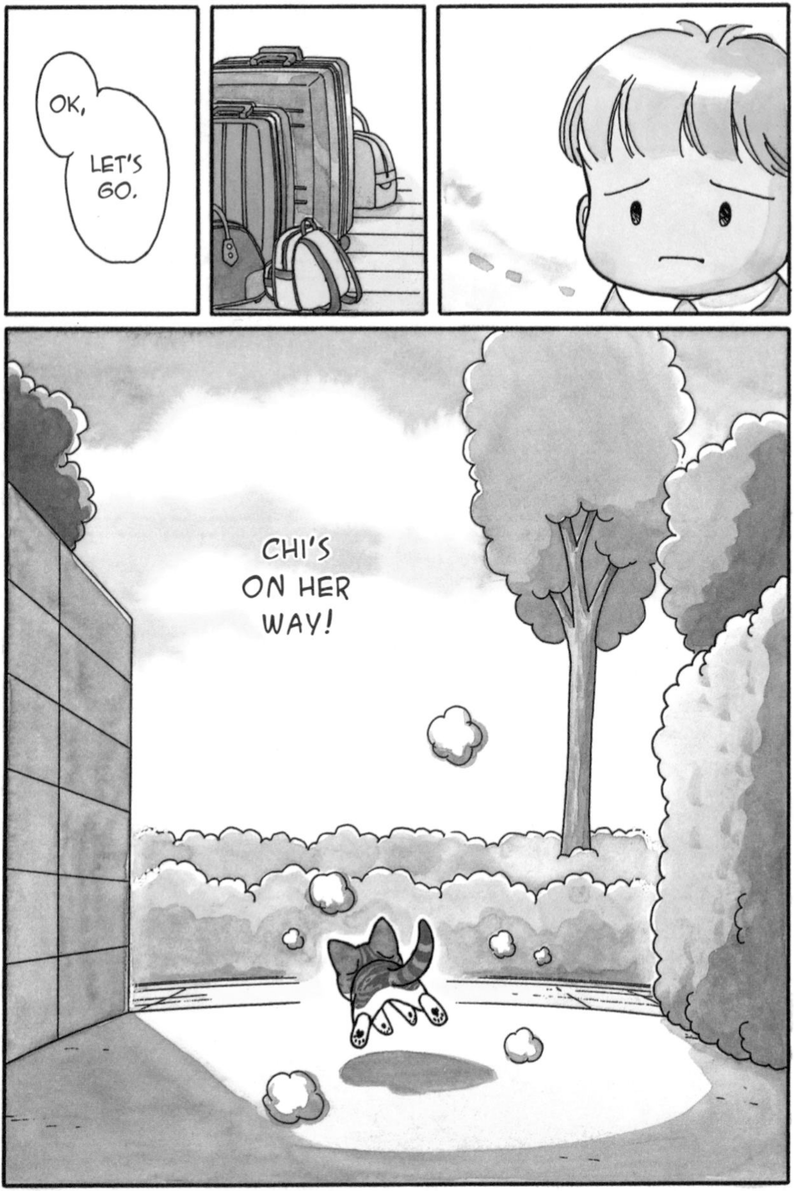
OK, LET'S GO.
CHI'S ON HER WAY!

the end

homemade 216: a cat continues to run

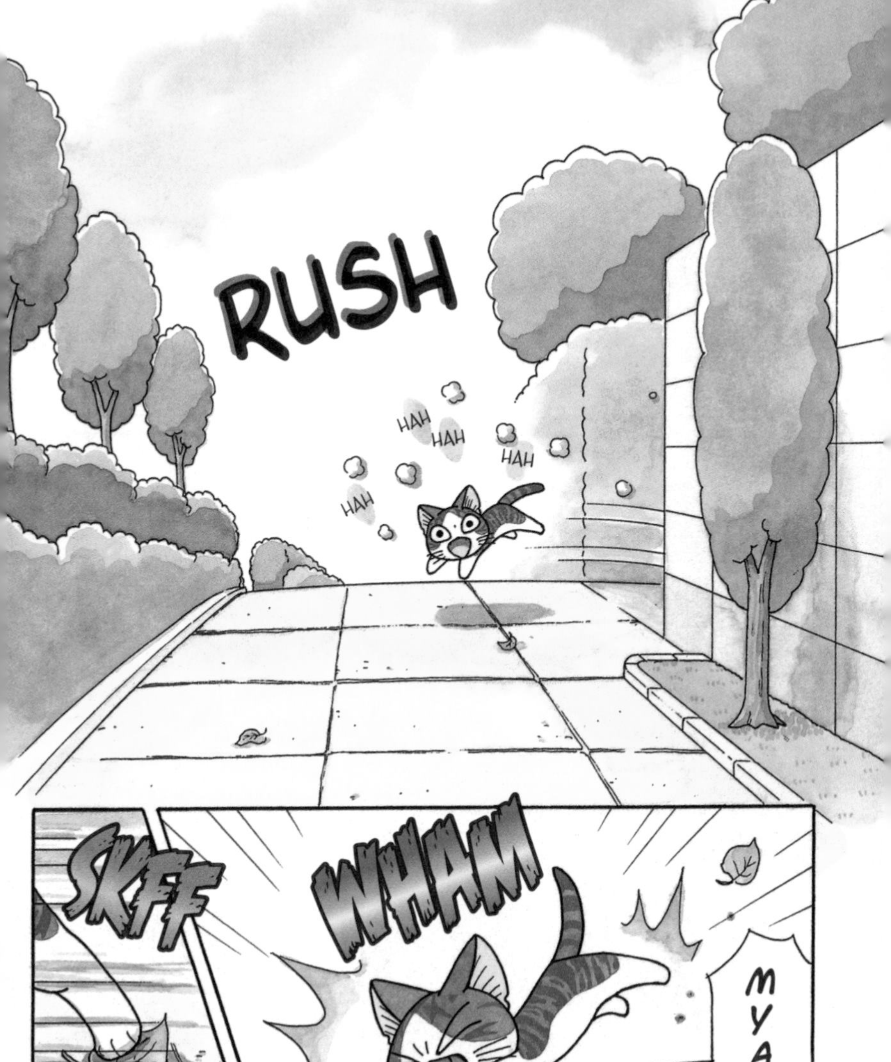
RUSH
HAH
HAH
HAH
HAH
SKFF
WHAM
MYAH

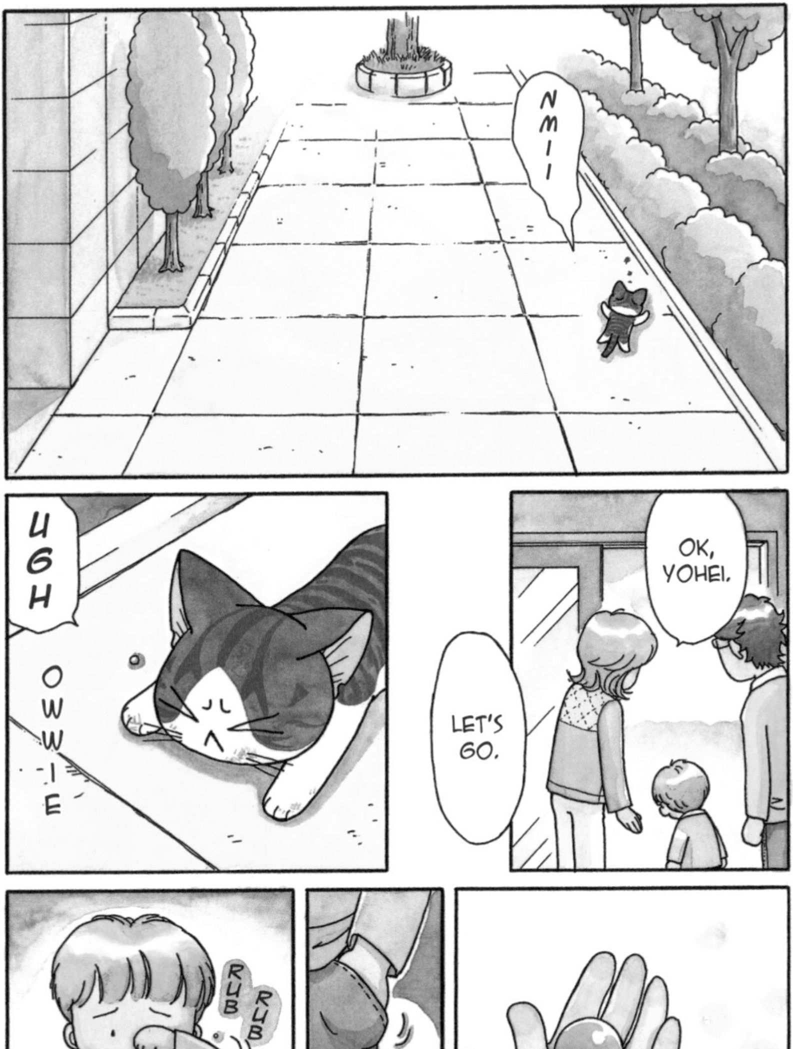
NMII
UGH
OWWIE
OK, YOHEI.
LET'S GO.
RUB RUB
RUMMAGE

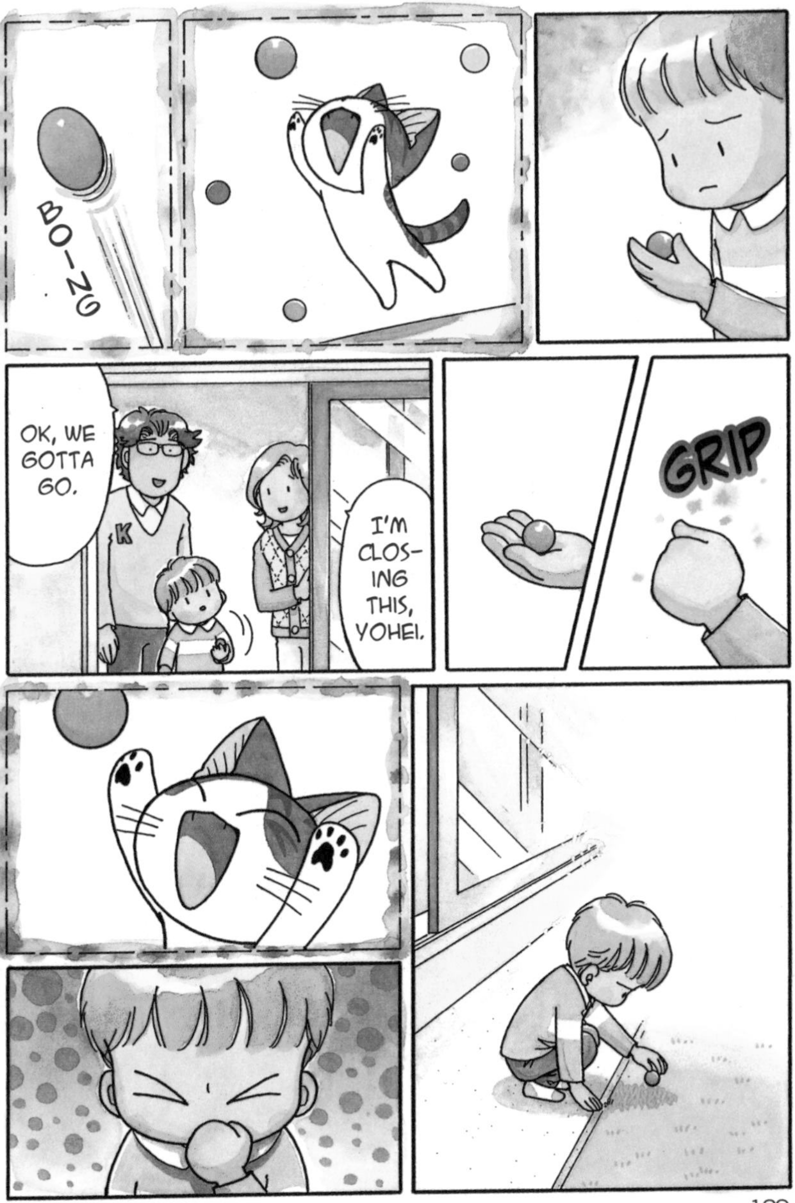
BO-ING
OK, WE GOTTA GO.
I'M CLOSING THIS, YOHEI.
GRIP

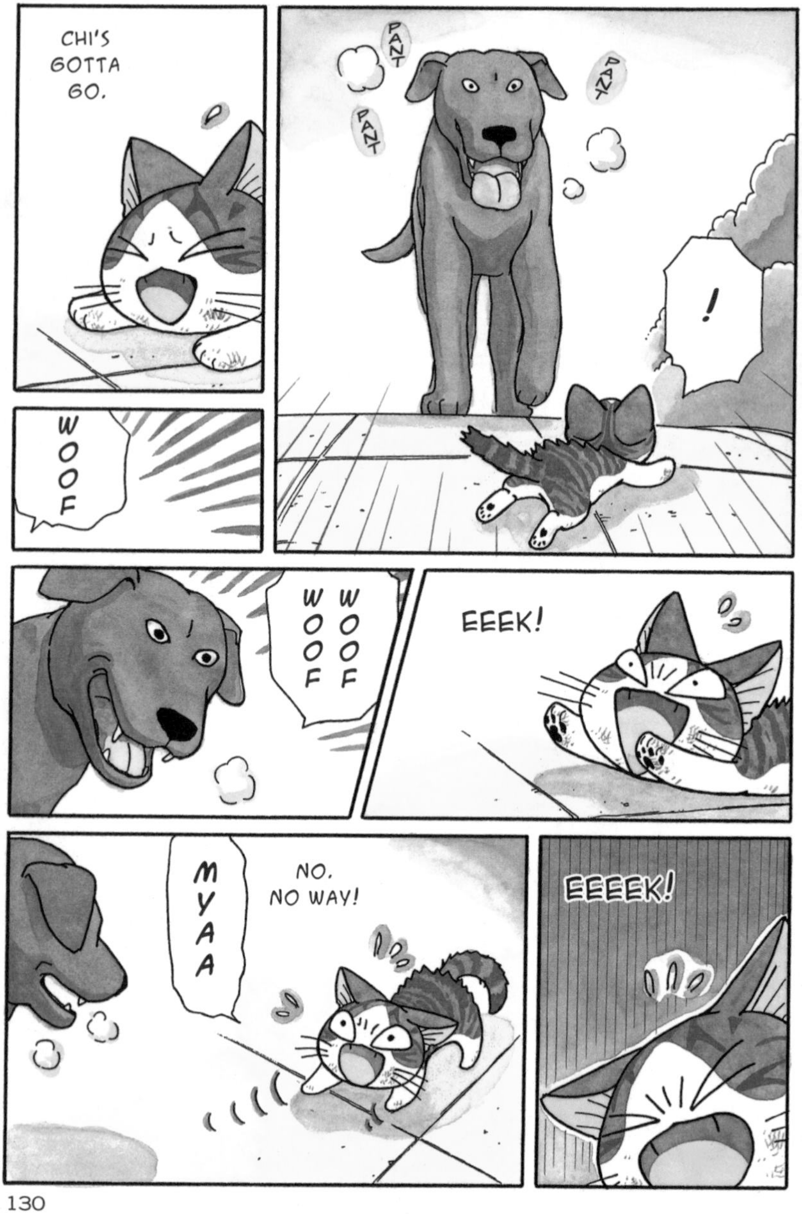

CHI'S GOTTA GO.
PANT
PANT
PANT
!
WOOF
WOOF WOOF
EEEK!
MYAA
NO. NO WAY!
EEEEK!

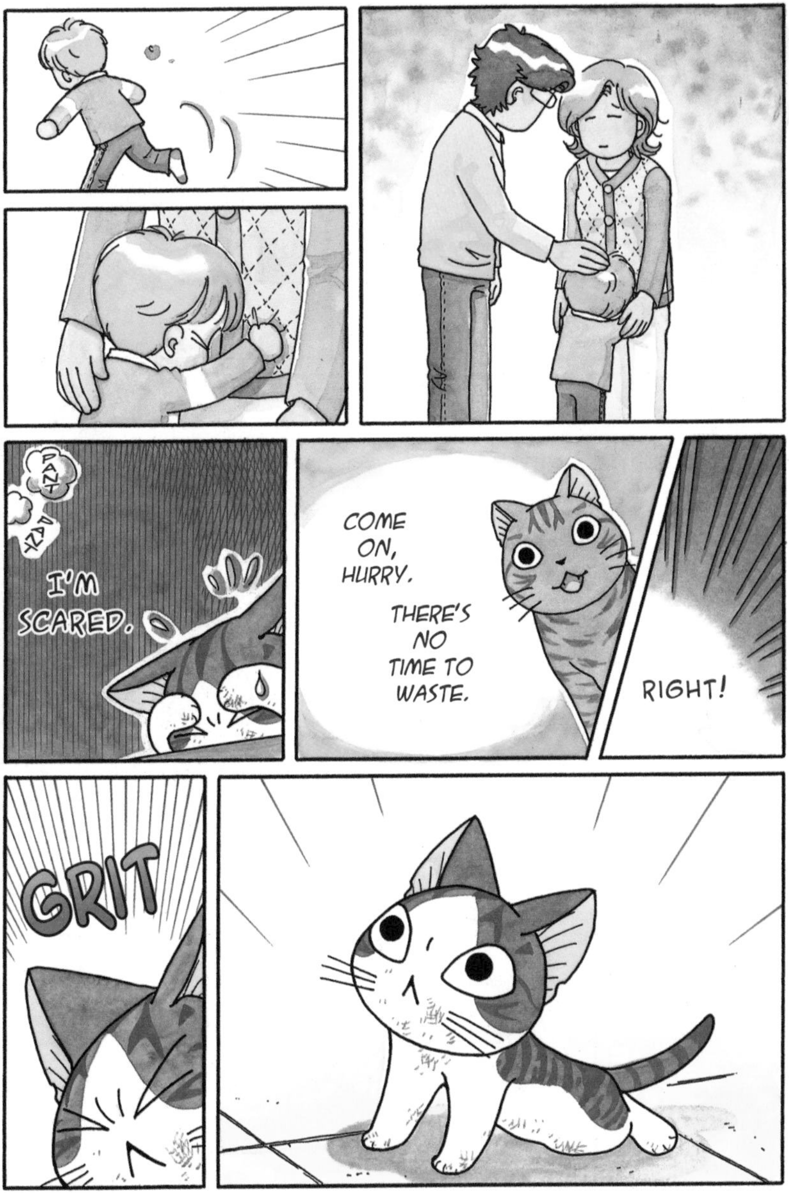
PANT
PANT
I'M SCARED.
COME ON, HURRY.
THERE'S NO TIME TO WASTE.
RIGHT!
GRIT

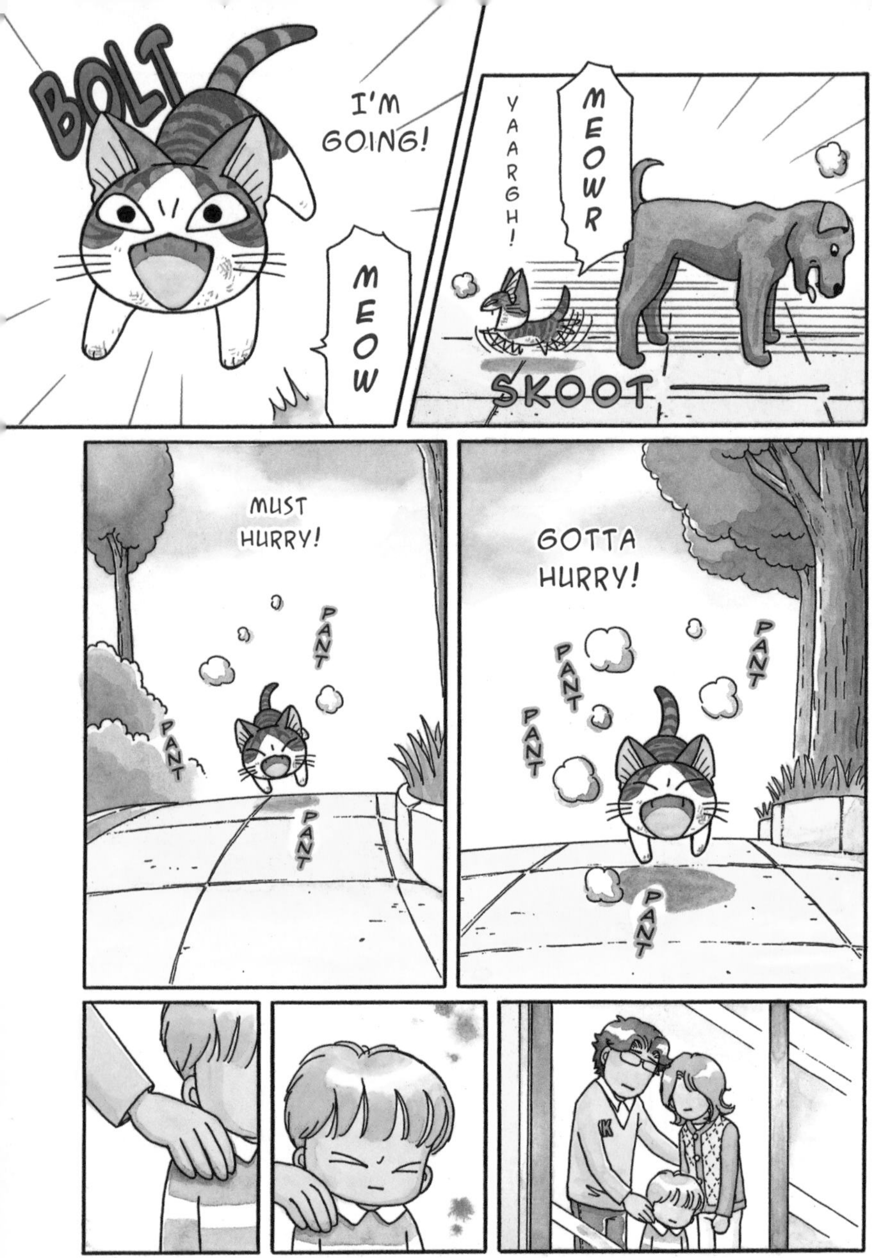
BOLT
I'M GOING!
MEOW
YAARGH!
MEOWR
SKOOT
MUST HURRY!
PANT
PANT
PANT
GOTTA HURRY!
PANT
PANT
PANT
PANT

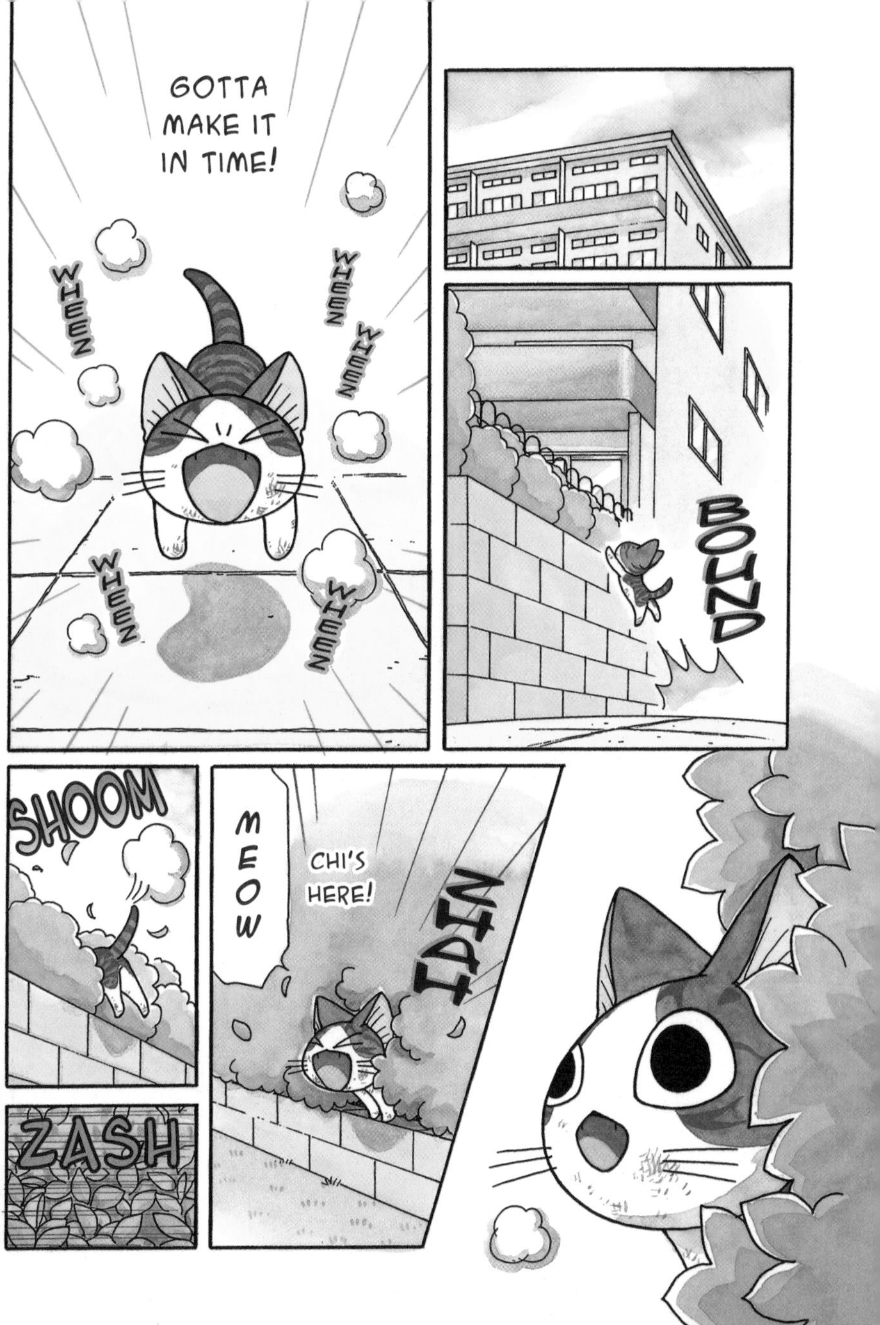

GOTTA MAKE IT IN TIME!
WHEEZ
WHEEN
WHEEN
WHEEZ
WHEEN
BOUND
SHOOM
ZASH
MEOW
CHI'S HERE!

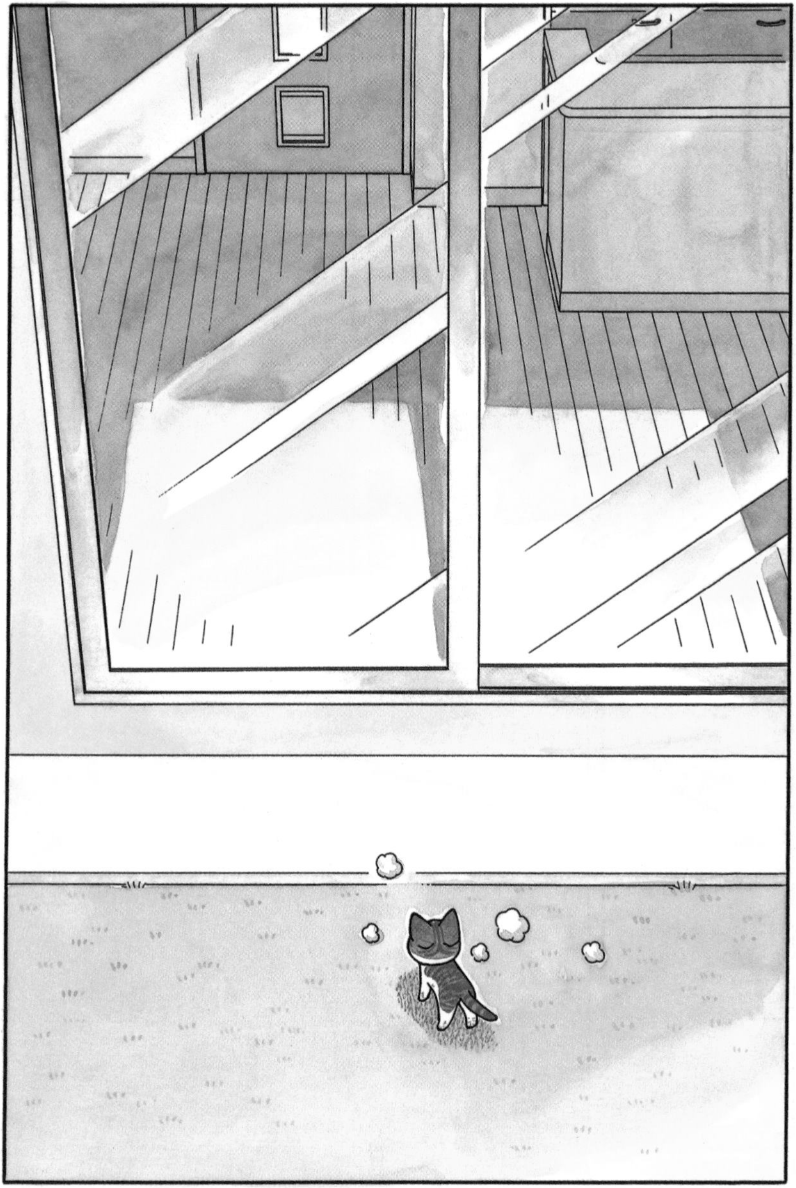

the end

homemade 217: a cat dwells

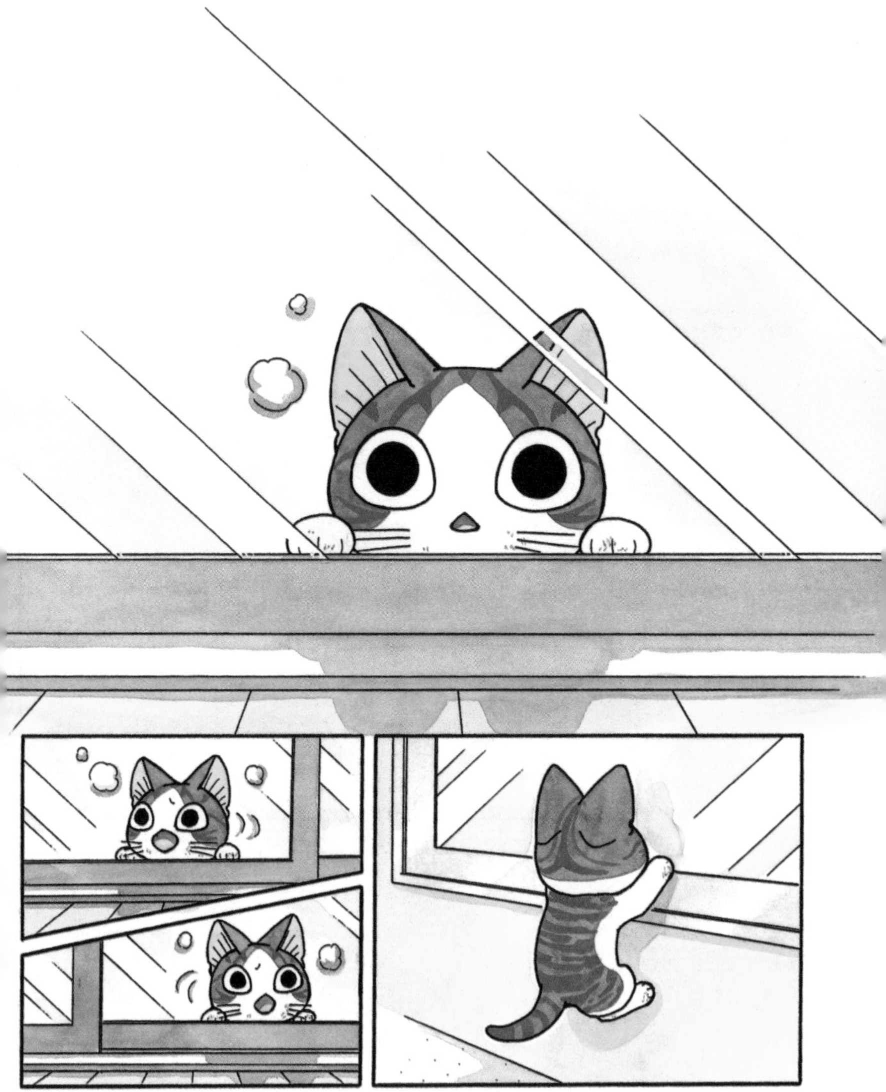

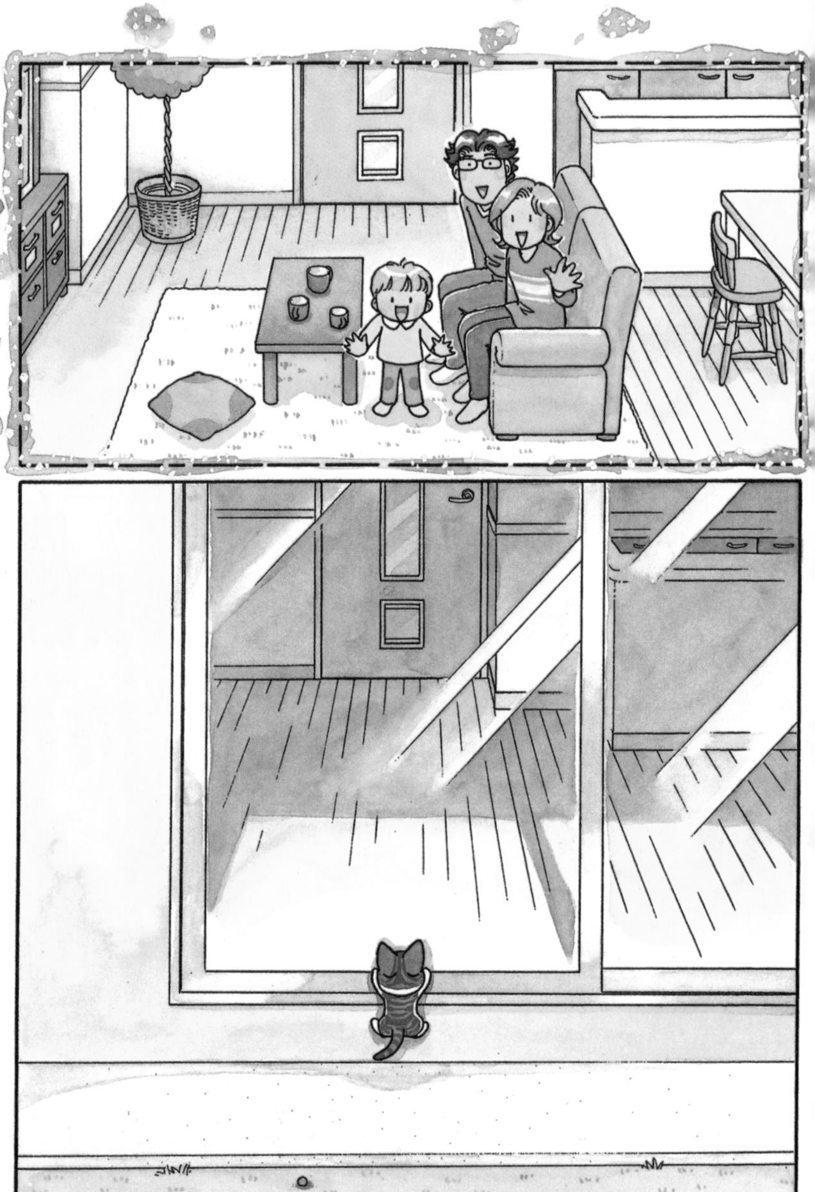

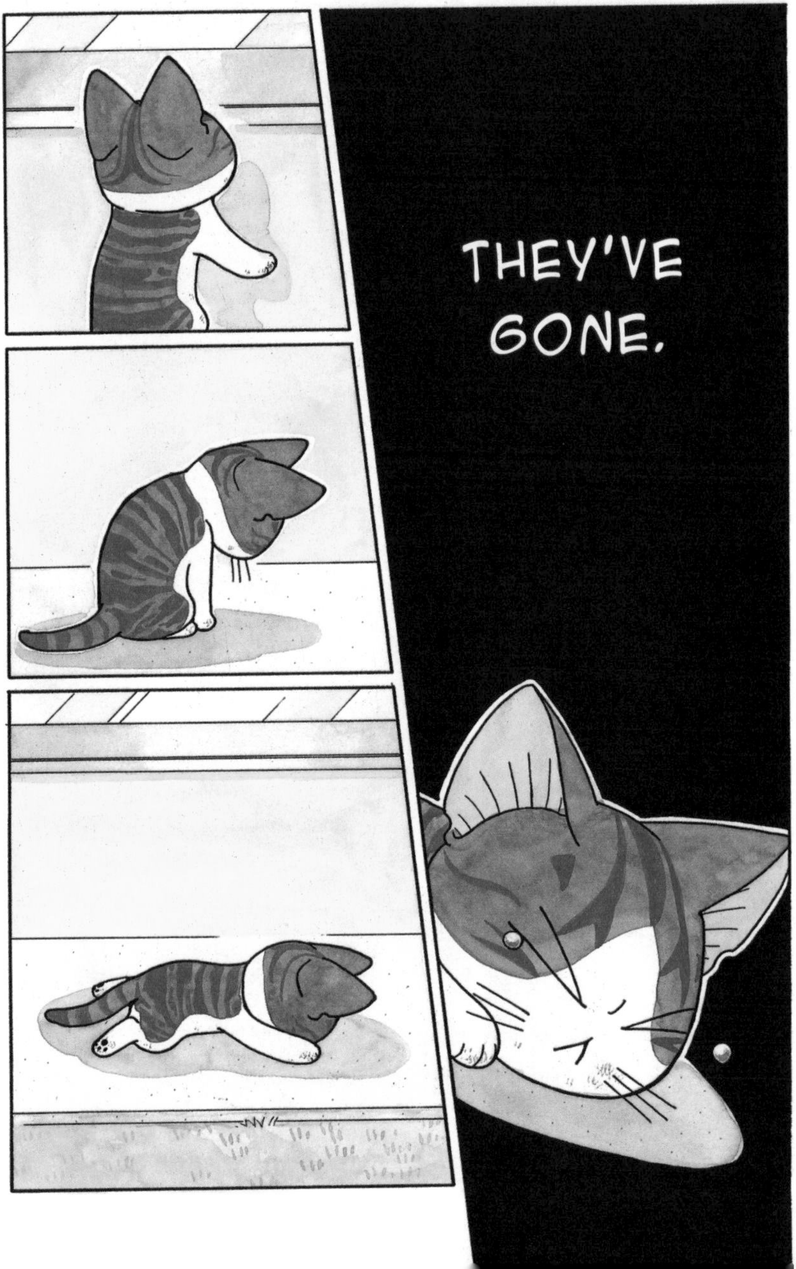
THEY'VE GONE.

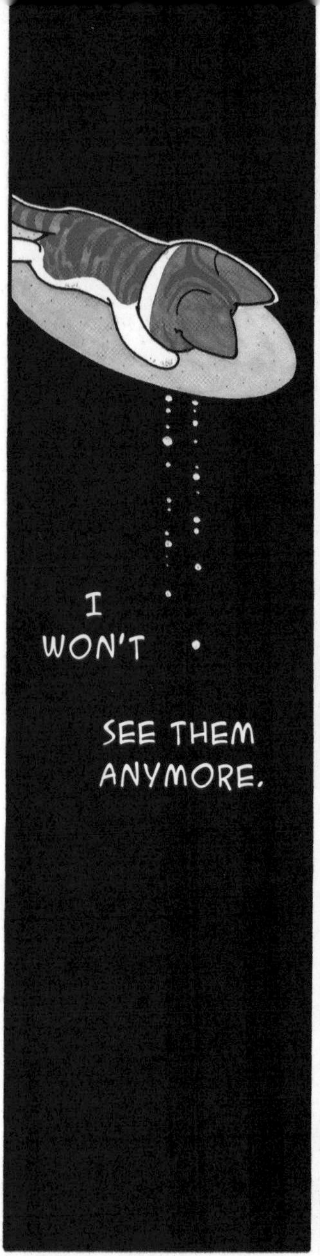
I WON'T
SEE THEM ANYMORE.
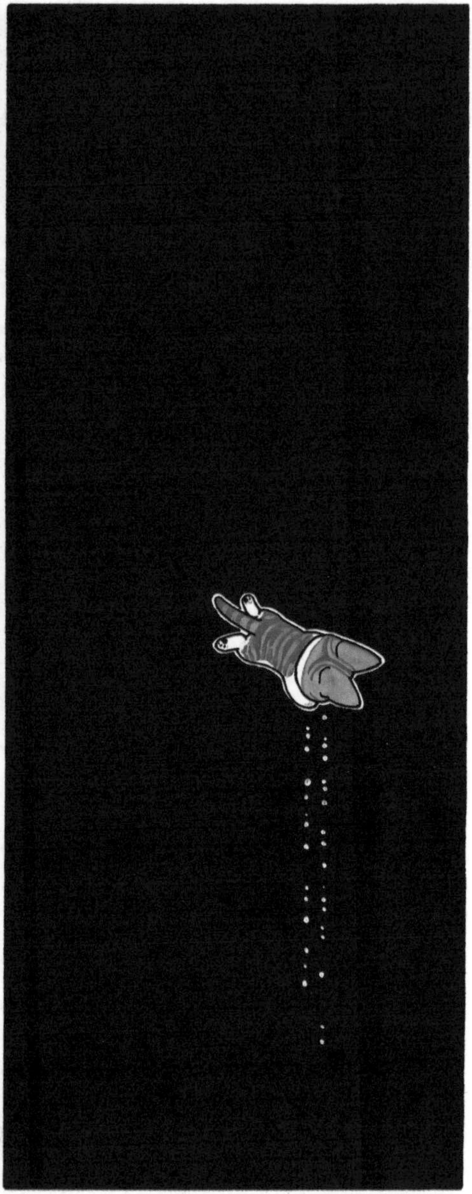

[redacted]

[redacted]

[redacted]

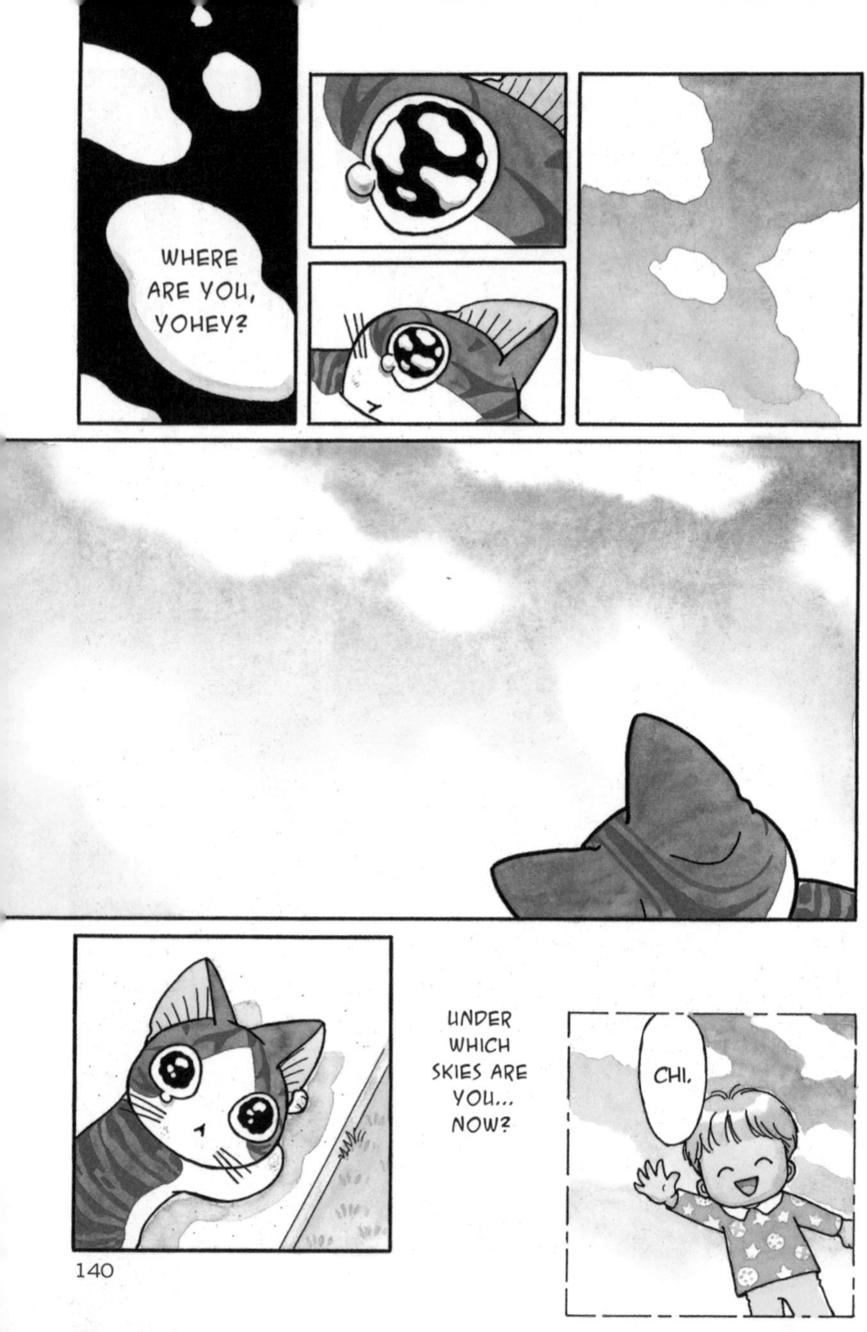
WHERE ARE YOU, YOHEY?
UNDER WHICH SKIES ARE YOU... NOW?
CHI.

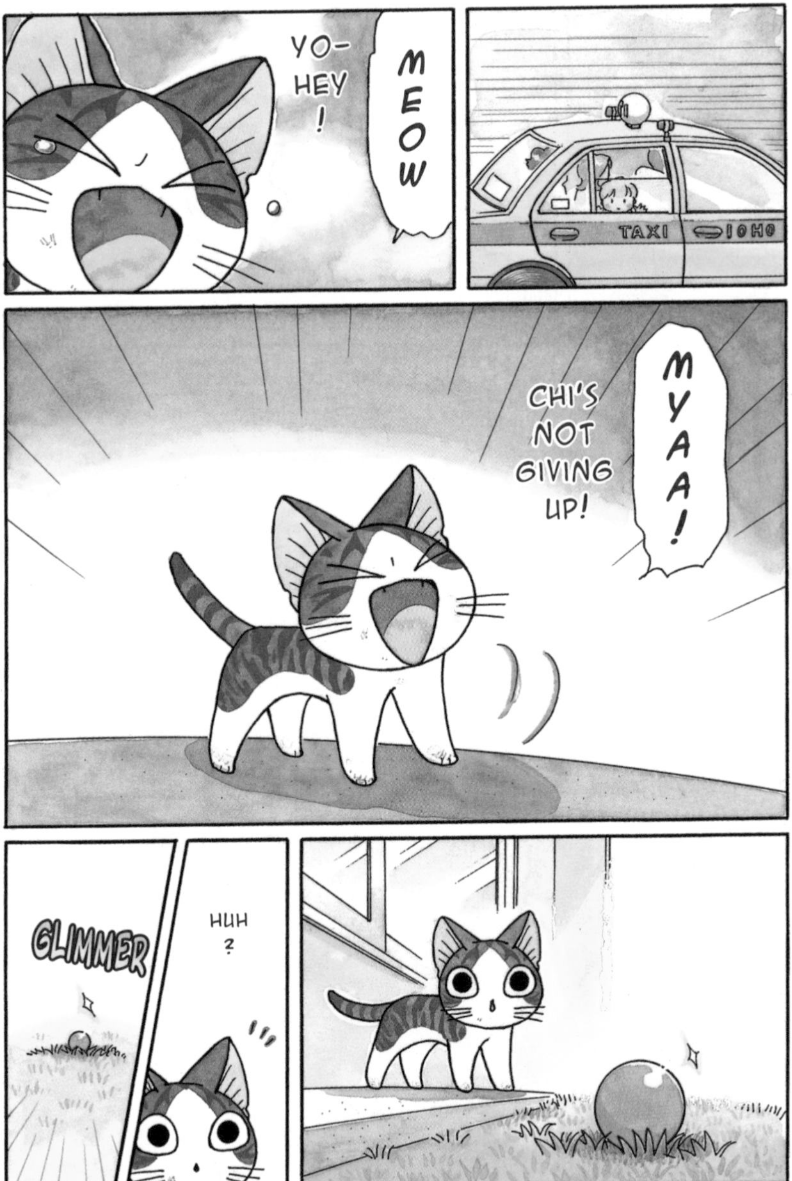
YO-HEY!
MEOW
TAXI
CHI'S NOT GIVING UP!
MYAAA!
GLIMMER
HUH?

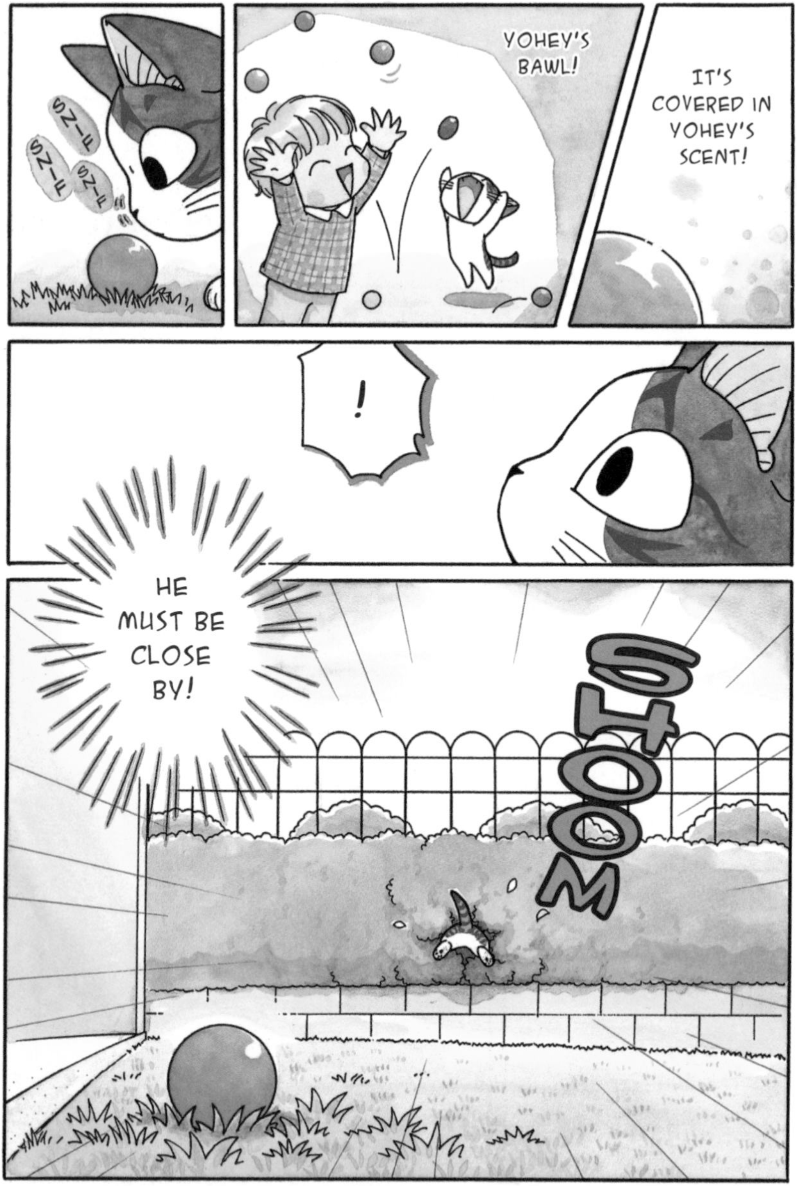
SNIF
SNIF
SNIF
YOHEY'S BAWL!
IT'S COVERED IN YOHEY'S SCENT!
!
HE MUST BE CLOSE BY!
SHOOM

the end

homemade 218: a cat comes home

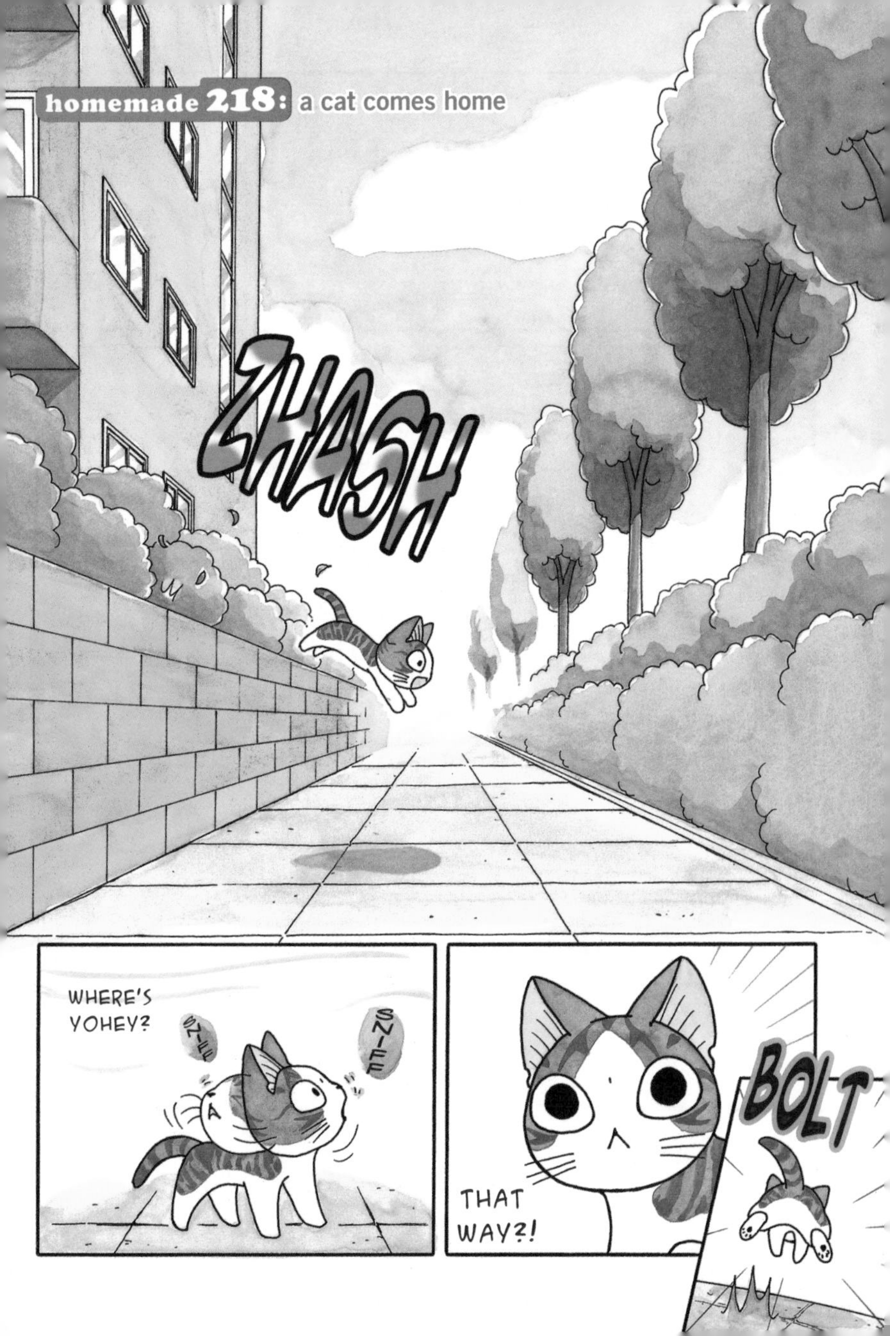
ZHASH
WHERE'S YOHEY?
SNIFF
SNIFF
THAT WAY?!
BOLT

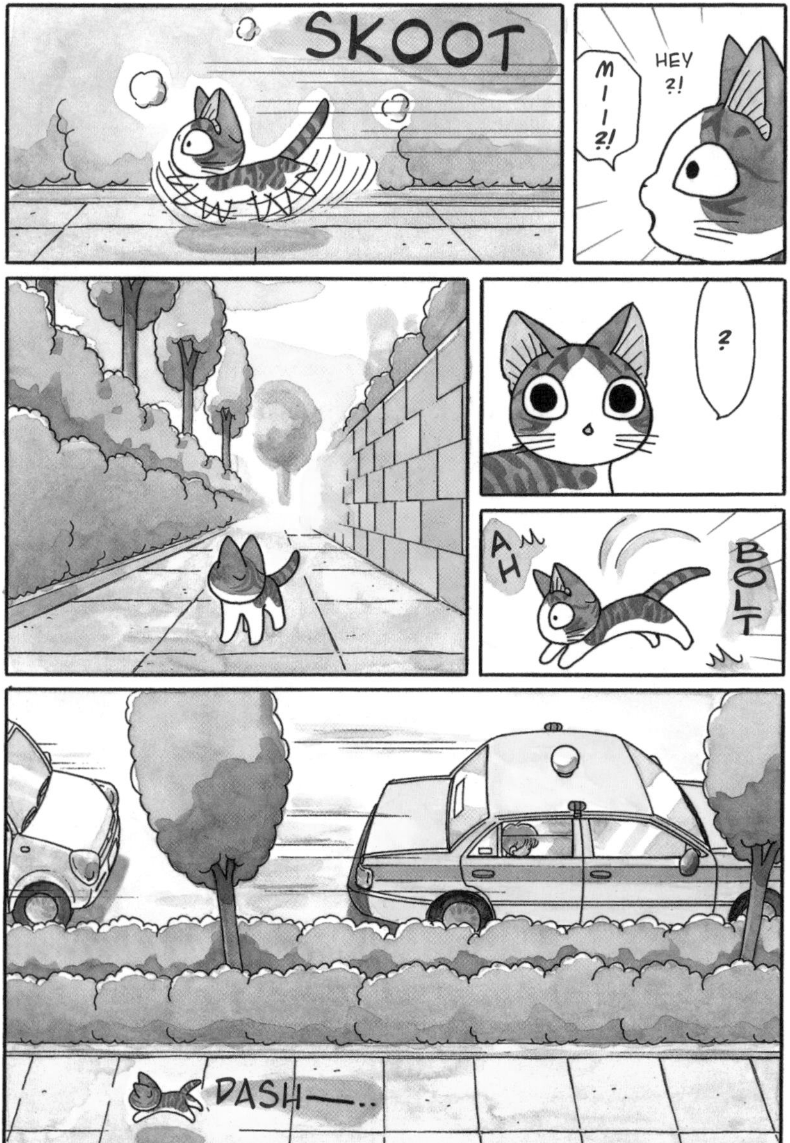
SKOOT
MII ?!
HEY ?!
?
AH
BOLT
DASH—..

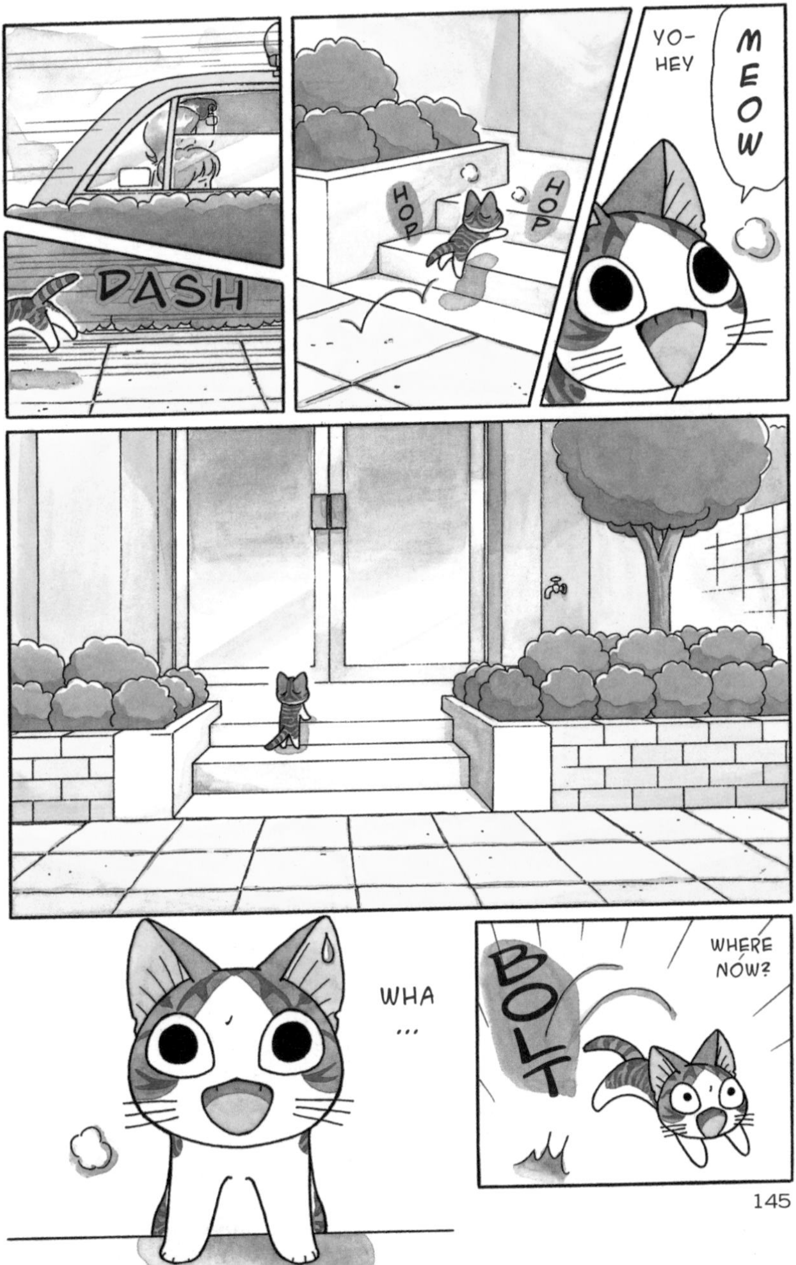
DASH
HOP
HOP
YO-HEY
MEOW
WHA ...
BOLT
WHERE NOW?

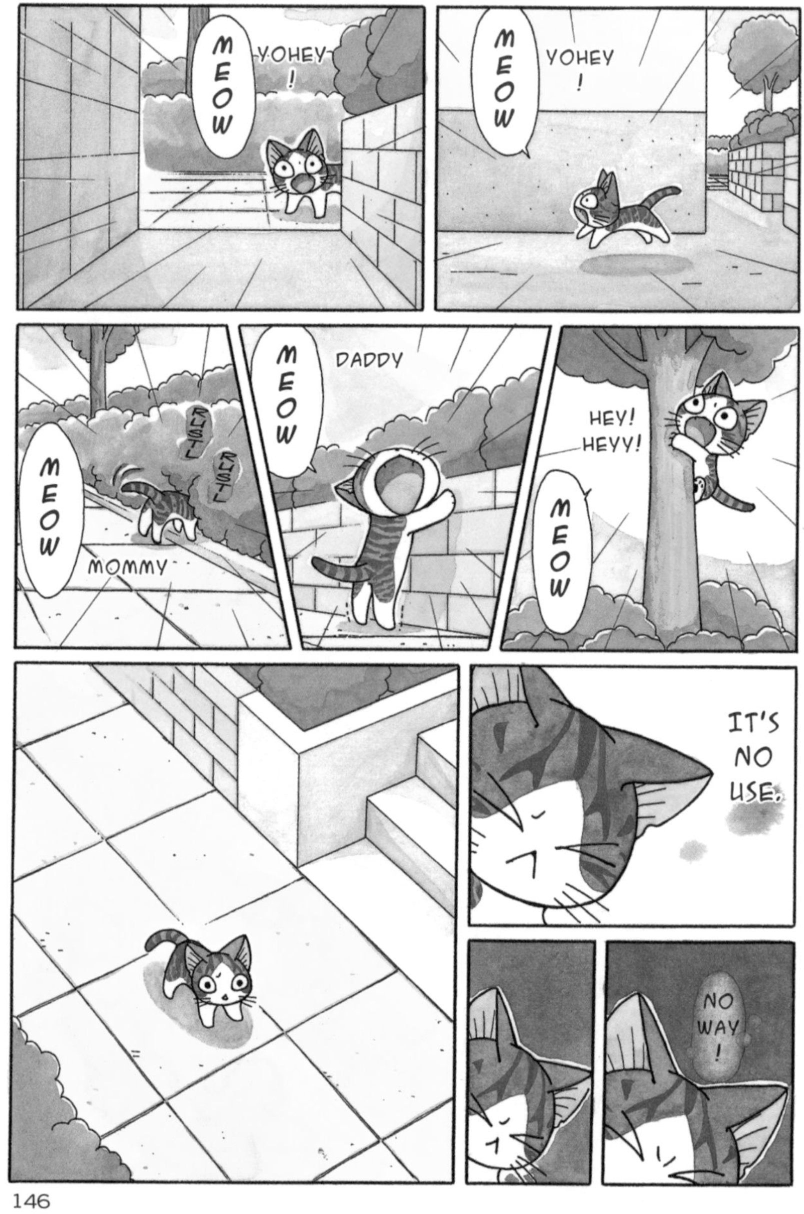
MEOW
YOHEY!
MEOW
YOHEY!
RUSTL
RUSTL
MEOW
MOMMY
MEOW
DADDY
HEY! HEYY!
MEOW
IT'S NO USE.
NO WAY!

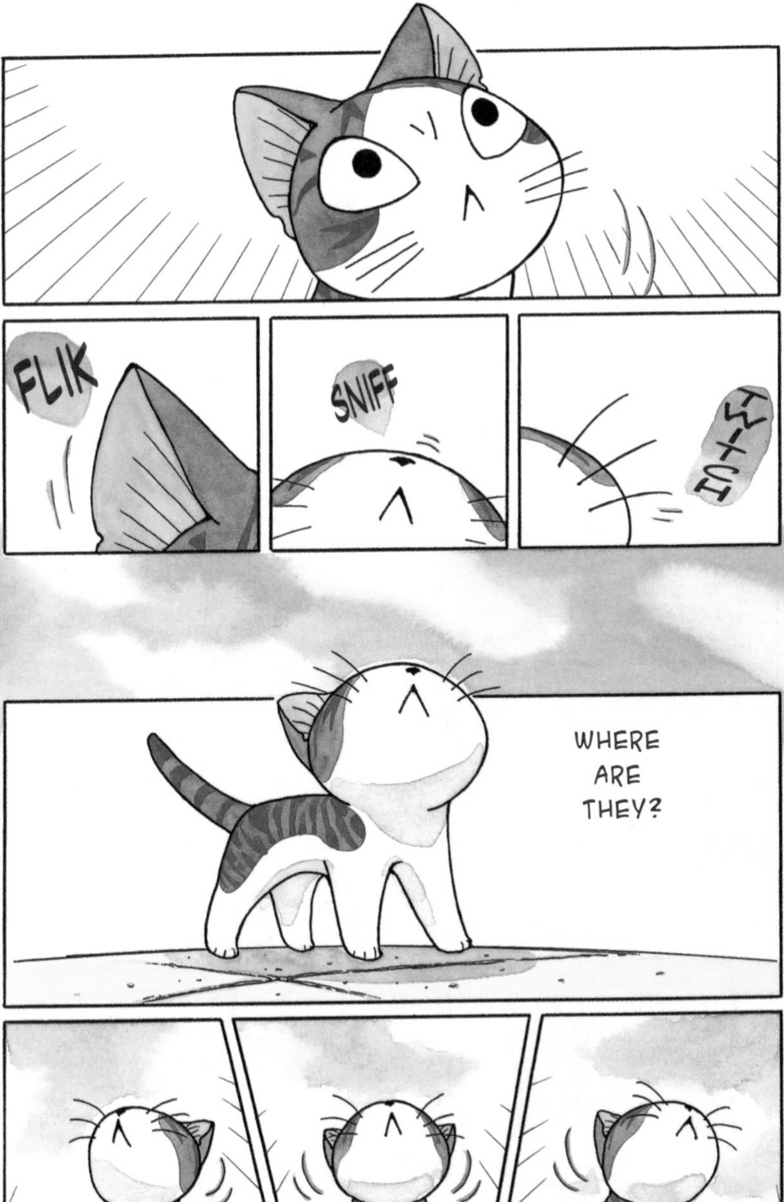
FLIK
SNIFF
TWITCH
WHERE ARE THEY?

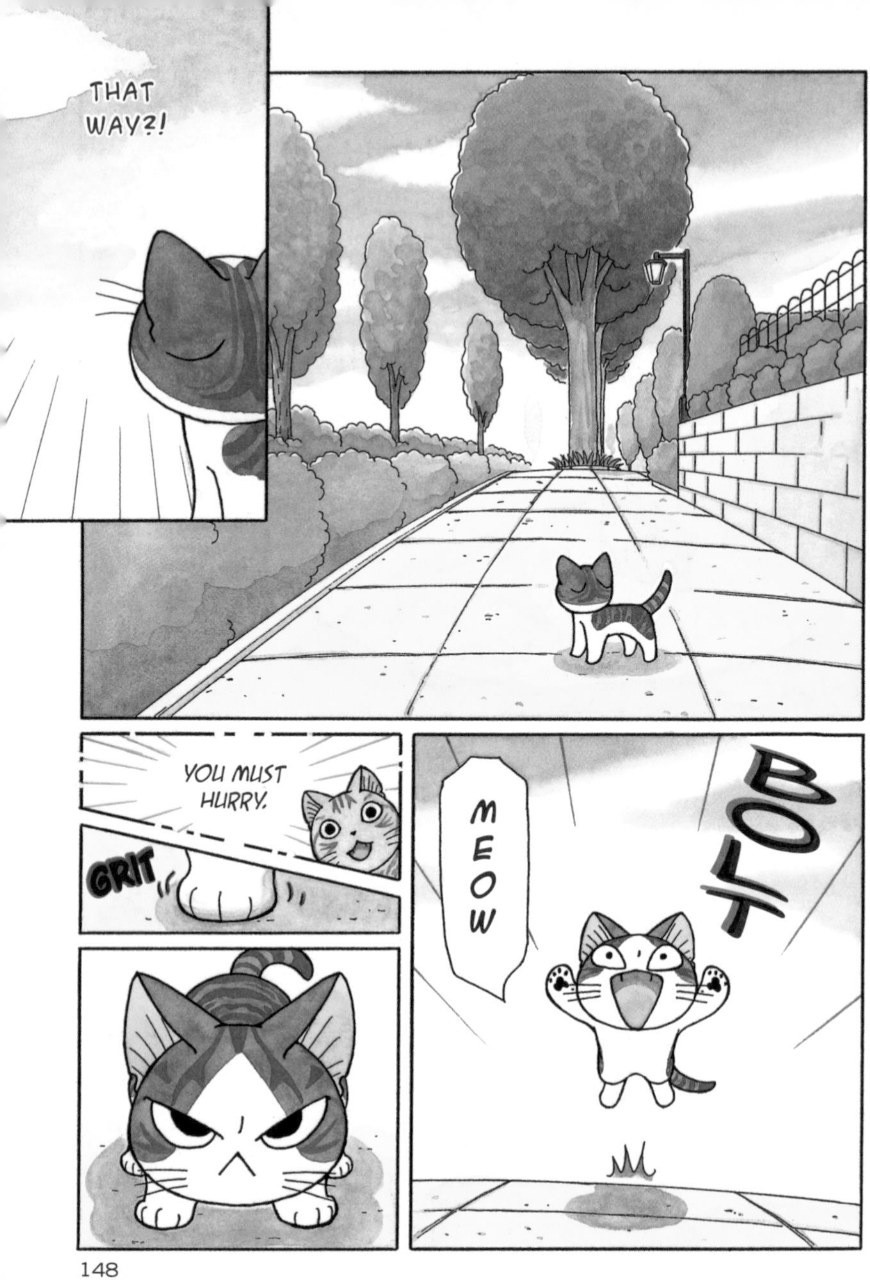
THAT WAY?!
YOU MUST HURRY.
GRIT
MEOW
BOLT

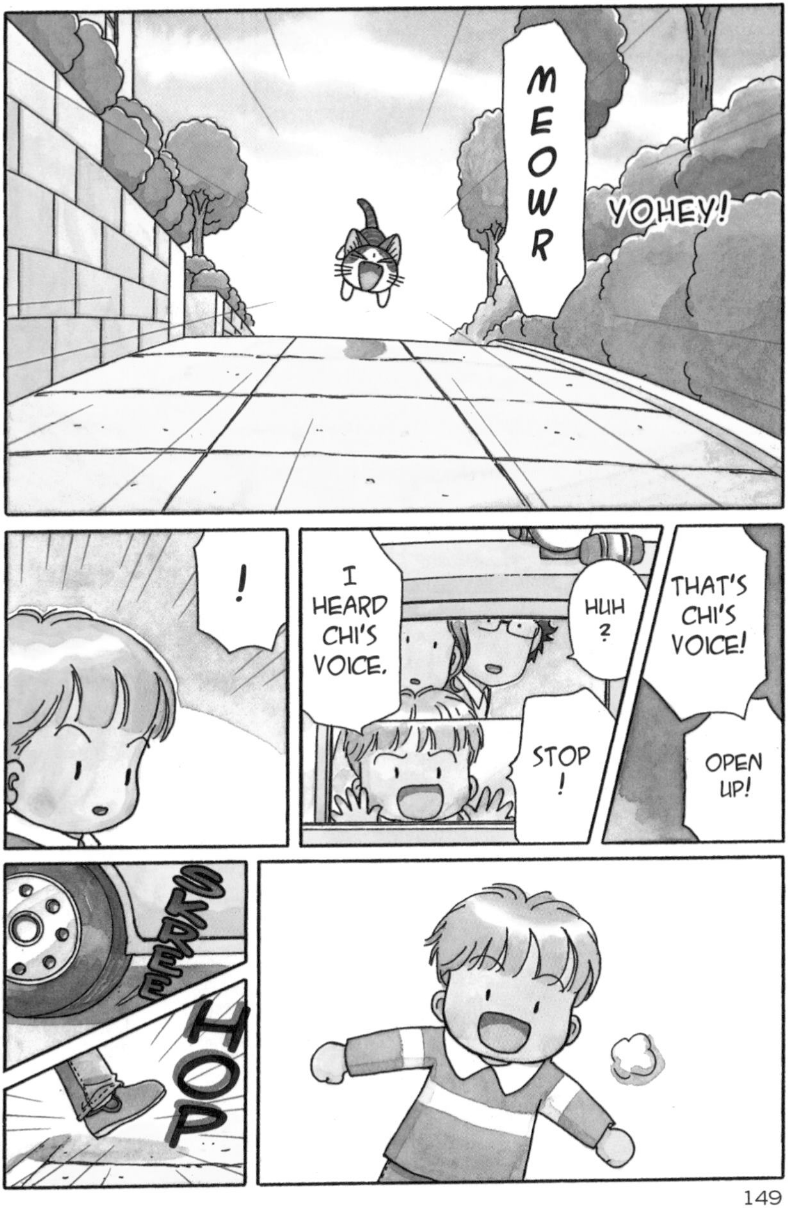
MEOWR
YOHEY!
!
I HEARD CHI'S VOICE.
HUH?
STOP!
THAT'S CHI'S VOICE!
OPEN UP!
SKREE
HOP

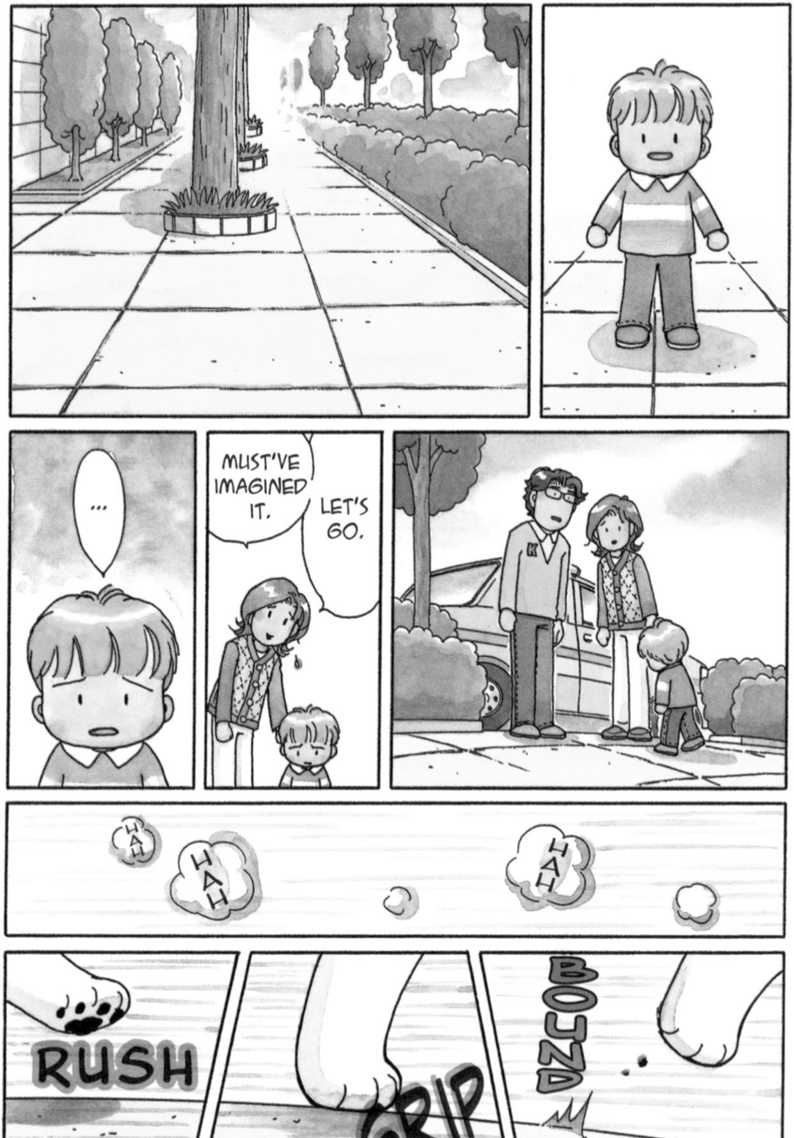
...
MUST'VE IMAGINED IT.
LET'S GO.
HAH
HAH
HAH
RUSH
GRIP
BOUND

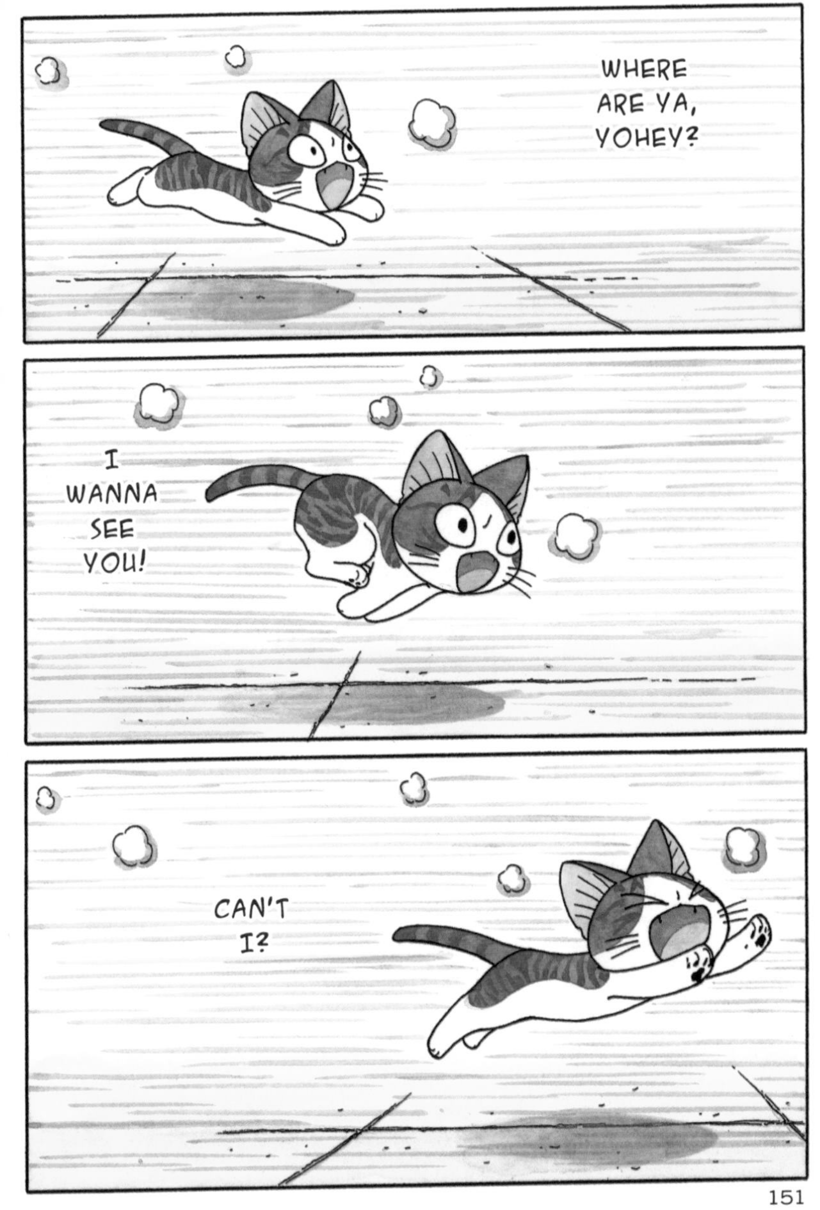
WHERE ARE YA, YOHEY?
I WANNA SEE YOU!
CAN'T I?

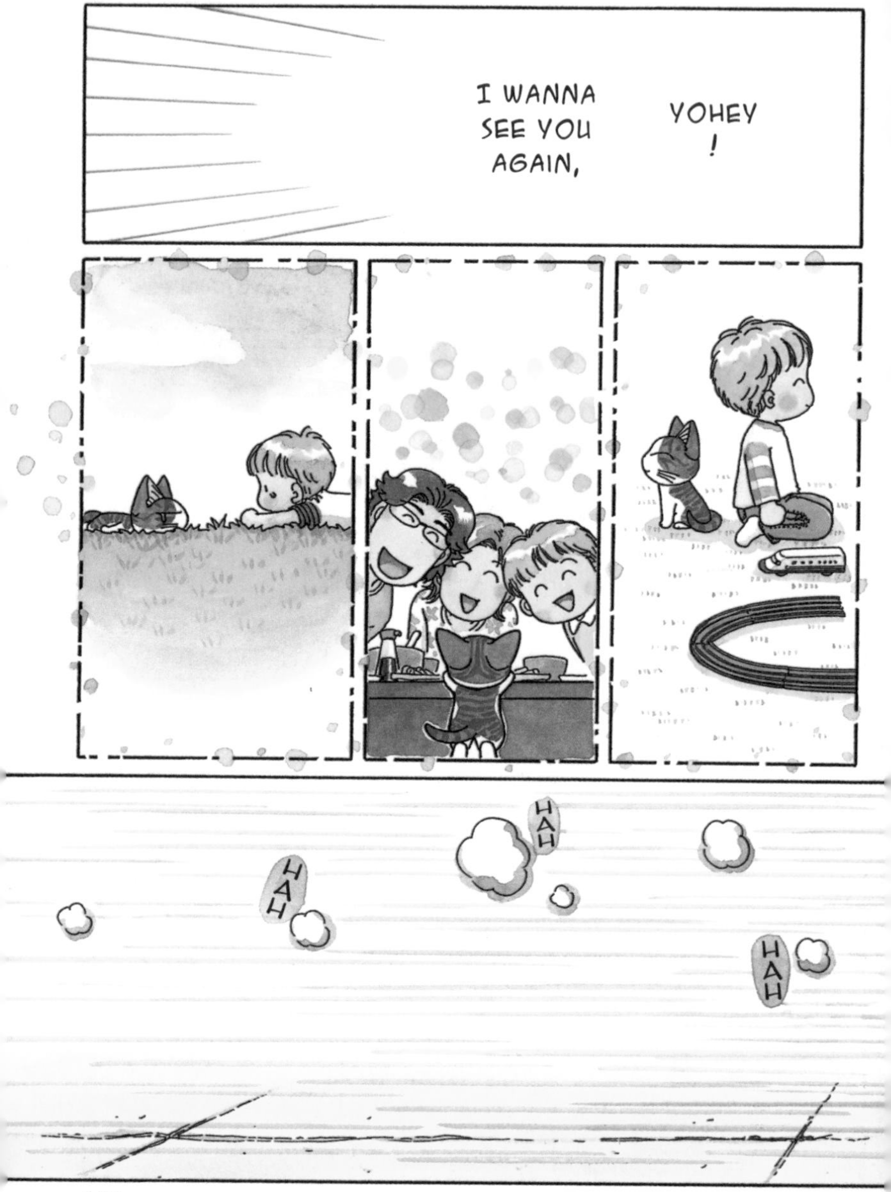
I WANNA SEE YOU AGAIN,
YOHEY !
HAH
HAH
HAH

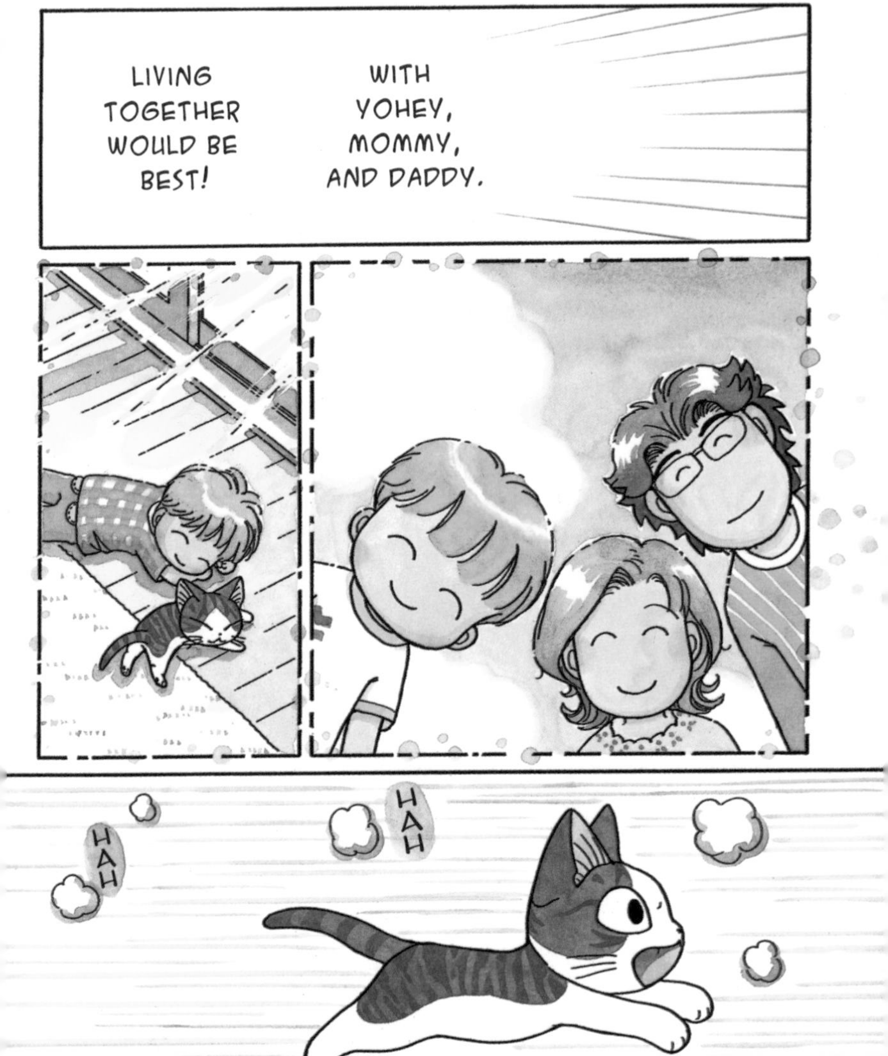
LIVING TOGETHER WOULD BE BEST!
WITH YOHEY, MOMMY, AND DADDY.
HAH
HAH

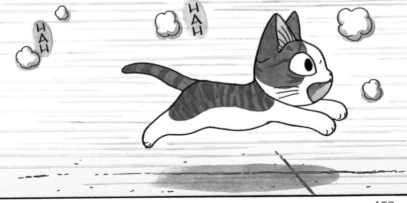

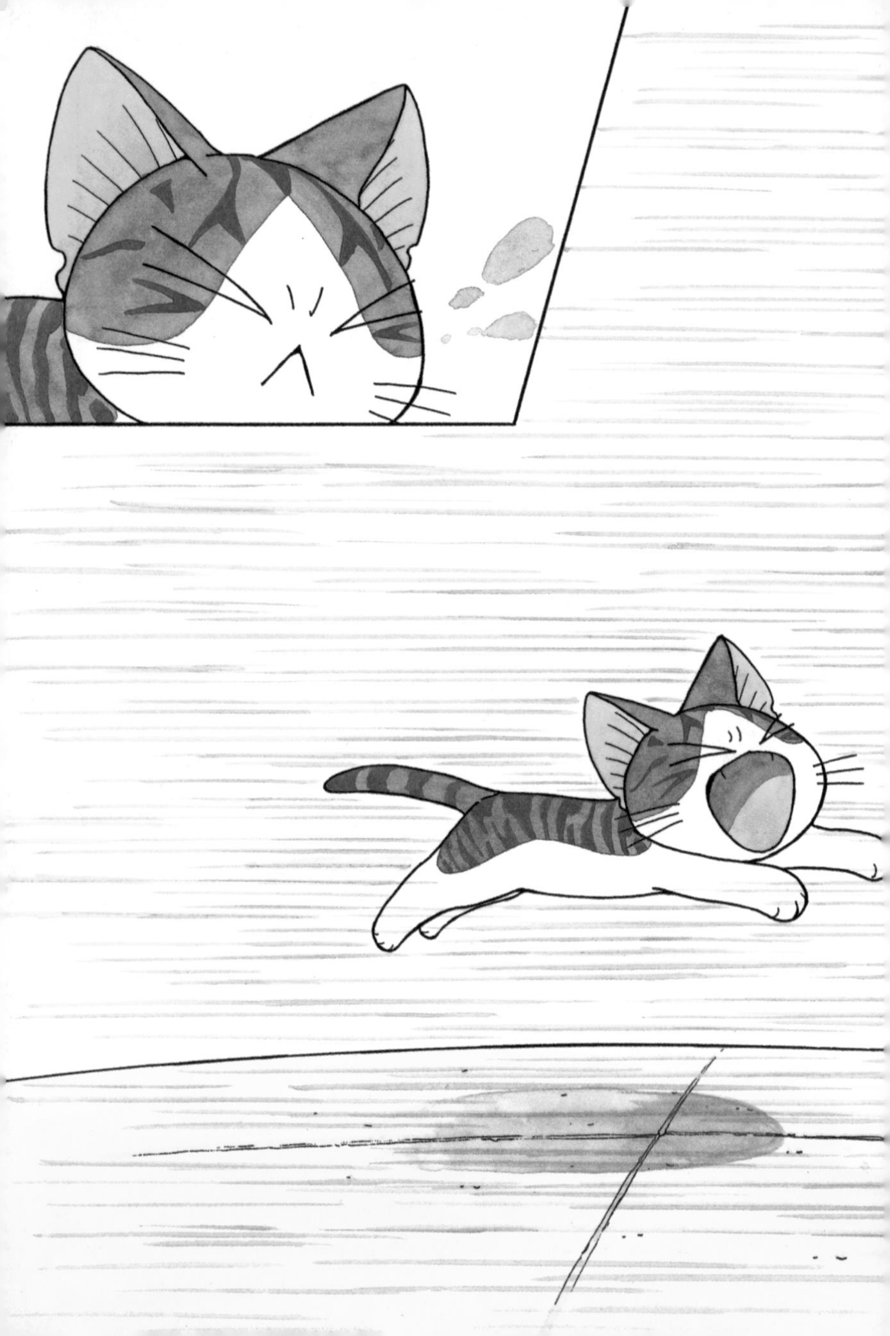

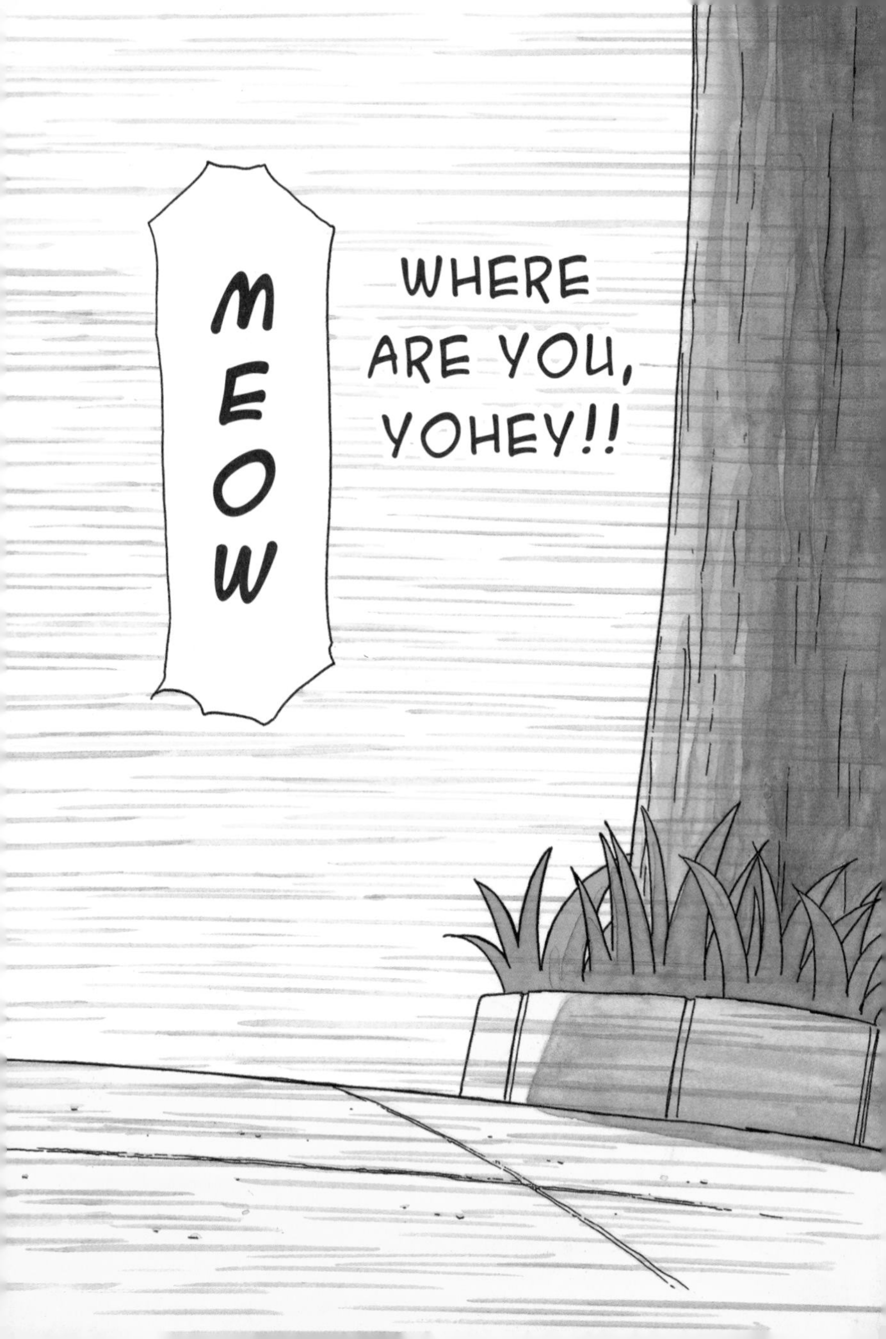
MEOW
WHERE ARE YOU, YOHEY!!

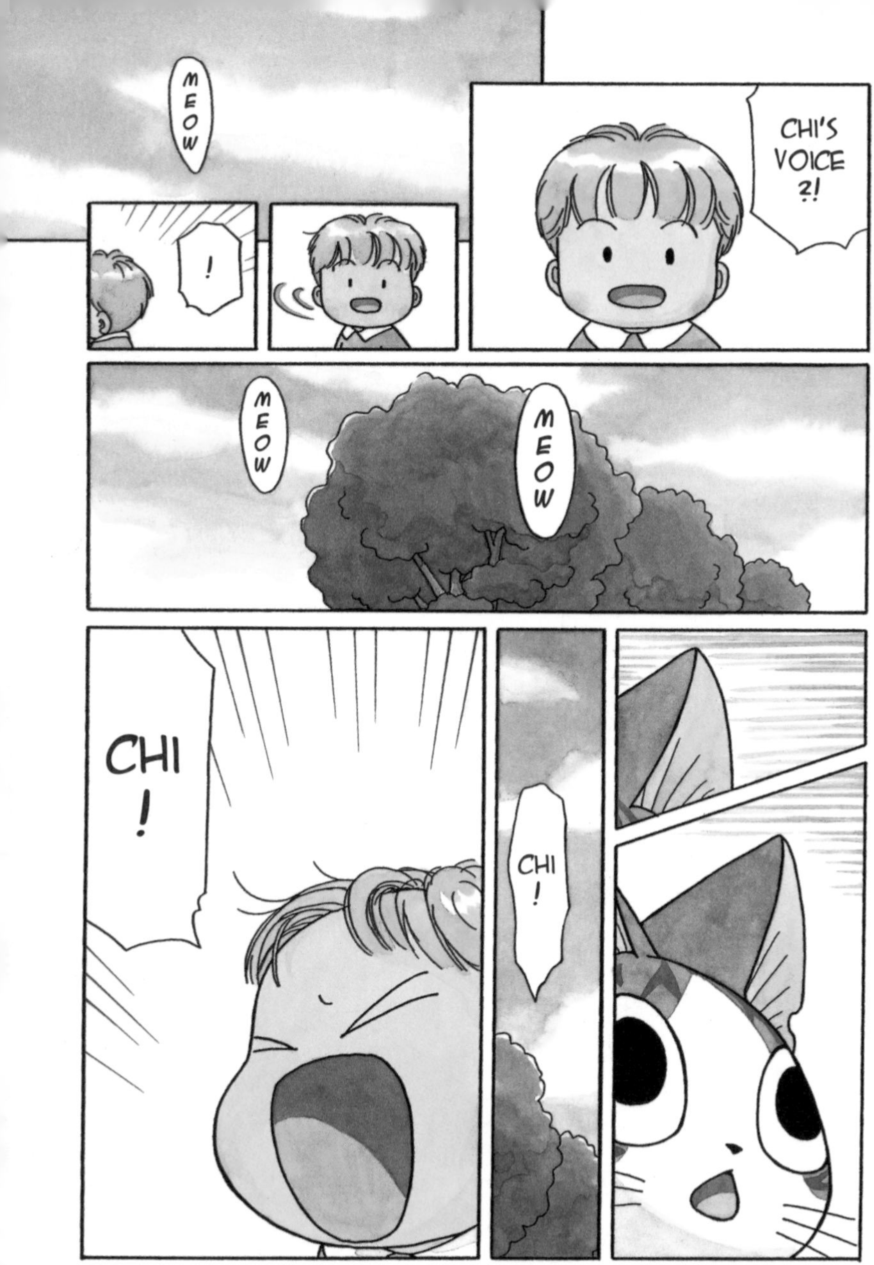
MEOW
!
CHI'S VOICE ?!
MEOW
MEOW
CHI!
CHI!

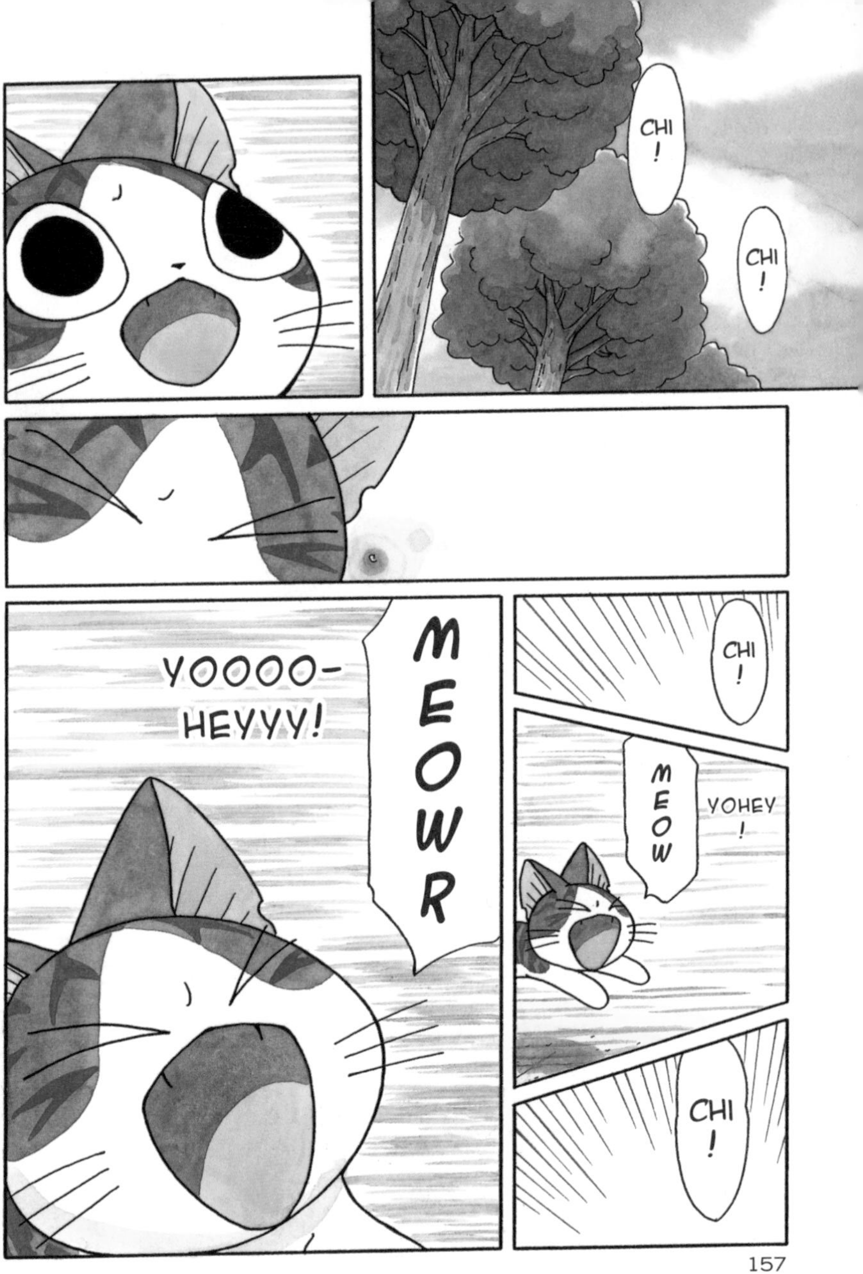
CHI!
CHI!
YOOOO-HEYYY!
MEOWR
CHI!
MEOW
YOHEY!
CHI!

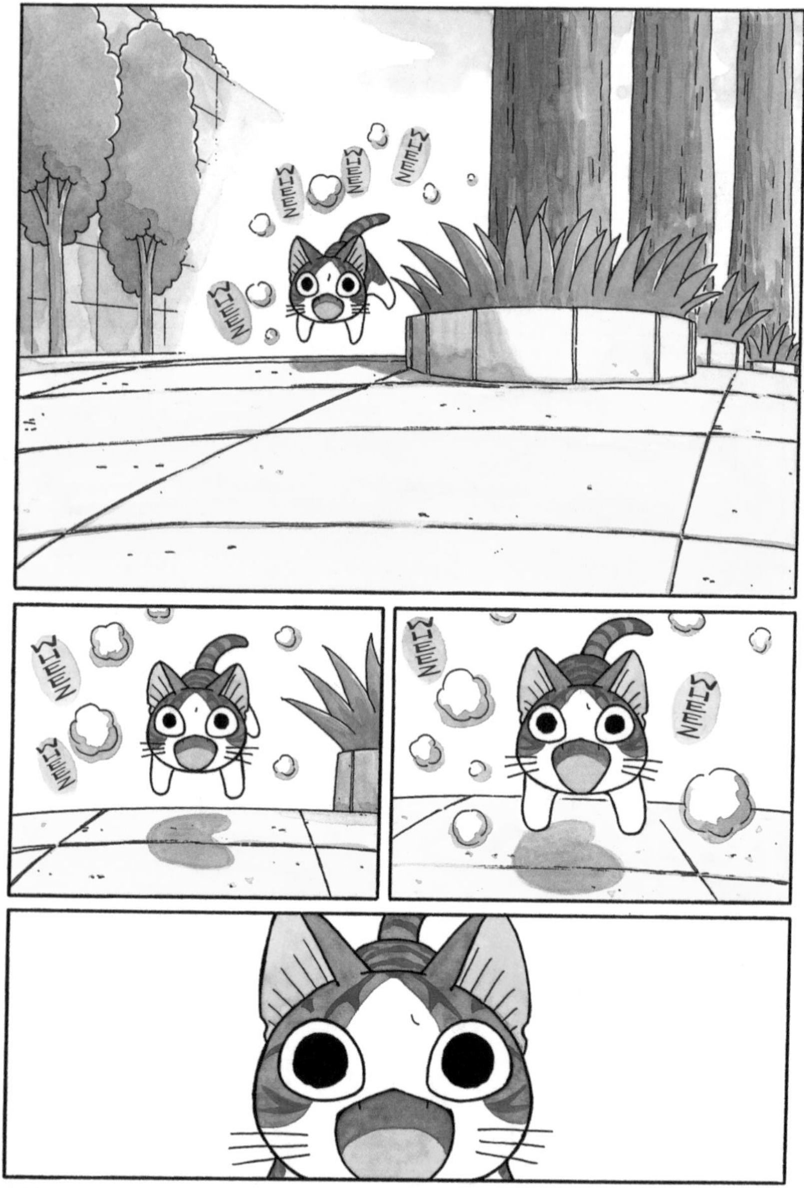
WHEEN
WHEEN
WHEEN
WHEEN
WHEEN
WHEEN
WHEEN
WHEEN

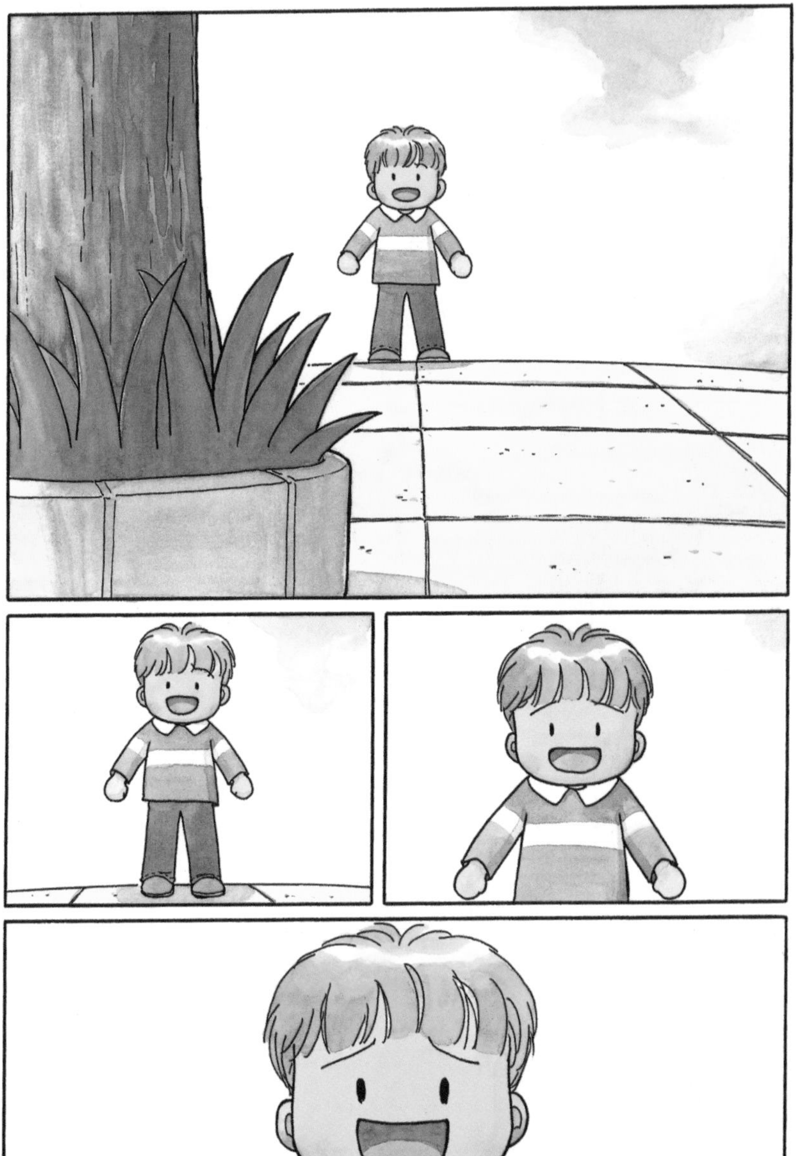

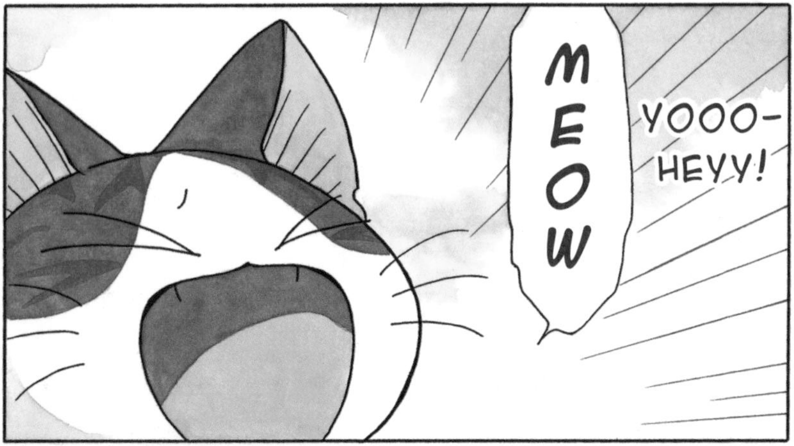
MEOW
YOOO-HEYY!
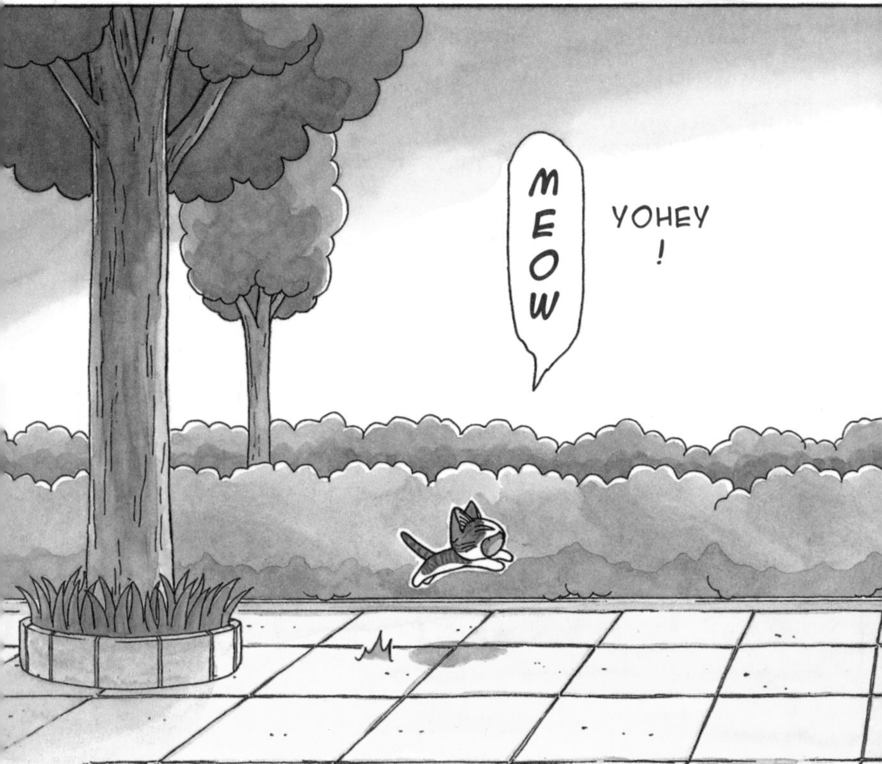
MEOW
YOHEY!

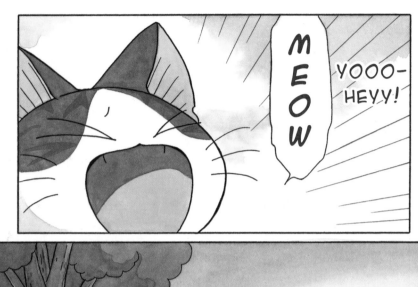

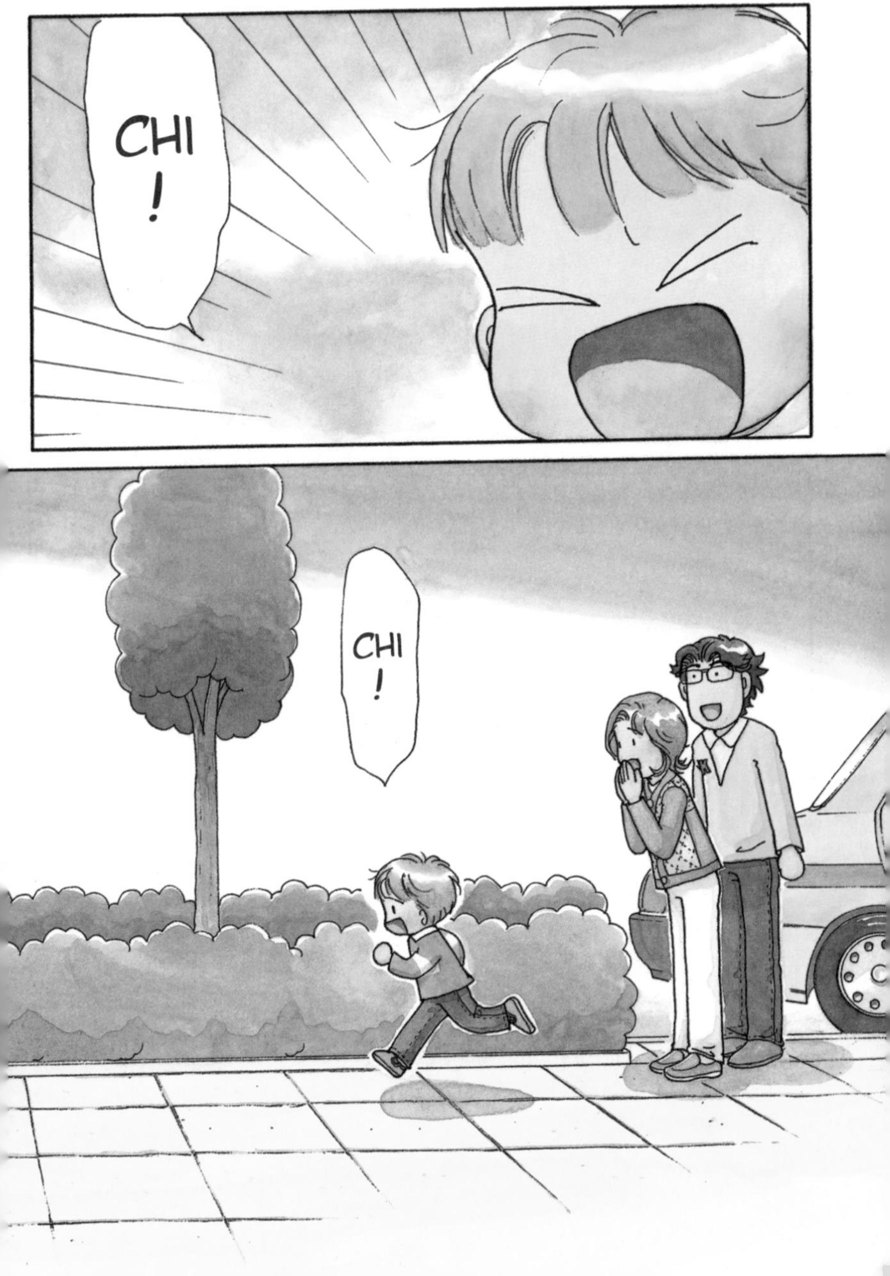
CHI!
CHI!

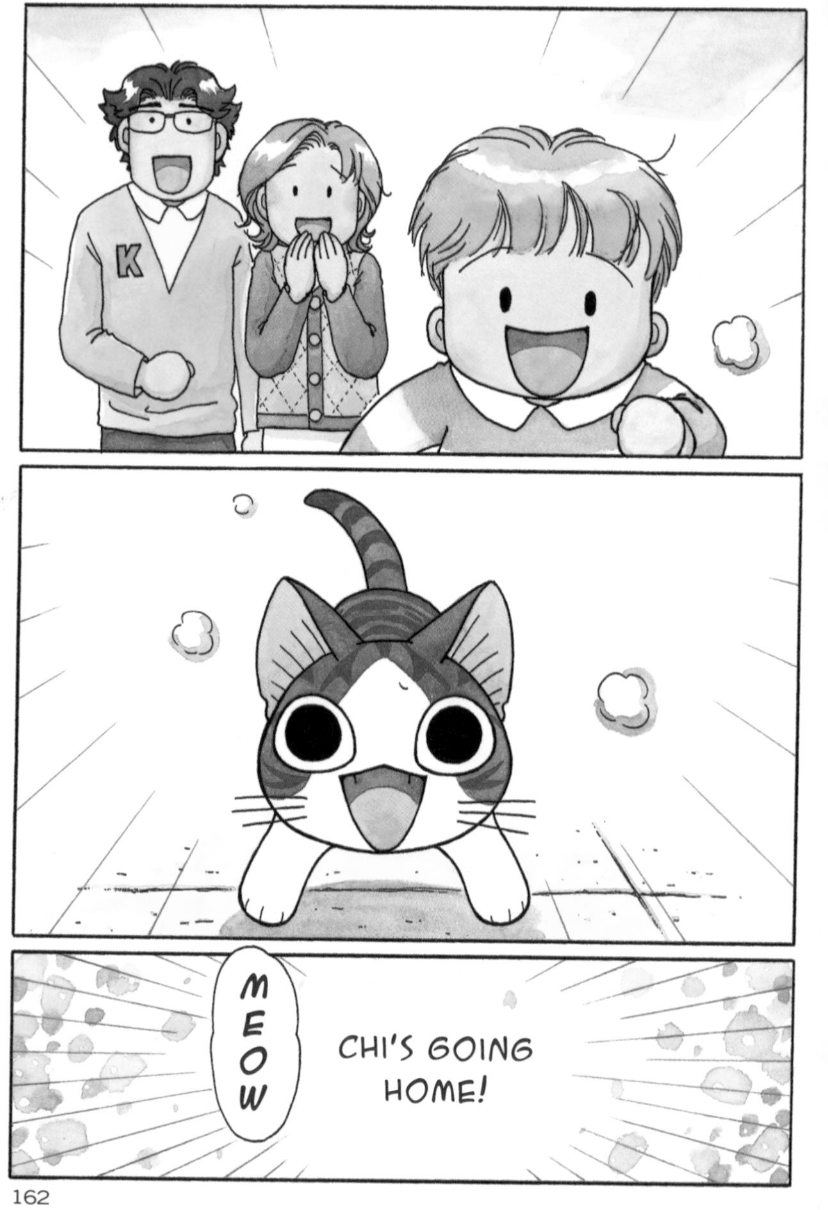
MEOW
CHI'S GOING HOME!

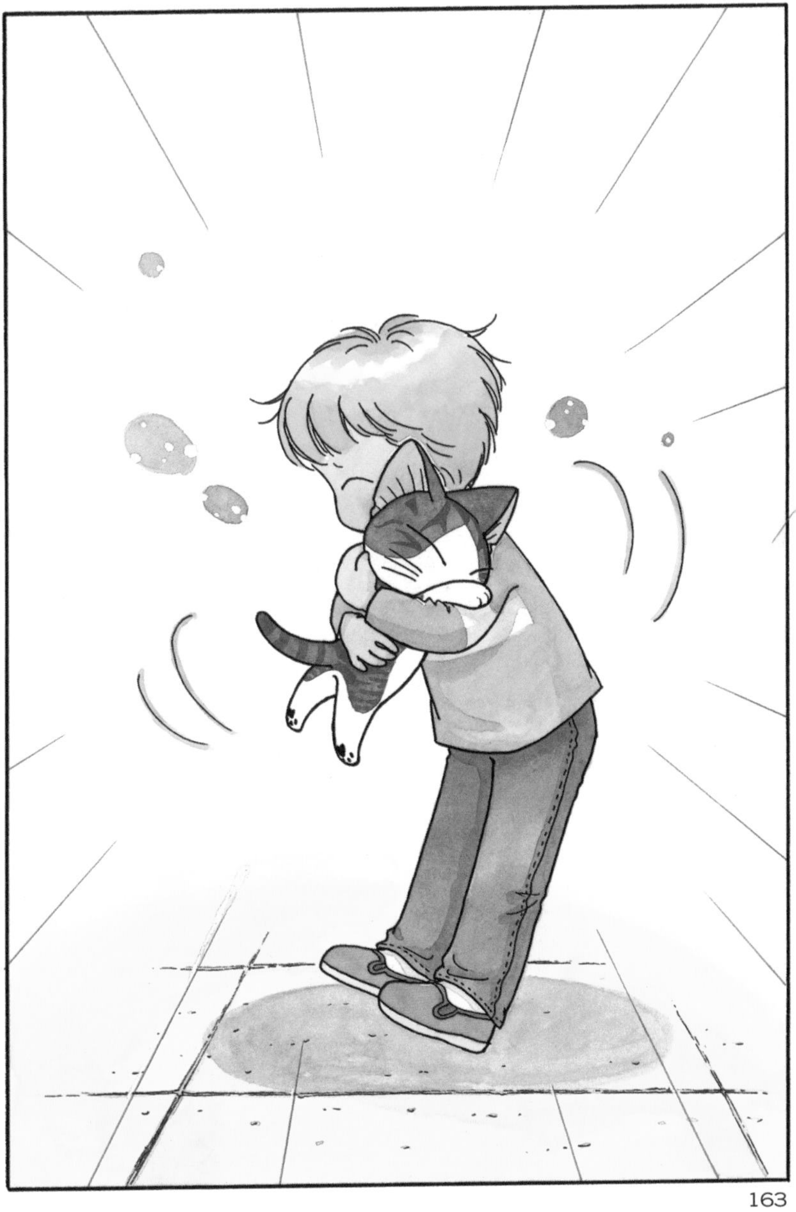

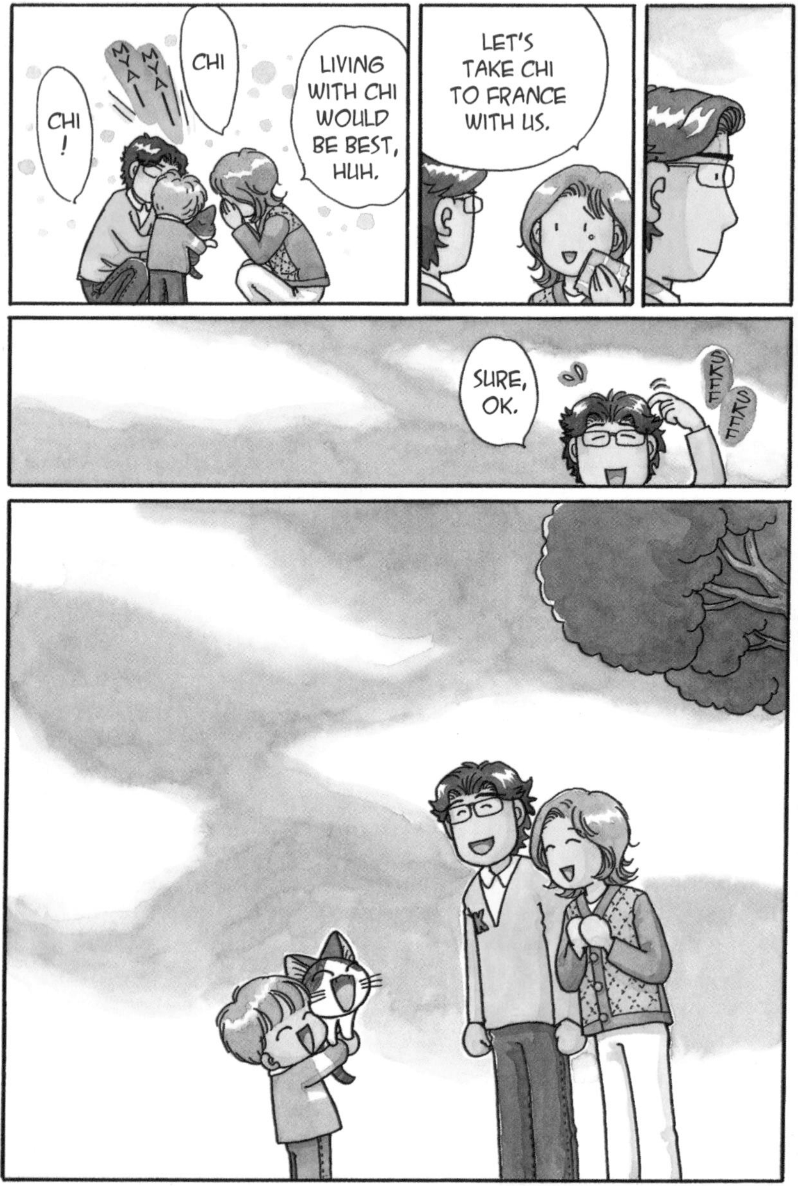
CHI!
MYA
MYA
CHI
LIVING WITH CHI WOULD BE BEST, HUH.
LET'S TAKE CHI TO FRANCE WITH US.
SURE, OK.
SKFF
SKFF

the end

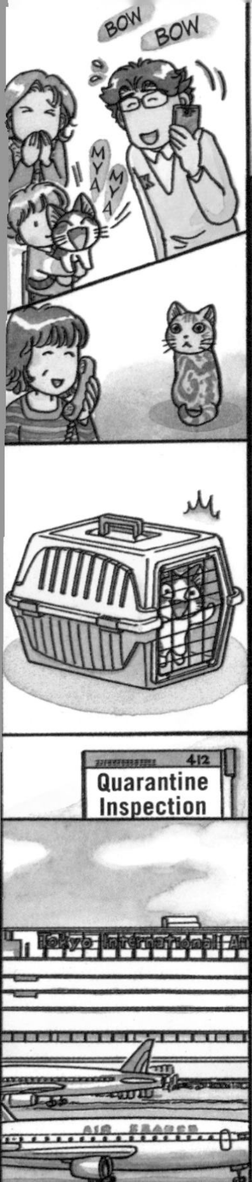
BOW
BOW
MYA
MYA
412
Quarantine Inspection

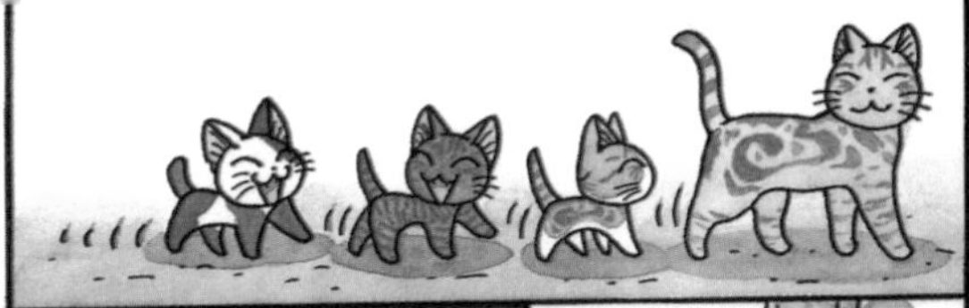

Special Thanks to:

JP Production Staff:
Kasumi Misuto
Masanori Mizuochi
Junko Tanaka

JP Production Support:
Mutsumi Tanaka
Riko Inaba

Design:
Kei Kasai
Megumi Shirakihara

US Production Staff:
Hiroko Mizuno
Aryaan Razzaghi
Grace Lu
Nicole Dochych
Laura Kovalcin

Others:
Press and Events,
Anime Production,
Goods Makers, Foreign
Publishers and Anime Localizers,
Foreign Merchandise,
and Many Others

And to the Readers:
Thank you so much for
our long time together.

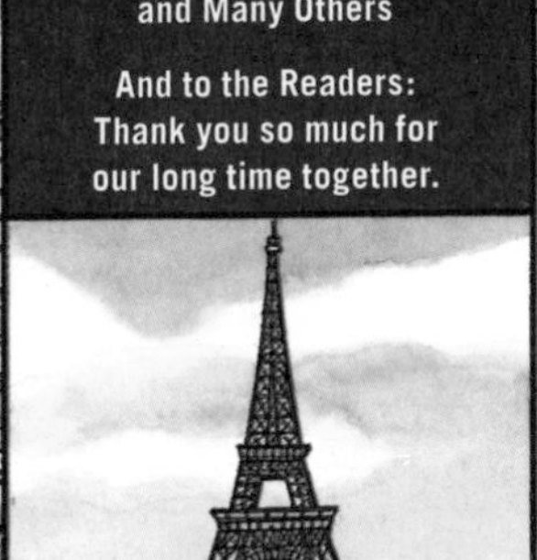

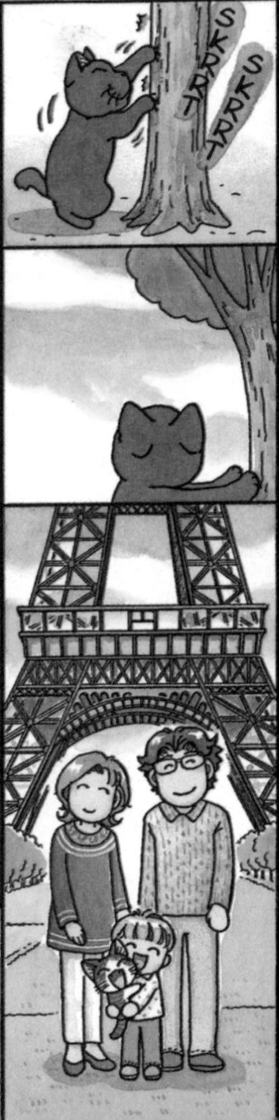
SKRRT
SKRRT

Chi's Sweet Home
Celebrating
the Conclusion

Konami Kanata Interview
—Chi's Sweet Home: Where it's been and where it's going—

"Ugo. Nyago, nyagogo. Ugo, ugougo.
Nyangogo, ugo, ugo, nya—ugo."

—(translation) Hello, Blackie here. How did you like the ending of "Chi's Sweet Home"? Chi started publication in 2004, was serialized for 11 years in the magazine Morning, and now, finally we've reached the final chapter. This is solely due to the support of you, the readers. Even though it's the final volume, for the first time in a long while, we're publishing an interview with the creator and author, Konami Kanata. I hope that you enjoy it.

Blackie: Ugo. Nyago, nyaago. (Alright, Konami. It's been a long time.)

Konami (hereafter KK): It has been a long time. When was the last time, I wonder?

Blackie: Ugo, nyago. (The last interview was compiled in the volume 2 release in 2005, so about 10 years ago.)

KK: Wow, 10 years. I'm shocked. Somehow all that time just flew by.

Blackie: Ugo, nyago? (So you've finally reached the final chapter, how are you feeling now?)

KK: Well. I don't actually have any strong feelings about it yet, it's a weird sensation. Somehow, I was finally able to struggle through, and I'm really

The picture of Pi-chan and Konami's son (4) attached to Konami's work desk. Like Chi and Yohei, they are sibling-like best friends.

Drawn especially for use in bookstore promotional displays: Chi being held tightly by Yohei.

happy that I was able to carry out my duty. A feeling like that, I guess.

Blackie: Nya, nya, nya. (That's so Konami, LOL). At the time of the volume 2 interview as well, you answered, "I want to continue to draw steadily and diligently so that I won't miss my deadline.")

KK: Did I really? Well, As far as I'm concerned, it really was a big ambition for me (laugh).

 A photo attached to Konami's work desk.

Blackie: Ugo, nyago. Ugo? (Because this is the final volume, let's take a look back on the eleven years of Chi. What was your inspiration for wanting to draw this story?)

KK: Morning's editor-in-chief at that time, Mr. Kutomi, asked me if I would draw something for the magazine, but what would I draw? Thinking about it, I thought I might try to draw a story about a kitten next. About 3 years earlier, a good friend of mine told me that her cat had just had three kittens, did I want one? It was the first time in my life that I owned a kitten.

"I'll keep the smallest but cutest one for you," my friend told me, and when I went to go see, it really was cute. Up until that point, I'd only ever taken care of adult cats, so I was uneasy about whether or not I could actually care for a kitten, but I planned to seriously give it my all, and accepted the kitten. I named it Pi-chan. She had only been born about 2 months before but she was really friendly, reckless, naughty, and more so than I expected, a cute beast.

At the time, my son was not yet 4 years old, and when the two of them were together, even though they were human and cat, they were like siblings. Everyday is fun, I thought, to the extent that our spirits rose and the feelings of myself, my husband, and everyone in our family became quite cheerful. Thinking it would be good if I could bring the fun of living with a cat to a manga, I decided to make a kitten the main character of the story.

Blackie: Ugo, ugogo? (The picture above was taken at that time, wasn't it?)

KK: Yes. That picture was on my work desk the whole time I drew the manuscript.

Blackie: Ugogo, nya~go? (In the volume 2 interview, you talked about taking a picture capturing the little beast's expressions?)

KK: Right, right. At that time, my son and Pi-chan were still small, but now the two of them have gotten bigger, and Pi-chan has completely settled down and now she has become like a grandma cat.

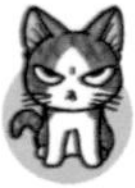

Friends of Chi around the World

Blackie: Nyago, nyago~. (The model for Chi's story was indeed Konami's family. From there, anime, foreign translations, and goods have come out. Chi really has gone on a big adventure, hasn't she?)

KK: Yes, she has. Basically, because the manuscript was drawn on my desk the whole time, I had the feeling that my world was just the desk in front of my eyes. It didn't really sink in that Chi was being read even in foreign countries, but then I went to events in places like Canada, France and Switzerland, and for the first time I met readers who were there for the events. I was astonished when I found out that it wasn't just the world on top of my desk.

Blackie: Nyago, ugo, ugogo. (In 2014, Chi also made an appearance in the global company Apple's TV ad spot, right?)

KK: Yes! The first time I heard about it was from the editor in charge of me. "A TV CM appearance inquiry came from the computer company Apple, and I'm guessing it's that Apple, but are you interested?" Unbelievably, it

The illustration of Chi used by Apple for a TV ad spot.

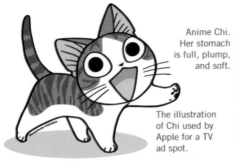

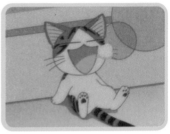

Anime Chi. Her stomach is full, plump, and soft.

really was that Apple that extended an offer to me. I couldn't believe it.

Blackie: Ugo, ugogo, nyago. (Chi would be appearing together with world famous characters like Mickey Mouse, Snoopy, and Hello Kitty (Laugh))

KK: It was an honor. When Chi got to make an appearance on TV while eating an apple, it was a really great feeling.

In the anime, Chi's became an old man?!

Blackie: Ugo, ugogo, nya? (What did you think when you first saw the anime?)

KK: The way that Chi talked was really cute, so I was very happy. I was asked about my image of Chi's voice by the people at MadHouse, who were in charge of the anime production, and when I answered "Korogi Satomi", a voice actress I love, they made it a reality for me.

Blackie: Nyago, nya. (The way Korogi Satomi portrayed Chi's voice was quite cute.)

KK: From the yawning to the voice used for humming, it's fantastic. And I love the way the anime deals with Chi's movements, especially the tummy-related actions. In the manga, when Chi's tummy was full, she'd just slump and lie down, but in the anime, she thumps her side like some old guy, it's original and fantastic.

Blackie: Nya. Ugogo. (Certainly. After the anime, even in the manga, Chi turned into more of a lazybones.)

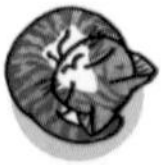

Chi's Art Director: Kei Kasai

Blackie: Nyago, nyanya. (All around the world Chi has books and anime, as well as a development of goods, but a lot of the designs are so wonderful.)

KK: That's right. Especially the design of the French products is really pretty and makes me happy. That Chi came to be this loved across the world owes a lot to Kei Kasai, who made me a cover design with the book's worldview in mind. When the editor in charge conveyed the image of a cake box, and soft colors in Scandinavian style, she polished off the design fantastically for me. Along with Ms. Megumi Shirakihara, who did the design for the text in the volumes, the two of them have been in charge of Chi's design since publication started.

Blackie: Ugogo, ugo. (I'm glad that you were blessed with a fortunate meeting.)

KK: Yes. And that's not all. Because I met Ms. Kasai, Blackie was born.

Blackie: Nya, nya? (Eh, is that so?)

KK: At the time, Ms. Kasai had a black cat named Higuma. But, Higuma was slender and handsome, so maybe if you saw him you wouldn't think he was the model (Laugh).

Blackie: Nya, nya?! Nyagogogo! (Wh-What?! That's so rude!)

KK: Sorry (Laugh). But because of similar meetings, others were born, like Alice and Mi-chan.

Blackie: Ugogo. Nyago? (The amount of friends just increased, huh? What about Cocchi?)

KK: Cocchi was, well, he started from a few words of my son. One day, he said, "Chi is lucky because she got picked up and became a house cat, but if she wasn't she'd have been a stray." In life, luck and misfortune exists, and it's sometimes hard to say which is which. Chi was picked up, but I wondered what might have happened if Chi hadn't been picked up, and that was how I came to imagine Cocchi.

Blackie: Ugo, ugogo. Nyago. (Cocchi saw Chi reunited with her family and his view of the world seemed to change just a bit. Because in the end, Cocchi was there with Chi's mom and siblings.)

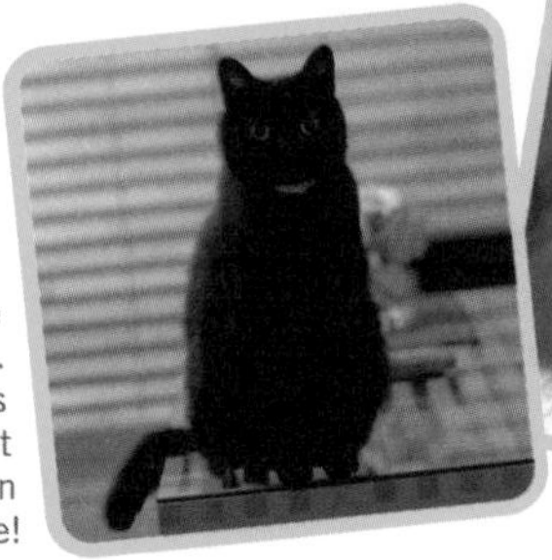

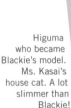

Higuma who became Blackie's model. Ms. Kasai's house cat. A lot slimmer than Blackie!

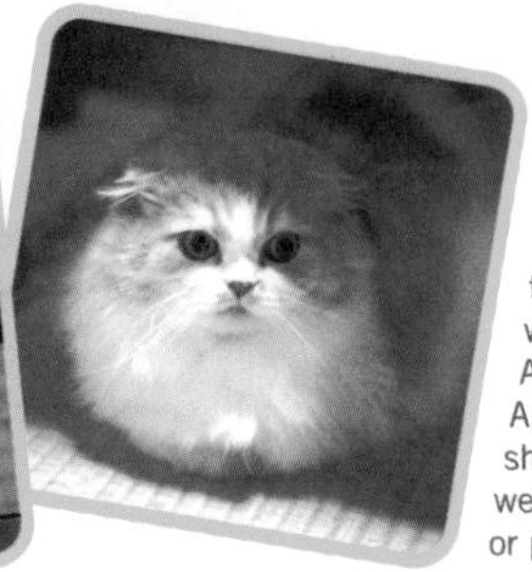

The editor in charge (at the time)'s cat who would be Alice's model. Apparently, she wasn't so well-mannered or polite.

KK: Cocchi loves his freedom as a stray, but now because he has friends, I think he can be even happier.

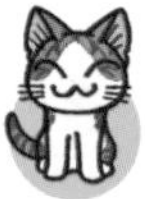

Having Finished the Story

Blackie: Nyago, ugogogo, nygo. (Well, how about a message for those readers that read until the end?)

KK: These books aren't about animals that are just well-behaved, but mischievous and free too, so if I was able to convey the fun of such animals, I'm happy. Another thing, the whole time I was drawing, I tried to respect the fact that cats are cats, and people are people. Because they are not the same species, they cannot communicate with words. Of course, because this is a manga, there is a human abundance of expressions, but, as much as possible, I wanted them to not be human-like, but animal-like looks. So I had to think what's the best way to express that, and it was difficult.

For Chi and the Yamada family, the words they use can't be understood by the other so there might be misunderstandings, but as friends and family, might not they be tied through their feelings? Together they have fun or they cry, and how nice if they ended up precious to each other. Supported by lots of people, I gave it my all and somehow got this far—that's how I feel. I think I was allowed to go beyond my real abilities. Thank you for reading over such a long time.

Interview & Setup: Yoshiko Tezuka

Chi's On Social Media!!

Even with the end of the manga series, Chi's adventures will continue. Fans of Chi can get news and information about the Chi anime, goods, international events and promotions via the four official Chi's Sweet Home accounts. Get to know more about Chi and experience more cute kitty art on these platforms!

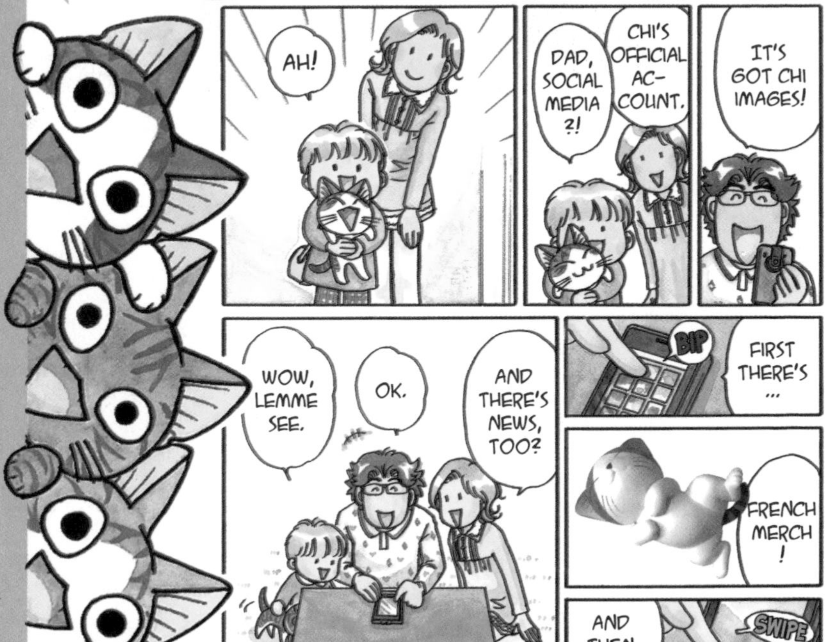
AH!
DAD, SOCIAL MEDIA ?!
CHI'S OFFICIAL AC-COUNT.
IT'S GOT CHI IMAGES!
WOW, LEMME SEE.
OK.
AND THERE'S NEWS, TOO?
BIP
FIRST THERE'S ...
FRENCH MERCH !
AND THEN ...
SWIPE
SUPER EXPRESSIVE CHI AND MORE.
IT'S FULL OF CHI NEWS!

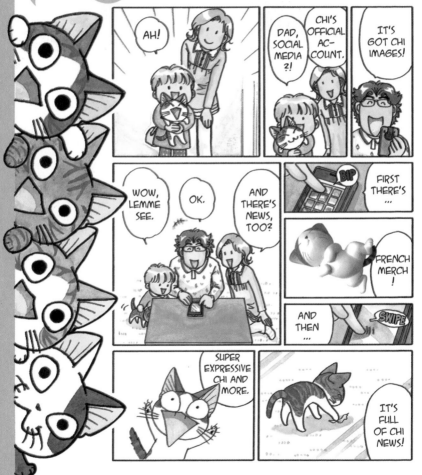

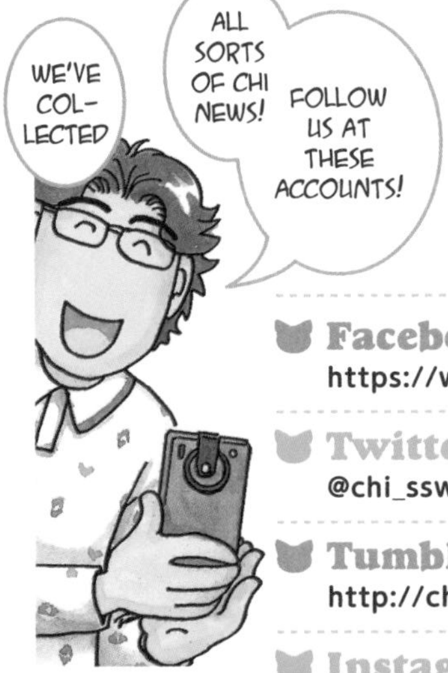
WE'VE COL-LECTED
ALL SORTS OF CHI NEWS!
FOLLOW US AT THESE ACCOUNTS!

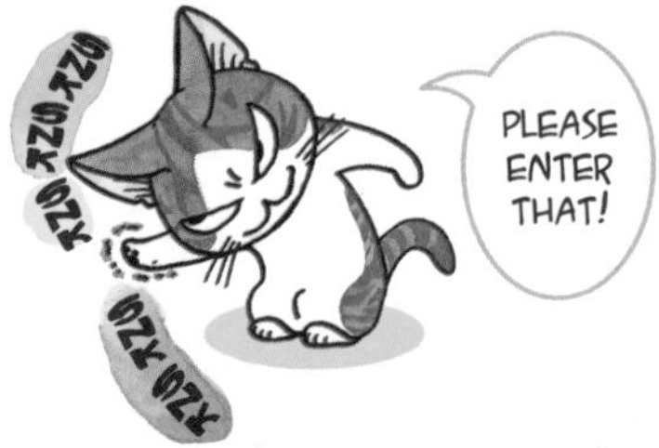
PLEASE ENTER THAT!

Facebook Chi's Sweet Home—Chi's Page
https://www.facebook.com/chissweethomeofficial

Twitter Chi's Sweet Home Official Account
@chi_ssweethome

Tumblr Chi's Sweet Home Official Tumblr
http://chi-sweethome.tumblr.com/

Instagram chi.ssweethome
https://instagram.com/chi.ssweethome/

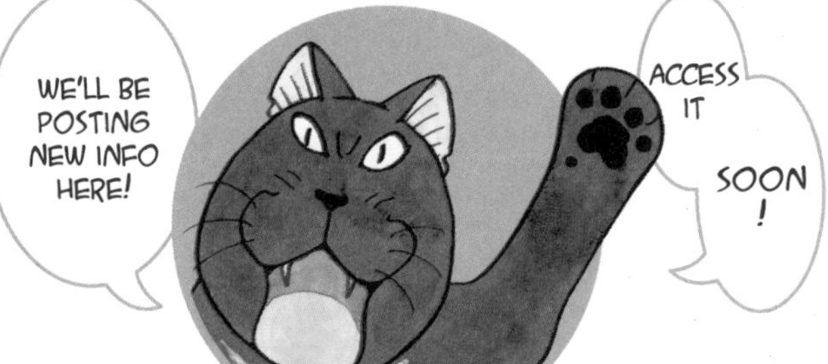
WE'LL BE POSTING NEW INFO HERE!
ACCESS IT
SOON!

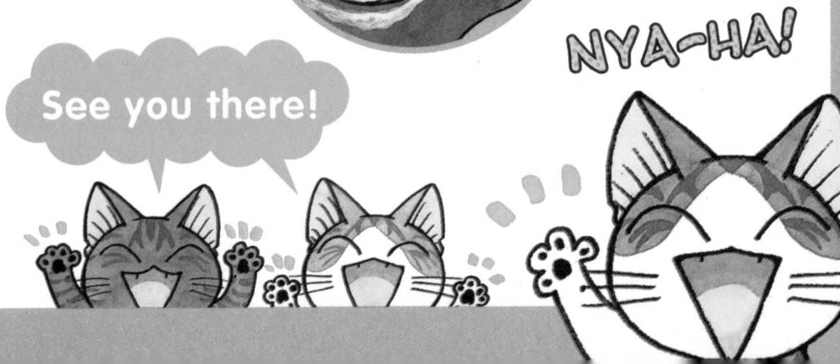
NYA-HA!
See you there!

Chi's Sweet Home, volume 12

Translation - Ed Chavez
Production - Grace Lu
Hiroko Mizuno
Anthony Quintessenza

First published in Japan in 2015 by Kodansha, Ltd., Tokyo
Publication for this English edition arranged through Kodansha, Ltd., Tokyo
English language version produced by Vertical, Inc.

Translation provided by Vertical, Inc., 2015
Published by Vertical, Inc., New York

Originally published in Japanese as *Chiizu Suiito Houmu* by Kodansha, Ltd., 2014-2015
Chiizu Suiito Houmu first serialized in *Morning*, Kodansha, Ltd., 2004-2015

ISBN: 978-1-941220-25-2

Manufactured in the United States of America

First Edition

Vertical, Inc.
451 Park Avenue South, 7th Floor
New York, NY 10016
www.vertical-inc.com

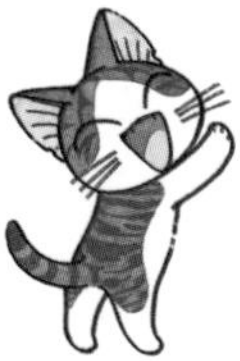

Special thanks to: K. Kitamoto

Chi volumes are now available in eBook format!

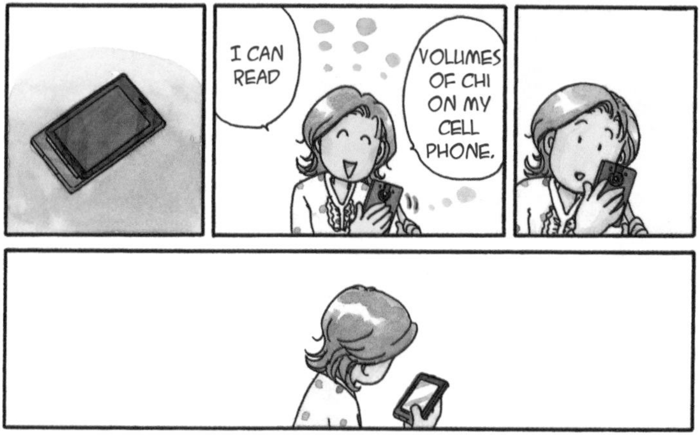
I CAN READ
VOLUMES OF CHI ON MY CELL PHONE.

With this new option how can you stop reading?! All twelve volumes of *Chi's Sweet Home* can now be enjoyed on your tablet or cell phone. Just access your favorite eBook retailer—Kindle, Nook, iTunes Bookstore, Google Play and more—and search for *Chi's Sweet Home*.

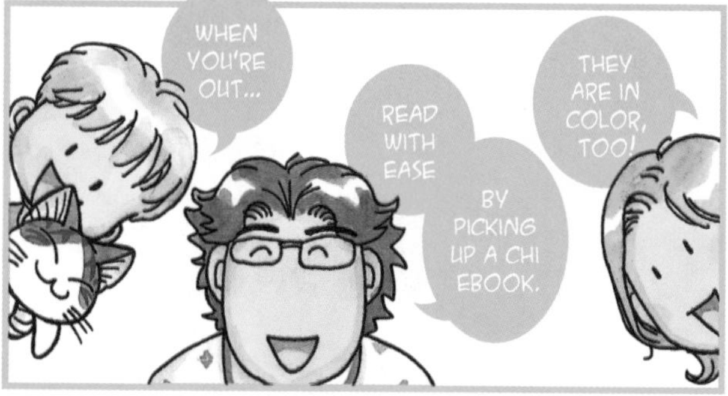
WHEN YOU'RE OUT...
READ WITH EASE
BY PICKING UP A CHI EBOOK.
THEY ARE IN COLOR, TOO!

★ Fold into 4 pages
★ Glue back sides marked with arrow below

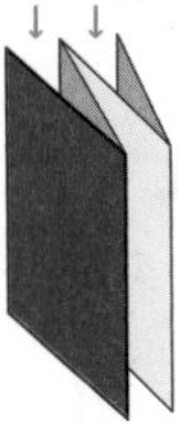

★ Round off the corners

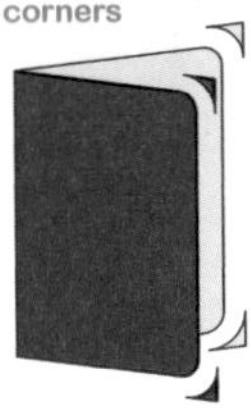

And your Chi passport is done!

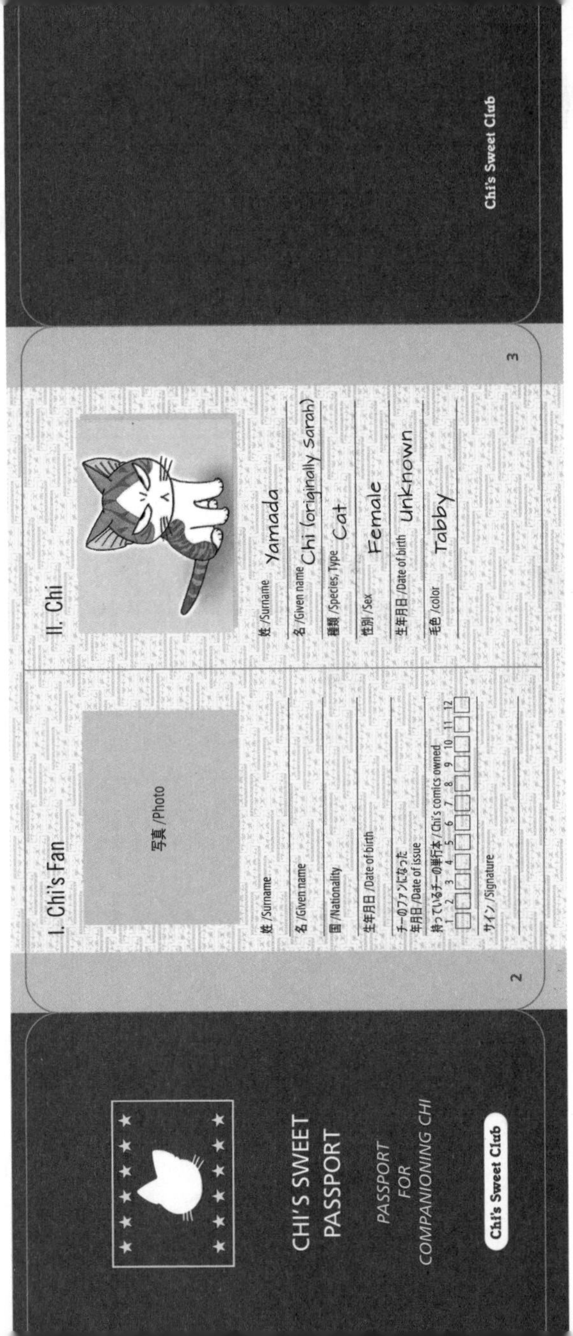
CHI'S SWEET PASSPORT
PASSPORT FOR COMPANIONING CHI
Chi's Sweet Club
I. Chi's Fan
写真 /Photo
姓 /Surname
名 /Given name
国 /Nationality
生年月日 /Date of birth
チーのファンになった年月日 /Date of issue
持っているチーの単行本 /Chi's comics owned
1 2 3 4 5 6 7 8 9 10 11 12
サイン /Signature
2
II. Chi
姓 /Surname Yamada
名 /Given name Chi (originally Sarah)
種類 /Species, Type Cat
性別 /Sex Female
生年月日 /Date of birth Unknown
毛色 /color Tabby
3
Chi's Sweet Club